SCORCHED TREACHERY

THE IMDALIND SERIES, BOOK THREE

REBECCA ETHINGTON

IMDALIND PRESS

Published by Imdalind Press

Copyediting by
Production Management by Imdalind Press

Library of Congress Cataloging-in-Publication Data Available
Library of Congress Control Number:
ISBN (print) 978-1-949725-02-5
ISBN (ebook) 978-0-9884837-5-0
Printed in USA
This Edition, July 2013

ISBN: 978-0-9884837-5-0

❀ Created with Vellum

THE IMDALIND SERIES

BOOK ONE: *Kiss of Fire*
BOOK TWO: *Eyes of Ember*
BOOK THREE: *Scorched Treachery*
BOOK FOUR: *Soul of Flame*
BOOK FIVE: *Burnt Devotion*
BOOK SIX: *Brand of Betrayal*
BOOK SEVEN: *Dawn of Ash*
BOOK EIGHT: *Crown of Cinders*
BOOK NINE: *Ilyan*

CONTENTS

1. Wyn   1
2. Wyn   17
3. Wyn   35
4. Wyn   45
5. Wyn   63
6. Wyn   78
7. Wyn   90
8. Wyn   100
9. Wyn   111
10. Ilyan   122
11. Ilyan   138
12. Ilyan   147
13. Ilyan   156
14. Wyn   165
15. Wyn   176
16. Wyn   190
17. Ilyan   203
18. Ilyan   211
19. Ilyan   222
20. Wyn   229
21. Wyn   247
22. Wyn   263
23. Ilyan   270
24. Ilyan   283
25. Ilyan   297
26. Ilyan   307
27. Ilyan   320
28. Joclyn   333

Also by Rebecca Ethington   347
About the Author   349
Imdalind Continues in Book Four   351

*To **Cassi**—*
Who is afraid of Trampolines.

-

*To **Anna**—*
Who was Amazing.

1

WYN

I T WAS THE SAME DREAM. Always the same dream. I had been having it since Cail first marked my skin with the curse, the night Ilyan saved me from my father.

The dream usually featured a beautiful little girl dancing in a meadow. She danced through the tall grasses with flowers in her blonde hair. After about twenty years, I began wondering if it was some repressed memory, but I didn't have blonde hair. My hair was dark; it always had been.

With time, it became clear that I was not the little girl. Instead, I sat and watched her with some guy sitting next to me. I would like to say the guy was handsome, but he was not Talon. No one could hold a candle to Talon. Talon was tall and built like a football player. This man was sinewy, his coloring lighter. Besides, the mystery guy from my dreams was dressed like Henry the Eighth and there was nothing attractive about that. He looked like a peacock. It didn't look good then, and it wouldn't look good now. Not like anyone would dress like that now.

The dream had always started the same; I sat next to the

man in my dreams as he talked, his lips moving, but no sound coming out. Then the dream would morph. The girl, the man, and I would move from the meadow to a village, then to a marble lined room, and then to the darkness. It was in the darkness that I would begin to hear sound. The only sound the dream ever had was in that room, when the little girl screamed as Edmund tortured her.

I would hear the screaming and see the man as he fought to save her, and in the back of my mind, I knew I was fighting, too.

The dream was the reason I had never consented to try to have children with Talon. Not only was pregnancy a strange and uncomfortable prospect, but I was scared of what Edmund would do to a child. Everyone was. It was the same reason so few children were born. People had seen what Edmund had done to his own children; it was not worth it to risk him doing the same to their own.

Up until a few weeks ago, when we first heard the screams of the woman in the tunnels below Prague, the screams of my dream had always ended in the dark room; but the more the woman yelled, begged and screamed, the more my dream changed. It lengthened until I watched the little girl succumb, her screams dwindling to nothing.

The screams in Prague continued, however.

We could only listen as the woman pleaded to and fought against those who attempted to make her give away Ilyan and Joclyn's location.

No matter how hard we looked, we could never find them. Our failure to find them, combined with Ovailia's decision to keep the information from Ilyan, led to her removal as the další v příkazu and the replacement of Talon in the ruling position—something I was not happy about.

Now, he was gone all the time, and the screams of the woman still echoed through the halls.

So, the new ending to my dreams stayed. The screaming moving from one person to another before I would wake up and scowl at the high ceiling of our room.

Except for this morning. This morning, I was rudely awoken by the blasting of Ilyan's phone playing 'In the Hall of the Mountain King'.

Wait.

Ilyan's phone.

His direct line.

I rolled over and kicked Talon, my magic surging through him. He jerked as I zapped him, my not-so-nice way of waking him up, shooting him out of bed. He moved to get back into bed, grumbling at me for a moment, only to jump when the sound of the music hit his ears.

Talon's fingers reached toward the phone as he sat down on his side of the bed, while I chose to stay lying under the covers, my eyes focused on him.

Yes, it was the middle of the day where Ilyan was. Yes, he was free to call whenever he wanted. However, the fact that he would have known it was the middle of the night here, and he was calling the white phone that was a direct connection to Talon, set my nerves on fire.

Talon pressed the phone to his ear, the skin contact triggering the magic and completing the call.

"Ilyan?" Talon asked, his voice drowsy but still on edge, my mood mirrored in his clipped words.

I waited, reluctant to move, hoping for something exciting, but knowing, absolutely knowing that nothing positive was going to come out of this call.

"Princess Mudgy." Talons voice was low, the statement

making no sense to me. For all I knew it was a code word, and if it was a code word...

I watched Talon as he listened to Ilyan talk, his shoulders knitting together more and more, his body language spelling danger to me. Talon stayed silent as Ilyan spoke, his voice a mellow buzz that slipped through the air until the line went dead. Talon never said anything more after the code words, his silence only making me more nervous.

He lowered the disconnected phone to his lap, his movements tense. Talon didn't turn to me; he didn't say anything. He just sat with the phone in his hands, his knuckles white from clenching the small, white box. I watched his broad shoulders flex, the tension never leaving, and found my own fears growing.

The silence was painful. I wanted to hear. I wanted to pry, but I knew it would not be right. I placed my hand on Talon's back, willing him to turn and smile, but knowing it wasn't going to happen.

"Meet you in my dreams," Talon said tersely. Not once did he look at me as he lay down and opened his arms for me.

I was seriously on edge now. Whatever had happened was monumental enough that neither he nor Ilyan wanted anyone else to know what had happened. I lay down next to Talon and closed my eyes, letting the magic of the Tòuha take me away to meet with him.

My mind pulled right into his, the large expanse of the Münzenberg Castle courtyard surrounding us. Wispy projections of people walked around us as Talon's memories fueled the Tòuha. The castle was whole and intact as it once was centuries ago, the cobbles of the road pristine. I was never alive in this castle's time, but this was Talon's mind, what he envisioned our Tòuha to be.

"Talon?" I asked as he wrapped his arms around me as we stood in the middle of the courtyard. His tense muscles strained against me as he held me, the movement not helping to ease my anxiety.

"They were attacked." My body froze, my eyes flying open in shock. The tension that now flowed between both of us was too much to contain, and the people around us zapped into vapor, colors floating through the air as they disappeared, leaving us alone.

"Are they all right?" I asked. I didn't want to hear the answer, I didn't. I did not need to hear of injuries or brutal battles. I could already feel what hearing this had done to Talon.

He had reacted the same way a few years ago when Edmund's men captured Ilyan. Talon had felt like a failure. He had been raised to guard Ilyan. It was his job, but Ilyan had dismissed him when he took me as his mate. No matter how much he tried, Talon could never move past what had been his entire life up until a hundred years ago. He still felt responsible for Ilyan, and blamed himself if anything went wrong. I knew he was doing it now, putting the words of guilt into his own head, even though there was nothing he could have done.

Ilyan was far more powerful than Talon. If Ilyan could not protect himself, then nothing could be done. Except now, there was Joclyn, too, and I had no idea if she was capable of protecting herself or not.

Talon shook his head no in response to my question, and I felt my stress intensify. His muscles tensed, his arms pressed uncomfortably into me as he lifted me off the ground to his eye level. I wasn't surprised to see the sparkling sheen in his brown eyes, the tears threatening to escape from him.

"It's not your fault," I said before he had a chance to let the words he was painting himself with become more of a weight against him.

He nodded once and held me against him again, his hold tight as his breathing slowed. He finally lowered me back down to the ground, releasing me. When he pulled away, the wetness was gone from his eyes, his composure back. He did not show emotions like that very often, but when he did, it was my job to build him up and always love him. I would always do that.

"Does he know who betrayed him?" I asked as Talon moved away from me and toward the large, carved stone bench we always sat on. I followed him, my bare feet slipping against the slickness of the cobbles that lined the courtyard, before sinking into the hard, unrelenting seat next to his.

"No," Talon answered simply. His hands brought my feet onto his lap and he began to trace the dark marks that graced my left foot, the jagged swirls matching the ones that ran along the entire left side of my body. "He wants me to watch for signs that someone might know what happened before we announce it. It is probably our best chance at tracking whoever it is down."

I nodded, not knowing how to respond. Everything Talon had said only re-affirmed that someone was inside of our perfectly protected shelter, someone who should not have been able to get past Ilyan's protective shield. You had to have Ilyan's blessing in order to get past the gate, you couldn't even use a stutter to get inside. Somehow, though, someone had managed it.

All it would take was one.

Get one of Edmund's men inside and then, like ants, the rest would follow. They would place themselves in dark corners and hide where no one else would go, waiting until the time was right. Then they would jump out and attack, and within moments, the last of the Skříteks would be gone. I had seen it happen before. There was a reason there were so few of the Skříteks left. It was probably the sole reason I still was not fully accepted in these halls—I had marched against them once upon a time.

I shuddered at the thought, for once actually wishing I wasn't so morbid.

"Are you okay?" Talon asked, his voice worried.

I ripped my eyes away from the blob of mud on the cobblestone path that I had been unwittingly staring at to smile at him, my smile more like a grimace. It seemed somewhat fitting, so I didn't try to fix it.

"Who do you think it is?" I asked, avoiding his question and moving to snuggle into him. He welcomed me into him, his arms wrapping around me as he held me tightly against him.

"I don't know, Wynny."

I didn't know what else to say. I didn't know how to phrase what I was feeling. I wished we could find the traitor, and fast. I wished I could tear their arms from their sockets and torture any of my kind they had let into the halls of Prague. It was my sanctuary now, too, my home after my father had exiled me and my brother had tried to kill me.

I felt my magic increase in eagerness beneath my skin, my heart thumping erratically in either excitement or fear; I wasn't quite sure which.

"I will keep you safe, Wynifred."

I froze, my breathing caught in my chest, my heart lost between beats. Usually, I would have screamed at him and clocked him upside the face for insinuating that I couldn't take care of myself, I didn't need him to protect me. I heard what he said between the lines, though; I heard how much he cared, and so, my frantic heartbeat continued. I listened to the sound of my full name on his lips, the promise of my safety heavy on the air.

"You promise?" I asked, not needing to hear the answer. I asked because I knew that he needed to know that I had heard him, that I had understood.

"I will protect you above all else."

"Even Ilyan?" I asked, unable to help the question and the accompanying laugh from seeping out of my lips.

"Even Ilyan. I took a vow to protect him the day he was born, but that vow was broken the day I sealed myself to you. It is the vow I made with you that is the most important bond to me. I will honor and protect that before all else." His voice was serious, his tone so true and honest. I felt it melt into me, and our magic surged with the feeling of love.

As our magic intertwined and seeped into our souls, everything inside of me caught fire. I felt a dulled version of this connection outside the Tòuha, but here, inside the Tòuha, everything was heightened. It was a feeling we could only get here.

I was not sure how long we spent in the shadow of the castle, but before either of us were ready, we were pulled away, only to find ourselves in each other's arms in the flesh, the door already being banged off its hinges.

I sighed as Talon left me, his další v příkazu responsibilities already in full force, just as I assumed they would be.

He was gone most of the day, leaving me alone to attempt to clean the huge mess I had made when I had attempted to make dinner the night before, something I never do.

Talk about a nightmare. I had cut my finger off when trying to chop carrots. Yes, *off*. Luckily, I was magical, or I would have forever been walking around reverse flipping people off. As it was, I just reattached it. Though, after the soup became inedible and more solid than it should have been, and I had burned the Galder, I remembered why I never heated food. It was better cold anyway.

The whole experience was a great reminder as to why I hated human food. It was gross, and the texture was so off. I don't know how or why, but humans can take a simple tomato and turn it into a slime-covered bit of goo. I mean, just leave it alone. Don't touch it. Just put it in your mouth and eat it.

Humans eat weird food.

After I had cleaned the house, it became quickly evident that I needed to wash the lace tablecloth. After the finger-loss induced bloodletting, it was clearly required. Unfortunately, the dratted thing was bearing the label 'hand wash only'.

Hand wash only!

Whoever had created such stupid fabric needed to be shown a washing machine. There was a reason that washing machines were created, and that was so hand wash only items needed no longer exist. Regardless, some fool decided to make an un-natural fabric that needed to be hand washed only. Then another silly fool—ah-hem, Talon—decided to buy a bright white tablecloth for his lovely wife —that would be me—made out of said abhorrence of natural fabric.

I took the tablecloth down to the old guards' chamber, the closest place that the freezing cold water of the underground spring ran. The dark grey stone of the cavern was jagged, unlike the rest of the tunnels we called home. The roughly hewn walls arched high above my head, the only light source was a small collection of magical orbs that floated and bobbed amongst the shallow cavities of the stone ceiling. The green light that blossomed from above gave the room a dark glow that cast hundreds of eerie shadows around me.

The underground spring ran through the lowest level of the tunnels below Prague—well, the lowest level that anyone dared to go to anyway.

This room and the ancient dungeon below were old relics of when Edmund had first declared war on all magic. In the beginning, the dungeons were used to house traitors, and Edmund's men that Ilyan had captured, but refused to kill. There had been at least ten of the Skřítek army in here at any time, guarding the prisoners in the rooms below.

That was what the Skříteks were after all, an army—an army with the sole purpose of guarding the wells that sat in the lowest points of these caves.

The wells of Imdalind, the center of magic.

Ilyan and Edmund were the last ones alive who knew the way through the labyrinth of tunnels that led down to the muddy wells, which is why it was so scary that someone could be letting Edmund's people in here. If Edmund got in, he could stroll right down to the source of pure magic as if he were walking into a Denny's.

Now, however, the dungeons were bare, the rooms below and the guard chamber I now stood in were only a reminder of how the war had started and how many magical beings there had once been.

Putting the tablecloth into the water, I scrubbed the fabric before letting the majority of it trail away with the flow of the water. I held onto the corner, letting the white lace swirl through the freezing water.

In only a few minutes, my hands had become a lovely red color, although I couldn't feel the burning tingle of the cold. If my skin was threatening hypothermia, I had no idea.

Everything inside me had heated when my skin touched the stone of the floor I kneeled on. I had always reacted to the stone of these caves this way. It was as if my magic sensed the deep magic of the world that was hidden somewhere far below me and grew in response. As far as I knew, I was the only one who did that, but there weren't many Trpaslíks around to ask. It could be perfectly normal, and I would never know. Besides, it definitely had its benefits. My personal explosion factor increased by ten when my skin was in contact with the stone. Not like there were many things to explode around here, but it was still cool.

"NO!"

I jumped—like, full on jumped—at the disembodied voice that bounced into the air around me. The high-pitched scream shot through my body with electricity that raised every hair on my arms to full attention, my heart rate jumping with the speed of a twenty thousand volt reaction.

"P-please, n... no."

The woman was back, which meant that whoever was torturing her was back, too. They were close, close enough to find me. Close enough for me to find them.

I didn't know why my heart was thumping so wildly. It was either the fear of discovery or excitement for the battle. I narrowed my eyes as my muscles tensed, definitely excitement. I dropped the wet wad of lace down to the stone floor and tuned my ears toward where I could only assume the voice was coming from.

I took a step forward without thinking, my nerves on high alert, eager to attack. If only I could find her, I could end all this.

"I... I... w-won't t-tell you!"

My head spun, the voice seemed to have moved from one area of the cave to another. This time, the voice echoed down a darkened hallway that led toward the dungeon. I looked at the dark cavern, my nerves mingling with fear. No way was I going down there alone. No way. For all I knew, that was exactly what they wanted. Last thing I needed was to run into someone in the dark and then accidentally collapse the cave with my magic. Yep, that would be just my luck.

Why did this voice, this woman, only seem to appear when everyone else was busy? It didn't make sense. I needed to get Talon; we needed to find her.

"L-leave me a... alone," her voice broke and stuttered as she once again begged for her life.

The timber of her voice was so close to that of the little girl that haunted my dreams that my heart tensed in a reflex reaction, the contents in my stomach spinning uncomfortably.

I went to take off toward the sparring hall where the pull of Talon's magic told me he would be, but my wet Chuck Taylors squeaked on the stone on the first step. I froze, waiting to see if the noise would alert whoever was down there to my presence, but the crying remained. The last thing I needed was to scare her off before I could get Talon, and we could investigate.

I began walking again, moving slowly this time until the volume of the crying had lessened enough that I figured I was out of earshot, allowing me to take off on a dead run toward the training hall.

The sounds of battle hit my ears before anything else, the grunts and explosions mixed with laughter as everyone enjoyed the spectacles of combat.

I barreled into the large hall and wove my way through the small groups of sparring Skříteks, each group covered by the shimmering orb of a shield. I worked my way through them, looking like a fool when I jumped at an explosion that rocked against a barrier near my head.

I smiled at the two Skříteks enclosed in the fighting space and made my way toward Talon.

"Hi, baby," Talon said softly when I ran up beside him. His face dropped at the look in my eyes and the transmission of my panic that I was sure he felt through our bond.

"I heard her again. I think she is in the old dungeons."

Talon said nothing more before dragging me behind him out of the training hall and toward the underground spring.

His feet moved quickly, his gait and cumbersome shape unable to be quiet as we bounded through one dark tunnel and another before arriving in the same large cavern I had just left, the dark entryway to the dungeons staring at us hauntingly.

"Are you sure you heard the voice from down there?" Talon asked, his voice shaking as he looked wide-eyed into the abyss in front of us.

I could only nod. Talon was scared, that alone was enough to freak me out. I had never been down there, but Talon had, hundreds of times I was sure. The place was probably full of more haunted memories than crazy, flesh-stripped skeletons. Although, I was positive there had been a few of those, too, there always were in dungeons.

"You're sure?" Talon asked again, and I felt my confidence waiver.

"Of course I am not sure, Talon. Her voice echoes around like an Olympic game of Ping-Pong. She could have been a mermaid in the water for all I know."

"Don't be silly," Talon said, his voice still shaking, although less than before. "Mermaids don't exist."

Talon took a step away from me, toward the cavern, and I could feel his magic surge as he put on a small shield. Dude, he wasn't thinking about going in there, was he?

"Talon?" I asked from behind him, my voice catching at the petrified anger on his face. "Baby, let's go. We can't hear her anymore; she's gone."

I pulled on him, but he didn't move. I waited, but he didn't respond. His eyes stayed glued to the dark opening as if they had been sewn there. It was creepy watching him stare at something so intently.

My heart rate began to accelerate to match Talon's, the quick pick up triggering a warning inside of me. I didn't know how much I could take, my heart was beating too fast, and even I was starting to feel some creepy vibe from whatever was down there.

"Talon?" My voice was weak with the heavy vibe of fear that Talon's stare had given me.

I couldn't do it. Like a wet dog, I shook off the anxiety that was trying to take hold of me and grabbed the sopping tablecloth from where it still lay on the stone floor by our feet. In one smooth movement, I threw it over Talon's head, the wet fabric covering him with a loud smack.

It did the trick. He howled and pulled the cold thing off him.

"Let's go, Talon," I said before he could get angry with me.

His jaw hung heavily for a moment before his brain clicked back into place, reminding him of what had happened before I hit him with the wet tablecloth. That was the problem with being married to such a big guy; sometimes, his brain moved a bit too slowly.

Talon nodded and put the tablecloth in the basket, only to freeze at the sight of something over my shoulder.

"What are you two doing here?" Ovailia spat with as much icy venom as she possibly could.

I whipped around to see her standing before us, her feet moving back and forth as if she was walking in place, her long arms folded over her slender torso. I instantly moved back into Talon, content to let him take the lead and thankful when he squared his shoulders defiantly against her.

I guessed that was the one good thing about growing up with Ovailia; he was used to her. When you can think of someone as a tantrum-throwing toddler with a stinky diaper, their fits as an adult didn't truly bother you.

"That is no longer your concern, Ovailia," Talon said simply, his voice making it clear he didn't feel the need to elaborate.

"What?" Ovailia said, her voice airy with surprise. Why she was surprised, I had no idea. I had always assumed it would take pigs standing and walking on their hind legs to surprise her.

"I do not need to remind you of Ilyan's proclamation regarding who is acting in his stead, do I?" Talon wrapped his arm around me, pressing my shoulder into him.

"No, I remember quite well," she said snottily, the airy confusion in her voice gone now.

I stared at Ovailia intently, the nerves in my spine jumping sporadically. Something about the way Ovailia shifted her feet was freaking me out. Her whole body was screaming, liar! Run! I couldn't tear my eyes from the icy blue of hers and the way her lips curled in warning.

"Speaking of Ilyan," Ovailia started, her voice hesitant, "how is my dear brother?"

"Wonderful," Talon answered, his voice pinched.

Ovailia smiled, but said nothing. Talon began to lead me out of the large room, the basket perched on his hip.

"Oh, and Wynifred," Ovailia sneered the moment we had passed her, "I wouldn't go poking around in corners if I were you."

"Is that a threat?" I hissed, my body pulling away from Talon as my magic surged angrily.

"Of course."

I wanted to lunge at her, but let Talon's strong arm around my waist serve as a warning. I let him drag me out of the roughly carved chamber and into the smooth stone halls that would take us to our room. I didn't feel comfortable just leaving her there, but something in Talon's body language begged me to.

I complied, choosing instead to stick my tongue out at the stone wall that stood between us.

Yes, sometimes I was just that childish.

2

WYN

I WANTED to curl up in a ball and go to sleep, but I couldn't. Joclyn still hadn't called.

It was probably foolish of me to expect her to, but I considered her my best friend. I knew she thought the same, and besides, she had called me about everything else. They had been attacked. I didn't even know where they were. It was getting hard to ignore that angsty, creepy crawly feeling that was working its way up my spine. She should have called. Maybe I should call.

I could call, but the way Ilyan was so hush-hush about everything made me question if I should. I was not sure I was allowed. Hell, I was sure I wasn't allowed.

So, I waited. I curled up in the blankets like a guinea pig and waited until sleep took me, the blonde girl and the Henry the Eighth wanna-be occupying my thoughts almost immediately. I watched the girl dance and the man laugh as he chased her.

He laughed.

He had never laughed before. He had never talked. I had

seen his mouth move every night that I slept, but no sound had ever escaped.

It was a dream and I shouldn't have cared, but even in the dream, I was acutely aware.

The image jumped and bobbed as I watched, the girl flashing from one side of the field to another, the man doing the same before he ended up right beside me.

"We should go," he said, his voice conspiratorially low.

I would have jumped at the sound of his voice had I been in control of my body. I wasn't in control, though, and I could do nothing. My voice spoke on its own. The dream me smiled and felt joy, while inside, I only felt more and more panic.

"Go where?" I said. At least I thought it was me. It came from me and sounded a bit like me, although the voice was different, more mellow, adult, not the electric youthful tones I had now.

"Away," he answered as he turned to look at me, his blue eyes smiling.

I tried to scream and push him away, but I didn't have control over my arms. My body didn't move. I could feel my lips smile, even though I didn't want them to. I could hear my mind think about his eyes, the eyes of his father, royal blue.

His father?

It was my thought. I felt it form inside of me, but it wasn't mine. It wasn't true. How could it be? How could I know, how did I know?

"We can't get away," that wretched voice spilled out from me again, even though I still fought to control the body.

"We can run." His voice was desperate.

I felt myself screaming, but the body I was trapped in didn't follow suit. Instead, the body smiled and touched his face. I screamed until my eyes flashed open, the silence of our dark room filling the air in the wake of my nightmare.

I wasn't sure what had woken me. Not the dream, surely? I always slept through those. Then again, the man had never spoken to me before either.

I lay still, my mind pushing away the images of the dream while still trying to recall pieces of it. Why would I want to recall that? It was a dream, and I was not a Drak. My dreams had no meaning.

"I understand." I jumped as the voice came out of the dark. Even though I recognized it as Talon's right away, I had not expected to hear it or the stress that lined the words behind it.

"Only a week? Is it that unsafe?"

I could tell Talon was trying to be quiet. The light from the phone lit up his face, making the deep stress lines look even darker. My heart clunked as his stress leached through our connection and into me.

So that was what had woken me.

"What about Ovailia? She has been asking questions—"

Talon's voice cut off as Ilyan interrupted him, his head bobbing in agreement with something Ilyan said. I pulled the blankets up around me as I watched him, fighting the temptation to go back to sleep. I wanted more information.

Only a minute later, he lowered the phone. The light from the screen went out, leaving us alone in the brightening yellow shades of dawn that seeped in through the vent in the ceiling of our cave.

"Is everything okay?" I asked, my voice startling him.

"I didn't know you were awake." Talon moved over to me, his weight indenting the bed enough to make me roll toward him.

"Yeah, someone's stress woke me up."

"Not mine surely?" He smiled as he moved to sit next to me, his arms draping over me as if he was locking me in place.

He looked down at me, and my stomach twisted. I knew what the fire behind his eyes meant, what the deep surge of magic I felt tumble through me was leading up to.

I smiled back at him, arching my back as I lifted my face to meet his, my lips pressing deeply against his.

My magic surged violently at the intimate connection, our magic rejoicing as they met their mates and curled around each other.

Talon lowered himself onto me, his body heavy against mine. I sighed as his hand moved up my arm to cup my face. His tongue dragged against my bottom lip before he left my lips and peppered deep, longing kisses along my jawbone and neck.

I couldn't help the moan that escaped my lips. I couldn't understand where this was coming from, especially with the stress that had lined his voice only a moment ago, but I wasn't going to complain. I was enjoying this far too much.

Talon kissed my neck once more before he stilled against me, his breathing deep and ragged. I closed my eyes and savored the way our contact moved through my body, the way every nerve ending felt illuminated. I could have stayed like that for hours, but I could still feel Talon's erratic heartbeat, and I knew he needed more from me.

"Are you okay?" I asked again, changing the question to get the answer I really wanted.

Talon shifted his weight, moving back to sit at the edge of the bed, his hand moving to cup my face. I looked at him, wishing he would answer, not even knowing if he could. His dark eyes glistened as more light filtered into our room, the sparks of dawn igniting around us.

"Talon?"

"I think I know who the crying voice belongs to." Talon's bold statement made my arms and legs feel like lead. I hadn't expected that.

I sat up and leaned closer to him, my heart thumping, desperate for more information.

"Who?" I asked, my voice only a whisper, the sound swallowed by my jumpy nerves. I could feel my magic skitter around inside of my skin, ready for a fight.

"All day yesterday, only one person asked me about Ilyan's welfare—several times, each more desperate. It was very unlike her to care—"

"No!" I gasped. His statement combined with what he had said on the phone a moment ago putting the name in my head. "Not Ovailia! I mean, she's wicked, yeah, but she wouldn't betray him, not again."

"What would stop her from doing it again?" Talon asked softly.

I held my tongue. He had a point. Ovailia's personality was not one that lent itself to loyalty; she would go where the chips lay thickest.

"Besides, the crying we keep hearing, it is like she is fighting against the bind Ilyan placed over everyone to keep his location secret."

I could only stare and nod. He had a point. Ilyan had placed that little touch of magic inside of everyone when he first went on the run, hundreds of years ago. I shouldn't be surprised it was still around and strong enough to keep Ovailia's tongue at bay.

"I'm going to go talk to her," Talon said, his voice making it sound as if he was walking into a death camp, not simply speaking with Ovailia. I didn't want to face Ovailia, not in the slightest, but I couldn't let him face her alone. This confrontation would not be pretty.

"Let's go," I said, trying to ignore the foreboding pulse of my nerves.

I jumped out of bed and took the two quick steps to my dresser. I didn't even look as I grabbed random items of clothing in my rush to leave: Styx shirt, red skinny jeans, black converse.

Talon, now dressed himself, nodded once before moving toward the door, my converses squeaking as I followed him.

Everything was tense inside of me. My muscles and magic were tight against my skin, just waiting for Ovailia to pop around a corner and attack us. Talon walked in front of me, his hulking form leading the way, his fists clenched to his sides. I wanted to reach out and hold his hand, but he did not need that kind of comfort.

We had just passed the orchard when a loud robotic song began to play from the pocket of my jeans. I pulled the phone out to find Ilyan's name lit up. On the screen was a picture of him and Talon from when they dressed up in some medieval armor they had found in a storage room.

Now? She would call right now?

I stared at the picture, a heavy need to talk to her temporarily clouding the fear of where Talon and I had been heading.

"You should answer that."

"But, Talon," I began, my voice laced with a whine.

"Stay here. Talk to Jos. She needs you."

I could only nod. I wanted to say that he needed me, too, but I couldn't. He was right. I wasn't very happy.

Talon ignored my surliness and leaned down to kiss me, a soft peck on my lips was his sweet goodbye.

"You will be back, right?" I asked, trying to put a laugh on my lips, but the way he had spoken was making me uncomfortable.

"I was raised to protect my king, and now my wife. I will return, Wyn; don't worry." He smiled before he left, his eyes shining with his promise.

I smiled at him as he left before turning back toward our room, pressing the phone to my ear.

"Jos!" I yelled into the phone as I made my way back down the hall. "Oh, please tell me you are okay! I've been so worried since Talon told me what happened. Then you didn't call me at all yesterday." I really wanted to yell at her, berate her for not calling me sooner, but I was so happy she was calling in the first place that a little berating could wait until later.

"I knew I should have gone with you!" I continued when she said nothing. It's not as if I gave her a chance, which is probably why she cut me off. "This never would have happened if I had—"

"It would have happened either way, Wyn," she interrupted, our voices overlapping a bit. "If you were here, you would have gotten hurt, too."

"Too?" I practically screeched. "You got hurt?"

"Nothing a little magic can't fix."

I breathed out like I had been holding my breath my entire life, my exhale loud and obnoxious.

"I can still come out if you want. An extra pair of hands doesn't hurt," I said as I moved into an old, empty bedroom, fully aware I was practically begging.

"No!" I jumped as she screamed in my ear, her panic taking me off guard. "Stay where you are. You'll only get hurt if you get too close to me."

What was that about? She was talking about herself as if she were a curse. I would have rolled my eyes and laughed at her, but I could hear the stress and the nerves in the undertones of her voice. Something had happened, something more than just being attacked.

"Joclyn?" I asked, my worry guiding my voice forward whether I wanted it to or not. "What are you saying? I'm not going to get hurt."

"I don't want to risk anything. People seem to get hurt around me."

I heard her sigh, and my heart broke just a little for her. Even though I felt like we were close, she had never genuinely opened up to me. I wanted her to do so now. I needed her to, for her sake.

"Is Ilyan okay?"

"He's fine." Her voice was dead, belligerent and lonely... so lonely.

What had happened? The last time I had talked to her, she and Ilyan had almost been buddy-buddy. Joclyn had gotten away with more around him than even Talon. I had never known anyone to yell at him to put on a shirt and stop leaving hair in the shower only for him to laugh. Maybe that was what she had needed, a friend. If Ilyan had been one for her before the attack, the stress of the situation must have zapped that out of him.

"Are you sure you don't want me to come out?" I asked again, careful to let just enough cheer into my voice, hoping to zap her buzz-kill attitude.

"I'm sure, but can you do something for me?"

"Sure! What's up?" I responded playfully, I would have jumped off a bridge at her request right then—but only because I could fly. I was ready for whatever she was going to lay on me. What she actually laid down on me, though, was surprising.

"Sing me a Styx song."

I laughed aloud. I couldn't help it. Joclyn not only liked crappy music like Katy Perry, she also never listened to music for the joy of it. I would have liked to believe I had magically converted her to good music—aka 70s music—but I doubted that was the case.

"You're a dork," I managed to squeak out through a laugh.

"I can't help it. You've got me addicted," she pleaded.

Nope. Sorry, babe, I still don't believe you.

"Addicted to Styx?" I asked.

"Yep."

Fine, prove it.

"All right then, when was their first album released?" If the girl was going to lie to me, she needed a test—okay, a trial by fire, but whatever.

"1840."

I laughed so hard I might have broken the phone's mouthpiece. *1840? Really?* I guessed when she lied, she went for the blatantly obvious I'm-a-funny-moron lies.

"Liar," I taunted once my laughter had died down.

"Come on, Wyn; just sing me one of their stupid songs." No way had she said that. No freakin' way. This girl deserved a full on beating.

I stood before I was aware of it, my feet pacing me around the room in my agitation.

"I thought you said you liked them?" I snapped, unable to keep my own irrational response at bay.

It took me a moment to realize that her voice had jumped back to the distraught tone she had started with. She was stressed, alone, scared and had just been attacked, presumably by Ryland. God, Ryland had attacked her, and I hadn't even asked her about it. I felt like the world's bottom-of-the-bar worst friend right now. I didn't know how to make up for that. Well, yes I did. I didn't ask. I didn't apologize. I just sang her a Styx song. It was not my favorite of their songs, but it was a good one, and one I hoped would help her. After all, the lyrics were far and away awesome.

"...Free to face the life that's ahead of me."

I was about halfway through the song when I noticed it; Talon's magic was gone. The pull that told me where he was only a moment ago had vanished. It wasn't gone like when he shielded himself because even then, I could have felt something that would have led me in his general direction; this was just gone.

I froze; everything inside me turned icy with dread.

The words of the song faded as my focus left it, my fear growing. "And, I'll try. Oh Lord, I'll try to carry on."

"Thanks, Wyn." I barely heard her.

"No problem. Are you okay?" I asked automatically, my mind and magic both distracted and searching for Talon. I was barely able to get the words out, barely able to focus on her.

"I'm better now."

"Good," I said a little too stiffly. "I've gotta go find my husband now, okay? I'll call you in few hours."

"Sounds good, Wyn." I had already pulled the phone from my ear when she spoke, her voice almost drowned out by the disconnecting phone.

I put the phone in my pocket and made my way toward the door, my fingers tingling as I turned the knob. I stood in the wooden doorframe for one solid minute as my magic searched for him, my heart rate picking up as no sign of him came. I couldn't focus, I couldn't think. What had happened?

I waited to hear something, almost expecting parades or riots, but heard only the buzzing in my ears as my stress took over.

Everything slowed down to a snail's pace before my brain moved into overdrive in my panic. My feet moved without asking, taking me nowhere before I was able to stop and attempt to refocus.

Talon had gone to speak to Ovailia. The last I felt of him had also been in that general direction, so I turned, my heart beating angrily as my feet ran toward him, my mind moving from panicked to focused with each step. I reached Ovailia's room quickly and found the door open slightly as several voices filtered into the hall toward me.

The voices overlapped each other and bounced around the smooth stone of the walls that surrounded me. The sound contained more than Talon and Ovailia's voices; I could hear at least two others in there, both male, their voices deep and scratchy.

I tiptoed toward the door, flattening my back against the dark stone of the wall as I closed my eyes and expanded my vision into the room. I had to work to press it that far, but what little I could see was enough to make the contents of my stomach turn and my heart thump against the thin bones in my chest.

My father and Edmund were in there.

It was not just henchmen that had made it in; *they* were here. Edmund and my father. I knew they wouldn't travel alone either; they never did. Somewhere, in the once safe halls of Imdalind, an army stood in waiting.

I clasped my hand over my mouth, trying to keep the panic stuck inside, my breath trapping itself inside of my chest. Everything inside me constricted, my body freezing in place even though my feet were threatening to run in and attack.

Don't move; don't let them know you are here.

Ovailia sat in one of her many large, carved chairs, filing her nails as if she was bored out of her mind. In the corner of the large room, a man was crumpled and chained, his own blood staining his clothes and dark beard. The beaten man moaned and rocked as his fingers clawed against the wood of Ovailia's floor, large scratches appearing as black sparks flew from his fingertips.

My father stood in the middle of the room, Timothy's short, squat frame barely enough to hold Talon's wavering form steady, his neatly trimmed beard glistening with blood I knew didn't belong to him.

My whole body jolted at seeing Talon. I saw him, but I felt nothing aside from my own fear. There was no magical pull alerting me to his presence, no surge that would have normally filled the air. Something had happened. They had done something to him.

Edmund paced the floor in front of Talon, his tall, muscular body draped in black as he smiled wickedly toward him. Edmund moved to slick his curly hair back against his head, and my stomach muscles tightened, his knuckles were bloody from having turned my husband's face into a punching bag.

I watched them for only a moment before trying to let my panic subside enough for my logical thinking to step in. I shielded myself the moment my rational brain burst strongly to the forefront of my mind. My eyes narrowed, my back straightened, and even through the fear and stress, I knew what I had to do.

The shield around me was strong enough to block me

from sight as well as hiding any magical signature I might have been broadcasting; at least, I hoped it was.

One breath. I let one breath escape my lips before I walked into the room, careful to keep my steps silent, my eyes watching the reactions of all those in the room, wary of being noticed. No one reacted or even looked in my direction.

My chest loosened, although just briefly. I was not walking into a surprise party—I might as well have been walking to greet my death.

"Tell me what I need, Talon, and I won't hurt her." I froze at Edmund's words, his voice dark and chilling, as I turned toward him, worried he had seen me.

His focus was not on me, it was on Talon, whose face was already swollen and bloodied at Edmund's hand. I restrained a gasp as Edmund pulled his arm back, his fist glowing white, before a strong sucker punch to the gut winded Talon with one shot. I froze as Talon grunted in pain, my hand flying to my own stomach as anger lurched up my spine.

"What about the rest of your men, Edmund? What would they do to her? I know how your deals work." Talon's voice was broken and pained, blood spattering around him as he forced out the words.

"Oh, we won't kill her if that's what you are asking," Timothy said, my father's voice full of pure enjoyment. Edmund only smiled at his response before wiping his hand on a bright white cloth, smearing it with red.

I moved toward the back of the room, my magic crackling under my skin as it kept the shield in place. The angry energy rippled through me in a raw need to defend my husband. My toes curled as I begged myself not to react, and to wait until the most opportune time. If I began an attack now, I would be dead before I could get within reach. It was all about the timing. Running in to face the three most powerful people in the room was only a death sentence. Hell, attacking them on my own was a death sentence. Still, I wasn't scared—a fool, yes, but not scared.

I stared at Talon's face as I moved. My conviction growing as my magic surged. I would protect him, just as he would me.

"And the others? Will you hurt them, too?" Talon asked, his voice continually fading.

I fought the urge to run to him, choosing instead to knot my fingers around each other, hoping the tension in the small joints would dispel the panicked anger that was building in my heart.

"Oh, what do you care?" Ovailia snapped from the chair she sat in. "It's not like you are their rightful leader anyway."

"Very well put, Ovailia," Edmund said with true pride in his eyes. "She was always my good child," he said, more to himself than to anyone. "Took us a bit to break through Ilyan's spell and get the information I needed, but we got there in the end."

"Will you hurt them?" Talon repeated, his jaw tightening.

"Save whom you can, Talon. Don't worry about the others. They will be in capable hands, I promise." Edmund leaned down close to him, his lip sneering only millimeters from Talon's face.

"Give me what I need, Talon," Edmund snarled.

"You better make it look good, Edmund." Talon laughed deeply, his voice loud as he taunted him, while Timothy strengthened his hold at the sound.

Talon's eyes widened and he attempted to fight against my father's hold, yelling out. The struggle only lasted a moment before Edmund placed his hand against Talon's skin, his struggle for release turning to one of agony as Edmund's magic seeped into him, the powerful attack torturing him.

No. I couldn't let this happen anymore.

The time was now. Talon had risked everything for me, but I had done nothing for him. Now I would.

I slipped my right shoe off, letting my skin come in contact with the floor of the cave. Even through Ovailia's carefully preened wood floors I could still feel the energy of the caves. It prickled up my spine and down into my arms. I smiled as it seeped through the rock of the cave and into me. It flooded me as the power controlled me. That was why I always had to wear shoes in this space, why I could never risk skin contact with the walls of the caves. The magic that rested in the belly of this mountain flooded through the rock and, in turn, me. It was only here, in this mountain, that this much energy was at my disposal.

Now. I lifted my toe and let it drop to the floor, a rumble spreading out from me as I shook the floor. Edmund swore as the energy hit him, the power rushing up into him. I focused as my magic spread from the floor and into Edmund and Timothy. It moved right into their bones, shaking them within their bodies. They called out as their bones grew and vibrated, the pain of my attack sending them to the floor.

Ovailia stood in fear just as I took a step forward, each hit of my skin against the ground sending more ripples of energy across the surface and into Ovailia as well. All three writhed with pain as I lifted Talon with my magic and pinned them to the ground. Their calls of surprise mixed with those of agony as his body lifted into the air in front of them.

"Wynifred!" My father's voice yelled as he fought against the painful restraints my magic held him in.

I moved forward to grab Talon just as Edmund broke the magical bond that surrounded him. His voice howled as he stood, his body moving to block my path to my mate, his eyes boring right into where I stood.

I wanted to say he couldn't see me, but the way his eyes seem to bore into me, I was sure he could. I froze, carefully calculating the possibilities and my chance of survival.

I knew it was low, but right then, I didn't care. Right then, I just wanted Talon, even if it meant we would die in each other's arms.

"You will live to see Talon again, Wynifred." I froze at the voice that rasped through the air, the familiar tones triggering some memory long forgotten. I didn't dare turn to see who had spoken. I trained my eyes on Edmund's fingers as they flexed and glowed.

Edmund sent a surge shooting toward me, without even a flex of energy. I threw myself to the side, the heat of his attack warming my skin as it grazed the air beside me. I caught my scream in my throat before it escaped me, as my body landed roughly against the wood floor.

The impact of my body against the floor was hard enough that a strong surge of magic rushed out of me unrestrained, the floor shaking as I sent everyone to the ground again.

"Run!" The voice came to me again, the yell pounding into my head.

I didn't want to listen. I didn't want to leave Talon. I could hear each beat of my heart as it begged me not to. I could hear the voice's statement echoing around my head. Talon would live. I wanted to believe him.

I needed to believe him.

I jumped to my feet before anyone else had a chance to find theirs. I looked one last time toward Talon, my feet feeling like lead as they carried me away from him. I ran down the hall, their screams following me as I bobbed and weaved through the web of halls.

I didn't look back. I didn't dare. I only had a matter of minutes before they would regain their strength. I needed to draw them off my path while I figured out what I needed to do next.

I attempted to slow my heartbeat as I ran, but it was no use. Edmund was inside the caves of Prague, and now, he was after me—if anything my panic only increased.

They were here. There was no safety here anymore. Edmund had gotten past Ilyan's protections, and Ovailia was the one to guide him through.

Ovailia had betrayed us all.

My soul froze as screaming began to fill the halls. The sounds of fear, loss and battle exploded through the once safe halls.

I could easily hide, stay back and stay safe. Even if I did though, it wouldn't benefit anyone. Not even me.

There was no safety here anymore. There was no place to hide. I needed to get everyone out of here.

I needed to get out of here, but I couldn't, not without Talon.

The screams increased as I continued to move through the halls. I knew bigger things were at play here, and I needed to stop them. Stopping my father, and stopping Edmund, was my only way to get Talon back.

The cave vibrated as the battle increased, screams ricocheting around the stone halls as the battle broke out all around me.

Edmund's final execution had begun. Only one race

stood between him and the wells of Imdalind, and if Edmund had his way, there would be nothing left by the time the sun rose.

Edmund had started a war, and I was not going to back down.

3

WYN

I RAN through the halls toward the screams, the shouts increasing in strength and number the closer I was to the battle. I couldn't deny the throb within me that wished to run into my father, to end this before it even had a chance to begin.

Each step I took thundered through the underground tunnels, shaking lamps and doors, each step recharging my magic and sending magical currents surging through my body.

Flashes of light filtered along the dark stone that surrounded me, the screams chasing the shapes as they rippled through the once dark halls. I passed a raging fire, not willing to see what was keeping the blaze going. I turned and ran, my feet taking me toward the loudest concentration of noise where I just knew I would find the battle; but the state of the hallway in front of me froze me in place.

This was where it had begun. I could tell by the splatter of red on the walls, the screams that still lingered in the air, and the lifeless bodies of my friends that littered the ground, left to die with no one to hold them.

I stepped around them, my eyes trying to look away from each heartbreaking expression, but unable to do so.

I fought the panic that rose in me, the hopelessness that tried to take hold; instead, choosing to let my anger and conviction fuel me. I tiptoed around at least twenty of my friends; selfless people who had taken me in and loved me after my father had tried to kill me. My father. He had brought enough Trpaslíks into Imdalind to begin and end a massacre in one swipe. My logic begged me to hide, to wait until the battle slowed, until I could find Talon and we could escape.

I turned into another hall as I pulled out my phone, my feet picking up pace. My heartbeat was erratic as hate and anger fluctuated through me in a surge that only hyper-activated my magic.

The phone rang in my ear as I ran, the loud thrum vibrating through my head and mixing with the frantic beat of my heart.

"Pick up," I growled to myself, turning a corner as I made my way toward a seldom-used row of apartments. "Pick up, Jos! Jos, pick up the phone!"

"Wynifred! What's going on?" I had never been so happy to hear Ilyan's voice. I could have kissed him, cried into him, and thanked him for saving us; but I knew he couldn't save us. I wasn't calling for a savior; I was calling with a warning.

"Ilyan? Oh, thank Heavens!" I yelled into my phone, one knot in my stomach loosening while another one tightened.

"Wynifred?" Ilyan boomed, his commanding voice seeping into me through the phone. "Where is Talon?"

"They got him, Ilyan," I panted as I ran, my eyes threatening tears. I would not cry, not right now. I hated that Ilyan asked the one question that would trigger the emotion in me right now. "They took him. I think..."

I turned from the darkened hallway into a place that was never used, a place I had hoped I could hide, only to find my father standing in the middle of the dark stone-walled room. My words dropped off my tongue as I saw him there; the fear that twisted through me lessening my power for a moment. It was a moment too long.

A loud crack echoed through my ears as a powerful attack impacted on my spine and sent me across the large room to collide with the rock wall in front of me. My head hit the wall, my bones and joints rattling hard enough to vibrate through me in a claw of pain. The pressure increased as I hung there, Timothy and Ovailia's laughter loud in the quiet space.

"No! Please don't!" I screamed, feeling them come right up behind me. The force on me increased and my scream followed, louder this time.

"Father! Please don't!" I shouldn't beg; I knew it was pointless. "Don't let them hurt me."

No sooner had the words left my mouth that I was flung through the air again, my hands sparking as I attempted to find someone, anyone, to attack. However the movement was too quick, the flight too short, and before I knew it, I was stretched out on the hard floor, my father restraining my hands above my head and Ovailia standing over me in an oppressive straddle.

I looked away, desperate to see anything other than the wicked sneer of the blonde above me, only to see the still lit screen of the cell phone reflecting off the dark stone.

"Ilyan!" I screamed, knowing I might not be allowed to live after this point, and hoping that my last warning was not my final goodbye.

Ovailia's eyes went wide, her head whipping around in fear as I yelled her brother's name.

"Run!" I yelled.

It did not take her long to locate the light, one pulse of her magic destroying the small box. I only hoped my warning had reached them before the line had gone dead.

"Nice try," Ovailia said, her voice heavy with indifference and anger. "But sadly, I don't think it's going to work." She smiled, and her face lit up like a maniac. Ilyan would get the same light when going into battle, but instead of giving hope, this one twisted my spine and rippled through my stomach.

I ground the feeling down to my toes, letting it come to rest inside of me, in a place that I didn't care about, and squared my jaw at her.

"You have no idea what you are up against," I snarled, happy to see her recoil a bit at my taunt.

"Oh, don't I now?" Her crazed energy came right back into her face.

I heard my father laugh from above me, the pressure on my arms increasing as he pulled them, the tendons in my shoulders pulled to their brink. I winced, even though I tried not to, and Ovailia laughed right alongside my father, the ringing of her cell phone drowning out the noise.

"I think I know exactly what I am up against," she said as she pulled the phone from the pocket of her designer jeans. Timothy's hold on my hands lessened as one of his hands moved down to cover my mouth.

"Now, princess," he said, the once sweet pet name spoken with acid, "don't try anything stupid." His hand cupped the entire lower half of my face, the pressure arching my neck back and making it difficult to breathe while also pushing my head painfully into the stone floor. I fought against him, yelled against his palm, but the pressure of his hand hurt worse the more I fought. I stopped struggling with a whimper. "Nothing stupid," Timothy repeated before increasing his grip even more. I winced and breathed in sharply but kept my mouth shut.

Ovailia smiled at me before putting the phone to her ear, her face and voice changing the second the line connected.

"Ilyan? Ilyan, where are you?" Ovailia said, her voice thin as she pushed emotion into it. "Please tell me you are all right."

She began to pant as Ilyan spoke, the movement of her voice making it sound like she was running.

"They took her," Ovailia said sharply, her voice panicked. She looked at me before firing a stream of light into the wall of the room, causing a giant explosion that rocked the floor of the cave. "They took Talon, too; I don't know where he is..." She gasped, panted, winced and screamed softly, each action perfectly placed to make it sound like she was fighting someone.

I knew I had to fight Timothy whether I wanted to or not. She was lying to Ilyan, leading him into a trap. My father's grip increased and I winced again, the action silencing me.

"I wouldn't fight if I were you," Timothy hissed in my ear, the heat of his breath uncomfortable against my skin. "You wouldn't want something to happen to that mate of yours."

My body relaxed as if on a switch. I could still feel the beat of my heart, hear the static of my stress as my brain clung to the panic, but my body relaxed. I felt like a puppet, a foolish, little girl who could only do what her father said.

"...But Timothy dragged Wyn off," Ovailia finished, her false exhaustion picking up.

"Father, Timothy," Ovailia said, and I heard Timothy's

faint chuckle from right above my head. "There are hundreds of them."

Hundreds. I knew it was true. I had seen the bodies, smelled the blood and the smoke. Edmund had planned this attack well. It was to be his final attack. He wasn't going to let anyone survive. He wouldn't stop until he killed them all.

"I don't know how they got in," Ovailia continued, giant crocodile tears rolling down her perfect cheeks and cracking in her voice. She smiled at me, the tears glistening as she flipped her hair.

My stomach clenched, and I felt my magic crackle between my fingers in anger. I hated her. I regretted never saying it before, never seeing who she truly was before. She was evil.

"Our whole city... I don't know how many are going to make it out."

I groaned and fought him again; I didn't care that he had told me not to. I heard Ovailia's words and knew she was telling the truth, though not quite in the way that she tried selling it to Ilyan. I wanted to claw at her face, to stop this, no matter how futile it was.

Timothy stretched his arm out and away from my head, pulling my arms until I felt the tendons in my arms pop. I screamed, and he released his hand from over my mouth just long enough to let the sound flow through the phone. It was all part of their game.

I panted as the tendons in my arms began to repair themselves, the pain lessening as my magic covered it.

"I can try," Ovailia said, her voice more disappointed than anything else.

She nodded once to Timothy who stretched my arms again. What little repair my body had been able to produce shattered as my scream rent through the air around us, the rumble of explosions overlapping with the sound of my pain.

"And you, Ilyan." Ovailia smiled and tucked the phone back in her pocket, her wicked eyes never leaving mine as she bent closer to me. Her hair fell around her like a curtain, the effect increasing the terror I felt at being trapped between the two of them. I sucked in breath as Timothy released my mouth, the hold on my hands loosening just enough to let my body begin to heal.

"We will destroy you," Ovailia said, her voice hard.

I just met her gaze. I had nothing to say to her. I could rebut. I could be scared and give her what she wanted. I did none of that. I did, however, choose to laugh. It wasn't the wicked laugh of my father or the taunting laugh that had just graced Ovailia's lips, it was light and joyful, the change in mood jarring.

Ovailia's face fell and she looked around, her shoulders stiffening in expectation. I took my opportunity and slammed my bare foot against the ground, the rippling energy moving around us again, sending Ovailia off me and causing my father to fall away. His hands released my arms as he fell into the ground.

I didn't wait. I spun away, regaining my balance as quickly as I could, and stumbled away from them. I called out for help, trying to ignore the gripping panic that was trying to stop the beat of my heart.

I spun around to where Ovailia and Timothy were attempting to get back to their feet. I sent another stream of energy toward them, hoping to restrain them before they regained their bearings, but Ovailia caught sight of what I was doing and blocked my weak magic with a powerful shield of her own.

I immediately moved to attack, sending a bright light toward them, only to have Timothy block it as Ovailia sent her own attack in my direction. I dodged and blocked the attack a moment before it would have hit me, only to see another force in my direction.

"Come on, princess," Timothy taunted, "let your ol' dad give you a present!" I blocked his assault, but just barely. I could feel the heat graze my shoulder as the muscles in my arms tensed, the warning of what my father's magic would do to me as clear as if he had said it. The attacks kept coming, one after another, and I knew what they were doing. I wasn't fast enough, wasn't strong enough, to fight off one, let alone both of them. I had walked into this fight knowing I was too weak, my anger fueling my desire, but now my only option was to play defense. I couldn't attack. I could only hope to hold off their attacks long enough to give myself enough time to escape.

I fell to the side, sending heat through the ground with my skin contact, the earth responding to my touch. I rarely had control over what my touch would do in these caves, but this time, I focused. I forced the magic into my desired outcome and watched as they crumpled to the ground, their mouths opened in horror as their bodies heated up from the inside.

I picked myself up and ran, stepping over them in my haste to get away, to find Talon.

I spun around the corner and slammed into the thick barrel chest of a man who smelled of death and smoke. I didn't need to look up at him to know who it was. I pushed my hand into his chest and sent a stream of fire into it, only to be met by a shield that blocked my pointless attack.

"My, my, Wynifred. You would think that after a few

hundred years you would know better," Edmund hissed, his thick fingers curling around my tiny forearm.

I tried to pull away, but I wasn't even sure why. There was no escaping now. His fingers met the small indentation of my spine through the skin in the back of my neck, and I felt the white-hot heat of his magic shock into my spine. His magic surged, numbing each and every one of my nerve endings and muscles before I could move even so much as an inch. I felt the ripple of the attack move through me before everything went dead, my body going limp as I fell into his arms. He held me against him, my head lolling. My unfocused eyes came to rest on the bruised, bearded man Edmund had been dragging around by the chains attached to his wrists.

I couldn't even move my eyes, I realized. I just stared at the intense green gaze of the battered man as Edmund placed a smooth stone on my tongue, his magic pulsing just enough to force a reaction that would make me swallow it. The tiny stone slipped down my throat and toward my stomach. The further it traveled into my body, the more numb and unresponsive my magic felt.

An omezující stone. The rare rock that was given to prisoners as a magical restraint.

I felt it as it lodged itself in my stomach, my numbed body unable to fight it. I felt my magic slow to a stop, freezing in place before it traveled to surround the rock, where it would stay until I could find someone powerful enough to remove it.

I could feel the wetness of my silent tears roll down my cheeks, my body accepting my defeat without my permission, accepting my loss.

"Wonderful," Timothy said as he came up behind us. "I was hoping someone would grab the little whore."

Timothy grabbed my hair and pulled my head back, my eyes drifting to the roof of the cave tunnel, unable to focus on their own.

Edmund chuckled at my father's comment. His rumbling voice vibrated through my head as he hoisted me over his shoulder and carried me down the hall, my desire to find my mate pulling me in the opposite direction.

4

WYN

MY BODY WAS STILL NUMB. Edmund had carried me into the dungeons below Prague after he had incapacitated me. The dark space was cold, wet and smelled of mildew. I had wanted to look around, see what horrors had made this place forbidden, but my eyes still would not respond to my commands.

I stared into the darkness as my hands were bound and chained above my head, the chain extended until I was pulled to a stand, my weight supported by my wrists, my weak legs not able to hold me. Even though I could feel the stone against the balls of my feet, I couldn't move my legs to try to stand against it.

They left me there, alone, strung up against the cold stone. I hoped that the mysterious power I shared with the stone of these walls would awaken and ignite, but the rock Edmund had forced down my throat had done its job. I was powerless.

I stayed like this for hours, with only the darkness for company, and an occasional movement or whimper off to my left. I couldn't tell if it was a rodent or the battered man that Edmund had been dragging around behind him.

Time passed. I was sure that if I could feel anything, my shoulders would be on fire, my wrists screaming and broken from supporting me for so long, and my legs numb from lack of movement. I felt nothing, and saw nothing but blackness.

I don't know if I had passed out or simply slept, but the clanging of chains woke me, and I felt the subtle pressure of fingers against my spine. I heard the sound, felt the touch, and everything inside of me woke up.

I had been wrong. It wasn't pain in my arms and legs that the numbness had taken away; it was agony. Without my magic to numb the sensation, it quickly moved to torture. I screamed as my brain registered the pain, the sound echoing off the dark walls. My scream hung in the damp air even after a wide fist collided with my face, leaving more pain at the heavy impact. I screamed again at the pain, only to have another punch join the first. I whimpered, and this time the hand hit me with a wide palm, the message as clear as day: *The less noise you make, the less you are hurt. Say nothing.* I did not need the words to understand the lesson that that hand had taught me.

The chains that suspended me clattered again as they were moved higher, extending my body until I was on my tiptoes, the stone cold and uncomfortable against my back. I screamed at the movement, whether I wanted to or not, the sound loud for a moment before the same hand smacked my cheek, the face of the hand's owner swimming into view.

"Silence, princess," my father sneered, his lip curling underneath his large moustache. "There are consequences."

He slapped me again, his movement unprovoked except in warning. My cheek stung, and my body screamed, but I said nothing, refusing to give him rise to the occasion, to let him win. I just stared into his eyes, the irises as dark as mine, waiting for more. None came, and his smile only increased.

"Aren't you going to say hello to your father?" he sneered. "I think I have taught you better manners than this."

I stared at him in silence, my eyes wide as I taunted him, as I dared him. If I was anyone else, I would have whimpered and given in to him; but I couldn't, something deep inside wouldn't let me.

Timothy's eyes narrowed at my defiant gaze, his confidence wavering at my stubbornness. Good. He might kill me, but I was going to put up a fight until the very end.

"Say, hello," he sneered again, the stubbornness I had inherited from him forcing him on.

I shook my arms; the fire burned through my arms, and I winced, my taunt lost as pain seared through me only to settle in my spine. I couldn't stop it; a groan escaped me as I fought back a scream, my jaw clenching painfully as I attempted to keep the scream behind my lips.

I should have just screamed. Timothy's fist collided with my face, turning the groan into another scream—a scream that triggered another impact of Timothy's fist against my cheek.

I froze, keeping the noise trapped in my chest, a lone tear escaping my eye—again, whether I had wanted it to or not.

I looked at my father with as much hatred, as much power as I could muster. I found the sleeping magic within me and prodded it, but nothing happened. My now mortal body was useless and strung up before my father for whatever torture he had in mind.

"Say, hello," he prompted again, his fists flexing by his sides.

I stared at him, my jaw clenched, ready for the impact to come... when he smiled.

"Don't you want to see your mate, princess?" he snarled, and my eyes widened. His smile only increased.

I hung my head, not wanting to let him win, but I had no other choice. This time he would win.

"Hello, Father," I growled from behind clenched teeth. He said nothing. He only nodded his head to someone in the dark and the chains loosened, sending me tumbling to the ground. My arms were still extended above my head, although not as painfully as they were a moment before. My body relaxed with the loosened position, and while I still fought the urge to scream and cry with the pain, it was manageable.

"You do what I say, Wynifred. I do not care what deal Talon worked out with Edmund. You are my child, and I will do with you what I please." His voice was soft as he came to kneel down next me, his finger pushing aggressively into the tender skin of my now battered face.

"You stay silent, you do as I say, and we may not have to do this anymore."

I glared at him, not willing to take my gaze away, not willing to accept the weak position he had set up for me.

He took my silence as affirmation, the pressure of his fingers leaving my face as he moved away from me. "Good girl," Timothy said, his voice making it sound like he was addressing a dog. "Now, your brother has just arrived in Prague, and I am sure he has news, if not a heart, for your master." He smiled once more before disappearing into the darkness, the heavy sound of his footsteps on the stairs announcing his departure.

I tried to focus through the dark, squinting to see anything through the black that surrounded me, but without the aid of my magic, I saw nothing. I eventually gave up and sank back into the wall, trying to ignore the fire that was thrumming in my shoulders and arms.

"Do what he says, Wynifred, and keep your secret safe." The voice came from the darkness where the movement had come from before, the sound deep and rough like sandpaper. I recognized it at once. It was the same voice I had heard in Ovailia's room, the one that had told me to run.

I turned my head toward the sound, but only saw darkness. My eyes squinted, but no shapes formed through the black.

"Excuse me?" I asked, not sure what the voice was talking about, my voice broken and muffled because of the swelling in my face.

"No talking!" The new voice was loud and powerful. The warning from what could only be a guard floated through the air toward me, causing me to shrink into the stone, wishing I had a way to attack him.

No magic to heal my body, no magic to increase my sight, and not even the slightest of pulls to signal to me that Talon was alive. I clung to the hope that he was still alive as I leaned my head against the stone wall, wishing sleep would take me, but knowing it wouldn't.

Without wanting to, my eyes floated back toward the darkness where the rough, male voice had come from. I could only assume it was the battered man Edmund had been dragging around with him.

I wished I knew who he was; or at least, part of me did. The other part was not so sure. I didn't want to know whose side he was on or what Edmund had done to him. I didn't want to know what Edmund was capable of, what was in store for me.

For years, I had watched them drag Skřiteks down to the pit of whatever house we lived in. I had heard the screams, seen the blood that they washed off their hands. Now I was on the receiving end. I didn't want to know what was behind the screams. I didn't want to see the blood being drawn.

Now I was going to. I had seen what they had done to the battered man, and to Talon. I didn't want to think about him because the thoughts only brought fear, but part of me was rejoicing that I wasn't alone down here.

The minutes stretched into hours and thankfully, my arms began to go numb. My head swam as my blood flow got all muddled, my body calling for water, food, and above all, a bathroom. None of which, I knew, would be provided.

I shifted my weight for the millionth time, the chains rattling as my joints surged with pain before settling back into the burn of numbness that was becoming normal.

Still, sleep did not come, no matter how much I wished it would.

I jumped as steps sounded on the staircase, the loud thump of feet cutting through the icy silence that had been the only sound since Timothy had left. The heavy sound of feet, many feet, increased as they came closer. Tension built in my stomach, the flare of fear working its way up my spine. My eyes looked through the dark, toward the sound, desperate to make out anything in this utter blackness.

"This guy is heavy!" the thick voice of a man filtered down the stairs, his voice deepened by the echo of the stairway.

"Stop complaining and use your magic," another one joined the first, causing my stomach to twist with uncertainty.

"This is ridiculous," the first man said. "Edmund is just going to kill them all anyway."

An impatient growl followed the first man's comment and a loud rumble of something being dropped on stone echoed through the cold, dark room.

"What is going on here?" A new voice, a voice I recognized at once, cut across the first two. Cail's voice was loud and angry as dozens of footsteps joined the first two who had clogged the stairwell.

My eyes were drawn to the only light I had seen in hours, a gentle blue light that got stronger as the voices got closer. It shone through the blackness directly in front of me, the light dim, but growing. I pulled toward it, like a moth, my desperation for sight rippling into my spine. Soon, the glow was enough to filter into the prison, letting me see what hell I had been trapped in.

The prison was a long, wide hall, one half broken up with thick metal bars that segmented us into five-foot by five-foot squares, with not even enough space to lie flat and straight. There were no windows, and it was obvious that nothing had been cleaned for centuries. I had smelled the mildew before, but now I knew why. A glistening sheen of wet covered the stone, the bars, even the large padded stool where a lone guard had sat.

My eyes burned a bit at the light as I looked around. All the cells were empty to my left, as well as all, but one, to my right—where the battered man I had seen before was chained by his hands against the wall. He caught my gaze as I looked at him, the bright green of his eyes startling even in the dark. His eyes pleaded with me from behind his unkempt beard and hair as he placed his finger to his lips. I only nodded; the need for silence was evident.

"Why aren't you two down there yet?" Cail continued, his voice rising.

"I'm sorry, sir," the first man said, his voice soft and pleading.

I couldn't help the twitch that moved through my spine as Timothy's voice joined the others. "Just get down there and do what you were asked."

"Yes, sir," the two men mumbled together, and the footsteps returned, the light increasing as they all moved into the prison.

The battered man's warning was lost the moment I saw them. The two men I had heard arguing a moment before carried with them a hulking form with a mess of sandy brown hair I knew all too well.

"Talon!" I couldn't help it; I screamed, I yelled, and I fought against my chains. The small space filled with my voice as I yelled for him, the rattling of my chains almost loud enough to drown out my panic.

He didn't respond. He didn't even twitch as they dragged him into the cell right next to mine, dropping him to the ground and not even bothering to chain him before they closed the bars that trapped him in the tiny space.

My body was on fire as I fought against the chains. Every muscle, every bone, pulled in agony. I barely registered the pain. My need to get to him was too strong. I needed to touch him, to feel his heartbeat, to prove that he was still alive. I screamed, battled, yelled and pleaded, knowing it was of little use, but still, I couldn't help myself.

"Will someone shut her up?" I heard Timothy yell above my screams. I should have seen someone coming, but I was so focused on Talon's limp body in the cell next to mine that I didn't know anyone had come into my cell until a foot collided with my stomach, the impact knocking the wind out of me and sending me back against the wall.

I stopped screaming as I groaned in pain, gasping for breath. The chains around my wrists clattered as I slid down the wall, my arms pulling back into their extended position above my head. I couldn't take my eyes off Talon. I panted with pain as I watched him, my heart pleading with me to find a way over to him, my mind yelling at me that it was impossible. I looked at Talon until a strong hand grasped my jaw, causing me to wince at the pressure he placed on the tender skin as he turned me to face him.

"Don't push me, Wynifred," Cail sneered right in my ear before his closed fist hit me hard against my cheek.

I stayed silent as I turned back to look at him, my eyes narrowing in fight and warning. It was a useless threat; there wasn't anything I could do to him. He smiled once before moving out of the cell to stand in the small hallway that lined the jail block.

"Ryland," Cail said, his attention turning from me to the black-eyed man behind him. My head whipped up as Cail spoke his name. I didn't know why I didn't expect him to be here. Ryland was just as much one of Edmund's puppets as my brother was now.

Ryland stepped forward, his face blank, his curls limp as they hung damp around his head.

"Go sit by Sain, and chain your legs together."

Sain? The first of the Drak? The one Ovailia betrayed? The one Edmund killed?

My head bounced between Cail and Ryland, hoping for a clue about who they were talking about.

Without a word, Ryland walked into the cell with the battered man, sat down next to him, and chained his own ankles.

Sain.

Sain. It couldn't be; it just couldn't. My mind begged me not to believe it, but deep down I knew it was true. Sain looked at me with those bright green eyes of his, his one glance daring me to deny what I already knew. He was Sain. I had no idea how, or why, but I was sure it was him.

Ryland's movements were stiff, his vision unfocused as he followed Cail's odd demands. I looked between all of them; my brother and father who were focused on Ryland, Talon's limp body in the cell next to mine, Ryland as a shell of himself, and Sain. His green eyes still bore into mine, the power behind them evident even beneath the blood-soaked hair and the bruised face.

Timothy moved over to where Ryland and Sain sat. Sain lifted his chained hands up to him. Timothy removed one of the chains from Sain's wrist and reattached it on Ryland's. Sain did not fight, and Ryland did not move. The eeriness of it scared me. I didn't know what they were doing, and I didn't want to.

"Ready," Timothy said as he stepped out of the cell, closing the door to the tiny space behind him and trapping the two men inside. "Turn him off, son."

"Yes, Father," Cail said obediently, and for one split second, the prison was quiet except for the sound of my chains as I looked between them. The sound of my heart was like a beating drum in my ears as the silence pumped me full of dread. They were waiting for something, and the mystery as to what was terrifying. The silence dragged before the air opened up with a scream so mournful that I jumped, my own tears threatening as my soul understood the absolute heartbreak that the sound encompassed.

I recoiled into myself as Ryland began to writhe and fight against the chains that he had bound himself with only moments before. Sain's emaciated body moved around like a rag doll with each of Ryland's spasms as he fought against his own restraints. Ryland screamed and yelled and howled, his now blue eyes panicked as he attempted to claw his way out of the cell.

I watched him as he reeled and fought, my heart thumping. This was like no side of Ryland I had ever seen. This was not the compliant Ryland that Cail seemed to control. It was not the aggressive Ryland that had attacked us at the party, nor was he the calm and loving boy that I had seen with Joclyn before this all began.

He was desperate, emotionally unstable and terrifying. It was the terrifying factor that affected me the most. That raw primal aggression was powerful as he repeatedly lunged against his chains, hitting his head against the bars in an attempt to move through them.

I scooted as far away from him as possible. My arms stretched painfully above me as I moved toward Talon, knowing he couldn't protect me, but needing to move away from the scene in the cell in front of me. As much as I wanted to move away, I couldn't take my eyes off him. I was not sure I would have been able to look away even if I hadn't been chained. I was not certain I wanted to. A part of me needed to see what they had done to Ryland, to understand what was coming for me.

"Joclyn!" he screamed, his voice weak and breaking. "What have you done to her?" Ryland continued to scream and writhe as Cail laughed, his footsteps heavy as he moved to stand in front of Ryland's cell, right next to our father.

"I haven't done anything to her," Cail said innocently. "What you should be wondering is what you have done to her."

Ryland froze, his jaw working in terror. "What *I* did?"

he asked, his voice barely above a whisper. "I did... nothing... nothing... I'm good. Not hurt..." Ryland rambled for a moment, his words disjointed as his head twitched around.

"What did you make me do?" Ryland asked, the sporadic action disappearing quicker than it had come on.

"I didn't make you do anything, Ryland," Cail taunted, his voice heavy with malice. "Did you hurt her?"

"You made me hurt her!" Ryland yelled, his body pushing against the chains that bound him so tightly. What little relaxation my shoulders had found left as I tensed away from the anger in Ryland's voice.

"Made me hurt... made me hurt..." he repeated, his voice clicking through the mechanic repetition.

"Now, now," Cail taunted, his voice calm and condescending. "I did nothing of the sort. I didn't wrap my hands around her neck. Did you?"

Ryland's voice broke for only a moment before he answered in a hiss, "Yes... yes."

"Did I break her arm?" Cail asked, his back arching as he lowered himself to Ryland's eye level.

"No," Ryland repeated over and over again. His voice had weakened in desperation, his body now only barely fighting against the chains.

"Did she try to kill me? Did I try to kill her?" I froze, my breathing catching at Cail's words. I knew what they were talking about, but it didn't make any sense. Joclyn tried to kill Ryland? She hadn't said anything about this.

"No." Ryland's voice was soft.

"Did you?" Cail taunted. It was not a question.

"Yes."

"Will you do it again?" Cail spoke to him like a psychiatrist, his words soothing, and yet, the intention behind them was heavy and as clear as day. "Will you hurt her?"

"Hurt her... hurt her... hurt her," Ryland repeated as he began to rock, the rocking stopping suddenly as he switched over again, his voice loud.

"No!" Ryland roared, his desperation coming back quickly. "No." Ryland yelled and screamed as he fought against the chains, pulling at the heavy link that bound him to the rock wall.

"Really?" Cail taunted, his back straightening as he stood. "But she hurts you in your dreams, doesn't she?"

"No. Nonono..."

"What about when she kissed me, when her hands were all over me," Cail paused, "that hurt, didn't it?"

Ryland said nothing, but looked around frantically, his eyes darting all over the dungeon as his breathing picked up, his fingers curling as he moaned a deep lament filled with agony.

Watching him was traumatizing. I found myself torn between pity, an insane desire to help him, and fear over the explosive nature of his moods. I tried to catch his eyes, hoping that maybe getting him to see me would calm him, but he didn't seem to notice anyone other than Cail. Sain, however, was staring into me with his bright green eyes, seemingly oblivious to the exchange going on mere inches from him.

I returned Sain's stare, not knowing where else to look, not wanting to see Cail torment Ryland anymore. I looked at him, silently hoping that the strong gaze of the old man's eyes would fill in the gaps I was so obviously missing.

"Or what about when she tried to snap your neck?" Cail asked.

"It wasn't her."

"But you just saw her, on the roof top of that little farmhouse, clinging to Ilyan," Cail continued to taunt, his lips turned in a sneer.

Timothy chuckled wickedly at the look on Ryland's face.

"Nonononono," Ryland moaned, his fingers curling again as he rocked back and forth, his head hitting against the bars several times.

"Do you think he's kissed her?" Cail whispered, the harshness of his voice hissing through the damp prison.

"No." Ryland's voice was strong, but forced, his belief in his words wavering, his body still rocking as he fought whatever demons had been placed in his head.

"I saw Ilyan kiss Joclyn. I looked into the window of Sain's mind and saw her kiss him. Her hands wrapped through that hair of his as he touched her, loved her and *kissed* her."

Cail spoke softly as if to a lover, but the tone of his voice only triggered Ryland's violence. His voice cracked and broke as he cried out at Cail's words, and he pulled at his hair and clawed at the shackles around his ankles.

I moved myself away from him as if his pain would infect me. His voice opened again into that same mournful whine, the deep hollow noise of it was the sound of heartbreak and betrayal. I jerked as the loud noise broke the silence of our prison, my sharp intake catching my father's attention. He glared at me in warning before returning to Ryland's fit.

"And she kissed him back." Cail barely got the words out before Ryland lunged at the door to his prison, his hands shooting through the narrow space between the bars as he reached for my brother. Ryland's fingers moved and flexed, intent on clawing out Cail's eyes, but he couldn't reach far enough, the chains that bound him to the wall and to Sain were too restrictive. I heard my father laugh and was sure that Cail was sneering, but I couldn't look away from Ryland.

He snarled like an animal as he continued to try to attack Cail. His eyes were feral, his growl deep and menacing. I moved away until my shoulder could move no more. The desperate violence in his eyes scared me.

"She loves him, Ryland. Joclyn loves Ilyan more than she loves you. What are you going to do about it?"

"Kill... kill... kill," Ryland repeated over and over, his body rocking again.

"What. Are. You. Going. To. Do?" Cail asked, each word stronger than the last.

"I'm going to kill him!" Ryland pushed and tugged against the bars, his voice deep through his clenched teeth.

"And what about her?" Cail asked, his voice still containing that menacing taunt. "Are you going to hurt her? Make her pay?"

"Yes!" Ryland yelled, and Cail smiled more. "Hurt her... hurt her!"

"She hurt you!" Cail yelled, his voice changing back into a taunt, and I knew at once what they were doing. Cail had gained full control of Ryland's mind. He was manipulating Ryland into believing things that he wouldn't believe otherwise. The lines of reality and manipulated horror were so blurred I could tell Ryland had no idea what was what anymore.

"Are you going to kill her?" Cail asked, the final brick in his bridgework laid.

"Yes!" Ryland yelled, his feral growling against the bars increasing for a moment before it dropped, before Sain's hand, unseen by both Cail and my father, touched his back. The touch brought him back down to earth. The frantic movements slowed. Ryland's body settled back onto the damp floor of the prison, his hands shaking as his fingers curled around his head.

"No," Ryland gasped, his face horrified at what had just happened. "Nonononono."

"No?" Cail asked, even though his anger at the temporary glitch was obvious, his voice still held that manipulative tone. He didn't miss a beat, and Ryland began second-guessing himself.

"But she hurt you," Cail stated, moving himself closer to the bars again.

"It wasn't her," Ryland said, yelling as he tried to convince himself as well as Cail. "Wasn't her, wasn't her, wasn't her."

"How can you be so sure?"

"I know." Ryland lunged at the bars again, but Cail didn't even flinch, even though the raw aggression had returned to Ryland's face.

"The way she knows you didn't just try to kill her, for the second time?"

Ryland's jaw moved as he tried to get the words out, but nothing came. Finally, two words left him, the conviction almost gone from his voice, "She knows."

"How?"

"She knows, she knows," he repeated.

"Why don't you show her?" Cail asked, his lips twitching with a pleased sneer.

Ryland's eyes widened as Cail pulled a double-sided blade from his pocket, the metal of the blade bright red. It had no handle and no finger hold. It almost looked like a shard of jagged stone, sharpened to a point on both sides.

Ryland looked at it as Cail extended it to him through the bars, his fingers twitching as he slowly reached to grab it. I couldn't take my eyes off the blade. I had seen these many times before I escaped, and seeing one again made my stomach turn. It was a knife made of blood and bits of soul. It had dark magic at its core, but I wasn't sure what they were doing with the knife. I didn't want to find out. I pulled against my chains, the metal clanking as I tried to move away, knowing there was nowhere to go. I couldn't take my eyes off the blade, my breath coming in short, little spurts as Cail held it between his fingers.

"Tell her the truth, Ryland," Cail whispered, the last words all Ryland needed to hear before he snatched the blade from Cail's hand.

Ryland held it confidently, knowing exactly what to do with it. He lifted his shirt to reveal his chest, the skin over his heart pock-marked with line after line of stab wounds.

Sain reached forward and placed his hand over Ryland's heart, the skin of his hand equally as scarred. I only looked at it for a moment before Ryland plunged the blade through Sain's hand and into his own chest. Both men called out in pain, and my screams joined them until the pair passed out, leaving my screams to fill the prison.

Timothy took the final steps toward me, his body coming to stand right before the now open door of my cell. I barely saw him. I couldn't look away from Sain and Ryland's frozen bodies. I couldn't stop screaming. I expected my father to punch me again. What I didn't expect was for him to unchain me.

"Why don't you join them, princess?" Timothy's voice was icy as he grabbed the chains that connected to the shackles on my wrist, one yank sending me to the ground as he pulled me over the cold, uneven floor.

I didn't have to ask what he was doing. I knew. I skirted away from him in my panic, trying to ignore the frantic beating of my heart and the tension that had moved its way to fill every nerve ending in my body. If I could have moved into the wall to get away from him, I would have.

I kicked and fought as he tried to take me toward them. My voice caught and screamed as I pleaded with him to leave me alone, to save me. It was useless. My fear seized into me in my desperation. Timothy just ignored my pleas, pulling me by my chains, my body dragging against the stone floor as my feet kicked in desperation. I screamed again as he plowed my flailing body toward the collapsed forms of Sain and Ryland, my pained body trying to fight him, but unable to.

"Are we ready?" I barely heard Edmund's voice over my screams as my father pulled my hand toward the protruding edge of the dagger. My body was unable to fight him, so my screams were the only defense I had against what was coming.

"Almost, Master." My brother's voice was cold, distanced and almost excited.

My screams turned to pleas as I felt the sharp point of the dagger press against the skin of my palm.

"No," I begged. "No, Daddy, please no."

"Sorry, princess," he said, although he didn't really mean it. "But you'll like this, I promise."

I heard Cail and Edmund laugh at his words only moments before Timothy pushed my hand into the blade, my scream breaking through the air as my soul was sliced apart.

5

WYN

I was floating.

I was gliding through mist and water. At least, I thought that was what it was. I couldn't be sure. After all, I wasn't sure where I was, or who I was. My body felt disconnected. Not separated from me, but separate. I couldn't tell where my arm extended to or where my leg was. I saw white and dark, and memories that I knew did not belong to me. I felt happy and sad and scared and anxious, but none of the emotions were mine.

I was lost in a sea of everyone, a mist of white that gobbled everyone up and mashed us together into the confusion I now felt. The dungeon was gone. The pain in my body was gone. It was just me, floating through the endless mist.

The last thing I remembered was the feeling of the blade plunging through my hand, the blade of souls. Is that where I was, trapped within the blade, just another nameless face to all those already killed by the dark weapon?

Yes, I supposed I was.

I floated and let the bits of souls wash over me, my body of smoke and cloud taking it all in, my cares gone.

I floated. I was, and yet, I wasn't. I was nothing and everything. It didn't make sense, but I didn't care that it didn't. I didn't care that everything was gone.

"Sain?" a voice cut through the cloud of white. I was sure it was Ryland's, but it seemed younger somehow.

I would like to say I turned toward the sound, but I was not sure I could. I was too lost in the fog, swimming in sea foam.

"I'm here." My consciousness peaked at the voice, my awareness clicking into place. "They brought Wynifred here, too, Ryland." That voice, it wasn't familiar, and yet, I still felt like it should have been.

"Of course they did," Ryland replied, his voice floating to me through the damp, white cloud. "She is their bargaining chip now."

"Wynifred?" Sain's voice called out to me. "Don't be scared, child. You are safe here."

I would have loved to respond to him, but I still couldn't figure out how to speak, what to say, or even if I had a mouth to use.

"You need to focus, Wynifred. Think about where your body should be, and it should appear for you."

I gaped at Sain's words, the instructions foreign and awkward. I wasn't a body. I was mist. I was bits of everyone, and at the same time, nothing. How could I focus on a body if none existed for me?

I heard Sain sigh and Ryland laugh, the sounds rippling through me. Why did they seem so normal? Weren't they screaming only moments before?

"She's more stubborn than you were, Ryland," Sain laughed, an impatient clip in his voice.

"I'm just lucky you were here, old man, or I would have stayed a floating blob of other people's emotions forever. Well, until Cail forced me out, anyway."

Was that what I was, a floating mass of other people's lives? Yes, I was. I had known this before.

"I don't know why you count centuries of torture as 'luck', but I suppose I will take your word for it."

"Did you feel that?" Ryland interrupted, his tone deep and panicked.

"Is Joclyn falling asleep?" Sain's voice was just as worried. "Is he here?"

"No, it's something else."

I heard their words. I liked the way they floated through me. It was not their words that I felt now; however, it was small fingers on my cheek. A cheek.

Once I felt my cheek, my body fell into place, my mind detaching itself from the mist and the group memories that had plagued it. I felt my legs connect and step onto something hard, my weight dropping to the ground as my legs chose not to support me.

My vision circled and flowed as colors took over the white, a forest floor crackling under my fingers. I had barely registered the pine needles before Sain rushed up to me, his hands moving to my shoulders as he inspected me for injuries.

"Are you all right?" I looked up to face Sain, his face clean shaven, his hair short, and everything about him clean and well taken care of. I wouldn't have recognized him if it wasn't for his eyes.

I nodded once.

"You will be safe," Sain said, and I couldn't help hearing the heavy inflection in his voice, the way his tone dipped and wavered into something deeper.

"So it is you?" I asked, the normalcy of my voice taking me off guard.

"Yes. I could tell you my life story, but we simply don't have time for it, nor do I think you want to hear my depressing tale right now."

He smiled sadly, his kind eyes still searching mine. I couldn't return the smile. I just couldn't. I was far too confused.

"Can you stand?" Sain asked, his hands wrapping around mine and pulling me up before I had a chance to respond.

"It can be disorienting at first, so don't try to make too much of it. We are only here for a few minutes."

"Where are we?" I asked.

"This is where we wait," Sain said as he steadied me. "He doesn't know we are able to materialize. He makes us wait before he uses us as his pawns."

"He?"

"Your brother." I winced at Sain's words. I tried not to, but I did. The memories of what had so recently happened to me were still fresh.

Despite the effect Cail's name had on me, I still didn't understand where we were exactly. I arched my eyebrows at Sain and cocked my head in confusion, hoping to prompt him to continue, but his face fell, his head shaking dejectedly.

"Nothing good happens now. What your father has done to you in the dungeon, that's just the opening act."

"I thought you said we were safe here," I said, looking around and still not understanding.

"Not here," he said. "Where he takes us afterwards. Just remember, it is only a dream."

I swallowed hard, the inflection in Sain's voice heavy with fact and warning.

"It's gone." Ryland's voice was loud as it broke our conversation apart, leaving my hundreds of unasked questions trapped inside me.

"What was it?" Ryland asked Sain, ignoring that I was there.

"You control this place, Ryland; you tell me. It's just my blood that makes the connection."

Ryland snorted and shook his head, his curls bouncing as he finally turned and acknowledged I was there. He stared at me intently, a million emotions set into his eyes.

"Is she all right?" he asked succinctly.

I leaned into Sain, not knowing what to say or how Ryland would react to the little I did know. While I would like to say he was safer here, more stable, I could still see the anxiety and the exploding anger behind his eyes.

"I don't know," I whispered. "She has been in hiding with Ilyan. I haven't seen her in months."

I watched as Ryland's jaw clenched, his eyes turning to the chilling color of ice. I could feel the anger radiating off him as he walked away from us, his fist colliding with a tree and then punching through it as the sturdy trunk turned to smoke.

"Calm down, Ryland," Sain ordered, his voice deep and fatherly.

"How can I calm down?" he yelled, his voice loud. I flinched into Sain, feeling weird for trying to find comfort in him. "It's been months, she says. Months! We have been tortured, used against her, beaten—for months. All while she has been on an extended date with her new boyfriend." I flinched at his words, taking a step closer to Sain. I really wished I hadn't said anything.

"That's not true, Ryland," Sain said, his voice a calming beacon that Ryland didn't seem to respond to.

"He has his hands all over her!"

"No, Ryland, don't give in to Cail's games. You know he is lying," Sain pleaded as he moved us toward him.

Ryland stepped forward, squaring his shoulders, but Sain didn't back down.

"How do I know?" Ryland spat, his anger fuming as he moved and paced.

"Remember what I told you?" Sain's voice was calm as he placed his hand on Ryland's shoulder, the touch once again triggering a calmness in him.

"Only Joclyn can stop my father." Ryland's voice was tight as he spoke, his eyes unfocused on something far beyond us.

"Yes, and who is the only one that can help her with that?"

The temporary calm that Ryland had found faded away as fast as a slap. His breathing picked up, and his chest heaved, his eyes darkening into a deep icy blue. "I can do it."

"Ryland, I—" Sain tried to interrupt him, but Ryland exploded, and I jumped away from him.

"I am strong, too. Stronger than him. The sight was wrong, Sain! It is me that can help her! I need Jos's power to stop him."

"No, Ryland!" Sain roared, causing Ryland to stop in his tracks. "You must not take her power. That was your first mistake—when you foolishly sealed yourself to her. At that moment, you were more in love with Joclyn's power than with her."

"Don't judge what you don't know! I love her!"

I was not one to hide by any means, but the volatility of

Ryland's emotions was terrifying. I looked around for somewhere out of the way, but all I could see was forest.

"You did, Ryland, you loved her. But when you found out who she was, your love changed—"

"No…" Ryland interrupted, his voice airy and desperate.

I took a step back instinctively, not liking the fiery sheen that was taking over Ryland's eyes.

"You loved her magic more than her," Sain insisted, his voice calm and level. "You loved what her magic could do for you."

"No, I need her magic." Ryland sighed and shook his head as if clearing the thought from his mind. "I love her."

"That may be," Sain said, his voice still low and comforting, "but this bond has only caused her pain. We have talked about this; you are not helping her now. You must trust in the sight if you wish her to end this."

"You just want Jos to be with a king, not a worthless prince." Ryland spun to face Sain as he spoke, the anger deep in his voice as he hissed at the old man, his face only inches from Sain's.

"I want her to live up to her true potential."

"And that is not with me?" Ryland asked, the deep root of his voice struggling to keep steady. Sain only shook his head.

"How do you know, Sain?" Ryland spat. "Have you seen something new?"

"You know I have no control over my sights anymore, Ryland. I see only what he would have me see." Sain's voice was a whisper against Ryland's outburst.

Ryland howled at Sain's words, moving away from us to smash his fist through several more trees that turned to mist at the impact. Ryland stood still after disintegrating his eighth tree, his chest heaving as he watched the white mist float toward the empty expanse of sky above us.

"Don't give in to Cail's taunts, Ryland," Sain counseled. "If you give in, then he has won. Use this time to clear your mind. It's the only time you are in control of yourself. Don't let Cail's words cloud you here."

Ryland stood with his back to us, his head bobbing once in understanding before he turned, his strides taking him right into Sain's arms. The older man embraced him, his hands wrapping around him tightly. They said nothing; the embrace enough to convey all that was needed. Ryland moved away and came right over to me, his giant arms sweeping me up as he squeezed me against him.

"I'm sorry, Wyn," he whispered in my ear. "I'm sorry I got so mad. I just can't see the lies from reality anymore." He dropped me and smiled. "My brain is a mess. All I can remember is Joclyn, but the details are all fuzzy."

I wanted to laugh at what he said; I could tell that had been his intention, but I couldn't. I heard the honesty behind it, and it broke my heart. Edmund had tried to delete Ryland's mind, but somehow Ryland had fought him. So instead, they turned to manipulation and torture. I felt my stomach swim, the lack of contents adding to my nausea.

"If it wasn't for Sain, I would probably be more of a mess." He chuckled again, but I could only smile.

Ryland's awkward chuckle stopped as he looked away. Both his and Sain's eyes turned outward as tree after tree began to vaporize, the white fog that surrounded us started as moving forward, seeping through the trees much faster than was natural.

"Remember, it's only a dream, Wynifred... Brace yourself." I barely heard Sain's words before the mist took me, the white mass moving into me and breaking me up into a million pieces again. This time, however, the feeling of carelessness didn't take me. I was aware.

I was aware as different trees began to form around me and aware of voices in the distance, these ones hard and menacing. I was aware of the change in my body and the hands that wrapped hard around my arms, aware of the fear that gripped my heart.

The voices in the distance raised as someone, a girl, yelled. The large hands that held me wrapped around me, lifting me off the ground. As soon as I started to struggle, one massive palm covered my nose and mouth. I could barely breathe through the pressure, so I stopped struggling, hoping for air while my brain caught up with my situation.

Had I left the dream that Sain had been talking about? This all felt too real. How did I get to this place? I could feel the bruises on my face return, the joints in my body scalding me with pain from my captivity and beatings.

Instinctively, I began to fight against the painful fingers that dug into my skin and the hand over my face. Whoever held me only held tighter, his fingers pressing into me to the point I was sure I was going to bruise. Sain's warning of this being a dream repeated through my mind. I wanted to believe it, but everything seemed too real to be a dream. It felt too real.

My captor began to move me through the forest, the heavy clomp of his shoes breaking through the undergrowth the main sound as he dragged me along toward the voices.

"Or torture," Cail's voice said from somewhere in front of me. I didn't know what we were heading toward, but I did know that I wanted nothing to do with Cail. My bruised and battered body called out as I fought my captor once more, my fight useless against his strong arms.

"Is that what Edmund told you to do, Cail?" I froze at the voice.

Joclyn's voice was filtering through the trees toward me. What was going on here? Where was I?

"To torture me?" Joclyn said, and my struggle against the man who held me resumed.

I was torn, I wanted to see Joclyn, but not like this. I wanted to fight and save her, yet I knew neither of those were an option right now. They spoke of torture, my brother's favorite game. Nothing good was going to happen here.

I yelled out to warn her, to help her, but my voice caught behind the man's large hand, my warning falling limply to the forest floor.

"Ryland told me you knew. He said you now know that Ilyan loves you. Is that true?" The man who held me stopped his advance. The voices were now loud enough to alert me to how close we were.

Trees surrounded us; our bodies gobbled up by a thick forest. I looked through the trunks of the trees that surrounded me, hoping to see something, anything, in front of us, but saw nothing.

"Ilyan doesn't love me. Not in that way." I heard a gasp to my right at Joclyn's words. I turned toward the sound, sure that someone else was there, but once again, seeing nothing but trees.

"Oh, so he hasn't told you," Cail taunted, the same babying tone he had used with Ryland earlier cutting through his voice. I cringed against it, expecting his verbal attack to switch to me at any moment, even though I was still hidden in the woods. "Could it be that I know more than you at this point in time?"

Cail laughed and I jumped at the high pitched sound, my whole body seizing in preparation for an attack.

"Ooo," Cail's taunts continued, "I would love to see your face when you figure everything out—what Ryland did, what Ilyan is keeping from you."

My ears peaked at his words. After seeing how Cail had manipulated Ryland, I wasn't sure I could trust anything he said anymore, but something about the way he phrased that sentence alerted me to a new danger. What *did* Ryland do?

Don't give into his games, Wyn, I said to myself. I wasn't losing my mind yet. I wouldn't let myself.

"This game just gets more and more exciting," Cail said excitedly, a loud clap sounding through the trees. Did he just slap her?

"This isn't a game!" Joclyn's loud voice broke through the trees, and I heard the same groan off to my right, followed by another more familiar one to my left.

Everything stopped after Joclyn's outburst, the ringing silence in the forest broken only by the small grunts and groans on either side of me.

"Not a game you say?" Cail's voice came out of nowhere, his voice cold and calculating. The sensation of ice trickled down my spine. I knew that tone in his voice. I wanted to scream at Joclyn to run, to leave, to escape Cail's web in whatever way possible, but before I could, my captor pressed me forward.

"Really?" Cail said darkly. "Well, what do you say we turn it into a game?"

I heard movement, but I wasn't sure where it came from or if it was just the sounds I made as I fought against the hands of the men who continued to push me forward.

"Bring them out!" Cail yelled, and our pace increased, the men trudging through the forest until they pulled me beyond the tree line and into a large clearing where Cail had Joclyn restrained against him.

I looked at her as I fought against the men, my fight all but gone as my weak body began to give out from the strain. Joclyn caught my eyes, her silver eyes staring into mine for only a moment before moving away to the others around me. My eyes followed hers as I looked toward Ryland and Sain to my right. Their bruises were back, and Sain's hair had returned to its wild tangles of neglect. Wherever we were before, this was different. I turned away from the two men to look at the groaning form to my left.

Talon.

My heart beat wildly at seeing him there, my urge to fight picking up for just a moment before the fingers around my arms restrained me. A hiss in my ear was the only warning I needed. I slowed my fight. I repeated to myself the words Sain had said only a moment ago. It was only a dream.

If I was here, and I was aware... then shouldn't Talon be aware, too?

I struggled, but my plight stopped when a swift hand exploded against my cheek. I sank down to the ground, my voice a whimper as I cried into the dirt.

"Four," Cail's voice brought me back to what was happening, his icy voice stinging through me. I forced myself off the ground to face Joclyn. I did not want her to see me like this. "We hold in our possession two of your friends, your lover, and even your father."

Her father? Jeffery? The man who had disappeared, who cued Ilyan in to her existence? I looked to where Joclyn so intently placed her focus. Her father. Sain was her father.

Sain was a Drak though, and he was also supposed to be dead. I gaped as I struggled against the hands, my movements weak as my mind tried to wrap itself around this new information. I looked between Joclyn and Sain, my eyes widening at the way their eyes met, and I knew it was true.

Suddenly the blood magic made sense. They had used Sain and Ryland's blood to infiltrate Joclyn's mind. It was why this 'dream' seemed so real. My soul was here, trapped here with blood magic. Everything was really happening.

"And who do you have? A protector? Someone who hasn't even told you the truth yet."

Joclyn tried to pull away from Cail the same way I tried to pull away from whoever held me, but it was no use. We were all held in place as Cail played whatever game he had carefully prepared.

"Let them go," she hissed, her silver eyes narrowing dangerously.

"Why?" Cail snarled, his lips moving right against the soft skin of her neck, gently, like a lover. He pulled her against him, and she hissed between her teeth. Cail didn't even seem to notice her reaction, his lips curling dangerously as he whispered something to her. Joclyn cringed away from him before Cail tightened his arm against her again. "We have the upper hand. We. Are. Winning. And you, you don't even know what's going on."

Joclyn snarled as she fought against him. I wanted to cheer her on. She was so different from the friend I had left crying on the floor of the forest. Her demeanor was different, and her confidence strong enough to stand up to Cail. I wanted to yell at her to kill him, to attack, to fight, to change the game. She was strong enough to do so; I could see it in her eyes. If this actually was her dream, then she had full control over it. However, she just stood there, letting

Cail taunt her. Why wasn't she fighting? I refused to believe that she did not know what was going on. I could see the strength in her eyes, the power that she held. She could do anything.

I struggled against the man that held me, knowing it was useless, but desperate to try something nonetheless.

"Now, now, don't go anywhere yet." Cail's voice broke through the forest like the hiss of a snake. "We still haven't gotten to our game! You see, we have four people in front of us, and you can pick one. One that you will not have to watch die right now. The others we will kill before you. You will not have to see the last die, but here is the clincher... whoever you choose will have to watch you die before we will release them from this nightmare and let them wake up."

Kill? Die? This was a dream, wasn't it? They couldn't kill us. They needed us. Bargaining chips, just as Sain had said. I looked toward Sain in a panic, desperate for answers, but he was focused on Joclyn, his body still as he studied her.

"Who do you choose, Joclyn? Who do you want to watch you die?"

I fought harder as Joclyn looked between us, barely registering when her eyes met mine. If I had been on my own, I would have pleaded with her for answers, but my only goal now was to reach Talon. I didn't care if this was a dream. I didn't care that the deaths we were enacting were fabricated. I needed to be with Talon. I needed to feel the touch of his skin against mine.

"My father," Joclyn said, her voice quiet to my ears. "I choose my dad."

"It's okay, Joclyn. I understand," Sain said, his soft voice almost gobbled up by my frantic attempt to get to Talon's side.

"Wonderful!" Cail said, his voice joyful. "She's made her choice. Dispose of the rest."

I didn't hear Cail, but if I did, I might have chosen my actions differently. The hands that had restrained me dropped, and I took my chance. I lunged toward Talon, my body falling hard on the forest floor as I clawed my way toward him, my fingers outstretched. I was inches from reaching his hand, his body still limp and unresponsive, when I saw the glimmering blade descend on his chest.

I didn't register when Joclyn yelled out; I only heard the static in my ears as I watched the sword plunge itself into the body of my husband, my own flesh separating as an identical blade severed me in two at the same time. I screamed at the pain, my body writhing as it racked through me, my muscles seizing before they began to relax.

Talon didn't even flinch at the impact. I continued to scream as I reached for him, my fingers uselessly clawing through dirt before my body gave out, my vision fading to black as the dream ended and my own hideous reality returned.

6

WYN

Ryland was screaming again.

All he did was sleep and scream. After we had all been released from the blood magic, we had been bound alone in our cells. Sain sat still in silence, Talon remained unconscious, and Ryland transferred between periods of waking and sleeping. His waking moments were spent screaming in agony about Joclyn, even strangling the bars of the cell as he attempted to kill her. What little he was awake, and not screaming, he always sat, rocking back and forth, as he mumbled promises to himself to both kill and protect Joclyn.

It had only gotten worse after the last time they had forced Sain and Ryland to open up a blood connection. Ryland had spent two hours muttering that he didn't love her anymore, that she didn't love him, before he had finally given in to the torture Timothy had forced him to endure and became silent.

Ryland had been driven mad by torture, the Vymäzat and Cail's manipulation. If it wasn't for Sain and his support, I was sure Ryland would be much worse. They had been imprisoned together for over three months. Ryland had only been let out when Edmund needed his magic to track Joclyn—when he needed him as a weapon.

And Sain... Sain's magic was weakened to nothing by years of Edmund withholding the clay mugs. Without the mugs, Sain could not produce Black Water. Without the lifeblood of his magic, he was left weak and useless.

We all were in the dark, both literally and figuratively, confined in small spaces, food never provided, a bathroom a thing of the past. The only luxury we knew anymore was the daily glass of water. One glass of filthy water and I dreamed of it as if it was wine.

The whole room smelled of vomit, human excrement, and the heavy mildew smell I had noticed on my arrival. The combined odors hung in the air, heavy and physical. It seeped into our tattered clothes, our hair, and lingered in our nostrils. I would like to say I never smelled it, that I had become immune, but the smell stuck to me. I had given up begging for water and food. I had given up begging for a bathroom. Each time I opened my mouth, my father would appear, the back of his hand at the ready and my query forgotten.

We were in the middle of another of Ryland's fits, and I could hear Sain whispering through Ryland's screams as he tried to calm him, to silence him before someone came down here.

"Shut him up, Sain," I hissed, my eyes peering through the darkness in their direction and then back to where I knew the staircase was. My ears listened intensely in the fear of hearing footsteps.

Sain whispered more, and I shifted my weight, the chains of my shackles rattling as I turned my body toward Ryland's cell.

"Shield him," I hissed, but Sain said nothing. It was a foolish idea anyway. They had already heard him, and if they found out Sain still used what little magic he had left, we would all be in trouble.

"Ryland," I whispered, my voice joining Sain's, "it's okay. Joclyn's okay."

Ryland only howled more, and my heartbeat froze. Footsteps sounded on the stairs, the pace fast and quick. I shuffled back to my wall, my hands directly above my head, as a blue light floated down the stairs. Cail came rushing into the room, his face hard and angry.

"Shut up, dog!" he yelled, the door to Ryland's cell swinging open without Cail having even touched it. Cail blinked once, and Ryland began to scream in agony, the magic attacking him from the inside. I looked away, not wanting to see the physical blows that were sure to come. They always did. We all had our fair share of bruises and broken bones, and with no magic to heal us, we sat, useless and mortal in the dark prison.

I pressed my face into my shoulder as the sound of flesh on flesh echoed around us. Ryland screamed until his cries turned to sobs, his sobs turning to whimpers, and then silence.

Cail laughed, while the grind of the metal as the cell door closed echoed around the rock. Then, there was nothing. I didn't move. I didn't flinch. I kept my head rolled into my shoulder, my eyes staring at Talon's sleeping form, silently begging him to wake up. I wasn't sure if Talon waking up would take away my terror or add to it. I didn't know what I would do if they beat him in front of me. I knew I wouldn't be able to keep my mouth shut.

I tried to focus on something good as I waited for Cail to leave, the prison silent with expectation. He didn't leave, though. I could hear his breathing as it picked up before the squeal of the door to my cell sounded, the door opening slowly.

"What did they do to you?" he questioned, I almost didn't recognize his voice.

I couldn't help it; I looked up. Cail walked in, and I recoiled. I wanted to plead with him that I had said nothing, I had remained silent, but I couldn't let the words filter to my tongue.

My brother looked at me, the hard line of his jaw gone, and his eyes soft. I saw the look of hope in his eyes that I had only seen a handful of times as a child. I glimpsed the look of the love and dedication that he had shown me as he raised me. He had given me the same look during the battle at the LaRue estate only a few months before. He had looked at me with sadness as he begged me to kill him. His hand had clenched over his heart, his voice howling as he gasped in pain when Edmund sent him a warning for whatever he had been about to do. I was as confused about his reaction then as I was now. My blood flared in curiosity, the sharp edge of fear cutting through my joints.

"Does... does it hurt?" he asked as he kneeled in front of me.

I couldn't trust this. Brother or not, Cail only hurt those around him. Always. Every part of me recoiled as he kneeled in front of me, his hand moving up to touch the metal bands around my wrists. I gasped as I moved myself into the wall in an attempt to get as far away from him as possible. My skin ached as I attempted to pull myself closer to the stone; my eyes wide and focused on the soft face of my brother who knelt right in front me. I felt the metal click as the shackles opened. My hands fell into my lap, my weak and pained shoulders unable to support them.

"I'm sorry, Wynifred. Dad is mean sometimes." I froze, my eyes wide as my breath caught, tears threatening. This was familiar, this voice and those words. This was the brother I had known as a child. He reached forward, my breath stalling in expectation of a hit, but nothing came; his soft hand reached out and rested against my cheek.

I stared into his eyes, the pressure against my cheek soft and gentle, and waited for my breathing to regulate. I couldn't seem to gain control of it. Everything screamed at me to attack him, to run. Deep down, I wondered if that would be what he would want. A reason to attack. Cail wasn't like that, though. He didn't need a reason. He just liked to cause pain. I couldn't trust this, I couldn't. I cringed away, trying to ignore the burn of tears that would never come, letting the sharp knife of pain dig into me as I attempted to wish away this trick that he was playing on me.

I felt my breathing calm and my heart rate slow. It took me a minute to figure out what was going on. Without my own magic to alert me to the change, I had missed the fact that Cail was calming me.

"It's okay, Wynifred," he said, his voice only a whispered breath against my skin. "I'll make all the bad go away."

I couldn't breathe. I could not force myself to inhale. I was too shocked, too scared. I felt the pain in my shoulders lessen, the fire in my wrists leave. My brother smiled at me, his face twitching just a bit.

I wanted to reach up to him, to comfort him, but before I could even move, his hand flew to the skin over his heart. He clenched his fingers around the fabric of his shirt as his face screwed up in pain. He backed away from me, his back hitting the bars that separated me from Talon, his eyes wide as he clutched his shirt, tears beginning to flow down his cheeks.

"Cail?" I asked, unable to help myself, not understanding what was happening.

I heard Sain gasp, in warning or curiosity, I wasn't sure, but it barely registered. I watched my brother crying in front of me, his hand clenched over his heart.

I moved forward, my body itching to get as close to him as possible.

"Save me." He hissed the words, and I froze as everything went on high alert inside of me.

"Cail?" I had barely moved before the back of Cail's hand connected with my cheek, the smack sounding loud and clear in the dark room.

"Shut your mouth," Cail snapped, the hard lines of his face back, his eyes hard.

He looked at me once more before he left my cell, the door closing with a loud snap before he went up the stairs, the light going with him and leaving us in the dark again. I looked toward the staircase, my eyes slowly adjusting to the lack of light.

"What was that?" I whispered into the darkness when I was sure that Cail had gone, not daring to say more and hoping that my voice hadn't traveled beyond my own five foot square.

I stared into the dark, my mind attempting to swim around the confusion that Cail had introduced. I tried to blow it off as a trap, a trick, but I couldn't, as much as I wanted to.

I exhaled shakily, rubbing the tender skin on my wrists, and then it hit me that I was unchained.

I waited, my body still curled in the middle of my cell. The footsteps were long gone, but I still dreaded the darkness, the possibility of someone waiting just beyond the black, out of sight. My breath picked up, and finally I could take it no more. I scooted across the small space toward the cell where Talon lay, my arms stretching through the bars as I reached for him. I clawed through air until I grabbed what I was sure was a shirt. I traced the fabric until I felt his skin, the warmth shooting through me as it always did, but without the magic behind it. Only my heart responded this time, the beats heavy and excited.

I didn't dare say anything until Sain gave the all clear. I had learned that the hard way. Any noise demanded a beating, and I had already risked enough with my whispered question. No one was stupid enough to risk talking without Sain's help. Ryland only howled because he couldn't help it, or perhaps because Cail made him; either was a possibility.

Why had my brother been so gentle with me? I wanted to find a rational excuse, a reason for what had just passed between us. Even as a form of torture, it made no sense. Why leave my hands free? Why give me what I want? This was absolutely what I wanted.

I traced down the skin of Talon's arm until I found his hand. It was limp, but I intertwined my fingers with him anyway, desperate for the connection. There was no wild flaring of joined magic when we touched. The omezující stone had done its job, but I didn't care. The touch of his skin, the feel of his fingers was enough for me for now.

A dim, green light flared from the other side of the prison, and I turned slowly toward Sain who sat with a tiny orb settled in his hands.

Sain's magic wasn't restricted; Edmund needed the use of his sight, so restricting it was useless. Sain was also weak and mostly powerless, so he couldn't do much more than give us some light and shield our voices.

I kept my hands intertwined with Talon's as Sain looked

up at me, his eyes barely visible from beneath his mat of hair.

"Are you all right?" he asked, his voice calm and low so as not to breach the shield.

I nodded once. "Was that a trap?"

"Cail?" Sain asked as he leaned over to check Ryland's body, whose chest moved as he struggled to breathe.

"Yeah."

Sain exhaled, the sound as shaky as Ryland's labored breathing. "Your brother is complicated, and strangely still with a conscience."

I exhaled, not really knowing what that meant, but Sain only chuckled.

"You will see what I mean soon enough, Wyn." Sain moved his hands through the bars of his cell as he reached for Ryland, his own chains rattling loudly as they hit the thick bars of the cell.

"Have you seen something, Sain?" I asked while trying to smile. I sounded strangely like Ryland. In Ryland's brief moments of lucidity, it was always the only thing he asked, what Sain might have seen.

"I have," he said simply. "I always see. I see you now sitting right in front of me. I see my daughter in a place of power. I see Ryland in his rightful place, and I see Cail finding his peace. You will see some of that, too."

He was always so cryptic. I had never been around a Drak before. I had been born long after their extermination order was given, but Sain was fascinating. I wasn't sure if it was just his way, or an attempt to keep us all safe by keeping us in the dark. I wanted to smile, but I couldn't find it in me. I couldn't smile in a place like this, with my wrists and arms covered in blood, and my husband passed out beside me. Call me pessimistic, but I just couldn't do it.

I leaned my head back against the bars, keeping my hand entwined with Talon's.

"You will make it out of here safely, Wynifred." I turned toward Sain, suddenly desperate for information, but he had already begun caring for Ryland.

"Ryland?" Sain asked softly as he ran his hands over Ryland's side.

Ryland shuttered at his touch, his body racking with even bigger sobs.

"No more." Ryland's voice was more of a cry than actual words.

"No more what, Ryland?" Sain asked, his endless patience enduring.

"No more pain. She hurts me... hurts me... hurts me..." Ryland wrapped himself up in a ball, his fingers clawing at his curls.

"I hate seeing him like this," Sain sighed as he attempted to stop Ryland's frantic movements. "It's so much easier when his mind is clear, before the nightmares."

"Why is he calm then?" I asked, remembering how much more like himself he had seemed for those few moments in that other place.

"Because all of his soul is together there, all of his heart is in one place. Now, like this, he is only part of who he truly is. He is broken, ripped apart."

"She hurts me... hurts me..." Ryland continued to pant, his pained groans pulling Sain's attention back to him.

"No, Ryland, no. She doesn't hurt you. It's all in your head, remember? It isn't really her." Sain reached up and touched the boy's hair, his fingers soft and gentle as he attempted to calm him. However, it had the opposite effect.

"Let me kill her!" Ryland's voice roared through the small, rock room, his body fighting against his chains as he moved from one barred wall to another; clawing, kicking and grabbing at the bars in his attempt to escape. "I'm going to kill her!" he roared.

I moved into the bars I was huddled against, my hands squeezing Talon's as I pulled him toward me, desperate for some comfort.

"Not kill, Ryland. Save. You have to save her," Sain pleaded, his volume increasing as he fought to convince Ryland otherwise. I could see his furtive looks toward the main door, his fear evident. Ryland's voice was going to break through Sain's weak shield, making our noise audible to those above.

Sain pleaded quietly with him, and my voice joined in, my body shifting toward him a fraction as I tried to steady him with my tone. I wasn't certain he could take another beating so soon.

"It's okay, Ryland. Calm down," I pleaded. Ryland didn't seem to hear; he kept rattling the bars like a caged animal. He looked at anyone he could as he yelled for Joclyn's death, his hands clawing and grinding through the air, Sain's soft voice barely audible from behind him as he tried to comfort him from his own cell.

I looked toward the staircase, terrified that someone would hear him and come down, but no one came. So far, Sain's shield was holding. It was obvious we didn't have much longer as Sain's orb of light began to flicker and dim.

Ryland's eyes began to droop as Sain's repeated muttered comforts began to sink in. His movements slowed until he dropped to the ground, his breathing still erratic and labored, but his voice now silent.

"Save her," he whispered, his voice strangely dead and monotone.

"No!" Sain suddenly yelled, the light disappearing. I

stiffened at his outburst. I didn't know much about Sain, but I did know this, he did not yell. He did not get scared.

I froze, my hands still intertwined with Talon's as loud footsteps sounded on the stairs. I didn't move as I attempted to regulate my breathing. I didn't know what was happening, but Sain was scared and that was enough to terrify me. I lay down and rested my body as best I could, hoping that feigned sleep would be enough to keep them at bay, praying that they would not notice me.

Part of me wished I could re-shackle my wrists, thinking this was Cail's game the whole time, but it was too late to fix it now. So I lay still as voices began to filter down to us.

"I like this plan, master," Cail said as he addressed Edmund, my insides turning to ice even more. "Trap her and dispose of her that way."

"Or at least turn her into a weapon," Edmund said, his voice light with a laugh. "Either way ends in her death, so what does it matter?"

A dim, yellow light filtered through my eyelids, but I kept them closed in the hope that they wouldn't notice me.

"And once she is dead—" Cail began, but Edmund's voice cut him off quickly.

"The end of the Mortals," Edmund finished, the sneer on his lips evident in his voice. "All I need is her blood."

"Yes."

Their voices were cut off by the deep grinding sound of a cell door opening. I tried to keep my shoulders relaxed, but was not sure it worked.

"Get out of there, old man." I heard a kick and a grunt after Cail's words.

I closed my eyes tighter, not even wanting to imagine what might have just happened.

"So compliant now, Sain," Edmund said, his voice full of

the same taunting malice I had heard in Cail's. "It's no wonder. You want some of that delicious water, don't you? You can't wait until I give you the mug."

I heard a groan of deep guttural need come from Sain as they locked him in with Ryland.

"Will you do something else for me, too? Do this and I will let you eat tomorrow."

I tensed in the silence, every nerve in my body on alert as I fought the desire to turn and find out what was going on. I squeezed Talon's hands, in a desperate attempt to alleviate my stress and wished the silence would end.

Then it did. I jumped, my body jerking as the sound cut through the silence in an ear splitting scream.

I recognized the scream at once, the same scream I had heard when Sain and Ryland had been forced to use the blood connection the past two nights, and obviously this one was no different.

The two howled, and I moved myself into the bars, my arms desperately grabbing at Talon as the screams died off.

"When will we end this, master?" Cail asked, his voice almost sounding bored.

"Ovailia is due back tomorrow," Edmund said, and my shoulders tensed on their own at the sound of his voice. "Let us see what she has to tell us and then we will make our final decisions. I still have many more tricks up my sleeve after all," he chuckled. "Now, let us go make the little girl pay."

"Yes, Master."

I let their words wash over me. Something infinitely more important was taking all of my attention. Talon was squeezing back.

7

WYN

I STARED into Talon's eyes, his beautiful, brown eyes. I felt his thumb rub across the skin of my hand as his other caressed every inch of the skin on my face, my neck. I wished I could move closer, I wished I could whisper in his ear, but I could still hear the guard pace in the dim blue near my head, and the deep breathing of Sain and Ryland as they remained stuck inside the blood magic. I shifted my weight and moved closer to him, my hands clenching his.

Talon's eyes had opened only moments after Edmund left. Cail, Ryland and Sain were still in the cell, though none of their consciousnesses were present.

I looked into Talon's eyes, my shaky finger pressing to my lips as I begged him to be silent, my eyes pleading with him to wait so I could answer everything under the protection of Sain's shield.

I could see the fear in his eyes, the terror at the first thing that I was sure he noticed. There was no magic flowing through his veins. No fire as our skin connected, and although I watched him try several times, no Tŏuha for us to retreat to.

His weak hand had moved to touch my face, tears streaming down his cheeks as he touched the tender skin. I fought the desire to look away. I didn't want to see the pain in his eyes, the way his jaw tightened, the truth of Edmund's lie stabbing into him. He had kept me alive, but little more than that.

I wanted to tell him it was okay. I wanted to promise him that I was alive, and that was all that mattered, but my lips stayed closed, the words trapped in my throat as I kissed his hand, hoping that was enough for him to understand.

With no words to say, we lay beside each other, Talon still too weak to move much, me too sore to try. We spoke with the subtle movements of fingers. A kiss—a promise. A glance—a vow. Soon, the language of touch was not enough to say what we wanted to say, so we settled into each other, content to hold hands and stare, happy to simply see each other again.

I flinched when I heard the gasp, the groan and the subtle laugh that escaped from my brother's lips as he returned to reality.

"Well, that was fun," he sighed, and Talon's hand clenched against mine. I stared at him, begging him to say nothing, do nothing, praying he would get the message and that he wouldn't even try to battle through the weakness in his body.

I lay still as I listened to stumbling feet and the grind of iron as Cail opened doors and shifted bodies around. I heard shackles replaced, doors closed, and saw a flash of red as the soul blade reflected off the blue light Cail had brought with him and left with the guard.

"Anything interesting happen?" Cail asked, his voice moving closer to where we lay. I closed my eyes, hoping

Talon followed suit, praying that we would simply look like we were sleeping.

"No, sir."

"Good. Come along. Let's go join the bonfire and say goodbye to the last of the Skříteks." Cail chuckled, and my shoulders tightened at his meaning. I didn't want to think about the end of the massacre that was occurring only a few levels above us.

I waited until I was sure that they were far enough away before opening my eyes, unsurprised at the absolute darkness surrounding us.

My fingers fumbled away from Talon's hand until I found his face. I knew what was coming, and I had an extremely brief window in which to act. My fingertips pressed into his cheek, the pads of my fingers following around his jaw until I moved him closer, pressing his face against the bars as my lips found the hollow cup of his ear. He winced at the pain that my movements had given him, his lips parting in a subtle gasp.

The pain passed, and I felt him tense, waiting for me to say something. Still I waited; this had to be perfectly timed. I didn't need to risk being heard. I waited, Talon's heartbeat pulsing against my hand as I kept my palm against his neck.

A groan and an exhale. Sain was awake.

I could count it like clockwork if I tried, but I didn't wait.

"Don't make any noise," I whispered into his ear, hoping that he could understand me with the speed I was getting the words out. They could count my whispered mutterings as Ryland's groans if I said them fast enough. "They beat you if you talk. I am okay. I love you."

I wished I could have said more, and I knew the time would come that I would be able to, but now was not it. The scream of agony I had grown used to opened up through the jail. The sound echoed and grew, Sain's whispered pleas adding to the noise as Talon clung to my hand, his fear at the sound evident.

"It's okay," I said through the yells, hoping it was loud enough for Talon to hear, but no one else.

"She's okay, Ryland. No one is hurting you. You are safe. She is safe. Joclyn is safe. She loves you, Ryland. It's okay." Sain repeated the phrase continually, but I knew it wouldn't be enough. The footsteps were already approaching, and Sain's words halted as he backed away from his friend.

The grind of metal, the whimpering, the crying and the sound of flesh on flesh, I heard it all, and I felt Talon's tears as he heard it for the first time. As silence took over the cell, Ryland's breathing equalized, the whimpers leaving him and unconsciousness took over. The grind of metal repeated and then there was silence, the long silence that stretched into the black.

I clung to Talon as Ryland's breathing changed to the deep pulse of sleep. Sain joined him, and reluctantly, even I fell into sleep, the darkness giving me no other option. The brutal reality of my life gave me no other escape.

It was the first night I dreamed since I had been imprisoned. I would have expected the dream to focus on the brutal torture of the little girl, but no, it was the meadow again. The girl danced through the daisies and poppies, her dress spinning as she twirled.

I watched her as her image moved from one scene to another before it shifted to an old-style market. I fought the urge to laugh, my dreams taking me to a medieval fair. The girl ran before me, her hair laced with wildflowers as she weaved her way through the crowd, her body jumping around as if I was watching a scratched DVD.

"Mama!" she yelled happily, and my heart clenched. Her

voice was beautiful, so sweet and innocent. "They have chocolate, Mama! Papa, Papa, come see!"

The image jumped. The Henry the Eighth wanna-be flashed as he smiled at me, his lips moving, but once again, no words came through. He suddenly appeared several feet in front of me, standing next to the little girl, pieces of chocolate in his hands.

Papa? Mama? I fought the confusion that threatened to overtake me. I pushed the need to know more aside and just focused on the girl, desperate to take something beautiful with me from the dream. I needed something happy to hold on to when morning came and I would awake on a cold stone floor.

"Here, Wynifred," the man said, suddenly closer as he handed me a large piece of chocolate. He smiled, and I felt my cheeks turn up in a laugh. No, no laughing. I wanted to look back to the girl, but I couldn't, there was only the man. Once again, I had no control.

The vision jumped again. This time the man was by my side, the girl back to dancing in the meadow.

"We should go," he said, his voice repeating what I had already heard. This scene, those words, this imagery, I had already had this dream before.

"Go where?" my voice asked. I tried to fight the words, but they came automatically, whether I wanted them to or not.

The image of the girl jumped a bit, her dancing moving statically as she appeared and reappeared.

"We can run." I felt his hand on my shoulder. My body turned to face him, the pleading in his eyes cutting through me, but I knew the emotion wasn't my own. I wanted to yell at him for taking my eyes away from the beautiful girl again.

"He would find us," my voice was simple, defeated.

"He will kill her."

"I know."

My vision flashed once, twice, and again and again. The images changed from the market, to the man in the meadow, a walk by the lake, and more—flash after flash.

I wanted to scream for it to stop, but I had no control over this version of me in the dream. The flashes continued until I woke up, screaming.

I heard my own voice fill the dungeon, heard Sain yell something over my screams, and then felt Talon's large hand clasp over my mouth. He pulled me against the bars, the gritty texture of his skin and the pain of the bars against my back alerting me to where I actually was and what danger I had just put myself in. My scream stopped as quickly as it had come.

It was not my scream we had to worry about now. My yell had awakened Ryland. His animal instinct took over, and his wails filled the air that mine had so recently vacated. Talon tensed as Ryland yelled and howled. He clanged his chains against the bars and rammed his head into them repeatedly.

"Let me at her!" he screamed. "Hurt... hurt... hurt..."

I could feel Talon's fear escalate as he grasped me to him tighter, his arms weak enough that it only felt like a gentle tug. He had heard Ryland scream once before, but it had been nothing like this. Ryland's panic at being awoken had opened up into a full blown attack. His messed up brain had unlocked, and he rambled and mumbled and pleaded and yelled.

"I have to save her," he howled, his chains colliding with the bars of his cell loudly. "Protect her... I have to hurt her..."

"Leave him," I heard Sain hiss through the dark, and my tension grew. I watched what little movement I could make out, Talon's arms encircling me and holding me close to him, when a bright, yellow light suddenly ignited the prison.

The light burned my eyes, and I shied away from it, my hands moving to cover my face in an attempt to keep the light out.

"Who woke him up?" Cail hissed, making me withdraw into myself even further.

No one answered him. We let Ryland's continued screams eat up the sound. I kept my face away from him, my eyes buried in my shoulder as my ears peaked to hear any noise.

"You hurt her," Ryland screamed through the silence of Cail's unanswered question.

I waited for the clunk of a chain, the hinge of a door. Nothing, but Ryland's continued howls filled the damp air of our prison.

"Who screamed before Ryland did?" Cail asked again, the wicked pleasure in his voice evident even above Ryland's screams.

Talon's fingers dug into me as he tried to move me closer to him, the bars digging further into my back at his attempt.

"What?" Cail asked, the mock disbelief in his voice unnerving. "No one is going to answer me?"

"You killed her!" Ryland roared, the metal of his cell clanging once more before his screams turned to sobs. "Killed her... she's gone... dead... dead..."

"That's all right," he trilled, the wicked pleasure dancing in his voice. "I'll find out anyway. More importantly, we have a new arrival in Prague. Did you know that?"

Ryland had all but stopped now. His sobs turned to whimpers as he rocked himself back and forth with his hands clasped through his long hair. I could hear each step of Cail's shoes against the ground as he paced in front of us. I could hear the gentle clicks of his tongue as he contemplated what to say next.

I stayed still, knowing that Sain and Talon were doing the same, each of our secrets held inside of our hearts.

"Oh, yes, our visitor has just come back from seeing Ilyan *and* Joclyn." The single word woke Ryland up again.

He jumped up, his hands hitting against the bars as he lunged for Cail.

"Ovailia just saw Joclyn, Ryland, and I guess Joclyn wants you back... do you want to go?" Cail's voice was quiet, and I felt my entire spine solidify. No. Cail was about to succeed, he had built a weapon and now was able to let it go.

"Yes!" Ryland yelled, his voice cracking in desperation.

"What are you going to do when you see her, Ryland?" Cail asked. I curled inside of myself, not wanting to hear what was coming. "What are you going to do when you see her, when you see Ilyan's arms around her?"

Ryland's breathing picked up as Cail spoke, his breath coming in deep heavy spurts as he threatened hyperventilation. I listened as the sound of his breathing turned into yells. The word 'kill' repeated over and over.

"Good," Cail sneered, the pride at a job well done evident in his voice.

I heard the click of Cail's foot against the bottom stair, the sound barely audible over Ryland's panic attack and continued panting. That one click clenched inside of me, my body rocking in on itself before it snapped, sending me to my feet. Talon gasped at my movement, his body too weak to follow, to defend me. Ryland stopped repeating his words, and Cail turned around, his dark eyes meeting mine as a sneer appeared on his lips.

We stood facing each other, Cail's dark eyes taunting me, warning me of what would come if I opened my mouth and did what I was planning. I knew better; he would do it anyway. I took the warning, magnified it, and sent it back to him, my eyes narrowing in a taunt that I was sure I didn't possess the means to follow up on.

I could hear Talon's whimper, feel his weak fingers on my ankle, but I ignored them. For my idea to work, it had to be me against Cail. I needed to get the knife, and we needed to warn Joclyn.

"You're going to let him go and make him kill her, aren't you?" I asked, trying to keep my voice as loud as possible, but knowing I was failing. "You're going to chicken out and make Ryland kill her for you."

Cail moved off the step and back in front of the cells. His hand wrapped around one of the bars of the door to my cell, and his face pushed awkwardly against the narrow opening as he glared into me. His lips curled, and narrowed.

I felt my heart clunk to a stop, the wretched thing forgetting to beat in its sudden panic. I ignored the pain in my chest and the desperate grab against my ankle. I ignored my better judgment and stepped forward, placing my face only millimeters away from his.

"You're weak, Cail," I spat, saying the one thing I knew would always be his trigger, the vice that Edmund had implanted him with. "You are nothing without Edmund. You can't even kill a little girl on your own."

I took another step forward, my hand extending toward the pocket of his jeans as he pressed himself against the bars, the door rattling ominously as his anger shook through him.

"I can kill a little girl, Wynifred. Or do you not remember?" he spat back.

I sneered, careful to keep his focus on my face and not on what my fingers were slowly maneuvering out of the pocket of his pants and into my own.

"Can you really?" I taunted as fear and hunger shook my legs. I knew I wouldn't be able to stand much longer, but that was okay, I had done what I needed to do.

Cail's lip curled as he shook the bars, his anger so close to the surface that even he could barely control it. I wanted to congratulate myself on my accomplishment. I had pushed him to this brink several times, but before, he was my loving brother. He would have never followed through then. Now, I was his enemy; I would be a punching bag.

I wanted to scream as the door swung open, his shaking body rushing into the cell. I held still, ready to take what was coming. Cail's hand clasped around my neck as he pushed me against the wall, my feet lifted off the ground as he held me there. The strong grip of his hand against my throat cut off the airflow, the blood flow, and started to cut off my life.

I heard Talon scream, and Sain plead. I heard their voices for one minute before the static took over, the blackness seeping into my vision.

It started slowly on the outer edges, but all I could do was smile. I didn't know why, but all I saw was the image of the beautiful girl. I heard Talon's voice, and I was okay.

As the black took over and zeroed in on Cail's face, I saw my brother, the boy who had practically raised me. I saw the soft lines of his face, the dark purple sheen of his eyes. Strangely enough, I still loved him.

8

WYN

"WYNIFRED?" Talon's voice was soft in my ear, his hand warm against my cheek.

I moaned and tried to roll over, but my body wouldn't respond. I stayed limp on the floor, my cheek pressed into the ground, and my eyes slowly opening to the green light that Sain held in his hands.

"She's awake," Sain sighed, his voice quiet as he tried not to wake Ryland up.

I blinked, letting my eyes adjust as I looked toward Sain. The intensity of his stare scared me. I wanted to look away. I wanted to move away from that look. But I couldn't make my body do anything.

Everything hurt.

Talon's hand grasped at my shoulder frantically, the pads of his fingers slipping on wetness and sending little pinpricks of pain down my spine.

I tried to move again. This time, my body allowed me to roll onto my back. The movement was only half managed though, and I landed hard as I half fell, half rolled onto the stone. I groaned as the impact sent a wash of agony through me. My teeth clenched in an attempt to keep the pain out of my voice. I wasn't sure there was a part of me that didn't hurt.

"What happened?" I managed to squeak out, my voice catching on what felt like sandpaper lodged in my throat.

"Cail beat you unconscious after you punched him, Wyn." Talon's voice was strained, the tone rough, making it obvious he had been crying.

"I punched him?" I asked, the words barely escaping.

I didn't remember punching him. I only remembered being pinned against the wall and then blackness.

I looked away from the filthy ceiling toward Talon. He lay on the floor of his cell, his body still pressed up against the bars, a new purple bruise forming on his cheek. I wanted to reach out and touch the dark mark, but couldn't get my sore fingers to respond. Just seeing it there told me the story I knew Talon wouldn't. Talon had yelled out, pleaded with Cail to stop hurting me, and in turn, he had been beaten, too.

He looked at me with glistening eyes and moved his arm closer to me. His face screwed up in pain as he moved, his arm only making it halfway before it dropped to the stone, his body not strong enough to support it.

"Yeah... and then he..." Talon's voice caught, his hand still reaching toward me, not quite able to reach. "Are you okay?"

I moved onto my side and pushed myself toward Talon as I gently moved to sit against the bars. Everything hurt as I moved, every joint, every bone, and every inch of skin that covered my body. I felt pools of wetness slip over my skin as I moved, my own blood washing over me and leaving glistening trails of bright red to swirl around the jagged lines of black.

I leaned against the bars, right by where Talon lay, and his arms moved to wrap around me. I felt his lips against my bare arm; they were wet from the tears of relief that moved down his face.

"Why did you do that?" Talon hissed, his voice panicked and weak as he leaned heavily against the bars in an attempt to be close to me. "He could have killed you, Wyn."

I cringed as I leaned my head against the bars, the simple movement igniting an inferno of pain in my body.

"He's going to kill, Joclyn," I said simply, hoping that my statement would be enough to pacify him, but knowing it wouldn't be.

"And you wanted to join her?" Talon asked; Sain's chuckle sounding strangely out of place.

"No, I wanted to save her." I cringed as I shifted my weight, a loud groan escaping my lips as I pulled the long, red blade out of my pocket. I held it up, letting Sain's dim, green light reflect off the surface, shattering a wicked prism of red around us.

"No," I heard Talon gasp, his fear and disbelief at what I held in my hands haunting.

Sain, however, moved forward, his hand grasping the bars as he tried to push through them, desperate to get through and reach what I held in my hands.

"You can go in and warn her," I said to Sain, his eyes widening as they flashed from the blade to me.

"I can't," he said simply, the energy not leaving his face, "but Ryland can. And, I think, without Cail to meddle with his mind, he might be coherent enough to get the message across. He has tried before, without the blade, but it has never worked."

I nodded my head once in understanding before moving forward, my body screaming as I moved. Talon stayed silent as I moved away from him, my body shuffling across the small space to extend my hand through the bars, the blade stretched toward Sain as I gripped it in between my fingertips. I felt his hand wrap around it, his hand encompassing it as he held it against him like a precious stone.

"Thank you, Wyn. We might be able to save my daughter now." I heard Talon gasp behind me, but ignored it. I wasn't even sure I understood how that one worked.

I nodded briefly and slowly moved back to rest against the bars of my cell, Talon's arm wrapping around me from where he lay, too weak to pull himself to sitting.

"My shield might be able to keep the scream at bay. It should be enough," Sain said quietly, his voice a mutter as he attempted to convince himself.

I said nothing, I only watched as Sain lifted Ryland's shirt, moving his hand over Ryland's heart. He hesitated for only a moment before plunging the blade through, the two men screaming in unison before they blacked out, the green orb of light extinguishing the moment their screams did. I froze in the darkness, waiting for footsteps, knowing they would come eventually, but hoping the shield had masked the noise enough not to draw immediate attention.

We had no guarantee that Joclyn would be sleeping. For all we knew, it was the middle of the day and we had hours to wait. Ryland and Sain needed all the time with her that they could get.

"Please let them find her soon," I said to myself, unable to keep the thought from entering my mind. "Please don't let this have been for nothing."

We waited in silence, with no shield to give us the ability to speak and with no light to see. I shifted down to the cramped floor of my cell, letting my arm entwine with

Talon's through the bars, a silent prayer for safety on my lips.

Thunk.

I felt the ripple of movement before I heard the sound of footsteps on the staircase that led down to the jail cell. The heavy tread was followed by Cail's loud voice as he sang happily while he made his way toward us. I moved away from Talon, ignoring his frantic grasping for me to stay, and shuffled across the floor to what I hoped was my original position.

Cail's voice grew louder as the light he brought with him brightened, his voice moving from song to speech as he stepped into the prison area.

"I have great news, Ryland. We get—What the hell?" His voice stopped mid-sentence and everything inside of me turned to ice, my heart thunking loudly in my chest.

I listened to his footsteps, to the iron grinding as the door opened, another loud exclamation from Cail and then silence.

Silence.

I waited and waited. I could hear Talon's labored breathing behind me, the shallow breathing of those on the other side of the bars and then screaming.

All three men's voices hollered. Ryland's in maniacal agony, Sain's in fear and Cail's in anger. They joined each other for just a minute before the only scream left was Ryland's, his scream morphing into wails of agony.

"Where did you get the dagger?" Cail yelled, his voice loud and oppressive.

"I didn't..." Sain muttered. "Ryland..." Sain's voice cut off as his body hit the rock of the wall.

"Don't lie to me!" Cail roared. Ryland's screams picked up at the increased volume of the room.

All I could hear for a moment was Ryland's screams, his mumbling pleas and the bang of his head against the bars. The sound loud, until it left, leaving us in silence.

"Sit down, Ryland," Cail commanded, and I stiffened.

Cail had reattached himself to Ryland's mind, turning him back into the black-eyed monster. I should be happy for the lack of screams, but I still remembered Ryland's cold and aggressive behavior from when we had tried to rescue him. With that one action, Cail had placed another enemy in the prison, in the jail cell right next to me.

"Now," Cail continued, leaving a long silence and keeping his voice calm, "who gave you the dagger?"

"Ry... Ryland," Sain panted, his voice tensed. I fought the urge to open my eyes. I really didn't want to see this played out.

"Don't lie to me, Sain!" Cail roared. "I don't like being lied to, and you have done it an awful lot recently." Cail's tongue clicked impatiently and I heard the clang of a chain, the groan of defeat.

"First, you lie to Ovailia and then to us about your first vision. Last, you lied about who your daughter was. Here I was thinking I was going to get to feed you today."

"No!" Sain begged. "Please, I need water."

"Then tell me who gave you the knife."

"Ryland," Sain's said before being cut off with a loud thunk as Cail pushed him into the stone wall at the back of his cell.

"Ryland, you say?" he asked, his voice heavy in warning.

I don't know if Sain heard the inflection or not, but his voice had lowered, "Yes."

"Interesting." I heard Cail's voice right outside of my jail cell followed by the creak of metal as he leaned against the bars, causing them to jerk against their joints. "Very interesting."

Sain's screams filled the darkness as Cail attacked him, but it was not an attack of physical blows. Cail was attacking Sain with magic. Sain's body jolted in pain as Cail laughed, the dry sound mixing with Sain's screams as it all echoed around the jail.

I curled up in a ball and pushed my fists into my mouth, desperate to keep the scream inside of me, to stop myself from yelling out. I needed to fight back, to save him, but I had nothing to fight back with. I did not know if I could survive another beating. I didn't know if Sain could either. Everything tightened inside of me as guilt seeped into my heart, tense anger washing over me.

I should save him, I should. I just couldn't make my voice come. I couldn't do it. I stayed still, waiting for the screaming to stop, while dry tears seeped from my eyes as I waited for it all to end, my shoulders finally relaxing when it did.

"Don't lie to me, Sain, or I will do it again! Who gave you the knife?" Cail asked, his voice loud above Sain's gasping breaths.

"It was Ryland, I swear it," Sain begged, his voice pained.

"Then I hope Ryland can give you the water you need, Sain, because you won't be getting any from me." Cail laughed, the loud sound making me jump.

"No!" Sain roared, the power behind his weak voice surprising. "I need water, Cail, please. It has been too long."

Sain was begging, and I knew at once that Cail had won. Cail knew it, too. I could feel the change in the electrical current that flowed through the air, the oppressive mood that Cail always brought lifting slightly. I tensed; I didn't know what to do. I couldn't move. I couldn't run. I could only lay there and listen to Sain as he whimpered my name into the damp air. I listened as Cail thanked him, his voice almost passing for genuine gratitude.

I didn't move. I didn't dare. I focused on breathing in and out evenly, keeping my chest from shaking, although I was sure that was impossible. Each of my ribs ached as they moved and my lungs were on fire as oxygen hit them with every breath. I listened to the methodical steps as Cail moved closer to me, the sound of the latch of my cell door unlocking, the squeak of the hinges and still I did not move. I was frozen in fear as I silently pleaded for mercy, pleaded that Talon would keep his mouth shut during whatever was to come.

"I can't say I'm surprised. It only makes sense that my pretty, little sister helped you." Breathe even. Don't rise to his baiting. Stay Still.

"N... no," Sain stuttered. I could hear the regret in his voice, the plea for forgiveness. I wanted to tell him it was all right, that I deserved it after not speaking up before, but I couldn't find the words.

I heard one tap of Cail's foot near my head and then my body flew through the air, Cail magically lifting and restraining me against the wall. I screamed as my body tumbled limply before slamming against the wall with such force that my vision went black. The movement of my body ignited every single new injury in a pressurized pain I couldn't focus through.

My eyes opened slowly, the bright light that Cail had cast on our prison illuminating everything. My eyes burned, and I tried to look away, but Cail's magic kept me so perfectly restrained that there was no hope of moving. I stared at Cail as he came toward me, his arms folded as he sneered.

"Hmmm, say, pretty, little sister, did you help them?"

I met his eyes, squared my jaw and glared at him. I wasn't going to tell him anything. He'd known it was me from the beginning. I was just going to take whatever punishment he doled out for me. I kept my eyes locked with his, wishing he would back down as I fought the shiver of fear that wiggled its way up my spine.

"It was Ryland," Sain gasped, his guilt making him take a regrettable back step.

Please don't, Sain, don't push him. I could see it in Cail's eyes; he was going to take everything out on me.

For one split second, his face softened, his hand moving up to cup my face. Then it was gone, the gentleness I had seen before leaving as the hand on my cheek turned into a slap.

My arms flew above my head of their own accord, my shoulders stretched painfully as the shackles wrapped themselves around my wrists and the chains lifted until my feet left the ground. I felt my big toe release from the ground just as Cail's magical restraints left me; leaving my shackled wrists to support my own weight. I screamed in agony as my body weight pulled against my shoulders and the heavy metal cuffs cut into my wrists.

My scream had barely left my throat before the flat palm of my brother's hand moved across my cheek, sending my head to the side before it dropped down to my chest in defeat and weakness. I let my head hang there, my scream forgotten, not wanting to muster the strength to lift it.

"Leave her alone!" Talon's weak voice echoed around the stone walls, making him sound much stronger than he actually was.

My head snapped up at the sound of his voice, my eyes

opening at him, pleading with him to just lie down and stay out of it, to save himself.

I knew he wouldn't.

He was slowly attempting to pull himself up, but his arms gave up halfway, sending him down to the ground. Cail moved away from me to squat down in front of Talon, the large, slimy bars of my cell the only thing between Cail and my husband.

"I guess I need to teach you a lesson, too." Cail didn't even move; he stayed squatted with his hands hanging limply in front on him when Talon started to scream.

I screamed along with him, trying to plead for Talon's safety, trying to fight back. My back arched as I screamed and tried to fight my way toward him, sending my body bouncing against the stone wall, my screams changing to my own agony at each impact.

Talon screamed as his body shifted on the ground, his weak muscles not giving him an option to fight back. Cail was hurting him without skin contact. I didn't want to start thinking about what else he might be capable of. I knew it wasn't his own magic he was using there—it was Edmund's. And Edmund was capable of just about anything.

Talon's screams died, and Cail's eyes widened.

I froze, my eyes stuck on my husband and on the limited movement in his chest.

"Talon?" I gasped, not caring about the consequences.

I stared at his chest, at the stillness of it. I couldn't tell if he was breathing or not.

"Talon!"

"Shut up, sister!" Cail yelled as he pulled himself back to standing. "He's only passed out. I wouldn't kill a perfectly good body, not when there are so many other chances to torture him."

He looked at me and smiled. I tried to control my breathing, I tried to settle down and scowl at him. I wanted to show him that I wasn't afraid, but I couldn't. For the first time, I was scared.

"Well, it looks like my work here is done," Cail said as he strode out of my cell, leaving the door wide open.

"I'll go get your reward, shall I, Sain? Be right back." He spoke like a friend, but his words were more of a warning than anything.

I watched him as he left, leaving his light behind to brighten the disgusting prison we were trapped in. My shoulders were on fire, and my head was spinning slightly as my body attempted to give into the pain.

Please let it give in soon.

9

WYN

"Is he all right?" Sain asked, his voice a whisper. I gaped at him, shocked he had the balls to say anything, and risk them coming back down to hurt us. Then again, it no longer mattered now.

"Yes." I looked away from the staircase to Talon. I still could not see the gentle rise and fall of his chest. I felt the thundering in my heart, and for one brief moment, it overrode the pain in my body. *Please just be knocked out. Please.*

"Are you all right?" Sain whispered from the other side of the jail, the regret I saw in his eyes earlier just as heavy in his voice now.

I was beginning to hate that question. I hated what it meant. I hated that it was the first thing we asked one another. I missed asking someone how their day was, or even talking about the weather. God, how I missed talking about the weather.

I didn't answer Sain. I rested my head against the rock wall, my arms tight against the skin of my cheeks.

"It will be soon," Sain said, and this time I looked at him. Something about his voice was different.

"What will be soon?" my voice creaked out slowly, the muscles in my throat burning as I forced air through them.

"When that life is lost, there will be a moment when you can do anything." His voice was strangely deadpan, his eyes focused on Talon and not on me.

"Sain?" I asked, ignoring the throbbing of truth that was burning through me. His words seeped into me and rattled my bones with a sob that wouldn't leave me. I pushed it to the side. I locked it away as my pride, and my fear, took over.

"No, Sain," I pleaded, not wanting him to continue.

"Follow the light, and you will escape. Follow the pain, and you will die."

"Sain!" I screamed his name, not caring if I was heard, not caring what beating might follow. I just wanted Sain to take his words back. I didn't want to hear them.

Sain turned his head to me, his hands wrapped around the bars as he looked at me. I barely made out the crinkle in his eyes as he smiled before footsteps started thundering down the stairwell.

I froze, regretting my scream and awaiting whatever new pain was to come. It wasn't pain coming though; it was something far worse.

My father bolted down the steps and right into my cell, his strides bringing him right up to me. His hand collided with my jaw, his dark eyes staring into me wickedly. He was daring me to challenge him, daring me to speak back, glare, anything. I couldn't. I couldn't see beyond the blinding words Sain had just unleashed on me. They leached out of the air like a poison and zapped all the fight out of me.

"Good girl," Timothy said, his lips turning up. He raised his hand and the chains that suspended me loosened, my body dropping to the ground as much as the chains would allow, restraining me to a high sitting position.

"Don't cause any more problems," Timothy spat as he walked away, just as more feet and voices echoed down to us.

"Oh God, what is that terrible stench?" Ovailia spat, her icy voice cutting through me and adding to my fear.

"The smell of fear and oppression, dear," Cail said, laughing as he walked back in. Ovailia, Edmund and one of their guards followed him in.

My father turned at Edmund's arrival, bowing slightly as Edmund surveyed the circumstances around him. I tried to look away, but couldn't. I stared at Edmund, knowing that defeat was evident on my face, knowing it didn't matter anymore.

"Lovely," he said, his voice stiff as he tried not to inhale. "I think you two have done a wonderful job."

Edmund moved around in front of us, his hands clanging each of our cells as he moved past.

Ovailia followed her father, Cail right beside her. As she moved past us, her eyes taking us all in, I caught her gaze. Her eyes crinkled as she smiled at the bruises on my face and the way I was strung up and immobilized.

"You're looking well, Wynifred." She smiled, and Cail laughed at her taunt before grabbing her hand and dragging her to the cell against the far wall.

"Hello, Sain," she said as she kneeled down in front of Sain's cell, bringing her eyes down to his level. The sharp points of her high heels stuck out precariously, the glistening of the black leather caught in the low light. I looked at the shoes, wishing I could grab just one of them and use it against her.

"How are you doing, dear? Did you miss me?" I could

hear the laugh in her voice, the taunt, but Sain only smiled, his eyes crinkling in joy.

"I never missed you, Ovailia." Even I could hear the lie and the heartbreak that his voice held.

"How nice," Ovailia sneered. "I have a gift for you."

Ovailia lifted her hand, and the servant that had followed them down put a large, brown mug in it. She lowered it down so that Sain could see, and he jumped, his body moving to press against the bars. Sain's chained hands reached for it, his desperate fingers unable to gain contact.

"Water," he gasped, the need in his voice showing a primal urge that I hadn't been aware he possessed. I watched as he grasped for the mug, his fingers reaching as Ovailia's smile increased.

"Thirsty, are we?" she asked, and the men behind her snickered.

"Calm down, Sain," Edmund said. "You know our deal."

The old man backed down, his chains grinding against the floor as he retreated to the corner of his cell. "What would you have me see?" Sain asked, his voice distanced as he recited words I was sure he had said a million times before.

"Ilyan wants Ovailia to give him Ryland," Edmund said. My head shot up, my breathing shallow. I moved against my chains, trying not to call attention to myself, but wanting to hear everything. "We need to know if the boy is ready for the job we have prepared him for."

Sain nodded once in understanding and then Cail swung the door to his cell open, letting Ovailia walk in with the mug in her hands. She walked right to him, her heels clicking loudly as she spat in the mug, her saliva dripping down the inside wall of the cup before she handed it to him with a wicked smile. He clenched it greedily, his fingers shaking as he held it against his chest.

"Not yet, Sain," Edmund said as he, too, stepped into the tiny cell. I could barely make out Sain from behind the forest of legs between us.

I watched in silence as Edmund took out a tiny silver dagger, cutting his daughter's finger and then his own, adding their blood to the mug before stepping out.

"Don't you want to try some, Ovi?" Sain asked, causing Ovailia to turn, her heels clicking to a stop.

"I never did, Sain," she sneered, folding her arms, her hair swinging as she glared at him. "I only told you that so you would think I loved you." She smiled and exited the cell, thinking she had won, but I could see the crinkle around Sain's eyes.

"You only lie to yourself to decrease the hurt, Ovi. Don't deny what you have felt for me."

Ovailia turned to lunge at him, but three pairs of hands held her back. Sain had already pressed the mug to his lips and was drinking deeply of the disgusting mixture of saliva, blood and Black Water. He drained the mug quickly, resting his head on the wall as he sighed in appreciation.

I heard the breathing of everyone accelerate as they waited, for what I didn't know. My eyes were as glued to him as theirs were, expectation heavy between us.

Sain opened his eyes, the large orbs of green now the purest black, the very center glowing with the red heat of a fire before extinguishing to deep black like the rest. I gasped. I tried not to, but it came out anyway. Thankfully, no one looked my direction; no one seemed to hear.

Sain had opened his mouth, a deep moan releasing before he began to speak, the deep, unnatural sound I had heard before taking over his voice. "Two men stand, one will fall. Blood will drip. The game is played, and those with the most pawns will take the stage. Take your man and play the game, but be careful where your trust is laid."

The same deep groan filled the halls as his voice faded out, his keening continuing as the voices of our captors overlapped each other, trying to decipher the sight.

I didn't hear them; I didn't even try to break words out of the mess of sound. I just stared at Sain, his eyes now back to their usual bright green. I wanted to make sense of the stories in those eyes. I wanted to hear the explanation and know what he had seen behind the black. He only stared, the sadness telling me all I needed to know. He had seen something, and it wasn't good.

"Stop." Edmund's lone word broke through the bickering, and my focus went right back on them.

"If I send him, I could lose him. That was always an option. I don't think Sain's sight says that however. Cail has used the same terminology about pawns with Joclyn, this is a chess game, and it is all about foresight. The pawns are certainly in our favor."

Edmund turned and looked over each of us, his eyes lingering for a moment on mine, the only one of the captives who stared right back. He smiled, the hatred in his face looking through me, into a future me, someone else. I could see the need to control me in his eyes, the same look he had in my dreams as he hurt the beautiful child. No one should be able to hold that much hate in their heart.

I looked away as he smiled, wishing the conversation would just end, and they would leave us, taking the suffocating hate with them.

"But, Master," Cail said, "it also said one would fall. What if that one is Ryland?"

"Then let him fall," Edmund hissed, Timothy laughing

at his outburst. "He was always just an expendable piece of property."

"Is he strong enough?" Ovailia asked as she walked up to his cell, bending at the waist to get a better look at Ryland. "He doesn't seem to be doing much."

"Cail is controlling him, Ovailia," Timothy said, his hands writhing together in excitement.

"What can he do?"

"Turn him off, Cail," Edmund said. I stiffened at his voice, knowing what would come after, my breath catching in my throat for one solid minute before I was able to pick it back up. "Let my daughter see what all of your work has done for us."

"Thank you, Master," Cail breathed, his voice awed and humbled. He bowed slightly before moving forward, his hands wrapping around the bars of the cage.

Everyone waited for the hold Cail had on Ryland's mind to dissipate, the silence dragging on and on. I couldn't look away from Ryland, from the calm way he sat until the first whimper escaped his lips, his hands already moving to claw through the air around his head.

"Joclyn," he moaned, the grip of his fingers increasing as he began to rock back and forth, his mumbling increasing.

"This is your weapon?" Ovailia asked. "A weeping child?"

"No, Ovailia, it's what the weeping child does that is the weapon." Edmund smiled and clapped Cail on the shoulder, his action making him look like a proud father. "Go on, Cail."

"Ryland," Cail taunted, "Ovailia's here. She saw Joclyn."

Ryland looked up, his whimpers turning to a howl as he stood and rammed at the cage, his voice opening up into a wail that only increased as Cail went on.

REBECCA ETHINGTON

I pulled against my chains, wishing there was a way to move away. My body screamed as I tried, and eventually I had to give up. I shouldn't still be scared of him, but I didn't know what Cail had planned for his little show-and-tell, and that worried me.

"Joclyn?" Her name was a groan on Ryland's lips, his hands gripping the bars in front of him so tightly that his knuckles had turned bright white.

"Yes, Ryland," Cail continued, "they had a nice dinner together, and do you know who else was there?" he asked, turning to Ovailia who smiled broadly and stepped up to the bars.

"Ilyan was there," she said simply. Ryland's grip tightened as he yelled, slamming his head into the bars over and over again.

"Yes, Ilyan was there, Ryland," Cail continued, raising his voice enough to be heard above Ryland's yells. "He was holding her hand and touching her face."

Cail stopped as Ryland's howls opened up, his body pulling against his chains repeatedly as he tried to get through the bars to them.

Cail smiled as Ovailia squealed with joy, her hand hitting the bars loudly in an effort to excite Ryland, his howls getting louder.

"He kissed her hand, Ryland," Ovailia said, her icy voice eager to jump in on what she obviously viewed to be a wonderful game. "He traced her lips with his finger. He touched her neck—"

"I'm gonna kill him!" Ryland howled, his voice rising with every beat of Ovailia's hand against the bars.

Edmund stepped forward to view his son better, his eyes full of pride as he watched his own flesh and blood writhe with torment and agony. "Perfect," he sighed. "I never thought I would say this about him, but he is perfect. If he cannot fight beside me, then I will use him as a weapon. With the power he has, and his lust for Joclyn, he is the perfect weapon."

Edmund reached through the cage as Ryland continued to fight to get at them. His hand ran along his son's face, a wicked gleam shining in his bright blue eyes, a gleam I hadn't seen in over a hundred years.

"Are you going to go kill your brother, son?" he asked. I froze, my eyes flashing to Sain who looked just as shocked as I felt.

"I'm gonna kill him!" he howled, his head knocking against the bars. "Kill... kill... kill..."

"And what of Joclyn?" Edmund asked, his hand leaving his son's face to curl around the chain that attached to his wrist. "Are you going to make her pay? Pay for hurting you?"

"Hurt her!" Ryland howled, his fingers clenching and unclenching in a halo around his head. "She's hurt me... hurt... she's gonna hurt..."

Ryland hit his head repeatedly in his agony, and the group in front of him laughed.

I couldn't watch anymore, I couldn't. I couldn't watch the beautiful boy who had been destroyed by his own family and turned into a weapon against the only person he ever loved, the only person who had ever loved him back.

I tried to drown out the sounds of his suffering, the sounds of his torment, but they kept coming. Ovailia's squeals of joy, Edmund's chuckles of pride, and Cail's constant taunts broke through the general cacophony.

I wished I could cry. I wished I had enough water in me to do so. Ryland needed someone to mourn over what he had lost, what he could never get back. I wished I could do that for him; there weren't many left who would.

"Let's finish this," Edmund suddenly announced. I heard two iron-barred doors open simultaneously, the grind of the metal closely followed by the clatter of chains.

"Are you ready to go kill your mate, son?" Edmund asked, the chains rattling as Ryland was led, writhing and screaming, out of the prison.

"Kill!" Ryland screamed. "She... she has to pay!"

"Come on, Sain," Ovailia spat, her voice so full of hate I could taste it on my own tongue. "I want to show you what I should have done to you in the first place."

"I hold no hatred for you in my heart, Ovi," Sain said.

"Don't call me that," Ovailia snapped as she led Sain out of his cell, his hands still shackled and chained.

"I am happy to see your love life has improved," Sain said, his voice light, as if he was talking to a long lost friend and not his former lover. "Cail is a much better match for you."

"Anyone is better for me than you were." Ovailia turned on him, her finger sparking as she shoved one long-nailed pointer in his face. I would have expected Sain to flinch away, but he stood still, his eyes focused on her and not the warning that flared only millimeters from his face.

"I quite agree; Angela Despain was a remarkable woman."

Ovailia's finger sparked; her face hardening as she jerked on his chains. His torso jolted down until her finger pressed against the skin between his eyes.

"Leave my love life alone, Sain."

"Then leave my daughter alone," he replied. Ovailia released her hold on Sain. I would have assumed the strength in Sain's voice to startle her, but I knew better.

"Haven't you been listening?" she asked, moving her face

closer to him. "Ryland is going to take care of her for us. Well, after he kills Ilyan anyway."

"We'll see," Sain whispered, his calm voice not missing a beat.

Ovailia's eyes widened for a just a moment before they softened. "You act like you actually control your sight, Sain." Ovailia laughed at the idea and left the cell, dragging the old man behind her.

"Oh," Cail scoffed once the sound of Sain's chains had ebbed away to nothing, "I almost forgot."

He laughed and threw something at me as the light began to fade. I stared at the loaf of bread he had tossed into my cell, unable to move toward it, my stomach rolling with need.

"Bon appétit, Wynifred," Cail spoke from the steps, his body already disappearing around the stairs. The shackles around my wrists opened, sending me tumbling down, and I landed on my chest right in front of the dinner-plate sized loaf of bread. The stale, mostly green surface crawled with maggots.

Bon appétit, indeed. I reached toward the loaf, my weak fingers curling around what was sure to be the only food I would see for another week.

10

ILYAN

I COULD HEAR HER. Joclyn's voice echoed within my head from the memory I had had since the first day I heard it, eight hundred years ago. The rise and fall of her tone, the way she said her Rs—it was an accent I wouldn't hear for hundreds of years after that day.

I had dwelled on her voice for centuries, allowed the memory of her to be my light in my darkest times, and hundreds of years later, I had basked in her voice when I heard it in my ears again. It came as no surprise that the first thing I could remember thinking about, that the first thing I had heard when the darkness came after the stutter had injured me, was her voice.

Trapped in the blackness of my subconscious, my thoughts were only on her. I wondered if I had been able to get her away from Ryland alive, wondered if my foolish attempt at taking her with me through the stutter had worked.

I had felt the warmth of someone healing me, but the touch was wrong. It wasn't her, and that only worried me more.

Until I heard her. Through the darkness that my body kept me in, I had heard her.

I heard her beg for me to live, and I wanted to tell her I was right there, beside her. I wanted to hold her and let her know that I would never leave her.

I had never been injured in this way. I had always been too strong to be hurt for long, and not being able to be there for her triggered my need, my determination, to leave the darkness. To protect her,

I listened to her voice. I listened to her fears, knowing that soon I would be able to calm them.

Every night since I had awoken, the memory of her words filled me. I heard her voice while I slept with her in my arms, and it calmed me, the way she had calmed me in Isola Santa two nights before—the way that no one had ever done. It was there I had felt her magic inside of me, mingling with mine. I had never felt that before, and the sensation was addicting. I wished I could keep that pleasant spark of her magic inside me forever.

I was so used to hearing Joclyn's voice in my dreams that when she woke me up by a simple call of my name, I heard her and my eyes opened. She looked at me with a face that I had memorized, and I blinked, waiting for my mind to clue me in to whether this was a dream or reality. It felt like a dream. Every morning, when I woke with her in my arms after so many years of waiting, it all felt like a dream.

I could feel the warmth of our body heat trapped against our skin and the cold of the cave against my cheek. I could feel her hand against my bare chest, her warm breath flowing over my skin. I could have died right there from the joy I felt.

"Jos," I sighed, happy at being comfortable enough to say her name so familiarly.

She smiled at me, but the smile was sad, the pain behind her eyes stronger than I remembered it being. Something was bothering her: a decision, a choice. I couldn't tell what. I had missed something.

My muscles tensed in alarm. I should have never let her wait so long between Tŏuhas.

I pushed my magic through her, letting the warmth slow her heartbeat. She looked at me with those sad eyes before the fear began to fade, a comfort taking over, her smile lighting her face.

I watched as the calm washed through her before I registered the light in the cave. It was morning. She had slept all night. My whole body felt light at the thought. Finally, she had gotten some rest. She needed it so very badly after all she had been forced to endure.

I had tried to give her that rest at the hotel last night, but the nightmares still found her. I grabbed her hand in surprise and held it against my chest, her skin warm.

"No nightmares?" I was hopeful. How could I not be? I had held her for months as the nightmares had plagued her, tried everything to help her, and tried everything again when nothing had worked.

"I am so glad," I whispered at the shake of her head, pulling her into me and wrapping my arms around her. The small movement must have triggered a million aches inside of her because I felt her back seize as she gasped, and my heart clunked heavily in my chest in worry.

I did the same thing I had done for months. I plunged my magic into her as I healed her. I wrapped her spine in energy as I repaired the tiny fractures that lined her bones and warmed her spleen as I jumpstarted it.

I had known it was foolish yesterday to let her wait so long, but I also knew why she was scared. I just hoped

Ovailia could bring Ryland back soon. Only his touch could make her whole again. I needed her whole. I couldn't bear to see her in pain, even if his return would take her away from me.

For now, I would keep her safe and protect her until the end.

"I'm scared, Ilyan." Her voice was so soft, so fearful. It triggered that deep protection instinct that was inside me, and I fought the need to hold her closer against me.

She spoke of the Tòuha as if it was a torture chamber, and to her, I was sure it was. It was now a necessity for her health and survival, and yet, it was always so full of pain and sadness. Not for the first time, I worried that I had made the wrong choice, wondered if I should have prompted her to break the bond. I wished I could take the pain away, give her health and healing, but it was not my place.

I leaned forward and pressed my lips against the skin of her forehead, her warmth shooting through me like lightning. I pulled away, much sooner than my heart begged me to. I had to remind myself that she was not mine for my heart to claim. As much as my heart called for her and my magic longed for her, she was not mine. Not yet.

She belonged to my brother. I was only serving as her safe harbor until Ryland was able to return to her.

"I will be here the entire time, Joclyn," I whispered to her, my soul lost to the doubt and fear that flashed through her silver eyes. "Be quick."

Something deep inside of me begged me not to let her go. I didn't want to see the pain on her face when she returned. After the last time, when she woke up bleeding, I had become worried as to what could actually happen within the shared consciousnesses her and my brother shared. A Tòuha was meant to be a place of intimacy and a joining of body and mind, but Joclyn had never been able to experience them the way they were meant. From the beginning, she had been forced into a place of loneliness.

I watched as she pulled the beautiful necklace my brother had given her from underneath her shirt, the jewel glimmering as she plunged her magic into it.

I could feel the power emanating from the immaculate stone, the strength of Ryland's magic. The jewel sparkled as his heart stayed with her, his magic surging through her as he protected her.

It was dark magic, but dark magic used for something good, and it had turned into something beautiful.

He had given her a piece of his heart, enclosed inside the shimmering surface of a diamond.

I had never told her what it really was. I wasn't sure she was ready to know the truth behind it.

She didn't look at me as she pushed herself into my chest again, my arms wrapping around her instinctively. Her body was stiff against mine before she relaxed, her mind leaving to connect with that of her mate.

I ran my hand over her hair, the thick braid I had placed in it only the day before all ruffled and frizzy from a fitful sleep. Neklidný spánek? No, that couldn't be. Joclyn had said that she had had no nightmares and the few nights without them, she had always slept so still, so soundlessly. Nevertheless, her hair was far more mussed than I had seen lately.

I didn't want to think that she might have lied to me; that she was hiding her pain. I wanted her to trust me enough to tell me everything.

I reached up to wind a thick strand that had come undone back into place, and her body shuddered against mine. The small movement was almost that of a sob. My chest froze at the thought of her crying again.

"Jos?" I pulled her limp body away from me, but her eyes were still closed, and she remained in the Tòuha.

I had almost pulled her back into me when she shook again, this movement heavier. Her head jumped and lolled a bit before coming to rest on my arm.

She had never moved like this during a Tòuha. It was always the nightmares that racked through her body and brought the seizures and agonizing movements. Tòuhas were gentle. I had seen so many of my kind enter them through my life span. The gentle way their bodies lay, the glowing, ethereal beauty that would overtake them as they visited such a pure eternal place.

Joclyn twitched again, and I brought her against me, my hands fanning against her back as her heartbeat fluttered inside her chest. It wasn't an excited flutter of pleasure; it was the heavy, racking thumps of fear, of danger.

"Jos?" My back stiffened when she didn't react, my hands moving to clench her to me, my muscles tensing against her.

Someone was hurting her. I could already feel my unbidden anger pulsing through me, the primitive need to protect her taking over my better judgment. She had only been gone a matter of minutes, but still, it was much longer than she had visited recently.

Now she was scared and trapped inside the Tòuha, with a heartbeat of a drum. She was in danger.

Her body shook again, her chest heaving as she gasped and coughed into the skin of my chest. Warmth spread over me as her breath spread away from her over my skin, leaving behind a wetness that stuck against my chest. I froze as I smelled it, the earthy scent of blood and the smell of all my fears.

I pulled her away to reveal a bright red patch of her blood on my chest. Her mouth was covered with it. It continued to drizzle from her gaping mouth and onto the sheet of the bed we lay in.

"Ne," I gasped.

I stared at the blood that trickled down the side of her mouth, the bright red vivid against her pale skin. My fear flowed into my bloodstream, igniting my fury, my anger.

Someone was hurting her. Someone was going to pay.

My magic pulsed once through her, in search of the connecting thread of the Tŏuha, ready to get her out of there, but I felt nothing before she began to convulse.

Her body shook violently next to me, her voice moaning and gasping as if she was being strangled. Her rough movements grew as I watched, my hands reaching out to steady her, comfort her, but finding no footing. The harder my hands attempted to grab her, the more she writhed, sending my hands away from her.

"Joclyn!" My voice broke as I yelled at her in a foolish attempt to wake her up.

Her body continued to writhe and seize, the moans turning into agonizing yells. My magic pulsed through to the Štít in desperation, trying to calm her, but her barrier pushed right up against it, denying me access.

I pushed with my full strength, knowing she could hold the power if the barrier broke, but nothing budged. There was no room to enter. She had somehow managed to lock me out in her most desperate time of need. The realization only fueled my alarm. It rocked through me in angry waves that grew the more they moved. My jaw locked in fear, my magic bubbling high above the power I normally held in reserve.

I moved myself over her, desperate to find a way to help

her, when her movements threw me from the bunk, her magic pulsing into me and sending me skidding across the cold floor of the cave.

I stood in one jump, my feet immediately moving to take me back to her.

Joclyn lay on the bunk as she continued to hack up blood. She had bled when Ryland had hit her with a chair. The same thing was happening again, but this time, much worse.

I needed to find the connecting fiber of the Tǒuha. I needed to bring her back, but I couldn't get close enough to do so. I yelled as I squared my shoulders, fully prepared to battle my way through her seizure and save her... until her hands began to glow.

If I wasn't so focused on her, I would have missed it.

The magic exploded out of her, an electrical current so strong it would have buried us all in the mountain in a matter of seconds. My magic burst away from me in a shield that cocooned its way around Joclyn. The force of her magic pushed me away from her as the transparent shell I sent toward her surrounded her, trapping a lightning storm of energy.

Her magic crackled and boomed within the protective layer I had created, flashes of light shooting over the dark walls of the cave. My fear grew as the onslaught I had just trapped Joclyn in got worse, and I realized the possible danger that she could now be facing alone.

I ran to her as I kept the shield strong. My magic pushed through the Štít in its desperate attempt to get near her, but still, it was restrained.

The powerful barrier I had placed around her was no match for her magic. The fact should not have surprised me, but given the situation, it only meant danger for her and for the rest of us around her.

I stepped back, although my heart called me forward. My jaw tensed as I looked at the danger before me, my blood ready at any instant to intercede.

"Dramin!" My voice was barely able to rise through the large space before the shield shattered. The loud crack of her magic hitting the stone resounded through the cave in a fearful rumble.

The sound rattled in my ears, the danger calling right into my gut. My muscles tensed and pulsed in my shoulders as the danger announced itself. My magic bubbled as my shoulders stiffened, my breeding guiding me toward her, toward the danger.

Dramin's footsteps were barely audible above the destructive sound of Joclyn's magic as she continued to writhe, the uncontrolled streams of power flowing out of her. The white hot torrents escaped from her fingers and out of her chest as they continued to tear through the mountain, the contact impact beginning to shake the ground beneath us. I stopped as many of her magical attacks as I could, my magic surging away from me as I attempted to protect us, but I was no match for the power that Joclyn held inside of her.

A rumbling sound ricocheted through the cave, echoing off walls as it intensified and the mountain began to fall apart around us.

Thom and Dramin called out from somewhere behind me when the shaking increased and sent us all to the ground, our feet unable to stay steady inside of the rumbling cave.

The current that now had a life of its own ripped the rock of her bunk apart, pieces of it falling around her and covering the bed she lay in as she unwittingly entombed herself in fallen rock.

I didn't think. If I had, I wouldn't have moved. My soul just stepped in, moving me forward in an attempt to save her. I dodged as the magic crackled in the air around me, yelling as one long tendril sliced deeply into my arm.

I could hear Dramin and Thom yelling behind me, begging me to stop, warning me of the danger, but I didn't listen. I ignored the blood that flowed freely down my arm. I ignored their voices. I could only focus on the girl who was fighting for her life right in front of me. I reached her just as the attack stopped and her arms went limp. I grabbed her body and brought her safely into my arms, the bunk shifting into a mass of rock and debris as it collapsed over where she had been only moments before.

Everything was silent. I held her in my arms as I let my pulse steady, as I accepted the safety of the girl I held.

One moment of silence and then the groaning of the cave opened up. The loud rumbling sounds had been a deep warning of what was to come.

My muscles tensed as my fear rose and swelled into a power I always tried to restrain, but not now. Now, I needed it.

The deep sound rumbled around us, ripping through our ears as it warned us of what was to come. I turned toward the two men behind me to see my own fear mirrored in their faces. Thom looked around as the groans increased and Dramin's head whipped around as a loud bang sounded through the cave as the roof began to collapse on itself. If we didn't move now, we would find ourselves buried in here.

"Get out of here! Jdi!" I yelled loudly in Czech, fully aware that I had placed the magical stream into my voice that would require them to comply. I knew that neither

Thom nor Dramin could perform a stutter, and I was not willing to leave them here to die alone.

Both men turned and ran, their speed increasing as more groaning echoed around us. I held Joclyn's body to me, praying she did not continue to attack her unseen assailant before I could get her to safety.

The floor shook as bits of ceiling continued to fall around us. The sizes of the stones increased as the mountain shifted; the groans responding to the destruction that Joclyn had caused to a now unstable cave. I listened to the groaning that echoed as we ran, the deep moans from the mountain warning us of the end.

I followed them as we attempted our escape. Thom's long dreads bounced around his shoulders, and Dramin's night robe flew behind him like a cape. Joclyn's continued jerks and spasms were masked by the jostling movements of my run as we dodged around falling rocks and dirt. I ran as I watched the intricate stonework of the cave crumble around us, the beautiful iron work that once hung from the ceiling crashing to the stone floor only to crinkle like paper left too long in water. We darted through obstacles as the noise grew until each of us had made it into the hall that would lead us out, only to find it blocked.

My heart plunged to see our escape route clogged with rock, the only way to safety encapsulating us in our danger. Thom and Dramin looked to me, fear and anger lining their faces. I ignored the emotion, stepping into my role as I had been raised to do.

"The training room." My commanding voice barely resonated above the groaning of the mountain, but even without the magical pulse weaved inside of it both men quickly obeyed.

The sound of the collapsing mountain had grown so

loud that I could barely hear anything above it. I shifted Joclyn's body up, leaving her dangling over my shoulder as the two men ran ahead of me toward the training room.

I watched them go, praying that the space to which they were heading would be free of the horrors we had just left.

Joclyn's body bounced on my back as I turned to face what little was left of the beautiful cave.

The palms of my hands came to rest on the cold stone that lined the dark hallway, the energy that the rock held inside of itself answering to my touch. The strong pulse of natural magic whirled inside of me, pulling at me for a fleeting moment before being sent back to speed through the mountain alongside my own. I closed my eyes as I focused, my magic pushing into the rock, moving it away. There was no way I could stop the destruction, but I could slow it down, stop what hadn't already happened. I could not fail.

I felt the shifting of the rock slow, the mountain answering to my call. I continued to push against it, sweat forming underneath my long hair as I forced the mountain to do what I wanted.

Boulders moved back into place, rocks piled up against others, and I heated and fused the rocks back together in a desperate attempt to stabilize the mountain. My mind moved each hulking mass quickly, stopping the fall in one place only to have it start in another. Even with the speed that my ability gave me, I wasn't going to be able to do enough to keep our way out free of more obstruction.

Slowly, the groaning stopped, the crashing of rocks ceased, and quiet filled the air. I kept my hands flat against the stone as my energy moved back inside of me, energizing me at its return.

I didn't dare move, not yet. I stood still, waiting for the

groaning to return. I could feel Joclyn's jolts against my back, her frantic movements continuing to alert me to the danger she was still facing. Her movements pulled at me, asking me to move, to go help her, but I had to make sure we were all safe first.

"Ilyan?" I didn't even move at Dramin's voice. I stayed still, waiting, needing to know that the mountain wasn't going to continue its attempt to bury us alive.

"Is it safe back there?" I asked through gritted teeth, still not looking toward him.

"Yes."

I felt his body only a step away from me, his energy pulsing through the air. I focused on his energy, my nerves tingling as I felt his arms rise, presumably to lift Joclyn from my back.

"Leave her." My voice was hard.

Dramin's arms dropped, but he did not move. His body was still right behind me. The minutes ticked by until I was sure that the mountain had ceased its implosion. My hands dropped as I turned to face Dramin, Joclyn's twitching body still hanging loosely over my shoulder.

Dramin looked at me, his eyes hooded with concern and fear. I ignored his expression, he needed no explanation from me, and I was not required to give one.

I shifted Joclyn's weight into my arms, her head lolling over my elbow as I walked passed Dramin, his energy following me into the bare cavern that had mostly been used for training until now. Now, it would be used as our home. At least, until I could find us a way out of here.

"What happened?" Thom yelled the moment I walked into the room, his words followed by profanities that no man should be aware of. I knew he was mad. I knew he needed answers. Right then, though, I didn't care. His anger didn't matter. All that mattered was making sure Joclyn was all right.

"Napadli Joclyn."

"What do you mean, Ilyan?" Thom yelled, his anger boiling out of him. "Your girlfriend just tore apart the cave and trapped us underground!"

I could feel the confusion and anger emanating off both of them as their magic peaked and their stress heightened the magical flow inside of them.

I was the only one of my kind who was strong enough to feel the subtle change in the powers of those around me. It was just another one of the curses my powerful magic brought me. Regardless, I wasn't focused on the gentle flow and pulse of Thom and Dramin right now. I was focused on the fact that I felt nothing from Joclyn. Her undercurrent was there, but the actual strength seemed smothered. It was more than when Edmund had been limiting her power through the necklace and worse than when her magic was dying. The thrum I felt now was weaker than when I had first felt her magical pull before her powers had even awakened.

My magic pulsed into her through the Štít, as well as the connection of my skin against hers. It flooded her. The strong barrier that had prohibited me from so much as calming her before was now weak and breakable between us like spun candy. Now, I could save her.

I scanned her body for the thin connecting line of the Tŏuha, my body freezing when I found nothing. I pushed into her, letting my magic fill her to every corner, the full extent of my power enough to kill any other, but Joclyn just lay there. I searched for the bridge to her mind, for injuries, for warning signs, for spells and curses—but found nothing.

I dropped to my knees, keeping her body in my lap, keeping her close.

"She is being attacked in the Tõuha," I provided, knowing I had to give them some sort of explanation as to why their lives had been torn apart.

"Ryland?" Thom accused, his angry voice bitter.

"No."

"Then who?" Thom's voice faded off as he asked the question because he knew, we all knew. We had all heard her retelling of Ryland as a black-eyed man, of how Cail was controlling her dreams. This wasn't a dream, however, and I didn't know how to wake her up. I didn't know how to help her. Somehow, Cail's control had moved into the Tõuha.

"So, she attacked him in the Tõuha and almost killed us?" Thom was angry, and I didn't blame him. "Is she going to do it again? Can't you just wake her up?"

"I can't find the bridge to her mind, Thom. I've been looking."

"How long ago did she go in?" Dramin asked, the confusion in his voice triggering my own.

"Ten minutes," I provided, knowing the short amount of time would sound silly. It did to me.

It wasn't just the time that she had been in there that had triggered my alarm; it was her actions, what had happened to her body. I felt my lungs constrict in stress as I looked at the still wet specks of blood around her mouth.

My hands pressed one of hers against the blood on my bared chest, against the dozens of scars that lined my skin. The pain flared through my chest as the pressure against the scars increased, the same way it had always done. I looked at our hands briefly before dragging my eyes back to her face.

"How is he doing it?" Dramin asked, letting the unspoken name float between us.

"I don't know. But I will find out." I looked up to the two men, looking from the deep sea green of Dramin's eyes, to the crystalline blue of Thom's—the color our father had cursed us with, the color of royalty.

The necklace Ryland had given Joclyn still hung around her neck, the large ruby glistening. *No, not a ruby*, I reminded myself. A diamond. He had given it to her with the intent that it would protect her, just as I had placed the Štít within her. Neither was doing her any good now.

After the protective shield of the necklace had faded, Joclyn was left with only a weak connection to my brother. I touched the stone lightly, knowing what it meant to her, but right then, I hated it. I hated what it had come to represent and what it had done to her.

It had been the bridge to his mind.

My heart rate increased as I stared at the jewel, my breathing stuttering as I attempted to control myself. Before I could stop myself, I wrapped my fingers around the necklace, breaking the clasp as I ripped it away from her neck.

I waited, waited for her to wake, waited for the bridge to make itself known, but she stayed as still as ever, the necklace dead and cold in my hands. I pocketed it quickly, returning my hand to her face.

"Why didn't that work?" Dramin asked, his voice making it obvious that he had already known it would not.

"He has been controlling her dreams through a blood connection, but a Tòuha? I didn't even know that was possible. I have never seen anything like this before, Dramin." I gave them as much of an answer as I felt comfortable giving, keeping my voice an emotionless mask.

"I have."

11

ILYAN

"Wнaт?" I moved to face Dramin, his words still melting into my crude understanding of what was going on.

"I have seen something like this."

I narrowed my eyes at him, and he took a quick step away in expectation of my anger.

"Where?" I asked, trying to keep my voice level, the anger and regality seeping out without me wanting it to. "Was it a sight, Dramin, or at some point in your living life?"

He hesitated, and I instantly knew why. Last night he had spoken in his usual guarded way about being needed; it was his reason for consenting to come to the Rioseco Abbey with Joclyn and me. I hadn't thought twice at the time, how could I? For hundreds of years, guarded words and cryptic answers had been his way. I had no reason to think that would have changed. I felt Thom's magic surge dangerously as his temper rose.

"You have seen this, haven't you, Dramin?" My voice was level, the regal tone I had tried to keep restrained for most of my life seeping through.

Dramin didn't answer. He simply extended his hand

toward me, his face pained as he gave me permission to use the full extent of his recall.

I placed Joclyn on the cold, stone floor of the cave to grab Dramin's hand and place it against my forehead. My eyes closed to blackness for only a moment before the vision filled me. I could see myself, standing over Joclyn, the stone walls of the Rioseco Abbey clear in the background. Her body was still, limp, and yet I was yelling at her, panic evident on my face and in my voice. I watched as Dramin walked into the room, his face calm for only a moment before he, too, panicked. Before I could see any more, Dramin removed his hand from my head, the vision leaving with it.

There was no sign of her waking up in the sight, only her limp body and my pain and panic. That sight could be in a week or in five years—I had no way of knowing. I re-ran the vision in my mind as I inspected every aspect: different clothes, my usual shorter haircut, the Rioseco Abbey.

"Why didn't you tell me, Dramin?" I ran my fingers through my hair, pulling hard on the long, uncomfortable strands.

"Tell you what?"

"Tell me what would happen! That something was wrong, something is..." I stopped, not knowing exactly what was going on. I was unable to put my lack of knowledge about what was happening into words. "We could have stopped this."

"How?" Dramin's voice was deep and accusatory. I could already hear the regular rebuttal of his kind on his tongue—the lack of knowledge, the inability to interfere with things to come.

"You could have told me," I said, knowing my reasoning

would be lost on him. "I could have stopped her from going into the Tòuha—"

"How was I to know it was Tòuha?" Dramin asked his voice rising. Anyone else would have recoiled, but I straightened in front of him, my height and heritage meant to terrify him. He, however, was so used to me he didn't even move.

"I showed you all that I have seen, Ilyan. There was no way to know—"

"Zastavit," I said loudly, prickling agitation moved up my body in a ripple. I let it take over for one weighted minute before I released it; unleashing my temper against Dramin would solve nothing.

"Does she wake?" My voice was a whispered breath.

"Yes." My head snapped up at Dramin's answer, hope running through me.

"Then we will wait," I decided when a small, feminine moan behind me pulled all of my focus away from Dramin and back to Joclyn. I spun around, part of me desperate to see her eyes open, her bright smile.

She was the same.

I dropped to my knees, pressing my hands against her arms as my magic flowed into her.

"Ne," I gasped when I found it. She had a broken bone in her leg. The break was clean and ran right through her tibia, and I was sure she had not had it when we entered the training room.

"What?" Thom had moved up to kneel next to her head, and strangely, the anger in his voice was leaving, concern seeping through in a slow trickle.

"Her leg is broken," I said, not willing to accept it myself.

"Broken?" Dramin leaned down next to me, his hand moving against her head. I could feel his magic move into her alongside mine, the heavy tendrils of the Drak magic cold against my own. He gasped when he felt it and withdrew his hand, his magic leaving with the loss of contact.

I wrapped the bone in a hard layer of my magic, giving it a strong internal cast to help heal it. I didn't know how long it would take with her strangely vacant magic unable to do most of the work itself.

"What is he doing to her, Ilyan?" Thom moved away as he spoke, his fear at the power of our father obviously affecting him.

Edmund was torturing her, hurting her, intentionally. He had done the same to me more than a dozen times— every time he had somehow managed to capture me. It was his favorite game, causing pain.

He had tortured and killed mortals in front of me, hoping to break me or drive me mad. For centuries, the only contact I had ever received from him had been meant to hurt me. Now he was doing the same to Joclyn, the only one my heart called to, the person I would protect with my own life.

Edmund had been hurting her, through Cail, for months in the nightmares, and I had held her as I took away the fears and wiped the anxiety from her mind. I had protected her in a way no one else could until I was able to find a way to make them stop. Now, Edmund had found a way to hurt her, really hurt her, in a place I could not follow.

Or could I?

"I need to get in there." I stood quickly, ignoring the gasps from the men on either side of me, my focus only on Joclyn's body.

"What do you mean, *get in there*?" Thom asked.

"I mean, go into the Töuha and get her out. Wake her

up." I squared my shoulders, still unwilling to look away from her.

"Is that even possible? You can't find the bridge." Dramin's voice was quiet.

"I will find it when I join my mind with hers, Půjde to?" I clenched my jaw, my mind working in preparation for what I was suggesting.

"This is ridiculous, Ilyan," Thom pleaded. "Tam jít tam, you would only be stuck in there. Dramin has seen her wake. We just need to wait."

"Wait?" I scoffed at Thom's reasoning. A few minutes ago, I had been content to do the same, but I could not stand by while she was being tortured. I couldn't let that happen to her. "Two hours there for every twenty minutes here. She has been trapped in that prison for six hours. They have broken her leg and hurt her enough to make her bleed internally. I can't leave her in there. Who knows what else they have done, or are going to do? I don't have time to try."

"I can't let you do this, My Lord." I turned at the sound of Dramin's voice, the desperate plea catching me off guard.

"I don't know what else to do. You are her brother, Dramin. As her brother, what would you have me do?" I didn't need him to understand, I could do it on my own. He was one of the first of his kind, and Joclyn's blood.

"He's her brother..." Thom said just as the thought crossed my mind. I could see what he was thinking, I knew where this was going, and I didn't like it.

"No, Thom," I said sternly, hoping to stop the thought in his mind before he found his voice.

"It's what our father is using to control the nightmares, correct?"

"Yes, but—" I began, but Thom swiftly cut me off. I

could feel my spine prickle at the lack of respect, but I ignored it.

"Then it must be what he is using to control the Tóuha." Thom's face was growing in maniacal intensity. I watched him closely, knowing I would have to put a stop to it soon.

"Using a blood connection is not an option," I hissed through gritted teeth.

"I don't see why not, Ilyan. It's what Edmund is using against her. So, we can use the same technique to save her."

"No, Thom. I won't let that happen, not ever. It's wicked, evil. Do you understand?" I spoke deeply. Blood magic was dangerous. The cutting open of hearts and souls to create stronger ties or to strengthen the bonds of what had once been a simple magic was inhumane. She had already worn dark magic around her neck for months. I wouldn't let her be objected to any more, not if I could help it.

I knew Thom wouldn't understand, he had lived under our father's rule for centuries, his viewpoint would always be somewhat skewed.

"It's just a blood connection, Ilyan. It is how Edmund is able to control Joclyn's dreams. They have Sain, but we have Dramin—"

"No. I will never allow you to cut open my heart or sever my soul in an attempt to save her. This is madness, Thom." Dramin's voice was panicked and scared. He knew what was involved in blood magic. There was a reason it was never done; a reason it was so terrible that Edmund had used it against Joclyn, that he had used his own son to perform it.

"It's the only way," Thom begged, his energy fading, if only slightly.

"No, Thom. You would mutilate her soul and mine, and destroy Ilyan's heart for only a minimal chance to save her. I can't let you do that." Dramin placed his hand on Thom's arm, but Thom pulled away.

"It is not futile. I have done it before." I balked at Thom's words, this fact about Thom disgusting me. To willingly use a blood connection... it was despicable. "It's the only way."

"No," I spoke hard, my power flowing over him as he sunk away.

His shoulders sagged, my magical barrier freezing his logic in place and allowing his better logic to finally be able to take over. I drew my magic away from him when he had obviously calmed, my jaw clenching that it had come to that in order to control him.

"Then what do we do?" Thom whispered, and I relaxed.

"We wait," I said, knowing there wasn't another option. Not anymore.

We looked at each other, each one knowing it was the only option, but none of us willing to say more than that.

I nodded once before moving away from them, my body taking me right to Joclyn's side without a thought. My fingers ran over the lines of her face as my magic swelled through her, my touch moving over eyes, her cheeks, and across the soft skin before her ear.

I lay down next to her, my body pressing up against hers, as it had only an hour before. The warmth from her skin counteracted the chill from the stone and caused my muscles to tense at the differing temperatures.

I pushed my magic into her, confident that I would not hurt her. For the first time in my life, I would not kill someone by filling them with my ability. I felt her magic push against mine, but the strength of it still seemed to be missing. It was still a substance within her, and the substance was healthy and alive, but there was not much more than that.

"Come back to me, Jos," I whispered to her, hopeful that my voice would flow to her as hers had to me. It wasn't fair what fate had planned for us; to take us from one hell to another, to tear us away from each other, to tear her away from her mate.

I let my magic settle inside of her for a minute before I moved it toward my target, fusing parts of myself with her, my magic connecting with nerve endings in an attempt to contact her. I let my finger slide down to connect with her mark, the jolt rocking through me as it always had, every day that I had touched it from the first. Even when she had felt nothing, I had always felt it. I sighed at the sensation and closed my eyes, letting my mind fuse with hers.

I would have yelled at what I found, but I was too scared to see the emptiness of her mind.

There was a reason I could not sense her power, her emotions or her soul. Nothing was there. Her body was an empty shell. I gasped internally at the emptiness, at the confusion and loss I felt from being inside of her like this and finding her gone.

There should have been memories, dreams and visions, but I saw nothing but blackness, the velvety color clear and dark.

If she had left to join her mate in some expanse of eternity, would it leave an empty shell behind? I was foolish to think that this would work, that even a blood connection would work. It couldn't work because there was nothing to attach to. There was no bridge to bring her back.

Edmund must have attached himself to Ryland before he used the connection. That was how he gained control. For us, it was too late.

I let my mind linger inside the black realm that Joclyn had left behind, searching for any way to bring her home.

As I searched, I sang. I sang the song I had written for her all those hundreds of years ago.

The song that was only for her.

I left the song inside of her head, hoping that it would, at least, welcome her home.

12

ILYAN

My stomach growled with the lack of food, but I just ignored it. I had gone longer without eating. Forced starvation was one of my father's favored techniques. I had been living in comfort for too long, my body had become used to consistency. Being trapped in a cave for the past few days had not helped to give it the consistency it now felt it needed.

I laid my head against the back of the cave, ignoring the hard, cold stone that pressed against my body and focused instead on the soft warmth of the girl that was curled against me. At least I could make Joclyn comfortable. I pulled Dramin's robe around her, tucking the edges under her in an attempt to trap her body heat against her.

Her heartbeat was steady against me. It hummed against my skin as it followed the rise and fall of her chest. I focused on it, waiting for her body to seize again.

I had slept with her here for the past few nights, her body warm against mine. Tonight, though, I could not sleep. I didn't know what was going on in the prison she remained in, but her body had twitched and moved more than usual.

Only an hour ago, her knee had been hurt so badly that the tendons had been ripped away from the muscle. I repaired it dutifully as she slept, wrapping it in heavy bindings as she twitched, and I sang my song to her. I let the words fill her mind, my voice imprinting inside of her whether she was there to hear it or not.

It had been the same pattern for the past four days— heal her and sing to her. Then, after every time, I connected with her mind in an attempt to find her. I would keep trying everything I could to save her, to bring her back to me. I would wait forever if that was what it took.

Her body seized again, and her chest racked as she coughed, more blood drizzling from her mouth. I wiped it with the back of my hand and then onto my jeans. With nothing to clean her with, my pants had become stained with a warm, red hue, her blood deepening the color every day.

My fingers clung to the once soft fabric of her shirt, pulling it down just enough to check the skin on her shoulder where the Štít lay inside of her, the dark red scratches deepening in color as I watched, a small trickle of blood appearing on the surface. I replaced the shirt and held her against me, rocking as I clung her to me.

Desperation, it was a feeling I had rarely felt in my long life. I had never really been hopeless enough to feel it. I was always the one in control, powerful and resilient. I laughed at battle and found joy in an impending death. With Joclyn's injured body in my arms, though, I only felt desperation.

If I had ever believed in God, now would be the time I would call to Him, beg Him to save her, to bring her home. I still didn't now, and whoever had called my kind to come forth from the mud had always been strangely silent.

"Have you slept?" I didn't even move at Dramin's

question. I kept my head curled against Joclyn, my hair falling around us.

"No," I whispered loud enough for him to hear me. I knew my voice would carry through the cave. "Last night was bad." I didn't dare elaborate.

"Any new developments?" He knew there would be none, just as I did. We were still trapped in the cave, and Joclyn was still trapped in the Tòuha.

"I can stay with her again today, if you would like? Thom can shift rock on his own for a while; it would give you time to rest." I knew he meant well, but I didn't need to be coddled. Resting while Joclyn writhed was not a possibility. I would rather shift rock with Thom as I did every day. At least then, my mind could focus on other things.

"I see you braided her hair again," he commented when I didn't answer him. I nodded at Dramin's question, waiting for what would come next.

I had braided her hair after some of her blood had dried in it. I had been able to repair the head injury easily enough, but the dark mass of curls needed to be washed. With nothing to clean it with, I resorted to re-braiding, weaving the clumps into the intricate five strand braid. I hadn't even realized what I had done until it was finished.

"The wedding braid is an interesting choice." I ignored him. "To match the shoes, I take it."

I leaned my head back and looked at him out of the corner of my eye, almost daring him to continue.

"You can imagine my surprise when she showed up wearing those things on her feet. They are excellent workmanship."

Dramin let his unasked question linger heavily in the air. I could feel it swirl around us, the intensity of it growing the longer I left it unacknowledged.

I knew I owed him no reply; it was not my place to allow insight into my every thought. Nevertheless, Dramin did not ask as a curious servant, he asked as my friend and Joclyn's brother, and in that regard, I did owe him an explanation.

"I made the shoes as a gift," I finally admitted, refusing to look at him. I focused on Joclyn's heartbeat as I spoke. The steady thrum moving through me.

"She had lost something I couldn't even fathom; I wanted to give her what was due her. What her husband should have placed on her feet on the night of the bonding."

"And so, with him gone, you tried to take his place." I could hear the accusation clearly, but instead of making me angry it only made me laugh.

"You know, that was never my intention, strangely enough. I made the shoes as a gift from her newfound brother, a wedding gift. Part of me fully expected Ryland to return, to fight Edmund and reappear as if nothing had happened. But then, when she wasn't recovering, when Ryland never came, I knew he was gone. Then, I had begun to make them for an entirely different purpose."

"As a gift from a husband to his wife."

I nodded. I knew it was a foolish line of thinking, and one I still resented ever having, but if that last visit into the Tǒuha hadn't cured her, I would have replaced Ryland's bond with one of my own. I knew that would have saved her because I had seen it done before. I would have gladly taken that role if it was necessary, but it wasn't.

It was not yet my place. She wasn't mine to keep.

"It is not my place, Dramin."

"Not yet," he said. I could only smile, letting the beautiful visions of the sight from so long ago wash over me.

"She is bonded to my brother, Dramin. That is a sacred connection and one I would never take advantage of. I will protect her for him. I will keep her safe as my soul calls for me to do, but I will never take her from him. She is not mine. I love her more than I have any other. I love her enough that I would rather see her happy than in my possession. My time will come."

I didn't doubt that any of my words were true, and it wasn't the fickle truth of having convinced myself to believe something. I truly believed it. I had felt it from the beginning when I had first seen Ryland swing her around on the grass at her school. I knew then that I could never take that away from her, that connection. It wasn't my place. Besides, doing things like that was not who I was.

"But she loves you, Ilyan." Dramin's voice was deep, almost as if he was trying to convince me I was making a wrong decision, but I could only laugh at him.

"I know, Dramin. She told me so," I whispered, my fingers moving to run over the soft skin of her face. "And those words flow through my head every night as I keep her safe in my arms, holding her until the right arms can take my place."

She sighed as I held her, almost as if she heard me, though I knew that wasn't possible, her mind was not there to hear me. I smoothed my hand over her hair and the soft skin of her face. Her deep breathing seeped into me, relaxing me as well. The heady beating of my heart slowed, the uncharacteristic relaxation making me feel more in love with her than before, if that was possible.

"It will be harder than you think, handing her over to him."

"I know." I couldn't help it, my muscles tightened around her, bringing her against me tightly. I knew Dramin was right, but no matter how hard, I still would not interfere. I would not break such a sacred vow. It was not mine to break.

"You are a better man than I thought you to be, Ilyan." Dramin sat up slowly, his back leaning against the cold wall beside me.

I looked at him curiously, not sure if his words were that of a compliment or not. He just looked at me with pride and knowledge lining his handsome face. I could feel my eyebrows rise as I waited for him to continue, sure that the threat on my face was evident.

"All those years ago," Dramin explained, "when I first saw the fate of what was to come for you, I was happy for you, so šťastný. But the heartbreak at her being with another... I thought you would purposefully tear them apart to get what was rightfully yours. I am sorry I ever thought badly about you. You are a man beyond words."

I smiled, but chose to say nothing. For years I had thought the exact way that Dramin had. I had been possessive, needy. She was mine, and no one was going to take her away from me. After all, I had waited for hundreds of years, what could one mortal do to stop me? It wasn't a mortal, however; it was my brother.

The child of Sain, the first of the Drak, the Silnỳ, the woman who was created for me, was in love with my baby brother. My brother who had stood up to our father and refused to torture me; who had fought him to give me a chance to escape. Ryland who had been poisoned at such a young age, a mere science experiment to our father. A boy who had known no love in his entire life had found that love, that sanctuary, in a girl I had been waiting for the majority of my life. I could not take that away from him, from either of them.

Once that realization had occurred, my heart no longer ached for her. It still longed, but it no longer ached. Because

I could see her face alight in love for Ryland, and that happiness was enough for me.

"Sain's going to love you, Ilyan," Thom's voice came out of nowhere, and we both jumped. "Of course, he had no idea it was his own daughter he was showing you when the sight was first delivered. Noble Ilyan, so kind to his only daughter."

"Am I detecting a touch of resentment in your voice, Thom?" I asked as he came to sit across from me, the light in the cave increasing a bit as we all woke up and the magical pulses inside it increased.

"Oh, always, Ilyan. As my perfect, older brother, I will always resent you." We both smiled, but it was strained. The bonds of family were always tense between us, between all of our father's children.

"Well," Thom began, leaning back on the palms of his hands, "I'm tired, bolák, hungry, and dying of thirst. What do you say we get out of here today?"

Dramin and I turned toward him, the looks on our faces showing our confusion. We had been shifting rock at the mouth of the cave since the collapse first happened. It was a long process. We had to make sure that what we shifted didn't cause more of a collapse while we tirelessly worked toward the exit. We had almost made it out yesterday, but another small collapse had hindered the process, and Thom and I had returned more dirty and disheveled than before.

I knew why Thom wanted to get out. We all needed food and drink; I could already feel my skin prickle with dehydration. Acting rashly wasn't going to get us out of here any faster; it was just going to get us killed.

"Brzy, Thom," I said, hoping to convey that a rush was not needed.

"Dnes, Ilyan," he countered, his inflection so modern it

brought a smile to my face. "I don't want to wait anymore. We almost made it through last night. If we had used all three of us, we might have been able to do it."

"What are you saying?" Dramin asked, leaning toward him. I could tell how interested he was, and that confused me a bit. He wasn't actually going to give Thom's idea his support, was he?

"If we all work together, we can make a hole big enough for us to escape through. Ilyan can carry the Silný, and we can all be in Rioseco by nightfall." He paused, and we just looked at him. I had to admit, part of what he was saying made sense. The small collapse from last night made me worry, however; the rocks might not have had a chance to settle yet.

"Just think about it," Thom prompted, "Skutečné postele, food and mugs for Dramin's poison…"

The silence stretched through the cave; it stretched between us until Joclyn moaned, her voice soft. Everyone's attention pulled to her as she twitched, blood seeping through the shirt over her shoulder. A quick check revealed that besides the scratches, she had a small skull fracture. I winced. I needed to help her, and being stuck in this cave was not going to give me that opportunity.

"Who knows, maybe feeding the Silný some of that poison will cure her." Thom let his words linger in the air, no one saying anything as Thom and Dramin each held their breath, waiting for a response.

It was the one thing we hadn't tried. The one thing we couldn't here. The pool in the hall of sight had drained with the collapse of the cave, leaving Dramin as starved as everyone else. I couldn't ignore the desperate need I felt. I needed to try it. I would try anything for her.

I leaned down to encompass her with my arms, my

cheek pressing against hers as I mended and braced the new break in her skull. Her body was so broken. So many of her bones were covered with the heavy magical casings I had been applying, so many tendons were still trying to join back together. If we were in the mortal world, she would be in a full body cast by now.

I only nodded once, knowing they were waiting for my approval, also knowing there was no way I could say no. It might not have been the best decision, but for the people around me, it was the right one, and I couldn't lead them astray. Those were the requirements of my position.

My inheritance.

13

ILYAN

WE WALKED DOWN THE LARGE, stone tunnel slowly, my ears attentive toward any sound. My fear of another cave-in was strong, much higher than it should be to attempt something like this. This area wasn't like the training room; this small, claustrophobic space could collapse at any time. We could be crushed to death in an instant.

I straightened my back as I walked, Joclyn held in my arms like an infant, my magic peeking into the rock as I monitored it. Although I couldn't do much with such a weak connection, I could at least give us warning if something was coming.

The light from the glowing orb that Dramin held in his hand flickered around the walls of the tunnel as we walked, the shadows moving and swaying like living hands coming to tear the rock down around us. I watched them for a moment before looking away, placing my gaze ahead of Dramin and toward the task at hand.

"I heard what you said back there," Thom said from beside me, his voice calm. I looked toward him, but he wasn't looking at me, obviously uncomfortable about what he was going to say.

So I said nothing. I just waited for him to continue. I was fairly sure he was going to be overstepping his bounds with what he was going to say, but I wasn't going to pull out any haughty orders, not right now.

"You really aren't going to force Ryland and the Silný apart?"

"No." I kept my answer short, my voice making it clear I wasn't going to elaborate. He had already heard what I said. I saw no reason to continue.

"I always wondered why you didn't after you discovered Cail was controlling her nightmares," Thom stated, and I tensed.

"I would never break her bond with another without her permission." I raised my voice a bit, letting my tone set the end of the conversation. If only Thom had picked up on it.

"Did you even ask?"

I tried not to fume at his off-hand comment. I kept my eyes ahead, and my fingers curled around Joclyn as my magic pulsed through her.

No, I had not asked. I was afraid to hear what she would say, afraid that she would get the wrong idea and think my intentions impure. Asking her to break the bond was the equivalent of sentencing Ryland to death. I could not ask that of her. I could not ask that of myself. My time with Joclyn would come.

I chose not to respond to Thom, instead hoping—once again in vain—that he would understand that our conversation had ended.

"What if the bond is what is keeping her in the Tŏuha?" He paused and I felt my muscles tighten. This wasn't a new thought. I had felt this line of thinking

cross over my mind several times before. I had
maintained my opinion on the matter. It was not my
place to break their sacred bond and doom Ryland to a
painful death. The Tòuha was caused by the connection
between Ryland and Joclyn. You destroy the bond, you
destroy the Tòuha.

"What if by breaking the bond, you would release her?"
Thom continued when I didn't respond. "She couldn't be
hurt anymore. You could save her."

"I have thought of it," I said, willing to give him some
insight. "But what happens if you break the bond and her
mind is still trapped... Co se stane potom?" I looked to him,
waiting for an answer, but he said nothing.

He hadn't experienced a bonding, as I had not, but at
least I was more aware of how a bonding occurred and what
the Tòuhas were.

"She would be gone." Thom sighed after a moment, his
own desperation showing in his voice.

Dramin's light bounced off the rock that surrounded us,
casting flickering shadows on the boulders that had begun
to obstruct our path. We weaved our way around them, the
path becoming more of a single file labyrinth full of jagged
stones and loose rocks.

We had been working in this tunnel for the past few
days after exhausting all other outlets of escape. This was
our only chance. Thom and I had shifted, melted and
moved the rock to make the narrow path we now traveled
down, but it wasn't enough.

"There," Thom announced when we had reached the
solid wall of rock that covered the exit. He pointed toward a
small space between two large boulders near the upper left
side where a small gap could be seen between them. The
space was large enough for no more than a mouse to go

through, but big enough to let in some of the fresh air from outside.

"Tight fit," Dramin observed with a chuckle.

I looked at him curiously, only to see him smiling widely. Leave it to Dramin to find humor and joy in any situation.

"We aren't going to crawl through there, Dramin," Thom said. "The crack is a start. If we work from there outward, we should be able to shift the rock enough to escape."

I could smell the snow and feel a million different energies carried on the wind from that small crack. My muscles tensed at the sensation, stretching tight over my chest. I could sense the crack through my connection with the mountain, but what I was sure Thom could not feel was the instability of the large boulder above it.

As large as a house, the mass rested on the crack, but the majority of its weight covered the roof above us. One wrong move and the rock would shift, crushing us in an instant.

"I am beginning to doubt if this is a good idea." I kept my voice low, suddenly aware of the danger this cave had now become to us. Chances were high that we would never make it out of here, not with the instability of the boulder directly over our heads.

Only Thom had returned yesterday after the collapse to assess the damage. If I had known the instability of this space was so bad, I would have never consented to bring us back here. I held Joclyn's body against mine, terrified we would have to run at any time.

"It's the only idea, Ilyan," Thom said quietly. "What would you have us do, sit in a cave until we all waste away?"

I narrowed my eyes at him, watching him as he pleaded with me. I didn't know what to say.

"What other option do we have? This is our chance; if we don't take it, then you have doomed us to death already,"

Dramin whispered. I knew what he was feeling. I felt it, too. Thom was right, as much as I hated to admit it.

I said nothing as I laid Joclyn's body down against the smooth rock next to me, her body settling into an unnatural position. I moved past them, their focus on me as I approached the opening, Dramin moving to stand next to Joclyn.

Neither of them questioned my motivation. Neither spoke or asked for clarification. They just watched as I placed my hands against the stone. I held my kouzlo there, ignoring my heartbeat that was racing in a desperate plea for me to stop.

The energies of the three bodies behind me thrummed through my blood stream. A keen awareness of Joclyn's weak pulse reminded me of everything else she was facing. This decision, to move the final rock, was dangerous. The selfish part of me begged to just stay, to find another way, but the leader I had been raised to become could not deny the needs of those with me and all those who still lived on the other side of our stone prison, few though they might be.

I needed to do right by them as well.

My magic surged into the rock, the powerful energy flowing away from me as I surveyed the rock more carefully. I tried to formulate a plan for the highest chance of success. The rock shifted and moved at my touch, the living elements within the stone responding to my very thoughts.

The shifting mass felt like a part of me, an extension of my own mind, thanks to the powerful magic that flowed through my veins.

Minutes ticked by as the rock obeyed my commands, as it yielded to my power. Then I felt it, the tiny shift, the start of what I had feared, what I had known was going to happen.

The mountain was coming down on top of us.

The large rock just above our heads, the one I had been fearful of since the beginning, began to shift away from the larger mass of the mountain that it was attached to. I grunted as I released more of my energy into the rock, hoping that I could shift it enough to fuse it more securely to the mountain it nestled against.

A large groan echoed through the cave, the sound loud enough to drown out the loud profanity that had spewed unbidden from my mouth.

I felt Thom and Dramin run from where they had been standing to either side of the cave, their hands flying to the rock as they, too, moved to assess the damage. Now that the rock had shifted, it only took a moment for them to find the weakness and for their magic to move alongside mine as the three of us worked to heave the giant boulder back into position.

My voice echoed around the cave as I yelled out, my strained magic weakening my body enough to cause me physical pain. I could feel the muscles in my shoulders knit together as I pressed against the rock. I pushed as if I alone was holding it up, attempting to make it move, my heart thunking in my chest in fear and panic.

Without having asked me, my eyes fled from the rock to Joclyn's still body that I had nestled into the rock.

She looked so peaceful. For one moment, her body didn't twitch, and her shoulder didn't bleed. Although I was sure the horrors she was trapped within were still a terrifying prison, right then, she was peaceful, beautiful. Just looking at her set the beat of my heart into a steadier rhythm.

I needed to get her out of here.

I knew what needed to be done. I always did, from the moment I sensed the boulder above our heads, I knew. As with all right decisions, there was a sacrifice to be made, wrong steps to take first. There always was. Making the right choice was never easy, but making it was required, and it was what I was raised to be.

A king, a leader to my people.

"I am going to blow the rest of the cave open," I announced, my voice loud above the incessant growling of the cave. I could see Thom and Dramin's heads turn to me in a panic, but I didn't acknowledge them. "I will be able to hold the ceiling for enough time for us to get out of the jeskyně."

"Ilyan... I—" I stopped Dramin's words with one stern look. The old man shrank into the side of the cave as the unbidden power in me escaped ever so slightly.

I knew what Dramin was going to say. I could hear the words on his tongue; feel the doubt in him. Doubt wasn't going to help us. I had run all other options through my head, each one enacted within my mind's eye as I watched Joclyn's sleeping body curled up against the rock.

"When I say go, vypadni odsud, and don't stop until you get to Rioseco. No matter what happens, do not stop." I kept my voice deep, the tones laced with the magic I always attempted to restrain within me.

Each man nodded in agreement, although I could tell that they doubted me. I could see the fear that lined their faces.

"And, Joclyn?" Thom asked, his voice soft.

"I will carry her. She is my responsibility." I turned to her, sending one small strand of magic toward her, lifting her body into the air and bringing her right into my arms.

What would normally only take less than a thought, drained me. So much of my concentration and magic was focused on keeping the boulder, and in turn the mountain, off our backs that even the smallest magic used could be felt deep in my bones.

I shook my head, sending my blonde hair swinging, as I focused back on the rock in front of me. I forced my mind off the people I was surrounded by, the people who were now fully relying on me to save their lives. I let the feeling of Joclyn's skin on mine move into me, the power of her touch lighting my soul on fire as it had always done. The contact increased my energy, the fire within me burning bright enough to take away the aches I had begun to feel.

I couldn't help the smile that spread across my face at the sensation. The light of the fire spread through my soul, igniting the rest of me, and I couldn't wait. I replaced one hand on the wall, wrapping the other carefully around Joclyn's head as I cradled her against me. I hovered my hand over her mark, the dark dragon shape staring at me through the dim light of the cave.

"Ted'!" I yelled the word a second before I let my finger touch the raised skin on her neck, the magical connection between us supercharging what remained of my magic.

I took the surge of power and sent it out in an explosion so great that I felt the floor underneath us rock with the energy.

The rock that had lined the exit exploded out in front of us, white snow suddenly visible only a few hundred feet out. Our feet moved before the smoke had begun to clear. I could hear the grunts and pants of Thom and Dramin as we stumbled and slipped on rubble in our desperate attempt to escape.

The cave filled with loud, resonating groans as my magic

left the rock above us, the sound extending beyond the blast. The rumble grew as the rock shifted, the sound of our footsteps lost in the sounds of falling rocks and the groan of death coming down on top of us.

Thom and Dramin were ahead of me, their frantic movements coming into sight as the smoke began to clear. The white sheet of freedom was blanketed with rocks from the blast, the rubble heavy between us and freedom.

The deep sound of the mountain grew as rocks just behind me began to collide with the ground, the air thick with the sounds of destruction. There was a heavy crash directly to my left, the impact rocking the ground and sending Joclyn and I sideways toward a wall.

One misstep and I had secured our death. I looked toward Thom and Dramin's retreating forms for one fleeting second before I pulled Joclyn to me, our bodies still falling toward the wall. I felt the tick of each moment like a death toll in my heart, every footfall ricocheting inside of me.

It was dangerous to take her with me through a stutter again so close to my recovery. I knew that chance of my survival was low, but I held in my arms the one person I would willingly die for, and I would do anything to save her life.

I didn't think, I just moved us into the heavy realm of the sub-dimension, moving our bodies away from the rock that would otherwise destroy us and, hopefully, into the warm sanctuary of the Rioseco Abbey.

14

WYN

No one came back. Not Sain, Ryland or even Cail. They all left and they never came back.

It had been at least a week since Edmund had removed the others from our prison and I still lay there, in the dark. At least, I thought it had been a week. There was no easy way to track the passage of time when you spend all of it, day in and day out, in the dark. I had slept six times, and someone had brought the daily glass of muddy water seven times.

One glass, not two, just like there was only one maggot-covered loaf of bread.

Just like Talon hadn't woken up.

A week alone in the dark, with only my husband's limp hand for company. I slept next to him, my arms around as much of him as I could reach as I dreamed of the beautiful girl and of the Henry the Eighth wanna-be, but never of the torture. I was glad that the dreams of torture had left. I had enough torture in my waking life.

I still hurt from what Cail had done to me a week ago. My joints still ached, and my skin was still tender to the touch. At least I could move, although not a lot and not very fast. I could manage to move from one corner to another; it was enough movement to enable me to reach the glass of water and still be able to lie next to Talon, which was where I had spent most of my time.

I clung to him in the dark, pressing his hand against my face, prodding him in the hopes that he would wake up.

He didn't. He stayed still, a high-pitched wheeze occasionally issuing from his mouth as his chest slowly rose and fell, his skin getting hotter and hotter. The fever that had appeared two days ago was increasing by the hour.

I ran my fingers over his skin, the heat feeling like hot stones in summer under the pads of my fingers. I kept hoping that he would cool down, but so far, nothing I had done had helped. Not that there was much I could do.

I was helpless. With very little water to cool him and no magic to heal him, I didn't know what I should try next. I wasn't even able to speak to him. I was trapped in a nightmare of torment, and all the while, Sain's words still echoed in my head.

It will be soon.

I refused to put thoughts behind the words. I refused to let the meaning behind them move into my mind. Even if it already had, I wouldn't accept it.

I shifted my weight and crawled slowly toward the filthy glass that sat in the corner of the cell. My fingers clutched at the stone floor, moving over sand, dirt and bits of what I could only assume were rodent bones, until they gently hit the hard surface of the glass. I fidgeted through the air until my hands wrapped around it, the grit on the glass feeling like slime underneath my hands. I clutched the glass to my chest, the small amount of fluid that was left in the bottom as precious as gold.

I shuffled back to Talon, my knees screaming in horror as my weight rested on them in my movements, the water suspended between my hands. I felt in front of me for the bars, terrified of going too far, of losing my balance and dropping the glass. It took a few tries and an extraordinarily large amount of pain before I found him again, the warmth of his skin heating the air around him.

With shaking fingers, I scooped the water from the glass and pressed it against his skin. I trickled it against his lips and into his mouth. Over and over, I moved, pressed and sprinkled the water over him, only to have it evaporate into the damp air the second it touched his scalding flesh. I held my damp fingers against him, hoping to keep the water there longer, hoping the chill of my own skin would serve as an equalizer.

Something deep inside of me was pleading for me to accept that this was hopeless, begging me to save the water for myself, but I couldn't. I couldn't abandon him. I would sacrifice myself for him until the very end. Half for me and half for him. Always.

"I love you," I whispered, my voice barely audible. It was all I could risk, but it was the most important thing to say.

I let the now empty glass clatter to the stone floor, my body giving out to collapse against the bars and slide across the slime covered surface to the floor the moment my job was done. A small gasp escaped my lips as I hit the stone floor a little harder than expected.

I turned toward Talon, my hands clinging to him as my body attempted to fall asleep.

I would have, if it weren't for the footsteps somewhere above me, moving toward me. I didn't know if it was the whisper, the clatter of the glass, or the groan as I had hit the floor, but something had reminded them of my existence. I had survived a week in relative security. Now that was being shattered.

The footsteps were faster than I had ever heard and the voices behind them louder, angrier. I clung to Talon, my overgrown fingernails digging into him as someone began their decent down the stairs and toward me.

"It's only been a week, sir," Timothy said, slightly out of breath. "You can't expect him to have finished her off by now?"

"I can expect anything I want, Timothy," Edmund spat, the footsteps stopping as he spoke, "Don't make me put you in your place, old friend. You have been with me from the beginning, but that does not mean you are on the same pillar as I."

There was a pause, a pause that lasted an eternity of heartbeats and tingling nerve endings. I had no idea what they were talking about, and I didn't care. The only thing in my mind was how close they were.

"Sorry, sir," my father gasped, the footsteps resuming almost immediately. Everything clenched as they came closer, my brain panicking in fear of why Edmund was coming down.

"I gave him a deadline, and I expect results. If he needs a little persuasion, then so be it." Edmund's voice grew louder as a bright light blasted through my closed eyelids. I held as still as I could, knowing that no matter how much pretending I did, it wouldn't stop them. The mere fact that Edmund was down here spelled danger for me.

"But are you sure this is the way?" Timothy asked, disgusted.

"You should have seen his face when I threatened to unbind the curse," Edmund said. "This is the way."

Their voices were right outside my cell now, their conversation ending as iron bars grated together.

"Put him in that end cell down there and then you can go."

Footsteps, the grinding of iron, and the rattling of chains. I heard Sain grunt and I fought the urge to turn toward him, my arm jerking on its own before I could stop it. They had brought him back. Ryland was not with him, which could only mean that they had begun their attempt to kill Joclyn.

"Get up, Wynifred."

I froze; my father's voice was deep with warning. I knew I needed to obey, but didn't want to face whatever Edmund had in store for me.

"Come on, Wynifred," Edmund coaxed, his voice sweet and condescending. "Listen to your father."

I didn't want to listen, but I also didn't want to push it. I moved a bit and began to push myself up to sit, my weak arms shaking as I lifted myself. My joints groaned at me as I moved, and I gasped before letting my body weight rest against the bars, my head flopping back as I looked at them.

"Hello, Father," I said with as much ire as I could, but my weak voice swallowed my pride.

"Why, Wynifred," Edmund said, ignoring my comment to my father, "you are looking well. Better than I think I have ever seen you." He smiled at me as he squatted, bringing himself to eye level.

I clenched my jaw and scowled at him, not wanting to know what was coming.

"Not going to say hello?"

"No. I'm not." I narrowed my eyes, daring him to continue, begging him to finish me.

"Not going to ask after my welfare?" His voice was still irritatingly calm.

I stayed still, my jaw clenched. A feeling I could not place was forming in the base of my spine. It was pure irritation blended with spite and it created an emotion I had never felt before.

"Hmmm, no matter," Edmund continued and smiled. "By the time I am done with you, you will be begging me to say 'hello'."

I didn't flinch. I didn't move. I just stared at him as the door opened, his body taking a few steps in before he towered above me.

"Stand, Wynifred." I almost laughed at him. It was a miracle I was able to move myself to sitting. Standing was out of the question.

"Not going to obey your Master?" Edmund asked.

I flinched, words that I knew I should never say to his face tumbling off my tongue before I could stop them. "You are not my Master."

"Well, not anymore, maybe..." He smiled, his hand patting the top of my head harshly. The weight of his touch sent me sliding down against the bars. "...but once upon a time."

I wanted to say something, but I couldn't. He was right. Once upon a time, I did bow to his every command. I looked away from his towering form, burying my face in the bars to look toward Talon, my eyes seeing for the first time what the darkness had not shown me.

His eyes were sunken in, and his skin was pale and covered with a thick layer of sweat. His eyes twitched as he lay still, his lips moving as he mumbled in his sleep.

He didn't have much time left.

I fought the desire to turn to him, to cling to him, even to plead with Edmund to heal him. Each thought was wiped from my mind as Edmund spoke, his next words barely having meaning for me.

"Years ago, you would do my bidding with only a smile and a swish of your hips." I kept my eyes on Talon as he spoke, my ears focused on the tap of Edmund's feet against the stone around me as he moved. "Well, until you betrayed me."

He stooped down beside me, careful to balance his weight on his toes and not touch the filthy ground that surrounded me. I kept my sight on Talon until Edmund's long fingers turned my head toward him, so that my eyes had no choice, but to stare into his. I would not give in. I would not close my eyes in fear, not in these last moments.

"Tell me, how long did Cail help you? How did you help him to block the Štít?"

My confidence broke, confusion weaseling its way into my expression as I looked at him. I had no idea what he was talking about. I wasn't going to tell him that, however. I wasn't going to give into the game he was obviously playing. I would not place myself inside of his trap.

"Did you do the same to Ryland?"

I waited, his eyes digging in to mine. He glared into me, his patience leaving as he slammed my head into the metal bars behind me.

"Answer me!" he roared, his hand pushing me back into the bars again.

I howled at the pain, my hands moving toward my head in an attempt to ease the pressure. They had only made it halfway before the heavy iron shackles snaked through the air to wrap around my wrists. The large bands jerked me away from the bars, my body dragging against the stone as the chains pulled me back against the wall, my arms extending above my head.

"What did you do?" Edmund roared, his face coming within inches of mine. I looked away from him and toward my father, who stood by the stairs with a wicked smile turning up his lips. I looked at Sain, who sat against the bars of his cell, his green eyes narrowed at me in both warning and expectation.

"I didn't do anything," I answered, my voice strained from the awkwardness of the position that Edmund had placed me in.

Edmund's eyes narrowed at me, his face moving in close until his nose was only an inch away from my face, his polar blue eyes the only thing left for me to focus on.

"Don't lie to me," he warned. "Tell me what else he did when he stopped your father's curse and tried to save your life. Tell me what happened when he put those pretty marks on your skin." Edmund dragged his finger along the dark marks as he spoke, his finger pressing painfully against my bruises.

I cringed against the pain, my eyes narrowing at him. Cail didn't try to save my life, he had tried to kill me. Just as my father had, but the curse misfired and instead marked my skin.

"N... no," I managed to stutter out, my confusion growing.

"What secret did Cail hide inside your pretty, little mind?"

"What?" I gasped, unable to keep my confusion at bay any longer. Edmund only smiled as he closed the gap between us and pressed his cheek against mine. I felt the uncomfortable warmth of his skin and the iciness of his blood pulsing just underneath the surface.

"Don't worry, Wynifred; you will remember everything soon." He smiled and moved away from me, the chains around my wrists tightening, lifting me up so I could only balance on the balls of my feet.

"I'm sorry, sir, but what exactly are you saying?" I guess I wasn't the only one who was confused. My father looked between us as he, too, tried to fit together the missing pieces.

Edmund, however, seemed to be enjoying keeping more than one person in the dark. He smiled as he turned to face me again.

"You remember that night, don't you, Timothy?" Edmund taunted, his eyes feeling like warm lasers cutting into my brain.

"Texas, 1867. A simple assignment—kill Thom. After four hundred years of flawlessly killing every person I commanded her to, Wynifred here missteps. She tells me Thom is in Texas and not in Italy as I had already ascertained. So off she goes to Texas, to kill the father of her child. But I see through it, and I follow her..."

My mouth opened automatically, my jaw working in disbelief. Four hundred years of working for Edmund, a child, Thom...? None of this was my life.

"That never—"

"That never happened?" Edmund asked, his cynical voice twisting the meaning behind my words. "You don't remember it? Then tell me what you do remember."

He arched his eyebrows, his lips curling in a wicked half smile as he waited.

That night. The night when I got the marks, I remembered it perfectly. The flash of light, my brother's face, the yelling. I remembered feeling scared. I remembered... I didn't... what was said?

My jaw worked its way open and shut like the jaws of a

fish as my brain tried to find the words to answer his questions.

"Don't remember what happened? How about your childhood? What happened then?" He had moved closer, but I barely noticed. My childhood...? I couldn't remember. I could see faces, feel emotions, but exactly what happened... how... there was nothing there.

"Can't remember, can you?"

"What are you saying, Edmund? We've always known about her memory loss—"

"Yes, but what if her memory loss, her change in personality, what if it wasn't a result of Cail's attempts to bind your curse. What if he did it intentionally to hide something?" Edmund ran his finger along my jaw, his eyes still boring into me.

I wanted to deny everything he had said. I wanted to tell him the truth. I just couldn't. I couldn't say something I couldn't remember... I couldn't remember...

What did I know?

I was Wynifred, born in about 1795, exiled in 1867. I had a father, Timothy, and a brother, Cail. Ilyan killed my mother in... He killed her because... My father gave me the marks because I was caught giving information to Ilyan... They caught me in... Texas?

Why couldn't I remember?

My eyes grew wide, Edmund's smile following suit.

"What secret did Cail lock in your mind, Wynifred?"

My eyes fluttered around the room, from Talon's still body, curled on the cold ground, to my father, to Sain, looking for anyone to give me a different explanation. Sain looked at me and nodded once. No, this couldn't be.

"Time to open the lock, Wynifred."

Edmund smiled as he placed his hand against my skull,

his magic rushing into me. I screamed as the pressure moved into my brain, the heat flooding through me as the force increased. I heard my own scream echo in my ears as Edmund's powerful magic threatened to rip me apart. It opened up my mind and let everything out.

My head throbbed and pulsed as things I had long since forgotten filled me. Memories that I had wanted to stay locked away came flooding back—the beautiful child's screams and the Henry the Eighth wanna-be suddenly made sense.

I remembered everything.

15

WYN

I remembered everything.

"What do you mean, *he wants us to have a baby*?" I spat, turning toward Thom.

Thom stood in the middle of my large room, that awful hat twisting through his fingers. Curse the ridiculous British king for such a style. It made Thom look like a peacock.

"Just that, Lady Wynifred. He has commanded it." I gaped at him, my mind working just enough to let me turn away from him.

I could see him through my mirror, his bright blue eyes boring into me from underneath that curly hair he had inherited from his father, and the sandy color that had come from his mother. He narrowed his eyes and went back to twirling the hat. The poor boy looked absolutely traumatized, and I didn't blame him. What was King Edmund thinking?

"You are sure this message is for me?" I asked, the laugh barely disguised in my voice.

"Yes." I could see him continually turning that hat in his

hands. Round and round it went. I shook my head and looked away, not wanting his stress to leach into me.

"Are we to be bonded then?" My voice was as uninterested as I could make it, my focus more on the ornate hairbrush Cail had given me for my birthday than on the prince behind me. It wasn't the first time Edmund had tried to force me into a bonding, but to use his own son this way was a little surprising.

"No."

"No?" I wasn't sure if I was more relieved or upset. This was the oddest request His Majesty had ever given me. You didn't often send executioners into a wedding bed, especially without a wedding. I guessed it was one of the perks of being a woman and under Edmund's control. He thought he could tell me who to sleep with as well as who to kill.

"Does this upset you?" I smiled, Thom's usual haughty demeanor coming back strong. It was unsurprising; men hated it when you insulted their masculinity.

"Be with a prince, but not be branded as a princess? Of course it upsets me." I glanced at him through the mirror before continuing my morning preparations. "Give me a name, Thom, let me take a life. That is what I am good for, what I thrive at, not this nonsense."

"Perhaps he wants you to have a challenge." Thom moved closer to me, the strength in his voice not leaving that time.

"Hmmm... Then let me kill his first born." I smiled, pleased when a bloodthirsty light flickered in Thom's eyes.

"Ilyan's mine." He grinned and I couldn't help returning the smile. Everyone wanted to kill Ilyan, but no one could get close enough to even attempt it.

"Why me, Thom?"

"You are the most powerful of the Trpaslíks, the only one who still possess the fire magic-"

"And he wants his blood blended with that strength?"

Centuries ago, the fire magic that the Trpaslíks had been born with began to disappear. It wasn't until my birth, over a hundred years ago, that the fire magic had returned. It was only me, though. It never moved beyond that, making my blood, my magic, a highly sought after commodity and one that Edmund greatly desired.

Thom nodded in answer to my question, the hat in his hand finally stopping its incessant spinning. I smirked and turned toward him, leaning against my dressing table.

"What of you, Thom? Does he want you to be stronger as well?" I stepped toward him, his eyes lowering as he looked me over.

"I think it is his hope."

I could only smile, of course it wasn't. If Edmund wanted Thom to be stronger, he would have insisted on the bonding. Then, at least, Thom would inherit my unique power should I die. No, Edmund wouldn't do that. He wanted my power for himself. He had tried to punish me after I removed his finger in warning when he suggested I bond myself to him. It was then that he had placed me as one of his assassins rather than his bodyguard, but I rather enjoyed the post. Not to mention, I was good at it, taking out a whole herd of useless Draks by myself had been much easier than I would have assumed. No, he wouldn't be so foolish as to give that power to one of his children. This forced pregnancy, however, was a different story.

It only took him seventy years to figure out a new punishment for my treachery. It was almost enough to make me regret burning off his finger in the first place.

I wondered how difficult assassinations would be with a

bulging belly. If this were Edmund's new punishment, then I would gladly shove it in his face.

When it was all said and done, I had expected to hand the child over to Thom and walk away back to my blood-soaked career path. What I hadn't expected was the reaction I had at holding a small wriggling infant in my arms. One look at the dark eyes of the beautiful baby girl and I was changed.

Rosaline.

Of course, she was cursed from the beginning. Her eye color was not the royal blue that Edmund demanded. He had killed so many of his children when they were born without the bright blue of royalty that a grandchild wouldn't make him bat an eyelid. I knew at once that she would be destined for the same fate if I didn't do something.

Fury would not be a word I would use to match Edmund's anger at his failed attempt at biology. It was much worse.

I was the one who would be punished. While Thom was left to raise our precious daughter, I was sent out on assassination missions, each one more difficult than the last. I continued to track the last of Draks with the forced sight of Sain. I tracked and murdered all of Ilyan's extended family, and even the family of his precious, clunk-headed bodyguard, all in an attempt to flush him out.

Through all the blood on my hands, it was the moments with my little, blonde-headed girl that meant the most to me.

"Mama!" I turned at Rosaline's voice. Her rosy cheeks, her dark eyes, everything about her seemed to glow as she ran toward us, her hair flowing in the wind. "Mama! Will you bind these flowers in my hair?"

"Of course, baby, why don't you go pick some more?"

Rosy smiled at me and danced back into the meadow, her hair flying behind her like ribbons of silk.

"She's like you." I turned at Thom's voice, his smile wide as he winked at me before turning back to our beautiful dancer.

"Are you training her in hand to hand combat while I am gone, Thom?" I asked, waving to my eager child as she plucked dozens of long-stemmed daisies.

"Oh yes, choke holds are her favorite." We both laughed, but it was strained, the truth of his words held a dark edge. "What I meant to say is that she does what she wants. She doesn't care what people think of her."

"Well, that *is* like me."

"Incredibly." Thom smiled at me before following after Rosy, scooping her up and swinging her through the warm summer air.

I had never had a friend before. Thom was my first. He taught me to care for my child. He taught me to laugh. He taught me to enjoy life. I had been raised to kill, raised to hunt people. It was all I knew, but Thom changed that. He turned me from a weapon into a person.

With him, I spent sunrises in meadows, evenings playing cards, days at pubs, and nights at gypsy parties. He showed me the world in a different light. I was amazed that so much life could be inside of someone.

I watched him kill men with my own eyes, but he was able to turn around and find something to smile about. I had never been able to do that before. I had always just dwelled in my cynical life, relishing it.

Part of me wished that Edmund had never changed that by bringing Thom into my life.

Our child had been born without the royal eyes and, what was worse, without my unique ability for fire magic;

Edmund's great experiment was useless to him. Useless things were disposable. Thom had tried to prove that she wasn't useless, that she was powerful, but Edmund never saw it. So, we made plans to escape, to take our child and run.

It would have worked if Edmund had not caught wind of our plan. As punishment, our child was tortured in front of us. My own father gladly took part in the hideous act.

I couldn't get her screams out of my head. Edmund had finally found a punishment that suited me; he had found a way to make me pay. He had done more than punish us, however; he had lost our loyalty. If only he would have guessed what we were truly capable of, perhaps he would have rethought his actions.

Thom left. I would have gone with him if it weren't for Cail's constant supervision. He never left me alone; his worry over me was paramount. He held me as I mourned the loss of the one beautiful thing, the one person, I loved.

I thought I would never recover, until Ilyan found me.

He stood before me, his face screwed up in a strangely alluring smirk. His sandy hair sheared short against his head. He balanced his weight on an ornate walking stick, looking like he had just been caught taking a stroll on his enemies' land.

I was one touch away from murder, my hand posed above the trunk of the tree, ready to send a million shards of wood into his skin; but I didn't, all because of that stupid hat. The hat he held in his hands—Thom's hat. He held it gently in his fingers, offering it to me.

"Thom asked me to give this to you," he said quietly in Czech. I looked around the forest that surrounded Edmund's estate, wondering how he had gotten in here. A large shape loomed behind him, probably that hulking bodyguard of his attempting to hide behind a tree.

"Thom?" I asked, the fabric of the cap soft in my fingers as I took it from him.

"Yes, he and Sain are in my care. I came to offer the same asylum to you." I clenched the hat in my fist, the feather turning to ash as my magic flared. I wanted to say yes. Oh, how I wanted to leave right then, leave the giggles that haunted my dreams and the perfectly laundered children's gown that still hung in my closet. I just couldn't. There was one thing I couldn't leave.

"I can't," I sighed, my own words stinging my throat.

"You want revenge." My head shot up, my heart thumping at his words. I wanted to ask how he knew, but I could see that he shared the same aspiration.

"Yes." My voice was a wispy pant of desire; it dripped off my tongue and into the air in a heady need.

"Then work for me." He smiled and moved the walking stick in front of him, where he leaned on it like the village boys would against a fence.

"Work for you?"

"Yes, I have something you want, after all." He smiled and leaned forward, making me fight the urge to slap him. His eyes were so much like Thom's. Thom, who had left me behind.

I laughed lightly, using the tinkling sound of my voice to draw him in. "What could you possibly have that I would want?"

He smirked, but it was different from the smirk that most men gave me. It wasn't a smirk of desire, the light in his eyes only showed strength.

"I can offer you a way to betray the man who betrayed you."

He kept his eyes on me, his fingers clenching and unclenching on that walking stick of his. I arched my eyebrow, my hand dropping just enough that my threat was lessened, but not enough that the danger was gone.

Then again, this was Ilyan; my threat to him might have never been present. I had watched him rip the arms off a man and wipe the brain of another only a decade before, all while still tied to a tree. There was a reason no one had done away with him yet.

There was also a reason my heart was thudding in my chest.

"What do you have inside that pretty head of yours, Ilyan?" I trilled, bringing my hands to the hips of the scandalous red peasant dress I had chosen to wear that day. "What would you have me do?"

He hesitated, his breathing level as he studied me. Part of me wondered if he was scared of me as well. The sheer tension of the situation made me smile. I popped my hip and raised my eyebrows at him before stepping forward. Ilyan stayed still, his hand still resting on the long staff in his hands.

"What do you want from me?"

"I don't want your power, Wynifred."

"You don't?" I laughed. I found that hard to believe. "What of your silent companion? Would you have him take my power to better protect you?"

I saw the hulking mass stiffen behind the tree. At least my words seemed to be affecting someone.

"Talon does what I bid him, Wynifred. If it wasn't for that, he would be driving you through."

A wicked smile spread across my lips at his words. Ah yes, Talon. So it wasn't my power, or even the fact that I was a woman that was affecting him, it was the murder of his younger sister not more than five years ago. Probably best not to mention how she moaned for him before I snapped her neck.

"So that's a no then?" Finally Ilyan smiled, his teeth flashing briefly before hiding themselves behind his lips.

"That's a no." Ilyan shifted his weight, his walking stick moving to rest against his hip, his long boots shifting as they crunched the pine needles of the forest floor.

"So if you don't want me for my magic, then what do you want me for?"

"Information."

"You wish me to spy?" I was flabbergasted. Yes, I wanted to make Edmund and my father pay for what they had done, but he was not only asking me to pass on information, he was asking me to put my own life in danger.

"Oh, it is not simply a request for a spy, Wynifred. You are my father's top assassin. You kill anyone who puts a toe out of line in my father's sights. Good or bad, you kill them all. And you do it well."

"I am good at it for a reason, Ilyan." I smiled, taking his compliment to heart. "It's not just death. Anyone can kill. Anyone can remove the beating heart of a magical being." I lowered my voice alluringly as I moved closer to him, wanting to test the boundaries of Ilyan's bargain. I was pleased when his jaw tightened uncomfortably. "No matter how much I enjoy it," I continued, "it's more about finding information, and I can do that above all others."

"Then find information for me." He lifted his chest toward me, his eyes flashing dangerously at his words, but I only smiled.

I liked this game of cat and mouse, but what I liked more was the very real possibility of destroying the carefully placed web that Edmund had created. My adrenaline surged at the very thought. I would make him pay.

"What type of information?" I asked coyly. As much as I liked the thought, I still needed to play my cards right to make this arrangement benefit me.

"His plans, his weakness, what he knows about the sight." My head snapped to his, my eyes narrowing, but he only smiled. "The name of your next target and everyone following."

I stopped my pacing, my head slowly turning toward Ilyan. All of that was doable; I could tell him most of the information now. The name of my target, though? Ilyan wasn't requesting that so he could do the job for me, he was requesting it so he could save their life.

My job didn't entail just destruction; Edmund required proof of the job's completion. He wanted the still beating heart of the victim. Edmund wanted their magic. If I were to turn the names over to Ilyan, then I would have no way of handing the hearts over to him. I would have no way to prove the job had been done.

"What would you have me tell my Master, Ilyan, if I suddenly stopped bringing him the hearts of his enemies?" I asked as I paced in front of him, careful not to let my eyes leave his. We might have been in the beginnings of a bargain, but I did not trust him, not yet.

"You will think of something," he smiled, and I couldn't help returning it. He was right, I would. I had already begun to think of possible ways to disguise mortal hearts as those of magical beings.

"Besides, he is not your Master anymore."

"And you are?" my voice snapped as I spun to face him, the fabric of my skirt dragging through pine needles.

"I am no one's Master." His voice was hard. Odd, he almost seemed offended by my comment.

"I think your muscle would disagree with that." The shadow shifted at my words, and I found myself drawn to it. Perhaps it was because Ilyan wasn't responding to any of my advances, and I needed someone to confirm that my techniques were still usable.

"He is free to come and go whenever he pleases."

"Then maybe I will steal him from you." I smiled, but Ilyan's face only hardened.

"Only if you wish to make acquaintance with his sword," he said through gritted teeth. I could tell right then that he would never trust me, even if he consented to what I was about to ask of him.

I stood still as our eyes locked, each one weighing the other. He was wondering if he could actually trust me, and I was wondering why he hadn't done away with me already. I had killed more than half of his army with my own hands, and yet, he let me live. I didn't know if it was pity or desperation that had brought him here, but part of me wished he would plunge me through already.

"Information?" I asked when the silence had become too much.

"Yes." He swung his walking stick once, slamming it into the ground as if to accentuate his words. I didn't even flinch.

"And not my magic."

"No."

I shouldn't have felt stung, but I did. It was not because all of my physical advances had yet to be effective, but because everyone wanted use of the last of the fire magic.

Everyone.

They all wanted my power and the upper hand it would give them, but the leader of the Skříteks stood in front of me saying he wanted none of it. I would be lying if I said I wasn't at least a little bit suspicious.

"Am I not appealing to you, Ilyan?" I popped my hip, testing him, watching him, needing to know for sure.

"I'm taken."

"So it would seem," I laughed, eyeing the shadow of the man who still stood guard behind him.

Ilyan said nothing, he only stood, jaw tight, his weight balanced on the narrow stick in his hands.

I stopped my movement, letting my hair fall down my back as I looked at him. So far, I liked this deal, but we still had my requirements to discuss.

"I will do this for you, as long as you give me everything I ask." Ilyan's eyes widened briefly at my words, his shock melting as he settled in to listen to my requests, a small head nod prompting me to continue.

"I will give you the information you need for as long as I can. I only ask one thing, after I am caught, you get me out alive. You give me the asylum you promised and wipe my memory."

His shoulders tensed at my last request, the muscles moving further toward his ears before relaxing down again. He didn't like that last part, not that I blamed him.

"You ask me to put a lock on your mind?"

"Yes, I don't want to remember anything. I don't want to remember Thom, my child, or the thousands of drops of blood that litter my hands." I held my palm out to him as if proving my sins, but his eyes didn't leave mine.

"I don't erase memories, Wynifred. That is a form of torture only my father uses."

"You can and you will if you want me to do this for you." I smiled, knowing I had caught him. "It is not a matter of power, Ilyan. I know you can do it."

"I can also bury you alive ten feet underground with one thought, but I don't." He smiled. "Or maybe I will."

I smiled back, but I wasn't going to relent on this. It was the one piece that I really wanted. I would gladly do all he asked for nothing, but then I would walk away with only my haunted memories for company. It was not a life I wished to lead. I would rather meet my death at my father's hands, but then I would gain nothing from this arrangement. I did nothing for free.

Even Edmund offered me his own form of payment.

"My memory for your information."

He exhaled, his muscular chest heaving as he contemplated my request.

"What would you do, Wynifred, once your memory is gone?"

"I'm not sure. Walk the world, discover a new land, perhaps I will join a nunnery."

The laugh that filtered out of his lips startled me, the humor heavy in the air. I didn't see the joke.

"You are not the type to join a nunnery."

"Oh, how would you know, Ilyan?" I snapped. "Once my memory is gone, I can be any kind of person I want to be."

That was the key, right there. I could be anyone I wanted to be, not what Edmund or my father wanted. Me. I could make my own decisions.

"Make your choice," I prompted, pulling a slip of paper out of my pocket. The white slip contained the name of the man I was on my way out to kill when Ilyan found me.

I twisted the paper as Ilyan eyed it, my actions forcing his decision, giving a good show of faith.

"We have a deal," he said, his hand extended toward me.

I closed the gap between us, his hand closing around mine.

"I will honor my deal with you as long as you honor mine, Wynifred. You have my word."

I froze, the sincerity of his voice shocking to me. No one had ever spoken so simply to me. Well, no one since Thom. I could hear his honesty, the commitment and the promise in his voice. Normally, I would have shied away from such emotion, but Thom had affected me in that way as well.

"You have nothing to fear, Ilyan."

"What is his name?" Ilyan asked, pointing to the paper that was still in my hand.

"Dramin, son of Sain," I said, ignoring the shock that lined his eyes and handing over the piece of paper to prove it.

"Good." He smiled, thrusting his walking stick into my hands. I clutched it automatically, the heavy wood igniting the magic in my blood.

"This will connect you to me. Use it whenever you have news for me."

I nodded once in understanding; Ilyan's smile the acceptance of my promise to him.

He said no more. He simply vanished into the air before me, leaving me alone with his shadow.

No wonder no one could ever find him.

16

WYN

Thomas Král

The name on the paper was moving, but I knew it wasn't the ink. It was because of the blood that was rushing to my head in my panic. My eyes couldn't seem to focus.

Thom had been sighted, and Edmund would have me kill him.

The sound of hammers and horses washed over me as I stared at the name. The construction of Edmund's new estate was progressing quickly after I had assisted Ilyan in burning down the last one. Why Edmund had chosen the American West as his new base, I still wasn't clear on. I now spent more time traveling over oceans than anything else.

"Is there a problem, Wynifred?" I looked up to see Edmund jump down from the carriage we had just been sitting in, the dust from the ground kicking up around us as he landed.

"Nothing is wrong, sir," I said, keeping my voice bored and defiant.

"Good," Edmund sighed as he wrapped his arm around

my waist to help me down, bringing his lips to rest against the hollow skin under my ear at the same time, "because I want his head."

"His head?" I asked, moving myself away from him. "What would you want with that ugly thing?"

"Think of it as a trophy, Wynifred. Sometimes a man wants more than a heart." He smiled and my insides froze at all that was said behind those eyes.

"Besides, I think it is about time you prove your loyalty to me." Another smile. What did he know? "Find him and bring me his head before my child is born. That should give you about a month. And if this one is born with eyes the color of mud, you can do away with it and its mother as well. Sounds like a full month for you."

He moved away from me and strode toward the new house before I could move at all, which was probably a good thing. The desire to kill him right there was too strong, but Ilyan had warned me not to take him on. I didn't know what reason he had for doing so, but I was more likely to trust him than Edmund at this point.

After three hundred years of espionage, I had seen more than my fair share of bad and had even developed what some may call a conscious.

"Where is my brother?" I asked one of Edmund's goons that was standing around, surprised my brother wasn't here to follow him around like usual.

"Try the bar," he said before shouldering me out of the way. My jaw dropped as I watched him go, my fingers buzzing with energy and a need to teach him a lesson.

No one dared treat me that way, not unless they wished for death. I would have asked what I was missing, but I already knew.

I strolled away from the construction site, my skin prickling with energy as the dirt seeped through my shoes and heavy stockings.

I didn't look back. I didn't dare. I walked right to the small tavern in town, where I knew my brother would be.

His back was to me as I walked into the bar, downing yet another tequila.

"Another!" he yelled into the empty space, it was far too early for the honest men of this town to be drinking.

"Make that two," I spat as I sidled onto the stool next to him, the bartender eyeing me as if I had asked him to hand over the deed to the place. "Now," I added when it became obvious that he wasn't going to pour the drink anytime soon.

"You seem to be in a bad mood," Cail commented, not taking his eyes off the small, dirty glass in front of him.

"Did you know about this?" I spat, not caring who heard me.

"Know about what?"

I slapped the paper down on the bar, letting my magic spread the paper flat until Cail could read the words. His eyes grew wide, and I felt the shield go around us. He held out his hand, and I took it, placing an even more powerful shield around his heart. His face relaxed the moment he touched me and his mind and body became his own.

"Of course I knew," was all he said, the small statement boiling my anger closer to the surface.

"And you didn't tell me?" I was furious. Cail had warned me of difficult assignments and helped to disguise the hearts of my victims for the past two hundred years by implanting some of Edmund's own magic within them, but this time, he had dropped the ball.

I couldn't disguise a head.

"It's a trap, Wyn."

"Of course it's a trap!" I spat, grabbing and downing the tequila the bartender had just set down in front of me. "He wouldn't send me after him otherwise." I swirled the empty glass around out of habit, refusing to look away from it.

"To death!" Cail toasted before emptying his glass, his head dropping to the table the moment he had drained it.

My head whipped around to face him, my eyes narrowing dangerously.

"To death?" I asked, surely he hadn't given up on me quite so easily.

"Ah, yes," he said, sitting up to pull a paper out of the pocket in his vest near his pocket watch. "You see, you are not the only one who has been given an assignment."

Dramin, Son of Sain

It *was* a trap, for both of us. I looked away, the buzzing in my ears growing briefly before I dispersed it, my jaw clenching as I shook my head and let out an irritated breath.

"Come with me." I didn't give him time to question me before I pulled Cail by the hand I still held, away from the bar and up to the long line of rooms above.

"Hey!" the bartender called out after seeing our ascent. "You can't go up there!"

"I'll pay you for the room after, old man, and it will be very worth your while." I smiled seductively over the banister and the old man paled, a small twitch in his lips telling me all I needed to know.

I towed Cail after me before closing the door to the small room behind us, my magic expanding to place a stronger shield around us while still keeping the one around the Štít in Cail's heart.

I pulled the small stone that Ilyan had enclosed in his walking stick out of my undergarments and held it in my hands, the stone growing warm for just a moment as I said his name, calling him to me.

"Do I need to be here for this?" Cail asked, the irritation heavy in his voice. "I only help you, not him, after all."

"By helping me, you are helping him," I reminded him, but he only ignored me, sitting back on the bed and putting his muddy feet on the clean bedspread. Great, I didn't want to see the bill for that.

"What is he doing here?" I spun at the thick voice, surprised to see not Ilyan, but Talon standing in front of the door.

"I might ask you the same question?" I said, my eyes narrowing at him.

"Ilyan is indisposed, so he sent me in his place." He stood straight and tall, his eyes focused on the opposing wall, anywhere but on me.

"You can stutter?" I asked, the impressiveness of that feat heavy in my voice, even I could not stutter.

"No."

"Then how did you get here?"

Talon narrowed his eyes at me briefly before glancing at Cail. His message was clear. He might trust me, which I doubted, but he did not, under any circumstances, trust Cail. There were not many who did.

"Why did you call for us?"

He still wasn't looking at me, a small detail that I wasn't going to push. It had taken him a hundred years to come face to face with me and another hundred not to draw his sword every time I was near. This was a marked improvement.

I handed over the papers silently. Talon took one glance before looking back to me, his eyebrow raised.

"These are the names of our next assignments."

Talon's eyes widened. "But Dramin was the first."

"Yes," I said knowingly, cocking my head at him. That was the point.

"And Thom." He crinkled the papers in his large fist before shoving them in his pocket. "Does Edmund know where they are?"

"I am not sure," I answered, looking back to my brother who was dutifully ignoring us with a newly lit cigarette in his mouth, the ugly American hat laid low over his eyes.

"He knows," Talon said, his deep voice quiet. I wasn't even sure he had meant to speak aloud.

"Excuse me?"

"They travel together, with Sain. It isn't a coincidence that these names came up together."

Lovely.

"So, your position with us has been discovered?"

I could only nod.

"Then you need to come with me." He reached forward and placed his big hand around my forearm, his grip too tight, hurting me. I zapped him, the small shock sending a warning, and he dropped me quickly, his eyes narrowing dangerously at me.

"We had a deal, Wynifred." Why was he pleading with me? That seemed a little out of character for him.

"What of Cail, Talon?" I spat, not even trying to keep the acid from my voice. "He has risked just as much for you and Ilyan, and one of those names was delivered to him, not to me."

"The deal did not include Cail," Talon said, his shoulders squaring as he went back to staring beyond me.

I sighed before my feet took me to pace around him, the irritation causing my movements to get jumpy.

"Then I want to make a new deal," I said after a moment, coming to a stop to face him.

"What could you possibly have that Ilyan would want?" Talon looked at me, and I stepped back. I wasn't one to step away from a man, but something in his eyes had changed, the subtly of it catching me off guard.

"The fire magic."

"What would I do with that?" Ilyan asked from the corner, causing me to jump, my hand covering my heart as I turned to face him. He sat on top of the high wardrobe, looking as thoroughly American as Cail tried to be, except the rugged look actually suited him. The limestone dust was a little much. There was authenticity and then there was trying too hard.

Limestone.

They were working on the estate. I couldn't help but smile at the ingeniousness of it all. What better way was there to gain knowledge of the layout of your enemy's fortress than to build it?

"I don't need your magic. I have no use for it," Ilyan said as he moved down to the floor, his tall frame towering over me.

"Then bind it, it is my payment to you for saving my brother," I pleaded, taking a step toward him out of habit.

"What if I don't want to be saved?" Cail's voice was loud from the bed that sat in the corner of the room, causing us all to turn to face him. "What if I like where I am at, because, no offense, Ilyan, but I don't trust you. You killed my mother in cold blood. Tsk tsk. Why should I trust you?"

"It wasn't cold blood, Cail. You know that as much as anyone."

"Yes, revenge is often a good reason." Cail lifted his hat to look at Ilyan, the metal of the bed frame squeaking as he sat up. "She breaks up your parents' bond, and you kill her. Seems honorable to me."

"She was your father's pawn," Ilyan said simply, his voice level. I looked between the two of them. Cail had always been good at triggering emotions from others, but Ilyan seemed immune to his taunts. How interesting.

"That, too."

"This is a strange game you are playing, Cail," Ilyan said, his body turning to address him directly. "Your sister has offered a sacrifice to give you asylum and to take the Štít out of your heart, and you don't seem to want it."

"I don't," Cail said simply, his eyes not leaving Ilyan's.

I took a step back, right into Talon's stiff chest before moving away from him automatically. How could Cail not want this? He had been helping me for a century, and to what end? He was now going to walk away, give us up to Edmund? My jaw clenched in frustration without me even realizing it.

"Why is that I wonder?"

"Simple," Cail said, his eyes still not leaving Ilyan's, the contest of wills and power strong between them. "With no one left on the inside, who is going to stop Edmund from coming after her?"

"I promised her asylum, and I will deliver that."

"You will? Against Edmund? Impressive." Cail nodded as he moved to the window, everyone's eyes following him. I could feel Talon tense in expectation. I knew he would do anything to stop Cail if he made a move to leave. He couldn't risk anyone finding out about Ilyan's location or breaking their cover.

"He is my father, Cail. I know his strength. You do not seem to see mine."

"Then you know about the Vilỳ?" Cail turned, his back against the window, blocking some of the light that was able to come in through the dingy, bottle-glass window.

"The what?" I didn't miss the confusion, the need in Ilyan's voice. I had to hand it to my brother; he played his cards well.

"Make me a deal, and I will tell you."

The room was silent except for the clicking of Cail's nails against the windowsill and the constricted breathing from Talon's chest as he fought the desire to protect Ilyan from my brother. I half expected them to just disappear and leave us both hanging, but they didn't.

"What deal?" Ilyan breathed out, his eyes narrowing.

"Protect my sister," Cail said without hesitation, his fingernails still clicking against the wooden frame. "When the time comes, I will stop the zánik curse that my father has already begun infecting her with."

I inhaled roughly. Cail had been holding back. No wonder he had been handed a death card. He knew far more than he had been letting me know. Even Edmund had never used the zánik curse. That level of pain and suffering was reserved for the ultimate of traitors, which I supposed I was.

"The zánik curse?" Ilyan asked, a wicked glow lighting up his face. "My, you *have* gotten yourself in some trouble, Wynifred."

"If you take her now, he will kill her before even you will have a chance to stop it," Cail said, fear lighting up his eyes even though his face was still hard. I wasn't sure anyone else would have caught his panic, but I could see it. "But, let us walk into their trap, and I will bind the curse and take my father's control from it. Then you can take her."

"Why wait?" Ilyan asked as he leaned toward Cail in an obvious attempt to establish authority.

"Now, Ilyan," Cail taunted smoothly, "do you really want to give up a chance to attack your father? Besides, if we wait, I will not only be able to bind the curse inside of Wynifred, but I will also be able to siphon the curse through me using Edmund's power. I may be able to curse him instead."

Everyone eyed Cail curiously, my breathing increasing at what he was saying. I was sure my eyes looked ready to explode from my face. What was he saying; siphon the curse? That wouldn't just kill Edmund; it would kill him as well.

"It will come at a cost," Cail continued, ignoring my panicked intake of breath. "You will have to remove her from my care quickly."

"What are you saying?" I gasped, my words lost in my panic, the hard edge that was always in my voice all but gone.

"I may lose my mind."

To use so much magic that his mind would crack—I couldn't let him take that risk. What was more, if he failed, then Edmund would live knowing that Cail had attempted to use his magic without permission. That alone was a risk I couldn't allow him to take. The Štít was there for control; he had been warned about what would happen if he utilized it any other way.

"Cail, you can't," I pleaded, knowing he wouldn't listen, even if he heard me.

"Don't show your emotions, sister; it is incredibly unattractive," Cail spat. I stepped back, my disgust still evident on my face. "Once my job is done, keep me from her.

Then, on the day the curse fulfills itself, when Edmund has died and when my mind has returned to its own, then you will get me out."

"Sounds fair enough," Ilyan said at once, my gasp of surprise echoing around us.

"There is only one hitch," Cail continued, finally stepping away from the window. "If I can only bind the curse, not send it into Edmund, and I die before my father, then the curse will be unbound and it will be unstoppable and Wynifred will die. To save her life, my father must die first."

"You drive a hard bargain," Ilyan said with a smile, his hand dragging through his hair as he contemplated everything in front of him. The minutes dragged on as we waited. I tried to catch Cail's eyes, to plead with him not to do this, but he avoided me, his focus only on Ilyan.

"I will agree to your request, Cail, if you both consent to my terms. Cail will bind the curse, with a future promise of sanctuary, and Wynifred will give up her fire magic."

"Deal," Cail said at once, his hand extending in an attempt to seal the promise.

I could not move. Cail was risking everything for me, putting his life on the line in a crazy attempt to get me to Ilyan and hopefully into safety. I could do nothing more than return the favor, even if it would be years before he could redeem it. I would do anything to save my brother, just as he would obviously do anything to save me.

"Deal."

"Tell me of the Vilỳs," Ilyan said the instant the word was out of my mouth.

"Edmund has found a way to make a Vilỳ strengthen his magic," Cail began, and everyone stiffened. Everyone knew that Edmund had captured the little things, but even I didn't know what he was doing with them.

"There are cages of Vilỳs he hides underground, harvesting their poison in the hopes of someday creating a child more powerful than you. He plans to inject his next child with enough poison to either kill it or turn it into a weapon. He also keeps a Vilỳ by his bedside, letting him bite him every night on his mark, in hopes of increasing his power."

Everything washed over me, the onslaught of memories coming in such a rush I couldn't help the wave of bile that expelled itself. I felt my stomach empty itself, heard the dull splat of liquid against stone, and my vision swam, the cold prison coming back into focus.

I heard the two men exclaim before Timothy laughed, his joy making the sound high pitched and girlish.

"Feel better?" Edmund asked. "Remember everything?"

I didn't respond. I just hung my head between my arms, the lack of muscle strength giving me reprieve.

"Now, tell me Cail's secret. Why will he do anything to save you?" I just looked at him, not willing to give him the information, knowing deep down that soon I wouldn't have another choice.

"Tell me what I can threaten your brother with, Wynifred." I felt his fingers rest against my spine, his magic jerking into my spinal column as he moved to take the information by force.

"If Cail dies first, then I die. If Timothy dies first, the curse unbinds itself." My voice was dead as Edmund forced it out of me.

"There now," Edmund sneered, the smile wide on his face, "That wasn't that hard, was it? Come along, Timothy. It looks like I have a job for you."

He moved away from me then, the door swinging shut behind him with a clang before the shackles around my wrists vanished, sending me to the ground in a heap.

17

ILYAN

I COULD NOT THANK Ovailia more for her foresight in adding modern bathrooms to the ancient chambers at Rioseco than I did right now. The room was still steamy from the prolonged shower, the air heavy with the mist of the okouzlený bush. I breathed in the heavy flavor of the wood, savoring the way it relaxed my heart and cleared my lungs.

I had let the water run for much longer than was strictly necessary as I cut my hair back to the short cut that Joclyn had said she liked, letting the steam move out into the bedroom where Joclyn lay on the large, soft bed. She looked so peaceful, and although I knew the magical properties of the bush would not wake her, I hoped they would calm her in the nightmare she was still restrained within.

Still she lay, unmoving and calm. Thankfully, we'd had no more injuries in the past few hours since arriving at Rioseco. I still couldn't believe we had arrived safely, my heart whole and unscathed. Magic like that had never been accomplished before, and to do so twice in such a short time... I had not expected to survive it. I did not look at this accomplishment as one to boast of. If anything, it only increased my ability to protect her.

Cleaned, cut and shaven, I walked out of the bathroom of my large suite into the bedroom, the sight of Joclyn's sleeping body welcoming me. She lay still underneath the heavy white covers; the bright white looking out of place against the ancient stone walls. Generally, I preferred white. I preferred the serenity, the hope and the reminder that you could always start again that it offered me. So many of my rooms were decorated with it, but here, in the ruins of the first abbey I ever lived in, I could not cover the brick I had laid with my own hands with such a trivial thing as paint. These walls reminded me of starting over in their own way, and that was enough for me.

Joclyn's clean hair fanned behind her like a dark stain of spilled ink against the white. My magic flared inside of her, moving to reach every corner of her body in an instant, the once powerful barrier now nowhere to be found.

Thankfully, her body was whole, but the absence of the barrier still worried me. It had been strong enough to keep me out of her when she was first trapped in the Tǒuha, only to fade the longer she stayed inside of it. Now, it had simply disappeared. I knew the absence meant something, but what it was, I couldn't place.

My father had found a way to work beyond my realm of thinking, his mind working faster than mine for once. Any other time, I would be glad for the challenge; but somehow, the brutal torture of a girl I loved, happening right in front of me, changed that. I didn't like to lose, and Edmund had upped the stakes in this game.

I lay down next to her, letting my magic flow into her mind as I joined myself to her, hopeful that this time I might find something. I knew the hope was slim, but I couldn't stop it from coming unbidden to my mind.

I let my mind seep into hers; the desperation, at once again finding nothing, gripping me to my very core. Her mind had still not returned; a path to retrieve it had not been found. I could still find no trace of where she could have disappeared to.

I had entered her soul, moved into her mind, reversed her magical line, healed her body, held her heart, and now the barrier had gone. The last thing I knew her to control.

She was a shell.

I had run out of ideas.

With all my training, all my power, this problem had stumped me.

We had one thing left, one thing we could try. Being at Rioseco had given us access to the mugs that could hold the Black Water, just as Thom had reminded us in the cave. As Joclyn's only food source, the Black Water might possibly be the key to awakening her.

I held her to me, my mind still wandering inside of hers, my song filling her mind, my words lingering as they echoed through her soul and vibrated through the tender muscles of her heart. I left them there, within her, before withdrawing from within only to hold her to me, her body pressing up against me.

"Jos, my love," I whispered to her, knowing it was no use. This was not like when I had been knocked unconscious by my overuse of magic. Her voice had called to me then, but I doubted mine could call to her now. There was nothing there to hear, not that I could find. I still couldn't stop the hope.

"Whatever happens, please know that I will always hold you in my heart. I now know I was not the one to save you, as much as my heart longs to be. But I will protect you, until the one who can awaken you returns."

I leaned forward and kissed her cheek, the warmth of her skin shooting sweetly through me in an electrical current that caught my veins on fire.

Before I could let my heart linger on my words, a soft knock filled the room, echoing off the stone walls.

Not a moment passed before Dramin walked in. As much as I hated the ritual bows and formal speeches, there were times when I missed the formalities my position usually accounted me, this was one of them. I had to remind myself that those luxuries were gone forever, as were my people. My father had massacred the ones I had been chosen to lead. I was all alone now, the last of the Skříteks, save my sister. Even at that, we were only half-breeds of the once powerful race.

Dramin smiled as I stood to face him, a mug of Black Water balanced in his hands. I couldn't ignore the banging in my chest at the possibilities feeding her might give us.

The water had awakened her true ability not too long ago; perhaps it was the key we needed to wake her up now.

"You ready for this?" Dramin asked, his dark green eyes looking at me over the mug.

I nodded once. Dramin needed someone to hold Joclyn still and upright. I had agreed without complaint, although it meant that I might get some of the poisonous water on my skin. The thought caused my muscles to tighten. I could still vividly remember the pain of the water as it lashed against my chest, the internal burning that plagued me for years afterwards. It was worth it, as this would be, if it was done for Joclyn's sake.

We moved toward the large couch, Dramin setting the heavy mug on the ancient table that sat next to the upholstered couch. I followed him, moving to shift Joclyn onto my lap where Dramin would need her.

"You are good man, Ilyan."

I only nodded at him, unsure how to respond. His simple statement was loaded with the implications of both past and future. I let the ire wash over me before arranging Joclyn on my lap, her head lolling against my chest as Dramin placed a towel beneath it. I only hoped the flimsy fabric would catch enough of the Water to prevent too much of an injury.

Dramin moved to the side of me, his jaw tight as he moved her head a bit. I held her head where Dramin had placed it, my skin warm where it made contact with hers.

"You can't move, Ilyan, even if it burns you. You move, and it will only burn you more." Dramin lifted the mug, and I cringed as the putrid smell of the deep brown fluid hit my nose. It smelled like rot, the heavy death smell of the body pits that had littered my home while the black plague ravaged Europe. The images of the time floated to mind, their suffering still fresh, even though the travesty had happened in my youth.

I closed my eyes against the imagery and held Joclyn's body closer to me, my body tense as I held her still. Thom had suggested we just restrain her magically, but I had swatted the idea away, wishing instead to be near her, wishing to help her physically. Now, I was second guessing my decision.

Dramin placed the mug against Joclyn's lips, his thumb and forefinger pressing against her mouth to open it slightly, the sag of her jaw making her look deathly and vacant. I looked away, not wanting to think of her being that way, of being vacant. Gone.

I looked out the high stone archways that led to my wide

balcony and to the misty Spanish countryside that lay beyond that. It all looked the same as when we had built this beautiful building. This place was like stepping back in time for me, one of the only places that felt like home. I couldn't deny the heady feeling from being here that was seeping into me. Of course, it didn't hurt that so many of the images in the original sight took place within these very walls.

In the sight given by Sain all those centuries ago, I had seen Joclyn battle powerful enemies. I had seen her bloodied and beaten, and I had seen her crying—tears streaming down her face before she kissed me. The images flashed before me now, and I could tell where each of them would occur, what corner of the ruins of the abbey she would stand in, many of which were only a few steps away.

The beautiful images were stolen from me as the deep, burning sensation of the Black Water shot across my arm. I called out, my voice loud and deep as I tried to keep my body still. I let my voice yell and swear, the rough Czech words bouncing off the stone, while keeping my body still as Dramin continued to work.

The burn moved deeper into me, the acidic fire burning into my blood stream where it ignited and moved all over my body in a matter of minutes. The pain was not as intense as I had remembered, but still it caused my muscles to tense as it passed them, the deep magic reacting with my blood. My magic tried to heal me, but it wasn't fast enough to fight the burn that shot through my veins.

There was a reason few of my kind had ever sought council from the Drak, and now I was being reminded why. I continued to yell, my only outlet in the battle against my own body that was desperate to move and flee the pain.

"H... he will... willl t... tear usss ap... apa... apart." The quiet, feminine stutter rocked through me. The hope that I felt filled me faster than the burning pain had. Dramin stepped away, the mug returning to the ancient table. Joclyn's body twisted easily in my arms, falling down to my lap as limply as she had been before. Was she coming back?

Her eyes were open, the endless black depths seeing something neither Dramin nor I could see. The pain and fear in her voice was strong, and I hoped the timbre of her voice had more to do with the sight than whatever was happening where she was.

My fingers curled against her skin, desperate to pull her to me, but also afraid of missing her awakening or that the sharp movement would hinder whatever progress was being made here.

"If... if... y... you w-w-wish to sssseeee th... the end, g... give m-me y... your heart."

"Jos?" I whispered as her eyes closed, hoping she could hear me, hoping that she would not return to her prison, but nothing happened. She stayed limp in my arms as her mind returned to the hell she was trapped in.

"He will tear us apart. If you wish to see the end, give me your heart." I had almost forgotten Dramin was standing behind me until he spoke.

I looked away from Joclyn at his voice, keeping my hands on her arms, not willing to be away from her, to lose contact.

"What do you think it means?"

I could only shake my head at him. It was obviously a sight as shown by the blackness of her eyes, and not the rambling nonsense that could happen while people dreamed. This meant the words were meant to guide. So the question remained; who was to receive the guidance, and what did it mean?

My hands pulled away from her slowly, my eyes widening at the large burn on my arm. My skin was raised in an angry, red welt where the water had touched me. The water that could unlock her sight; the touch of the water against my flesh, one that would trigger it.

Dramin saw me looking at the welt on my arm, his inhalation confirming that my thoughts were headed in the right direction.

"It's for you." His voice was awed. The water had called her from a dark place, and my sacrifice had been the one to have done that.

"He will tear us apart. If you wish to see the end, give me your heart," I repeated the words softly, the tender words sounding like a message rather than a warning on my tongue.

A message from her; from Joclyn.

She was still in there somewhere. I just needed to find her.

18

ILYAN

I WAS out of bed before I had registered what had happened. I had heard the soft knocking in my sleep and sat up, my body tense and ready as if expecting battle. I could still feel the warmth of where Joclyn's body had been pressed against mine, the heat leaving as the chilled night air that came in through the open archways swirled against my skin.

The knock sounded again, the taps soft against wood. A familiar energy seeped through the door, and my body relaxed.

I made it to the door in two steps, throwing it open to reveal a very disheveled looking Thom. His dark dreads were pulled back into a ponytail. The ear buds of his iPod were hanging out of his shirt, where I could hear the occasional twang of a guitar. Normally I would laugh at seeing them there—Thom always kept his love of country music hidden—but the concern on his face trumped the humor.

"Thom?" I questioned when he didn't say anything.

Thom looked over my shoulder to where Joclyn lay in the bed before looking back to me.

"You need to come with me."

It was very strange how one sentence could put each nerve in my body on high alert. My muscles tensed as I stood taller; my back straightened in an inadvertent attempt to challenge him.

Thom reacted, but not in a way I would have expected from him.

"Shield her, and follow me."

"Thom? What has happened?"

Thom's eyes darted around uncomfortably, the action only adding to my heightened awareness. My muscles tensed in expectation. I looked down the hall behind him, expecting Edmund to be standing right there.

"I found something outside." His voice was so soft and unsure that I barely heard him.

"What?" I asked, Thom jumping at my voice. His uncomfortable jitters seemed to be growing rather than receding.

"I'm not sure. I want you to see."

I looked at him sternly for one minute before backing off. I would receive a clearer understanding of what was happening by following rather than demanding answers. Although I didn't like going somewhere blind, it was my best option.

"Následuj mě." Before I could say more Thom had begun to walk away, his steps short and panicked, suggesting trouble. Everything prickled inside me in warning, but I wasn't one to second-guess Thom. He had proven his worth to me, and that was enough.

I glanced back at Joclyn for only a moment before watching her body vanish from sight; the heavy shield I covered her with ignited inside of her, as well as around her.

Thom's steps were short, the sound muffled by his quick,

soft movements. I followed him in silence as we moved from the renovated space on the northern side of the abbey to the ruins that existed on the far south. What had once been a beautiful cathedral was now reduced to a few exquisite arches and some tile work, most of it destroyed by war, neglect and tourists of the later 1800s.

"You better shield yourself," he whispered, his body stopping to face me.

My back straightened as he looked at me, my eyes boring into him in a silent threat. My desire not to begin dishing out orders was almost trumped by my distaste at being given them. I saw him wilt a bit, but not enough. He shook his head and disappeared before me, the heavy feel of his magic moving away from me.

I began to follow him, my steps mirroring his in timbre as we moved. We moved through a large, open area. I could see the tree line of the forest that surrounded the abbey clearly and the moon that hung above the trees, the face of the sleeping man I had grown up whispering my secrets to so clear on the textured surface.

As I followed Thom's lead, my magic peaked at some distant power I could not place. I fought the need to stop and investigate the new, unwanted energy that was buzzing through the air, but continued on. I could usually determine anyone I had met before by the feeling of their magic, but this was either too far away, or someone I didn't know. I brushed the feeling away, my nerves readying themselves for an attack.

Thom tiptoed through rubble as he led our way to the only remaining turret in the area. The tall pillar of stone still housed the large cathedral bell. The tower worked best as a guardhouse, which is what Thom had been using it as. The muscles in my face tensed as we climbed, the silence dragging on and on, leaving me to worry about what Thom had found.

I could desperately grasp at the hope of seeing Ovailia burst through the trees that surrounded the abbey, Ryland's body in her arms, but I knew better. Thom would have given me more information if it was good news.

The large, wooden door at the top of the spiral staircase opened of its own accord, and I felt Thom move beyond it, up into the large opening. Moonlight filtered through the rounded stone opening, casting confusing shadows on the walls around us. The ancient bell hung from wound rope the width of my arm, dust sprinkling down around it as the rope creaked and moved in the breeze.

I followed Thom's energy pattern and the dust footprints that lined the floor until he came to a stop, our backs to the bell as we looked out on the forest.

"Are you there?" Thom whispered, his reluctance to be heard flushing through me like ice.

"Yes."

"What do you see?" I fought the urge to command Thom to simply tell me, reminding myself it was not his way, just as commanding people to do my bidding should not be mine.

I scanned the trees in front of us at his request, the dark shapes of the trees barely visible amongst the black mass of nature. I looked above them in hopes of finding what he was talking about before returning to the trees, a bright light having caught my attention.

The yellow-gold flickers of a fire were nestled between the trees, casting a shadow through the dark stumps and making long, bright fingers amongst the strips of black. Several bodies cut off the light as they moved around it, making the intimidating shadows flicker and move.

I watched the light for a moment, trying to make sense of it in a non-territorial way before another light flickered through the trees. One after another they appeared, disappeared, and re-appeared as bodies and objects moved in front of them, cutting off the light that reached my eyes.

My heart thumped heavily in my chest as I watched the lights flicker, the magical pulses going on and off. The magical current I had felt before washed over me again, the strength of it tingling up my spine. My muscles tensed as I focused on it, my eyes narrowed at the lights before me. The magical flow wasn't one I recognized. The concentrated nature of the icy flow made it clear it was from more than a dozen of the same species, Trpaslíks.

I couldn't help the wicked smile that spread across my face, the pulse of my magic as it alerted me to its wish for battle. I knew it had been foolish to give Ovailia our real location after her eyes had shaded over and her lies had given her away. I had no choice at the time; I wanted Ryland. Now, that want had turned into a need.

Unfortunately, that need was going to trigger the beginning of the war. I had foolishly hoped we would have at least a decade, but Edmund was obviously a very impatient man.

"How many camps?" I asked, making sure to keep my voice low.

"Eight," Thom began, his frustration seeping into his deadpan voice. "They weren't there when we first arrived, so they must have come sometime in the last few days."

I sighed heavily. We hadn't been keeping as heavy a guard as we should have been. Our first two nights here we had taken turns at watch while the others ate and slept, but last night we hadn't posted one at all.

I watched the lights for a moment more before turning

to leave, using my magic to pull Thom behind me. I moved quickly, my steps much louder than they should have been, but I was keen to put some distance between the assembling army and us. I separated the pulses that flowed through the air around me, my magic registering exactly what forces lay beyond us. Two dozen Trpaslíks camped outside the wall of the abbey, waiting for the chance to strike.

They knew we were here, and no amount of tiptoeing could keep them from pounding down our door when the order was given to attack.

I could feel Thom behind me as I moved, his energy spiking as the anger that I felt brushed onto him and fed his deep rooted anxiety.

The second we moved past the open stretch of rubble, I released my shield, bringing my body back into sight.

"It was Ovailia, wasn't it?" I didn't turn at Thom's voice, the hardness of it expected. I could feel the same anger rippling through my body, just under the skin.

"Of course it was." I kept my back to him, allowing my magic and my internal sight to keep him in my mind. I could see him standing, his hands flexing as his brow furrowed.

Thom stood still, the small movement of his hands the only sign of his anger. He kept it restrained, controlled and hidden, the way he had done since he had escaped our father, since Sain had shown him what his temper could cause.

"So what do we do?"

I turned to face him, my taller than average frame towering over him. He looked up to me, his eyes, so much like a child's, wide and pleading.

"There is not much we can do. We stay here. We wait for Joclyn to wake and hope that Ovailia brings her mate to her."

"Ovailia? You want to *wait* for her?"

I nodded once before turning away from him, my steps taking me back the way we had come.

I could feel Thom follow me, his steps quick as his shorter legs tried to keep up with my longer strides.

"Why, Ilyan?" he said as he came up beside me, his legs still working double time. The muscles in my neck tensed at his question. I really didn't need to explain myself to him, but his question was understandable given their history.

"Because she will have Ryland," I said, keeping my voice strong and distant. "Ryland is the key to waking Joclyn. Once Joclyn wakes, we will be able to face the Trpaslíks that surround us."

I smiled at my words, the visions from the first sight flying into me. Saying it aloud somehow sealed her fate, making her the one that would defeat my father and assuring that she would become the beautiful warrior I had seen in my sight.

"Why can't we just attack them now?" Thom asked. I couldn't help but laugh, the hearty sound of my voice sounding odd against the tension that still rippled off both of us.

I stopped again to face him, the door to my suite only a few steps away. I could already feel my heart pull me toward the door, my magic stretching to ensure her safety.

"You would attack twenty or more Trpaslíks with only you, me and a Drak?" I raised my eyebrow at him, the dare for him to answer evident.

While I might be able to defeat more than half that amount on a wet day, I knew Thom had always struggled with his ability. Being the son of an un-bonded mortal had always made him weaker than the rest of us. Dramin would prove little help at all. Draks had no defensive magic. There was no other way to put it. It was the reason my father had been able to exterminate them so easily.

Thom shook his head and looked away from me, his answer evident in his eyes. I ignored the bristle I felt at his lack of respect, but kept it at bay, reminding myself that my role as a ruler had died with my people. Not like I had taken it seriously in the first place.

"We will watch them. We need to set a more consistent guard—which between the three of us may prove impossible, but we must do what we can." I set orders as I always had, Thom's back straightening in preparation to obey. "If we can make an adequate map of where their camps are, it will help us to attack without incident when the time comes."

Thom nodded once in understanding, the nervous energy that was flowing off him receding with my words.

"Thom, get some sleep. I will watch from here, dnes večer, strengthen our shield and develop a clearer plan."

Thom said nothing. He only nodded in respect as he turned from me, the thick strands of his hair swinging as he walked down the hall toward his room. I watched him put the tiny buds back into his ears before he turned the corner, leaving me alone in the dark corridor.

I couldn't ignore the thrum of my heart any longer, the pull moved against my skin like the crawling of a hundred emotions washing over the surface. My shield released from around Joclyn as I entered the room, bringing her back into view.

A few more days and she would wake.

If Edmund had already sent Trpaslíks after us, then Ovailia couldn't be more than a day behind. Soon, I would wake her.

If Edmund had sent Ovailia at all.

I wiped the thought from my mind. The stress that such a small idea gave me was overwhelming. I straightened my back and walked away from her, toward the window.

I could still feel the need to be near her, but for now, I needed to prove that I was stronger than my desire. I had to remind myself that she would not be mine for many years to come.

The breeze that came in through the high arches of the windows swirled around me, the mingled magic of the men who stood around us in preparation for attack evident to me now. The power was weak, but it was there. I could feel their anticipation, the nerves and excitement.

The danger had followed us to our door once again, but I knew what the Trpaslíks who guarded us did not. The time was coming, closer and closer. I could feel the tick in my blood, beating like a clock, signaling its arrival.

The hairs on my arms prickled as my energy rippled over my skin, my alert power tingling , desperate to be used. I always kept so much of my magic restrained for safety reasons. It was only in battle that I could freely feel my magic flow through me, that I could be free. My energy rippled now; the maniacal energy setting me on fire in eager anticipation.

The final battle was knocking on our door. The sight had shown me that.

We just needed Sleeping Beauty to wake.

"He will tear us apart. Rozdělí nás. Jestli chceš vidět konec, dej mi své srdce.." I spoke the words of Joclyn's sight silently, the words sounding like a deep prayer of mass when whispered in Czech.

Give me your heart.

Hadn't I done that already? Hadn't I promised her every

beat that it possessed when I first held her in my arms during the sight eight hundred years ago?

Yes, but I had also taken it away.

I had taken away her claim on me when I made the decision not to break the bond between her and her mate. My brother. Could I break that bond now, after all I had sacrificed, after all I had promised her? No, it was not in me to be so cruel.

My back was still toward her as my heart beat for her. I felt love and confusion swell inside of me. I didn't need to look at her to feel my conviction continue to cement itself within me. I could see her beauty, her strength, her power. I could see her weakness and the hold it had on her vanishing slowly every day. I could hear her laugh and see the way she wrinkled her nose. I could see the flash of her silver eyes when she was upset.

She was amazing.

I would do anything to protect her, to help her, to let her become what she wanted and needed to be. I would give her my heart, if that were required. She had it until it beat its last.

The tops of the trees reached toward the moon, the shadows dark and deep. I loved this view, the natural beauty of the world that modern man had destroyed. There were so few places on earth where you could find that peace anymore. Places that I had walked through, loved, worshiped and explored through my hundreds of years had all been overrun with what others were calling progress.

I could feel the energy of the earth radiate from the ground, the natural force strong here; whereas, in the cities of the world, the natural power was covered and poisoned until it no longer existed.

The thought came to me before I could stop it, the desire

to hold Joclyn as we looked out at this beautiful view, as we felt the magic of the earth together, because I knew she could. So many of our kind never could, but she would. I wanted to see her face when she did.

I wanted to show her the beauty in the world, not just the sadness. I wanted to give her my heart openly, and I wanted her to take it.

19

ILYAN

For hundreds of years, this abbey had housed the brethren that came to worship their own silent God. They farmed, they prayed, and they worshiped until the year the troops drove them away, leaving my beautiful home abandoned. It had been ransacked, the stained glass windows were destroyed, the gorgeous pews burned, and the stone walls carved with crude declarations of love. What had been my home, my personal place of sanctuary, was now only a discarded, forgotten place.

I could see one of the carvings now, a roughly drawn heart and an unintelligible figure carved amongst it. It was bright against the stone in the evening light, the last of the day's sun bouncing off the angles of the ruins like glittering jewels. I stared at it as I sat on the rubble strewn floor, my legs crossed in front of me in a style more common amongst the Chinese worshipers.

I had intended to restore this portion of the building, giving life to the ancient arches and restoring the glass back to what it had once been. Now, it seemed to be too late.

What could be rebuilt would only be ruined and destroyed within a matter of days.

I breathed in the smell of earth that lingered heavily in the air, the density of it filling my lungs before dispersing throughout my body, the heavy earth magic lingering with my own.

My feet had brought me here after the nerve endings in the base of Joclyn's neck had been severed from her spine. I had felt them snap, one by one, my magic working tirelessly to repair them as her heart began to go into cardiac arrest. If I hadn't been singing to her at the time, I would have missed it. She would have died in my arms as I slept.

My heart longed to stay next to her, but I couldn't. I couldn't look into her face and not blame myself for being unable to release her from her prison.

Ten days.

She had been trapped in her prison for ten days. We had escaped the cave in Italy only for her to remain trapped in her solitary prison. For her, it had been more than a month, more than a month of what I could only assume would be consistent torture.

My hands lay on my knees in meditation. My thoughts were on the desires of my heart, while my power focused on the natural magic that surrounded me. It was the only religion I knew, the only deity I had found in this world—the magic in the earth.

I had to hope it was enough. I breathed it into me, pulling the heavy ancient power through me only to transfer it to Joclyn, to move it through the Štít and into her.

When I first came to this place, almost a thousand years ago, my heart was heavy, broken and guilty. I had taken a life, and part of me felt power in that. A wicked ribbon of black that I could feel attempting to infect my soul. If my father had gotten his way, it would have. But I had seen that maniacal light in his eyes then, the joy at what I was able to accomplish, and the look scared me. If I had any wisdom at the time, I would have seen what he was capable of then, and I would have stopped him, but I was only a child.

A child who ran away from home, ran from what I was supposed to become, to build a monastery and find inner peace. Sadly, I was still not sure I had ever found it.

"Ilyan?" I kept my eyes closed at Thom's voice, his magic adding its own ebb and flow to the air around me. I breathed it in, adding it to my own.

The crunching of Thom's feet against the destroyed bits of the chapel came closer, his magic heavy with insecurity and yet steady, always steady. He sat down next to me, and while I still did not move, I opened my eyes, hoping the small gesture could be taken in greeting.

"Dramin told me what happened." I could only nod, not sure I wanted to talk about it, not sure what to say. "He's on guard now, but... I wanted to see if you needed anything nejdřív."

I kept my vision forward, although my magic flared to Joclyn, covering her through the Štít as I reconfirmed her safety. She still slept, her body continuing to heal as she lay.

I couldn't be mad at Dramin for leaving her, although part of me wanted to be. If we didn't keep someone on guard at all times, we would soon be overrun. Trpaslík camps had been popping up every night, each one bringing our enemy closer to us, each one giving us less time before they would attack.

"Ilyan? Můj Pane?"

I sighed and looked at him out of the corner of my eye, one quick glance before returning to stare at the graffiti on the wall. He obviously wasn't going to leave me alone. He was worried, but I couldn't help feeling his worry was misplaced. I could handle my own issues.

"I'm fine, Thom. Já jen..." I stopped. I never opened myself up to anyone. It exposed too many weaknesses, too many weapons that could be used against me. I had heard the mortals use the phrase 'skeletons in the closet' for hundreds of years, and that was sometimes how I felt—as if I had skeletons in my closet. Except it wasn't one or two hung up on a coat rack, it was an armada. If I could ever control them, I could take over the whole world.

I had surprised myself when I had begun to open up to Joclyn, when I had told her of my past. The only people who knew such things about me were those who had been present my whole life: Dramin, Ovailia, Sain and Talon. Even they did not know the whole picture, but Joclyn, I wanted Joclyn to know everything. I wanted Joclyn to understand me, to trust me, so that when the time came for her to rely on me and trust in my judgment, she would do so without question. I didn't want to have to command her magically as I sometimes did all the others. I had done so once, after she had first lost Ryland, and I still regretted it.

Thom continued to look at me expectantly. I could feel his eyes burning into me. I stayed still, my vision forward, my breathing even. As much as I trusted Thom, as much as I loved my brother, I didn't want to let him inside my head.

"You'll find a way to get her out." I couldn't help but smile at Thom's words, at his easy confidence. After all, he had been so set on simply destroying her not long before.

"You believe that, do you?" I could almost feel him twitch beside me at my words. I had overheard him talking to Dramin last night, his fears about the inaccuracy of sight spoken aloud. It might have been wrong to eavesdrop, it might have been wrong to bring up what I had heard, but my regal blood demanded one thing, while my logic another. The distinction was never clear to me anymore.

"You know I only fear our father," he said, the wavering in his voice surprising.

"Vím že." I suddenly felt bad for bringing it up. "I do, too, which is why I am still alive and why I can't bring myself to look past the terror that Joclyn is trapped in."

My muscles tensed in anxiety the second I finished talking. I had spoken too plainly, opened myself up too much to him. The words had come unbidden from my mouth, and now I was to face the consequences.

"Do you remember Rosy?"

Thom's quiet voice caught me off guard, the subject matter startling. Rosy was never spoken about, least of all by Thom. I had never met her, but I had heard the story, saw the terrors from Thom's memories. Unsurprisingly, Thom was now looking intently at the crude carving in the stone before us.

"Ano," I said.

"When she was three, Wynifred and I used to take her to visit the serfs in the country side." Thom's voice was distant, his mind lost in his memories. I could feel my heart tense at what was coming. I might not know the whole story, but I did know the outcome.

"It probably wasn't the best day trip for a child," he laughed, "but she enjoyed playing with the other small children. I could watch that smile on her face for days. She looked so much like Wynifred. Those crazy dark eyes; they would shine more than you would ever think possible."

I cringed, but stayed silent. Edmund had not allowed Thom to bond himself to Wynifred, and they were left separated for much of the time. She had been the most powerful of the Trpaslíks, chosen specifically for Edmund's first experiment.

"I loved to watch her dance. She was so graceful—we all thought so, even Edmund. His first grandchild. He was so proud. Except..."

Thom's words faded as the memory grew darker. I could see everything in my head, everything Thom had told me when he arrived under my protection. Rosy was the way he had to explain his allegiance for me; the pain over the torture and murder of his small daughter the reason for his defection. In coming to me for help, he had also given me something more, a link to Rosy's mother. I knew she would stop at nothing to get her revenge. I still remembered my anxiety at meeting face to face with Wynifred. I sighed heavily, the reason for Rosy's death almost too simple to even comprehend.

"She didn't have his blue eyes," I finished for him. The blue eyes. The sign of royalty. The sign of Edmund's lineage. So many of my siblings had never had a chance to live simply because they were born without his eyes. His obsession was over something that meant nothing, leaving a trail of blood behind it.

"I was so lost in what our father was doing to her, to my child, that I couldn't see beyond it. I couldn't focus. It became just another way for him to control me, but I didn't see it before it was too late. Suddenly, she was gone, my willpower tied to her life. When she was gone, all I had left was my anger, and it covered me. If it weren't for Sain, I would have been killed, too. The way..."

I knew he was about to mention Wynifred, how he had left her behind. She couldn't leave Rosy's memory behind. Her soul had been tied to what Edmund had done.

I reached up and clapped him hard on the back, needing to comfort him as a brother, not as a leader.

"He's doing the same to you, Ilyan," Thom said, looking straight at me.

"I know, bratr." I couldn't say much more than that, the tight restriction in my chest wouldn't let me.

"Don't let him."

"You are a wise man, Thom," I said, feeling humbled by the strangely perfect lesson I had just been taught by my younger brother.

"I've had a lot of years to perfect it."

I could only nod. After all my years on this earth, after all my lessons, studying, and worshiping, my younger brother had become wiser than me. He saw the world in the way I always wanted to.

"Well, you've done well."

"Not really," he said, surprising me with a rare laugh. "Sometimes, the things you need to hear have to come from others. You can't give yourself good advice, after all."

I turned to him, stunned. He looked at me for only a moment before looking away, obviously embarrassed.

"You've done it again, Thom."

"Whatever," he said grumpily, the modern word sounding odd in Czech.

He stood quickly, his stalky frame unraveling awkwardly. I looked back toward the crudely carved heart as Thom's ebbing magic signaled his departure, his direction making it clear he would sit with Joclyn until my return.

He left without another word from either of us, neither knowing what to say. Someday I would thank him for everything. I would find a way to let him seek his revenge, to let him find a way to fill the hole in his heart.

He deserved that, we all did.

20

WYN

"WHY DIDN'T you tell me, Sain?" They were the first words I had spoken since waking up, since Edmund had left with the last piece of the puzzle, the thing he needed to prompt Cail to kill Joclyn faster and give him even more power over my brother.

I had sat in silence, the dull, green glow of Sain's light keeping me company as I thought through the experiences I now possessed and let who I had been blend with who I had become in a mashed up jumble of personalities and experiences.

I couldn't even bring myself to touch Talon. It wasn't because he had lied to me about my past, it was because I had murdered his family, and the guilt was eating me up inside. I didn't understand how he could have forgiven me for something like that.

So I sat with my back against the cold wall as I let everything wash over me. I tried to find balance.

"Would you have believed me if I did?" Sain whispered from across the prison.

The answer to his question was clear; no, I would not. I

had been an assassin, a whore, a keeper of magic, stronger than many, who had become a fun-loving friend. Fun-loving, Thom had taught me that and Talon had perfected it.

"Who am I?" I asked the question more to myself than to Sain, but he laughed nonetheless, his answer coming quickly.

"You are Wyn."

I fought the urge to roll my eyes, to groan, to yell, to threaten, or seduce. Every single emotion was there, every desire, and they blended together so seamlessly that it wasn't confusing, but somehow, Sain's response made sense.

I am Wyn.

I smiled at the thought, the wicked sneer I had long forgotten sprouting on my lips as I looked at Sain from beneath my eyelashes. He was right; I was Wyn, and I would not just sit here and take this.

Sain returned my smile, his own power shining from beneath his eyes, the silent conviction we both shared strong and defiant.

Then Talon groaned.

I heard him and my heart called out, my guilt forgotten. I was at his side in an instant, my hand wrapped around his. His burning flesh scorched my skin, but I held on anyway, pressing his hands between mine as his eyes slowly fluttered open.

"Talon?" I whispered as his eyes stayed unfocused on the ceiling. I heard Sain's chains rattle as he attempted to move himself closer, desperate to see.

"Talon? Baby?"

His eyes were still unfocused, but his lips had begun to move, the limp movement subtle.

"W... Wyn..." he said, finally able to get my name out after several false starts.

"I'm here. I'm here." Slowly, his eyes turned toward me, the color of them clouded over as he seemed to look through me.

"I thought... I hoped you had gone," he gasped, his voice wheezing as his chest struggled to give him enough air.

"No, baby, I would never leave you. I'm here," I whispered, my hand clinging to his.

He coughed a bit, small drops of blood lining his lips. My eyes widened at seeing them there, my heart clunking at the thought of what they could mean. What they *did* mean. I squeezed his hand between mine, the warmth painful, and yet, somehow comforting.

"It's going to be okay." It was an empty promise. I knew it. I had heard Sain's proclamation as clear as day, and now, with my memory returned, there was no way I could deny the words. I couldn't pretend they hadn't been released into the air between us.

I looked toward Sain unwillingly, my subconscious mind begging him to shake his head, to somehow promise that his words were false. He only looked at me with his bright green eyes, the lines on his face sad.

"It's going to be okay," I said again as I turned back to Talon, trying desperately to ignore the tightness in my chest.

Talon said nothing; he only looked at the air behind me as if he was seeing my face there, his eyes drifting in and out of focus.

"Wyn?" he asked, his voice faltering after only one word.

I breathed in slowly, my emotions causing my chest to shake. The burning in my eyes signaled tears that would never fall.

I grabbed his hand and placed it against the filthy skin of

my cheek, needing to feel him, to be close to him. His skin was fire against mine, his palm flat and strong for only a moment before it went limp again.

I clung to him, watching his eyes drift before they finally came to rest on me, a small smile playing on the corner of his lips.

"Wynifred..." Talon began, his eyes coming into focus. This time, the clouded irises met up with mine, his limp gaze looking right into me.

"I love you, so much." *No.* I couldn't let him say this. Not now.

"Don't start, Talon. Please," I said, but he didn't even hear me. He plowed on.

"I never thought I could love you..."

"Talon, no."

"I want you to always be happy."

"Talon." My voice was lost in a sob, my hands shaking around the palm of his hand that I held against my face.

"I want you to laugh every day. I want you to find a reason to... to..."

I tried to speak. I tried to talk. I tried to control the sobs that racked my body. Nothing could escape the shaking that had taken control of my lungs. Nothing could escape the panic that held me together.

I clung to him, holding on to his hands as tightly as my frail body would let me. I pushed myself against the bars, desperate to be closer to him, to hold him.

"Clara." His voice broke as he said his sister's name. His vision moving beyond me, his eyes on something that no one else could see.

His sister. She had come to take him home.

"No, Talon. No." I pressed my shaking hand to his, my words distorted through my sobs.

"Be safe, Wyn," he gasped. "Be happy."

He paused as he wheezed, his breathing stopping before picking back up, my hand shaky against his.

"You've done so well, Wynifred. You amaze me."

I sucked in breath, my voice shaking as the sob released it in an almost inaudible burst.

He smiled. "You know when I first loved you? When I knew?"

I couldn't answer. I couldn't try. I just sat and cried.

"When you gave up your magic to save your brother. I had seen the good in you for years, but that's when I knew."

I gasped at the knowledge, my sobs racking through me as I tried to get the three words out. The three words that were the most important ones I could say, the ones I wanted him to hear before it was too late.

"I love you. I love you, Talon."

"Clara."

His voice faded to nothing, his eyes drifting out of focus for the last time, and the heat of his flesh left me as his hand dropped to the ground.

The air was silent, my sobs forgotten, the wheezing in my husband's chest gone.

He was gone.

"No!" I cried, suddenly able to let it all out. I sobbed as I yelled. I clawed at him through the bars, trying to pull him toward me, but his body wouldn't come. I couldn't reach him. The bars of the prison that had killed him still kept me from him.

"Talon! No!" I shook the bars, hitting myself against them in vain, willing myself closer, to be strong enough to reach him, but it was useless. I clung to Talon's hand. I held it to my face, but no life came back into him.

Talon lay lifeless in front of me.

The thought gashed open my heart and poured out the loss and grief that had been sheltered within me. I felt everything, raw and fresh as if for the first time. The loss of Talon and Rosaline burst together in a mixture of sorrow so deep it threatened to incapacitate me.

I didn't care if someone heard. I didn't care if they came. I didn't care if this was the end. I screamed out my pain in a keening moan that ripped open my throat and rattled my vision.

Edmund had taken them away from me. My father had taken them away from me. They had taken everything from me.

Everything.

No. Not everything.

I could already feel the boil of my magic as Talon's soul left him and his magic released from his body. Free from the omezující stone, his magic found its mate for the last time, the strength of him rumbling through me. A new emotion roared within me, a new power, a new strength.

Talon's magic.

My sobs stopped as a warmth—the heat as strong as his fever—moved into me. It filled me from my toes to the tips of my fingers. The feeling was so foreign, so forgotten, that my body almost rebelled against it.

I keeled over onto my hands and knees as my stomach heaved. My throat lunged and my body was racked with spasms as I vomited, the vomiting turning to dry heaving, as a steady stream of pain ran through me, my body fighting against the magic, against the pain.

I opened my eyes to a pile of sick on the floor in front of me only to gasp at the small, black stone that rested amongst the disgusting mess.

Talon's last gift to me.

I felt his magic settle into my blood. Taking its rightful place as my own came back full strength, the rush of it knocking me to the ground, the power that rippled under my skin strong and painful. I hadn't felt power this strong since Ilyan had bound it inside me. I had almost forgotten how powerful I felt, how powerful I was.

Edmund had made one giant mistake. When he had unbound my memories, he had also unbound my power.

He had unleashed me.

I gasped as the sobs left me. My anger squashed my pain and turned it into something violent. Something that normal people would rebel against, but not me. I was ready for it. I needed it.

"I love you, Talon," I whispered against the skin of his hand, the last contact I would ever have with my mate, the only closure I could ever hope to receive.

Talon's hand fell to the floor as I stood, my fingers wrapping around the small stone on the floor, clenching the slippery surface in between my gritty fingers. I felt my body heal as I stood, my magic knitting muscles, bones and skin back together. I felt bruises disappear.

I flexed my fingers as my determination took over.

I didn't care who came.

Let them come.

I opened the doors to each of the cells, the shackles that still bound Sain's wrists falling to the ground with a clatter as I released him. I watched him stand in my peripheral vision, his feet bringing him straight to Talon.

He kneeled down next to him, closing his eyes, and then he kissed his forehead. Any thought of my doing the same was forgotten as the footsteps that had begun thundering above us came nearer.

"You ready?" I asked, surprised at the deep timbre of confidence that had come back to my voice.

"We will need to get to the Rioseco Abbey," Sain said as he came to stand by me.

"I don't suppose you know where that is?" I asked, trying to keep the irritation out of my voice.

"It is in Spain." Great.

Spain. Half a continent away.

I didn't look toward him. I just stood still, unwilling to move as the footsteps thundered down the stairs.

I could feel the strength of the earth flow through me, my control of the fire magic stronger than I could ever remember it being. I let it pulse through me, building to a flame. When the guard appeared at the foot of the stairs, his eyes wide and confused as to what had happened, I didn't move. I just let the magic surge, turning the man into ash.

I smiled. I couldn't help it. I had forgotten how addicting taking a life could be.

"Was that really necessary?" Sain asked, his voice torn between disgust and humor.

"He would have done the same to us," I answered as I began to move forward, Sain following right on my tail. "If you don't like it, don't travel with a trained killer."

"As long as that assassin doesn't turn her skill on me, I think I will be happy." He wasn't worried. His voice was light and airy, and I could tell at once that he had seen something.

I took one last look at Talon, at the body of the man I loved, the only one who was strong enough to love me back. My heart beat once in silent farewell, the heavy pulse thick against the fragile skin of my chest.

It was one last goodbye.

I ignored the sadness and let my anger fuel me. I led us

up the staircase and into the thankfully empty guards' room. The room looked the same as it had the day I washed the sheet, the eerie light bouncing off the jagged edges of the stone.

I let my magic surge outward, searching for anyone nearby. No one else was close, but it wouldn't stay that way for long.

"We should move," Sain spoke from behind me, and I didn't challenge it.

I walked out of the room and into the first of many dimly lit halls with Sain on my heels. I kept my magic alert, each step of my bare feet against the rock on the floor giving me a clear map of where we were in relation to everyone else within the mountain.

There was a clear path laid out, a direct path, right to the exit—to freedom. As it stood, we wouldn't run into anyone, we would simply leave.

I began moving us in that direction before I felt it, the gentle tug of a magic that I knew all too well. It surged through my feet as it called to me, the magic of the earth making its presence known. Cail and my father were tucked away somewhere deep in the caves.

Cail's sacrifice ran through my head. Kill Timothy first. I raised my left hand and stared at the marks on my skin, the jagged edges strong where the zánik curse was bound into my skin. My brother had done that and in doing so had severed his mind into two halves. He had done it to protect me, in the hopes that he would someday be saved in return.

I had two paths before me, one to certain freedom, and one in the service of my brother.

With the power in my veins, the only thing that could stop me was Edmund, and he was safely tucked inside the bowels of the caves in search of the wells of Imdalind.

Imdalind.

I don't know how, but he hadn't found them yet. I could stop everything before it even began.

"Which have you chosen?" Sain asked. "The path of light or that of dark?" The reference to his sight was jagged and unwanted.

"I don't know what you are talking about, old man," I said, my voice hard. "I am choosing the path that makes the most sense."

I tapped my toes once against the ground, a surge of power and energy rushing away from me. It flowed through the rock before it exploded into the large cavern that held the orchard, the whole thing going up in flames with a loud explosion that shook the entire mountain.

I couldn't help but smile at the surge of power, while Sain jumped at the distant noise. His sharp intake of breath increased my smile before he laughed, soft and joyful. I guess that meant I made the right decision.

I tapped my toes against the stone once more, confirming that my father had moved away from Cail in his attempt to find out what had happened. My jaw clenched as I felt him move closer, the wicked desire for blood I had lost when my memories were bound coming back strong. I was ready. Timothy would be walking in front of us in three... two... one...

His quick steps moved him through the tall doorway of an adjacent hallway, but he didn't even make it past the archway before my magic had grabbed him and pulled him into the darkened space Sain and I hid in, flattening him against the rock.

He caught one sight of me and opened his mouth in a scream, a scream that never left his throat. I placed my hand against his mouth, my magic pushing the small, black omezující stone into his belly before it flared and burned his vocal cords to a crisp and he could draw breath.

"Hello, Father," I taunted, cocking my head to the side in amusement.

His eyes widened as he tried to move against my bindings, the strength incapacitating him. I smiled, my eyes flashing at the sudden reversal of roles.

He deserved this. My blood pulsed strongly in expectation and my smile grew.

"What? Are you not going to say hello?"

Timothy's pupils dilated in panic as he looked at me, the scream of pain and fear that he could never muster lost somewhere deep inside of him.

I placed my hand against his stomach, my palm pressed against the fabric of his shirt. His eyes widened as I pushed against him, my magic shooting a blade of fire into him. My eyes flashed with glee and then I pushed harder, dragging my hand against his belly as my magic sliced a large gash through him, the heat of my magic cauterizing the wound instantly.

"Choose light, Wyn." I froze, the advance of my hand stalled at Sain's voice.

Fine, I would choose light, but that didn't mean I would leave him unaccountable. I would not leave him free to repeat his same sins. He could die alone in the dark. The way he deserved to die.

"Goodbye, Father," I spat before sending his body flying back toward the empty room we had just come from, his back snapping as he impacted with the wall. He slid down and fell into a heap, his lack of magic making it easy for me to leave him to die.

"This way," I hissed, grabbing Sain's hand and pulling him behind me.

One step against the stone and I could see a quick layout of the caves, my magic pulsing at the realization that Edmund was moving directly toward us. It was no surprise. The man was smart and he knew me well, too well. I altered my route, pulling Sain into a connecting hallway I hadn't planned to use in an attempt to get away from Edmund.

If only the hall had been empty. Four of Edmund's guards were running through the hall in their attempt to get to the blazing orchard, their feet stopping the second we came into view.

I pulled Sain behind me as each of their faces registered our presence, their hands rising in unison. They looked between each other and back to me, their faces lighting with an eager anticipation. They thought they were going to take me down, but they had no idea who they were really up against.

"You aren't going to try to kill little, old me, are you?" I asked, a little pout entering my voice and, in seconds, each of their faces fell. Now they knew. Most of them were old enough to remember what I had been capable of, what Edmund had trained me for.

The Trpaslík at the back wasn't going to risk being near me. One look and he took off in the other direction, trying to escape before I unleashed my full power on him.

Let him run, it wasn't as if I wouldn't face him eventually. Besides, the other three seemed to have recovered nicely.

I smiled, waiting for them to attack, letting my magic surge as I prepared to breeze past them. The one in front raised his hand, his fingers shaking as he tried to pull together enough strength and confidence to attack me.

It was pitiful to see, and if I hadn't hidden all my emotions until I had time to deal with them properly, I would have felt sorry for him, but I didn't. I reached my magic out toward the wall of the hallway, the cold stone warming under my fingertips. The heat inside my body grew as my magic moved into the stone. I liquefied it, the rock heating to an extreme temperature before it melted into a stream of molten lava that seeped away from the wall and over the floor toward the guards.

The man that had come to the front opened his mouth in a scream as the fast moving molten rock ran over the stone floor, covering his feet and working its way up his body. He screamed as the heat of the liquid rock hit him, as the pain incapacitated him, and one last time before it hardened over him in a coffin of rock.

"Whoops," I whispered, sending the last of the guards running in the opposite direction, tripping over their own feet in a panic to get away.

"Don't say anything," I warned Sain as I pulled him past the molten man, making our way toward where I hoped Cail still was.

My feet picked up pace, knowing the fire in the orchard would only keep them busy for so long. Edmund was already onto me. I could deal with his minions, but I didn't want to test my newly remembered strength against him directly so soon, if I could help it.

I ran forward, trying to focus on where Edmund might be, but he seemed to have disappeared.

The halls grew darker the closer I got to Cail's magical imprint. The normally brightly lit lamps were covered and dark, the yells from the orchard fading into nothing.

I rounded the last corner only to come face to face with Edmund. I had hoped we would beat him here; obviously, I had been too optimistic. He stood between my brother and me, his arms folded over his black leather jacket as he looked me up and down. I could see Cail on a large bed behind him, the jagged red blade protruding awkwardly out of his chest.

I clenched my teeth as I glared at Edmund, hoping my face would be enough to issue a warning, but he only smiled, my challenge greedily accepted.

"Out of my way, Edmund, or you're going to lose another finger," I growled, my magic moving through the rock toward him eagerly.

"You really think I am just going to let you leave after I worked so hard to dispose of everyone else in these walls?" Edmund's voice was deep, as a wicked gleam played in his eyes. "You are the last one, and you are going to die, just like the rest of them."

"Move, Edmund." I felt my fingers flex as I watched him, unwilling to look away for a second. I wasn't going to step down. I would not back away, not after I had come this far.

"You would risk everything for him, wouldn't you?" he asked, my warning rolling off him like water. "Just as he would do the same for you?"

"Out of my way," I snarled through my clenched teeth.

"Very well," he said casually, shifting his body out of the way and giving me a full view of the stone room at the end of the hall. I glanced at Cail's sleeping body, my feet ready to take me forward, when a man moved to stand beside him, a large knife poised in his hands. I took one step forward without thinking, my blood pulsing with desperation.

"Nonono," Edmund taunted. "Remember, he dies first and then you die, and if I am not mistaken, Timothy still lives."

Edmund and his games, I should have known better. I should have expected this. I was a fool to have hesitated. My father should have been dead by my hand. The fact that he wasn't, and that there was some way he had lived through his fall was mildly disturbing.

My jaw clenched, my eyes glaring at him for a moment before moving back to look at where Cail lay on the bed. Choose light, Sain had said. What was he thinking? Light and dark. I thought I had chosen correctly. Had I really chosen the wrong path? I wanted to say no, but I could hear the footsteps of Edmund's army surrounding us, and I felt Sain cower by my feet, his practically useless magic no help to me.

That was fine. I had enough power for both of us.

I narrowed my eyes at Edmund, my lips turning up in eager anticipation. I felt the army surround us as their magic surged through the stone. The large stone cavern was now protected from every angle, trapping us in place.

For the moment.

Forgive me, Cail.

I surged my magic into the rock I stood on, sending Sain into the air as I tapped my toes to the ground, a deep rumble spreading out away from me like a ripple on water. The rock shifted as it opened up and swallowed those around me to the waist before solidifying again and trapping them in the stone. I didn't wait, I knew I only had a matter of minutes to use this diversion, and we needed all the head start we could get. I took off into the air, grabbing Sain around the waist and cutting our bodies through the air toward the exit.

I heard the yells and explosions behind us as the rock I had trapped everyone in was blown apart, releasing those I had trapped from their temporary prison.

"Wynifred!" I felt the ripple of Edmund's magic travel through the air behind me, my body turning as I dodged, afraid of what the magical current he had placed in his words might do to us.

REBECCA ETHINGTON

It was too late anyway, I had gained the time I needed. There was only one way in and out of these caves, through the gate. You couldn't even stutter in entrance or exit, Ilyan had seen to that.

The massive reflective carving that served as the gate into the underground circuit of caves towered above us—the large man sitting astride his horse, surrounded by a large intricate arch.

I angled us toward the carving, toward what appeared to be a wall of solid rock. Without stopping, I pulled us through the rock and into the large canyon on the other side, right into a large group of tourists that had hiked through the moss-covered trench to see the mirror image of the carving that we had just passed through.

Shouts of surprise echoed around us as a few tourists at the front witnessed our miraculous appearance from the stone.

I pulled Sain behind me as I plunged into the thickening crowd of people, the initial shouts drawing others from nearby. I didn't care about their mortal worries right now, I had bigger problems right on my heels. Of those that had seen us appear, many stepped away in fear, while others came closer, their curiosity bringing them dangerously close and slowing our progress. I glared at each of them, unleashing the full anger of my eyes on them.

We were attracting too much attention, and I knew Edmund and the guards he had left were not far behind us. I shielded us quickly, the decision only causing more screams of fright to echo round the dark stone of the canyon as we disappeared from view.

I moved us through the horde of tourists that had congregated around the ancient carving at the end of the damp canyon. The carving was known as the dwarves' door

244

to the tourists, but was known as the gates of Imdalind to my kind. It was those gates I needed to seal.

At this point, I did not care about the upset I caused. If I had, I might have been more careful, but my only goal was to get us in position before Edmund could find us. I needed him out of the cave before I could block the opening and seal him away from the wells of Imdalind.

I pushed people out of the way, causing more fear as people reacted to being manhandled by an invisible entity.

We reached the end of the line of tourists and moved around the edges of the crowd back to the side of the ornate carving we had just emerged from.

My heart thumped in anticipation as I locked my jaw. The tourists had begun to settle down, forgetting what they had seen quickly, as is the case with magic—their fully mortal brains unable to process what had happened. There were a few others, the ones with un-awakened abilities in their blood, who were still so worked up that they were lingering on the edge of panic.

I watched and waited, trying to control my breathing as I placed my hands against the rock face. My magic surged under my skin, the pulse of it matching the hectic beat of my heart. I felt the magic surge again as it prepared to burn the rock and destroy the portal. I needed to find him first.

It was only a matter of minutes before I caught sight of him, my chest tightening at seeing Edmund in the middle of the crowd. He had appeared there, having shielded himself to get through the gate, but unable to maintain his cloak as he moved through the panicking tourists. Edmund was out. Timothy and my brother were still inside.

I narrowed my eyes and let my magic swell , filling the rock behind me with the heavy fire magic, the rock melding and morphing as I urged it to shift. I was careful to keep the labyrinths of mazes intact, careful to keep Cail safe. I moved the rock until I was sure I had covered the entrance, hoping to block Edmund from the wells of Imdalind. Of course, I was also trapping Cail inside, and I was leaving Talon's body behind.

Perhaps forever.

21

WYN

ONE MOMENT. I took one moment and risked closing my eyes to say goodbye. I looked into the blackness behind my lids and said goodbye to my brother. I thanked him for what he had given up to help me and then silently prayed he would be all right and that I would see him again. I said my final goodbye to Talon, the man who had loved me no matter what and had protected me from myself for a hundred years, helping me grow as a person and learn to love life. I placed my hand against the cold stone of the mountain and felt my magic surge, the heat behind my eyes growing as I fought back the tears.

Then the moment was gone. I shoved the pain and loss into the black pit of my icy heart and opened my eyes to the crowd of tourists. They snapped pictures of the carving, made crude signs in front of their cameras and complained about their lack of water. I heard them, but let it all wash over me as my eyes scanned for what I was really looking for.

My magic ran through the ground, serving as my sensor.

It did not work as Ilyan's did; it did not alert me to any power nearby. I had to scan.

It rushed through the ground as I searched for him. My eyes narrowed as I found him near the edge of the crowd, surrounded by at least twenty of his men. Edmund stood still, presumably looking through the crowd for me.

My jaw set in a scowl as I looked at him, my magic pulsing in excitement.

I could take out at least three of Edmund's guards before he would notice, if the tourists surrounding them didn't notice the men turning to pillars of ash right beside them. I doubted that would happen. Besides, I wasn't sure that causing trauma for innocent bystanders was really my thing anymore.

I didn't want it to be.

As much as I could fight, as much as I wanted to, I also knew it wasn't the best choice anymore. I had lost Talon, Ryland was gone, and I had trapped Cail in the caves of Prague with my father.

I stepped closer to Sain as I weighed my options. I needed to get us out of here.

I ignored the stubborn ache in my chest and continued to glare toward Edmund, wishing that I was as heartless as I had been once upon a time.

I needed to get to Ilyan and to Joclyn, so that together we could end this. As much as regaining the fire magic had benefitted me, Joclyn was the only one that could stop the wicked man. I needed to get back to her. Which meant fighting was not an option for us here.

Our best chance was to fly toward Ilyan's ancient evacuation tunnel hidden in the catacombs of St. Vitus Cathedral in downtown Prague.

There were a few problems with this plan. First and

foremost, it was in downtown Prague. We were currently tucked away in the mountains, and it would take me at least fifteen minutes to fly us there, if Edmund didn't track us right away.

The Cathedral also sat in the middle of one of the busiest squares in the old town, and at this time of year, it would be flooded by tourists. I would have to be careful. I couldn't let Edmund follow us, too many people would die. Too many people already had.

"St. Vitus." Sain's voice was a whisper next to me. I had almost forgotten he was there. I turned to face him, not daring to keep my focus off the crowd in front of me for too long.

"Excuse me?" I asked, alarmed that he had somehow seen into my head, which given who he was, was a distinct possibility.

"We are going to St. Vitus, but we need to go by the Orloj where Kadan put his clock. I must retrieve something or this escape will have been in vain." His voice wasn't normal. It wasn't like when he was given the Black Water, but more like when he had told me of Talon's death. I couldn't doubt that what he was saying was true.

Considering what Edmund had done to him over the centuries, it was amazing his sight was still part of him at all, but if this was how the remains of his power chose to make itself known, then I would take all the help I could get.

I grabbed Sain's frail hand and held it in my small one. Our best bet was to fly, and if I could do this without detection, it would be a miracle.

I tensed my bare toes into the loose dirt that I stood on, letting the power inside me build. It bubbled and boiled until my body felt like it was vibrating; the anger and power bleeding together in a torrent that flooded out of me, through the dirt, and into one of the large wooden benches that someone had placed on the side of the path.

The second the power had filled it, I sent a pulse, one strong surge of magic that boomed through the air in a violent explosion. Fire filled the sky as screams of the tourists sounded, the noise barely able to be heard above the echo of the blast that bounced around the small canyon.

Tourists screamed and ran in their mad attempt to escape the blast. People ran into each other, children and women screamed as frantic men trampled over them. I could just make out Edmund as he turned toward the explosion, his eyes scanning the crowd for me.

I wasn't stupid enough to expect him to run toward the blast. He was smart, and hundreds of years of working with him had taught me his weakness.

I dropped the shield around us, the lack of security making us visible to him, but making it easier for me to merge with the crowd. I didn't wait to see if he had noticed us because I knew he would.

I took off running toward the now destroyed bench, my hand tight around Sain's as I weaved us through the terrified hoard that was fleeing the scene.

Please don't let anyone get hurt.

I shielded us again, hoping that our brief stint of visibility was enough time for Edmund to have noticed us and then sent my magic into a bench on the other side of the canyon.

This time, I didn't wait for the pressure to build. I just sent the pulse into the wood and sent the shards of wood into the air in a fiery explosion.

The effect was instantaneous. The remaining tourists screamed and turned to run toward the narrow opening in the canyon that had led them here, the only way to truly escape. They panicked and screamed as they ran, and I was swept up with them as they fled toward safety, their exodus taking Sain and I along for the ride.

Edmund and his guards were forcibly turned about and separated as the crowd intercepted them, forcing them toward the bottleneck that was now forming in the crowd.

At any other time, I might have expected Edmund to attack. He saw mortal life as useless, but they were his cover as much as they were mine. He was being smart.

So was I, and I couldn't wait any longer.

I stomped my foot into the ground, sending out a pulse of energy that shook the mountain. It rippled away from me and sucked the energy out of the legs of all those within range. Mortals fell as the power surged through them, their primitive minds signaling an earthquake as they screamed in fear.

I kept the shield strong around us as I took off into the sky, Sain's body unsupported as he dangled below me. I couldn't risk bringing wind to support his weight as that would be much easier for Edmund to detect. Sain would have to wait until I was sure we were not being followed.

Edmund and his men had fallen to the ground with everyone else, my unexpected magic pulse too much for them to fight against, but he recovered quickly, and instead of searching the people on the ground, he was scanning the skies.

He lifted his hand as his eyes moved, a surge flowing through his palm as he searched for us. His magic waved through the empty skies, and it would only be a matter of seconds before it would intercept with me, signaling to Edmund exactly where we were.

I felt his magic wash over me. It was the sign of the end, but I wasn't going to give up without a fight. I turned abruptly in the air, changing course, hoping that he would assume I had continued in the same direction. Sain dragged through the air below me, my magic making him weightless, but still not able to support him without drawing attention.

I sped us through the canyon and over the farmland that surrounded the beautiful city I had been born in.

"Are they behind us?" I asked, careful to keep my voice low and controlled. "Are we being followed?"

"I don't know..."

My jaw clenched. Of course, we were being followed. It was a stupid question really. My only hope was that they were following the wrong glare of the sun, the wrong gust of wind, that their guess as to where we were going was wrong.

We sped through the air as farmland slowly turned to city. The red-roofed buildings of Prague looked up at us as I moved over the narrow, cobbled streets and right to the center of the city, the small bend in the river serving as my compass.

I set my jaw and increased my speed. I could see the cathedral now and the clock was just on the other side of the river.

We were almost there.

"Wyn! Look out!" Sain screamed, his voice ripping me from my focus on our goal and straight to the car that had exploded away from the ground below us, the large heap of metal making a beeline right for us. I screamed at the sight and reacted, my fear controlling my actions more than my logic.

I blinked once in reflex, and the car exploded in the sky. The weapon that had been hurtled at me turned into a ball of fire in the sky.

I swore loudly and spun out of the way of the explosion, drawing wind to support Sain as I flailed and fear caused my shield to evaporate. Not like it mattered, they obviously knew right where we were anyway.

I twisted my body through the air, searching for them, only to see Edmund streaming toward us, about three hundred feet behind us. For one stupid second, I rejoiced that it was only him, but then reality caught up.

Edmund was right behind us.

I sent my hand out, my magic surging through the air in a line of fire that worked itself into a wall, a barrier that I hoped would slow him down. The wall moved toward him, the attack lingering in the air as I grabbed Sain and dropped us toward the crowded streets below.

"Is he following?" I spat as I dragged the old man behind me by the hand.

"What kind of question is that?" he yelled as we landed in a large courtyard in front of an ornate fountain, cherubs and snakes shooting water behind us. We landed roughly near a large group of people, causing several of them to scream in surprise. "Of course he is following us."

I ignored the group of people. I ignored the screams. I tuned it all out and turned toward the man who was now falling through the sky toward us.

"Your magic... Can you help me?" I asked Sain, my eyes trained on the wicked man who was set on killing us both.

"Not unless you want to know what you are going to have for breakfast."

I couldn't help the smile that spread across my face, the wicked gleam floating up to Edmund who only smiled more.

"Get to the clock. Meet me at the Golden Gate."

I didn't wait for his response. I didn't make sure he could do it; after all, it wouldn't matter if he could get to the clock if I didn't stop Edmund. Or at least slow him down.

That was realistically the only thing I could hope for.

I swung my arms wide, sending what was left of the tourists and residents away from me. They slammed into buildings and landed in the fountain, but I didn't care. If I didn't get them away, something far worse was going to happen to them. Broken bones they could recover from, melting skin they could not.

I let my magic surge through my feet. It connected with the magic of the cobbled street I stood on and grew as it rushed through the stones, shaking me as the road vibrated. The cobbles that had been laid thousands of years ago rattled and pulled themselves out of the ancient plaster they had been set in. They hovered above the ground as my magic seeped into them, heating them, melting them.

I watched Edmund's hands rise toward me, his palms growing white as he prepared to rain down acid through the air around me.

He had his trick, and I had mine.

The molten rock flew toward him as the white light grew in his hands. I shielded myself from his attack, my magic pushing me out of the way as the lava intercepted with him, the molten clumps of rock colliding with his powerful shield. His shield flashed and flickered as the boiling hot earth wove its way through it. It splattered against his hands and his face as his momentum flew him into it, his body falling to the ground as the white magic disappeared.

I could hear the yell of his pain, the agony behind it. He was definitely injured, possibly weakened from the attack, and for one moment, I thought that I might be able to turn him to ash, not just a single finger as I had done once before. I knew better, though; he would recover quickly thanks to the Vilỳ poison he infected himself with every night. One bite to strengthen him and then he would throw the creature's lifeless body away until there were none left.

I moved without looking at him, my bare feet turning to take me in a run toward the river. I ran through the narrow streets of Prague, the beige rock fronts of the buildings a mellowing calm over the frantic beat of my heart pounding in my chest.

My feet padded against the stones, and with each step, I let my magic flow through the rock, tracking where he was. I had only barely turned the corner before his signature disappeared from the ground. He had already recovered and was chasing after me.

I shouldn't be surprised.

I brought my magic to me and increased my pace as I raced and weaved between people. I pushed them out of my way, throwing them into walls and small cafes as I jumped and raced away from him. Each step increased my fear, my expectation, but still Edmund had not reached me. As much as I wished I would be the one to kill him, I knew it wasn't my destiny. My only chance for survival was to get away from him.

I could see the break in the buildings, the grey of the river, and the Úřad vlády České just on the other side.

I had just turned the last corner toward the river when his warm body collided with mine, the force of the impact sending me headlong into the white bricked wall I had been running next to. A loud crack echoed in my ears as the impact split the stone.

I felt my skull crack, my magic congregating at the wound as it repaired the damage. My head swam for a moment as the painful headache grew and then ebbed, my magic doing its best to keep me in one piece.

Edmund turned to face me. I couldn't help smiling at the

red welts of melted skin that lined his face and arms. The angry red marks boiled and blistered where the scalding rocks had hit him, the largest gashes healing visibly as his magic surged.

"Wynifred!" he howled as he slammed his hand into the wall by my head, another crack growing to join the first as he pinned my arms above me.

"Yes, Edmund?" I said causally, as if we were just enjoying a romantic stroll.

"I am glad to see you're back to yourself, now stop attacking me and get back to work." He moved his other hand to rest against my cheek, and I smiled. I smiled at him the way I had for centuries before letting my magic flare through my cheek and into his hand.

He yelled out in pain, his grip on my wrists increasing as his own anger flared.

"You can't have me, Edmund," I growled.

I felt the heat behind his hand grow, the temperature scalding me. It hurt, but I refused to scream. I simply smiled at him, narrowing my eyes in a challenge. His anger grew and he howled before my body flew into the air as he threw me away from him only to land in the middle of the murky waters of the Vltava River.

My body hit the water with a loud slap that seized through me in an agonizing ripple and cut all sensation from my muscles. I sunk into the cold water, kicking and squirming as I fought the sinking of my body into the river. Suddenly, a warm hand wrapped around my neck. The strong hand pressed roughly against my water-filled windpipe as it pulled me up through the waves and held me just below the surface of the lapping waves.

I looked into Edmund's face from where he held me under the grey water, my last breath held in my chest, his crazed face mad with victory. I attempted to fight him, but the lack of air made it more and more difficult.

"Think you can escape me and go back to that little half-breed? I will never let you win. Never!" he yelled so loud, his voice bellowing from above the water, as his manic power convinced him of his imminent success, but no, I was not ready to let him win just yet.

I wouldn't give in that easily.

The bubbling energy of my magic moved through my veins, boiling within me. I could feel the fire magic taking over.

I smiled at him from beneath the murky water.

His face paled, his crazed energy flickering before growing again, convinced there was nothing more I could do. The light from my body grew, reflecting off his face as I gazed at him from underneath the murky waters.

The water began to boil around me, the river turning into a boiling pot around my super-heated body. Edmund yelled out and attempted to release his hands, but I held them in place, my hands moving to wrap around his wrists and hold them down.

"No!" he spat, his voice muffled through the water in my ears. I felt his hands pulse, and my body convulsed underneath the water, the electrical attack frying the tips of my nerve endings.

Pain shot through me in a million volts. It buzzed painfully around me.

My mouth opened as I yelled in agony. The sound waves of my scream reverberated through the water as they burst from me, the water splashing away and splattering Edmund's face with scalding water. Edmund yelled again as the attack hit him, but he flattened his hands against my skin and sent pulse after pulse of paralyzing energy through my body.

I screamed with a jolt that rippled down my spine, wave after wave they incapacitated me. I didn't know how much I could take.

I let go of his wrists, my mind struggling to send the command to the weak grip I now had. Slowly, my hands loosened as Edmund laughed maniacally, believing his attempt to kill me was succeeding.

My lungs burned for air as my hands flew toward Edmund's face, the urge to kill him pulsing through me, my magic strong as it plunged into him.

Anyone else would have turned to ash, but I knew that with Edmund, this attack would never end in his death. The best I could hope for was a few lost fingers, maybe a singed ear lobe, and the time to get away.

He yelled out as the pain hit him, my energy a pulse that sent him flying through the air away from me.

I pushed myself out of the water, my magic taking over as I threw myself into the air. I hacked and gasped as I flung myself through the sky like a ragdoll, only to eventually right myself and quicken my pace as Edmund's yells behind me increased.

I turned my body toward the green copper roof of St. Vitus cathedral, the golden arches of the south entrance glittering at me in the distance. The tall, stone arches sparkled in the sun, the sandstone appearing as bright as gold in the setting rays of light.

I could hear Edmund yell from somewhere behind me, the sound increasing as he got closer.

Please let Sain have made it to the gates already. I didn't have time to wait, and I was going to have to seal the gate once I passed through it. I just wished I had enough time to complete the process.

I dropped my body closer to the earth, my heart beating quicker when I saw Sain standing near the large golden stone work of the gate, a large earthen mug clutched against his chest.

"Run!" I screamed when I was within distance.

Sain looked up at me, confused for only a moment before he turned and bolted down the hall, toward the large chapel.

I didn't slow my speed for landing. I flew right into the courtyard, my hard landing exploding bricks into the air at the rough impact. I straightened myself and turned to face the courtyard just beyond the gates.

The few tourists in the courtyard looked through the rubble. For the most part, confusion covered their faces.

Edmund was right behind me.

I set my jaw and raised my hand, a shimmering shield flowing from my fingers to cover the large opening of the golden gate.

My magic surged out of me as it spread in a curtain between the giant arches. I looked through the magical barrier to see Edmund change his course in order to intercept me.

He was almost here, and the shield had not set yet. I pushed harder, my teeth clenching as I grunted through the pressure, yelling as the exertion hit its maximum and my magic pushed and pulled to escape from me.

My mouth opened as I screamed, the shield setting itself into the stone the moment Edmund's body hit hard against the barrier. The impact of his collision rumbled through me, shooting me away from the shield and slamming me into the high wall behind me.

I straightened myself the same moment Edmund did, his jaw as set as mine as he turned to face me. His eyes stared into mine, the whites blood shot with anger and power. I had never seen him this worked up. I could tell at once that this shield would only hold for a matter of minutes once he decided to come at me.

Edmund uncoiled his body as he faced me, his hand lifting to his face. A large chunk of his arm was missing, the edges blackened with ash. Even with all of my power, that was all I had been able to accomplish against him.

He smiled at me as he bit down on his finger, the one I had burned off all those centuries ago, the replacement forcibly taken from one of his many servants. He bit down on it and pulled, the flesh separating slowly, his hand dripping with blood as he ripped the finger from his hand.

"I have a present for you, Wynifred," he sneered, his breathing shallow as some power-based insanity threatened to take over him.

"Keep it," I spat, turning from him. I didn't want to be on the receiving end of whatever he had to give me ever again.

I had barely turned my back on him before I heard the heavy clang of an attack against the gate.

I didn't turn to see what he had done. I let the angry yells that Edmund filled the air with wash over me as I ran. The clangs and yells of Edmund's attacks lessened the further I moved from the barrier, but I focused on them, knowing they would grow the second the shield collapsed.

I overtook Sain quickly, his pace quick in the panic that seeped off him, but his body not up to the strain.

"You will have to seal the door to the tombs. Otherwise, we will not have enough time." Sain's voice was low as he spoke, his pace not nearly fast enough for us to get away.

"You think I don't know that already?" I grabbed his arm,

knowing he was too weak to move fast enough, and pushed him forward through the ancient chapel we had entered.

I would have loved to walk quietly through the massive space, bask in the ancient architecture of the buttresses and stained glass windows I had known since I was a child. However, the manic yelling of the man behind us was a heavy reminder of the desperate situation we had found ourselves in.

The calm heads of the pious people turned at our frantic movements and the yells that followed us in. I saw the ancient priest step forward in his long black robes, his hands extended in welcome and worry.

He was sweet and kind. All of these people were, and I knew Edmund would kill him.

"Utíkej!" I yelled to the old priest. His face opened in horror as the high screech of my voice broke through the relative quiet of the cathedral.

He wasn't moving. Fine, I would make him.

I lifted my hand as we passed him, his body lifting ten feet into the air before I sent him tumbling into a confessional.

It was enough.

Edmund's growing screams mixed with the new fear of those in the chapel. I saw people cowering against walls, hiding under pews, and a select few darted toward the main door to the beautiful room.

I didn't wait to watch them hide. I kept my attention in front of me. There were only a few rooms to go before we would reach the catacombs, only a few minutes before we would reach Ilyan's tomb. We could make it.

We could.

Sain and I turned at the ancient pulpit at the head of the chapel to dart through the heavy, wooden door to the left of one of the many sandstones statues. I heard the door slam behind us, and for one brief moment, we were trapped in silence. I listened to my labored breathing, Sain's panting, and felt the tightness of my chest adding to the panic I felt.

"To the door," Sain whispered.

I nodded once before continuing to drag him behind me.

My heart beat and sputtered as we moved through the small, bare hallways of the offices and apartments of the clergy before coming to a lone, black, stone door at the end of the empty hallway.

The catacombs.

My hand touched the ancient knob of the door as the door several halls behind us opened, releasing the screams we had trapped in the main chapel back into our ears.

He was coming.

I caught my scream in my chest. The door swung open and I shooed Sain into the dark, damp space in front of us, closing the door behind us as quietly as I could.

The smell of ancient death hit my nose. The long forgotten smell of loss ignited my panic even further.

I sealed the door, my magic closing the cracks and melting the stone together into a solid slab of rock.

It was pointless really; Edmund knew where we were going, but anything I could do to slow him down, I would.

22

WYN

Our breathing escaped in a rush as our feet moved us down the winding stone steps and into the depths of the tombs below the cathedral.

"Faster," Sain panted. I didn't know if he spoke to me or to himself, but I took it at as a warning and let my magic flood through both of us, increasing our pace.

We flew down the staircase as the air became damper, the light dimming as it welcomed us into the home of the dead. We reached the base of the staircase, the dark expanse of the tombs a vivid reminder of the prison we had just left behind—the prison I had left my mate in.

I couldn't think that way.

Death filled my lungs as we moved past the large, dark stacks of bones that made up the walls of the labyrinth we had walked into. Skulls smiled at us, each one a casualty of plague or war. The bones served as a warning to grave robbers, but it was not one I needed to heed. We were going into a tomb, not taking things out of one.

My magic heightened my sight as we moved through the maze of bones, while Sain's green light once again shone brightly in front of us as it led the way. We moved quietly through the deathly green hues, waiting for the sound of the door exploding off its hinges.

The sound never came.

My heart beat wildly within me. I was having trouble keeping my focus. Edmund should be here by now, something was wrong. My nerves prickled as my heart called out 'trap', putting me on high alert.

Sain's feet stopped in place, our intertwined hands pulling me to a quick stop in front of him. I gasped at the sudden stop, the sharp intake of breath echoing around the open space that surrounded us.

"He is here," Sain whispered, and my whole body turned to ice. "Do not fight him, or we will not survive."

We stayed still in the labyrinth of bones as Sain's words settled into my mind. Edmund had moved beyond the door.

The sound of our breathing joined with a drip of water that was falling somewhere around us. The sounds bled together as they bounced off the bones and amplified themselves.

I took a hesitant step forward, the heavy thump of my heart against my ribs causing me physical pain.

We took one step after another, my bare feet flooding with magic with each contact with the stone of the floor. Sain stayed close, his breathing heavy in my ear. I was his only protection.

We moved through the labyrinth of bones at a snail's pace, my head peeking around each corner before we moved, my feet dragging through puddles of stagnant water in an attempt to keep my connection to the earth's magic.

I shivered as we moved into the large space of the catacombs, the ceilings higher, the roof speckled with small windows that let ribbons of light into the ancient hall.

I froze in place as I searched for him. But I felt nothing, saw nothing. I wanted to believe that Edmund was not here —but I felt Sain's tense body beside mine. I couldn't doubt Sain's sight.

"Where is he?"

Sain said nothing in reply, the quiet that surrounded us only interrupted by the occasional echo of a drip of water. I turned to face him, his eyes wide as he focused on the bright white coffin that the mortals had buried Ilyan in when he resigned as their ruler, faking his own death more than six hundred years ago.

I turned toward it, expecting to see Edmund standing right beside it, but the large hall was still empty. The room was silent except for my ever-increasing breathing.

I took a step into the room, Sain following as he cowered behind me. My bare foot accidentally slapped hard against the smooth stone of the floor, the sound echoing around us. I froze. If Edmund was down here, I had just given away our exact location.

"Ruuuuun," Sain breathed out, his voice shaking as his whole body began to convulse.

His words were lost as my pulse quickened. I turned toward him, only to see his body shake, his eyes darkening into black and then fading back into green. His body convulsed beside me as his eyes flashed between colors, his mouth opening in a silent scream. Sain's eyes widened as if his whole face was being stretched.

I forgot to breathe as I stared at him, the panic taking away my ability to process what he had said.

"Ruuuuun," he repeated again, his voice deep and hollow.

This time the word sank in; it ignited inside of me and sent my feet moving in a panic, Sain's body dragging behind me as his feet stumbled in a blind attempt to follow.

Our feet hit heavy against the floor, our breathing mixed with the hollowness of our steps. Each sound hit my ear, the urgency of each one increasing as we made our way toward what was now our only chance of escape.

"I'm going to hurt Cail, Wynifred." I froze at Edmund's voice, my feet coming to a stop only inches from the tomb that would lead us to safety.

"I'm going to rip his body apart, piece by piece. Hundreds of years of disloyalty needs to be punished after all." His voice was loud, his heavy breathing making the desperation, the madness, heavier in his voice.

I couldn't move as I listened to him, as the echo of his words hit my ears over and over. I fought for control. I fought to recall the words Sain had said only moments ago.

"I am going to make him pay."

"If you can get in," I said simply, unable to control my mouth as I took the last step toward the tomb.

"You think a little fire can stop me? I will be back in there before nightfall, you little slut. Then I will do to Cail what I did to Rosaline. I will remove his soul from his body, as slowly and as painfully as I can."

"No!" I couldn't help the sound that came from my mouth. I turned around to face him, my fingers clawing at my thighs with the need to rip his eyes from his face.

Edmund stood at the entrance we had just come through, his smile wide as he watched my panic. His eyes flashed as he watched me, his dark hair loosened from its usual tightly gelled style, his hand dripping blood from where he had ripped the finger from his body.

This had been his plan. He knew I wouldn't back down from this threat; he knew and so did Sain. Sain wrapped his arms around me as he attempted to keep me back, to stop me from attacking.

"Do not fight, Wynifred," Sain hissed in my ear, the reminder of his sight from only moments ago barely grazing the surface of my panic.

"I will rip him apart, limb by limb, until there is no more blood to shed, until his soul has given up. I will take his soul, Wynifred, and I will use it the way I use Rosaline's. I will keep it in a place you will never find it. Not that you will be alive much longer than he is."

"NO!" I fought against Sain, his weak body using up the last of his energy in an attempt to keep me at bay.

"I would do the same to Talon... if he was still alive."

I could hear Sain mumble behind me. I could hear him gasp as my magic surged under my skin, burning him on contact. He didn't budge. He endured the pain as he attempted to keep me safe.

Stay safe, Wynny.

My fight left me as Talon's voice echoed through my head, his words joining Sain's in a jumbled mess that pulled the fight out of me.

I stopped struggling against Sain's hold. I looked down to the stone floor of the catacombs, my eyes scanning over the tombs that littered the floor in front of us before I raised my head to look at Edmund.

Edmund smiled at the look in my eye, at the way my lips pursed. He believed he had won, that I would fight him now and he would win. He was a fool to think I was so easily predictable anymore.

I wasn't who he still thought me to be.

I was Wyn.

My eyes locked with his as I sent my magic surging through the floor of the tomb, the ancient magic in the stone collecting with mine to supercharge the pulse, which hit in a surge that shot him straight into the air.

Edmund yelled as his body impacted with the roof of the tombs, the magic still flowing through his body painfully.

I pulled Sain with me as I turned, the lid of Ilyan's coffin lifting just enough to allow us passage inside.

Edmund's screams died as we slipped ourselves through the opening, the magical barrier of Ilyan's protection washing over me as I moved through it.

There was no way Edmund could follow us here. For the moment, we were safe.

"Wynifred!" Edmund yelled. I turned, my eyes peering at him through the gap in the lid. "I will make him pay."

"I will retrieve both of their souls, Edmund, right before I rip your heart from your body."

He balked at my statement, his face going white before the lid to the coffin dropped, enclosing us in the dark space.

I listened to Sain's breathing equalize alongside mine as we waited for a sign that Edmund was trying to follow us, as we waited for his attempt to break through the barrier Ilyan had placed around the tomb.

But none came.

A deep green light flared in Sain's hand, and I looked toward it, my heart calming to see the relief on his face. We just looked at each other, neither of us having the words for what had just happened.

Sain turned toward the tunnel that opened up behind him, the long, dark abyss that would lead us safely underground and right into Italy. His light flickered along the walls of dirt and stone until the tunnel faded into an endless stretch of claustrophobic black.

In any other situation, I would have been scared at

seeing an endless enclosed space. Instead, I felt my heart relax at the promise of safety it held for us.

"We'd better hurry," Sain whispered as he stepped into the tunnel, the first step of a long journey.

I rushed to catch up with him, his words sending ice down my spine.

"What do you mean?" I asked, dearly hoping he hadn't seen anything else.

"We don't have a lot of time." Sain didn't look at me as he spoke; he simply continued walking, his slow pace taking us straight forward.

"Is he coming?" My voice slithered over my tongue, the fear rushing right back to the surface.

"No," Sain answered as he turned to face me, "but you have less time than I originally thought."

Sain reached forward and grabbed my left hand, lifting my arm to eye level. I looked at him in confusion, trying to make sense of his words. His eyes darted to my arm.

"Sain?" I asked, my eyes following his to my arm and then returning to him as I tried to make sense of what he was saying.

"Edmund has plans for your brother. We must get you to Joclyn before it is too late."

23

ILYAN

THE LARGE MAP of the grounds that surrounded the abbey took up the majority of the expansive table that stood at the end of the long kitchen. I stood over it, facing the crumbling stone ovens and fireplaces that had once been used by the monks of Rioseco for food preparation. I stared at the map, ignoring the twinge of guilt from using this room as a planning room for the battle that was coming closer and closer.

It had been seven days since we had been found and the first eight camps appeared. Now we could see twenty-two. Each one was marked by a small, red dot on the map, the number of how many we assumed to be in each camp marked in quill pen beside it. The camps kept coming, and still no Ovailia.

Joclyn had been trapped in the Tôuha for almost two weeks—three months for her. For three months, Edmund had been torturing her. I had healed her after every attack, but the injuries still kept coming. Last night, they plagued her over and over until, in the end, I had to restart her heart, my magic manually pumping it in an attempt to keep her alive. Futile, that was how it felt.

My only hope for her now was Ryland.

I scanned my eyes over the paper, trying to find a rhyme or reason to the pattern, but once again finding nothing. That didn't necessarily mean anything though. It could simply mean that the Trpaslíks did not follow instructions, which was common.

I snatched a strawberry out of one of the bowls that held down the massive paper, moving around to the other side of the table, hoping another angle would help.

"One new camp last night," I said as Dramin walked in, his energy slow and lagging from having just woken up. He came up beside me, and I pointed to the newest red dot, the ink on the number six still drying.

"One is better than ten," he chuckled, his reference to yesterday's surge making me cringe.

Yes, one was better than ten, and after they had come so steadily, it only left me worrying about what was still coming. I stretched my hands out to hover above the map, trying another view, but nothing jumped out at me.

"Do we have a plan yet?" Dramin asked, but I only laughed humorlessly at him.

At this point, if Joclyn didn't wake, it would be me against upwards of a hundred Trpaslíks with a little help from Thom. While I had defeated that number before, it was not without grave injury, something that would take time to recover from, and I had been alone at the time. There were many other considerations when I had to protect the people around me. With the impending assault my father had planned, I doubted I had any time on my hands for either healing or complicated strategy.

"Does all this happen before or after Joclyn wakes?" I asked.

"Does it matter?"

"It might," I prompted, careful to keep my voice light. "When does she wake?"

"Soon." Dramin grunted a bit as he sat down beside me, his hands already wrapped around a full mug of Black Water. I stared at the water as if it had offended me. We had given Joclyn the water for the past four days and nothing had happened. No waking, no more sights. She stayed still every time, laid out on the wide couch that had been placed in one of my side rooms years ago, now used only to supplement Joclyn's nutrition.

I sat down heavily next to Dramin, my eyes still focused on the poison in his hands.

"Do you suppose," I began, careful to keep my voice level and innocent as I didn't need a commanding tone to set Dramin on his guard, "myslíš, žeif we could give her another sight, she might wake? We could pour the water over my skin first." I cringed internally as I spoke, the pain from my last burn still strong in my veins. Most of the time it was just a dull hum of an ache, but sometimes it would flare up in agony.

When I had been given the sight about Joclyn eight hundred years ago, I had experienced the painful burn of the Black Water for centuries; shadows of the pain still plagued me when something would rub against the scars, namely fabric. There was no reason to expect anything less this time around. I was mad to even suggest it.

"I'm not sure what that much Black Water inside of anyone other than a Drak would do," Dramin said simply, but his words set me on high alert.

"Uvnitř?" My voice must have sounded much deeper than I thought because Dramin chuckled, his dark green eyes and youthful face turning toward me.

"Yes, Ilyan, inside. Why do you think it still burns? It will burn until your magic has changed it enough to let it flow comfortably through your veins. Even then, it is still Black Water. It's just more you than Imdalind at that point."

I stared at him wide-eyed. I had never heard this before. I was raised to be King, raised with all the knowledge of our kind so as to be able to lead them. But this, though? I had never heard this before.

"I just entrusted you with our only secret, Ilyan. You better keep it that way." Dramin smiled at me, but it was sad, his eyes were shaded by something... Regret? I couldn't see Dramin ever regretting anything, but then, he had just released a secret the Drak had seen fit to keep from everyone since the beginning of time.

"So what does that mean for me?" I asked, my eyes narrowing at him. Dramin only laughed at me, his usual joyful timber coming back into his voice.

"You have had Black Water flowing through your veins for eight hundred years and now you worry? Nebojte se," he said as he patted my hand in a grandfatherly way, an action that did not match his appearance. "You will be fine. All I said was that I did not know what would happen. If there was a threat of an additional head sprouting on your shoulders, we would have never consented to give you, or anyone else, access to the sight."

He laughed and I felt everything relax inside of me. He was right. I had feared the possibility of a greater ability. I did not need more power. I already feared the strength of the magic that flowed through my veins.

"Well," Dramin began before draining the last of his mug, "I'll go get Joclyn ready. Come to her after you finish with Thom."

"Thom?" I questioned, not understanding.

Dramin nodded once before standing, the sound of Thom's yells reaching my ears as he did so.

"Ilyan!" The excited yell of Thom's voice echoed around the stone hallways before reaching the kitchen.

"I guess I'll go see what he wants, shall I?" I laughed alongside Dramin as we both left the kitchen; Dramin leaving to go toward my suite where Joclyn slept, and I moved toward Thom's frantic yells.

Thom's voice ricocheted around the stone hallways. To anyone else, the bounce of his voice would have made it impossible to know where he was, but I could sense his magic. His deep earth energy was strong with excitement as he moved closer to me, the excitement mixing with panic the closer he got.

I had almost reached him when his odd mix of emotions hit me hard, setting me on high alert, and I moved faster. Curiosity and panic mingled inside of me with each step.

Thom turned the corner at a dead heat, his feet sliding as he caught sight of me. His face was wide and alert in excitement, but I could hear the rapid rate of his breath in my ears, the pace too quick to be purely excited.

My curiosity left as fear took its place, a million possibilities leapt to mind, but deep down I knew—they were attacking. My heart pulsed once in desperation, begging me to simply take Joclyn and fly away—to save her. The thought was only a breeze from a bird's wing before it was gone, before inheritance and responsibility took its place.

We said nothing to each other; I just picked up my pace, and followed him as he turned back the way he had come. His short legs moved fast as he ran, his magic pulsing through him as he quickened his pace. It wasn't until he turned toward the large garden on the west side of the chapel that the fear in me shifted.

The camps were arranged on the north side. Had we missed something? Something new, bigger?

Everything thumped in time with my footsteps, my heart beating in my ears and my breath moving in time with my steps.

Without thinking about it, I moved my magic to check on Joclyn, shielding her as much as I dared.

We turned one more corner before Thom stopped, my feet halting right behind him before I collided with him.

This was not what I had expected, it was worse.

Ovailia stood in the middle of the hall we ran through, her long, blonde hair down to her waist and a smug smile in place, as if she expected me to praise her for a job well done. However, it wasn't a job well done. It was a nightmare.

Ryland stood right next to her. *Stood.* His eyes were bright blue. His hair was damp with sweat, making the dark curls he got from our father longer than usual. He looked at me with understanding, with knowledge, and with eager anticipation. He was awake, and he remembered me.

"Where is Joclyn?" Ryland's voice was eager, panicked. I could feel his need and longing as it settled deeply into his voice.

I would have gladly taken him to her right then, except that his alertness was a signal to something much worse. Joclyn was still asleep, trapped in a Töuha that she supposedly shared with Ryland.

"You're awake." I couldn't help the panic that edged into my voice. As much as I needed to be the royal leader right then, I just couldn't. I saw Ovailia's brow furrow, but she said nothing.

"Yeah." He took a step toward me, ready to plead his case, ready to see her.

"But, the Tòuha?"

"Dad broke our bond... last week... I..." Ryland's voice trailed off as my soul turned to ice.

I said nothing as I turned and ran down the hall. I didn't know what to say. I didn't know how to explain. How could I when I had no idea what was wrong?

I heard footsteps behind me, knowing they would follow, knowing I could not stop them, but I couldn't waste time trying. I barely heard them; I could only hear my panicked breathing. I could only feel my heart clunk against the frail bones in my chest. Everything was falling apart inside of me.

I passed the ancient architecture, passed the ornate window I helped set. I passed it all without seeing. I ran without knowing. I followed the beat of my heart, the pull of my soul. My magic had already gone to her; it filled her completely, checking for something I might have missed. She couldn't just be a shell, she couldn't.

I slammed the door into my suite open, not bothering to close it, not bothering to say anything before moving into the small side room. Joclyn's body was still and small on the large couch. She didn't move, didn't turn. Could she not hear my heart beat for her? Could she not feel my terror?

When I entered, the room was empty accept for Joclyn. Dramin had obviously gone for something, leaving the large mug of Black Water on the table beside her. I grabbed it without thinking, my fear and worry taking over my better judgment.

"Mi lasko!" My voice was loud. The panic in me, scared me. I had never felt this afraid. Hearing my panic so deep in my own ears shook me.

I moved to sit over her, my legs on either side as I lifted her head, settling her onto the couch in a more comfortable way. My hand moved to her face, my finger tracing her lips for only a moment before I opened her jaw, her mouth sagging. I placed my fingers just inside, cupping my hand before her mouth, like a bowl, a bowl for poison. I tilted the mug, focusing on the determination in my soul and the steady beat of her heart before I poured the water into my hand, the slope of my skin forming a ramp into her mouth.

The sound of my pain exited my body with a howl of agony and misery. My voice hit stone and glass before bouncing back to me, but I barely heard. The sound of my agony that now shot through my veins only grew before the water had gone from the mug, leaving her face wet and dripping. I yelled as I willed the pain to die down, the burn only growing. I held my hand up in fear, my mouth opening at the sight of the seeping blister that now covered the palm of my hand, my voice continuing to howl at the agony that was threatening to incapacitate me.

This pain was worse than the brands on my chest, worse than the accidental drip on my arm. This was torture. I howled as I collapsed onto her, my body tensing as it attempted to manage the pain that I was now racked with. I held her to me as every muscle seized, as my throat burned with the howls that escaped from me.

The water tugged at me, pulling something out of me and took it into her. The heavy strand of magic moved the pain through me and centered it over the Štít, over our connection. The burn grew as the water pulled at me, changed me. I could feel her more acutely than I had ever done before, her heartbeat bounced in my ears, her breathing moved over my chest. I felt her inside of me as well as alongside me, my mind aware of her as if I was her.

The connection pulled stronger and stronger, unlike anything I had ever felt before or anything I had ever heard of. I focused on it as it grew and encompassed me. The water that flowed through my veins connected with the water that now lived inside of her. It was all I could focus on; her body, her soul, the thin thread of her consciousness that trailed far away, and next to that... the thin thread that connected her to the Töuha. I had found it.

"Mi lasko! Snap out of it! Get out of there!" I could feel her, somewhere deep inside. I could still feel that thread, the clarity of it shining at me like a golden ribbon.

Joclyn's heartbeat increased inside of me, the sound of my voice increasing the tempo for only a moment before she relaxed again. At least, I hoped it was my voice she was reacting to. *Please let her hear me.* I said the words to myself, a silent prayer to a silent deity.

"Joclyn! Come back to me!" My tears flowed unbidden as I looked at her still body and felt the slow ache when her heartbeat did not respond. "Joclyn!"

I could feel the bridge that the water had created between us leaving, the strength of the connection moving away from me. I couldn't stop my movement as I pressed my hands to her face, the angry burn on my hand pressing itself against the soft skin of her cheek.

The strong pulse of her magic surged through the raw skin of my hand at the touch. It rocked through me and my spine straightened, the power rough and violent as it filled me.

I could feel the warmth of her body, the silky texture of her skin, but more than that, I could feel her again. I could feel *her* inside of me. Somehow the water had bridged me to her, connected my body with hers.

"Dramin!" I yelled his name, knowing he wouldn't know what this was, or how to keep it, but he would have water, and perhaps the water could strengthen the connection again. The water had brought the clarity; I needed the water to keep the clarity strong. "Dramin! Bring the water!"

Dramin ran into the room before I could even finish talking, his face calm for a moment before he saw me kneeling over Joclyn and the tears on my face. I could only imagine how I must have looked, how desperate I must have seemed because I felt it inside me. I could feel the pain, the anguish, the desperation.

I looked at him with all of my weaknesses on my face, no façade, just me. He looked at me for one minute before the realization hit him and his own panic took over his face.

"What in land's name is going on here?"

"Ovailia has returned. It was just as Joclyn said... Ryland's here." I tried to keep the emotion out of my voice, tried to regain my composure, but it didn't seem to be working. It didn't want to take. "He's awake."

"What do you mean he is awake?" I could hear the confusion in his voice, and it made sense. Joclyn was sleeping, so Ryland should be, too.

"Joclyn!" I yelled. "Ovailia brought him. He is fine. But the bond is gone. Edmund broke it weeks ago."

My voice bounced around the room before I looked back at Dramin, hoping that he would understand me by the desperation in my eyes. He only stared at me, his heart breaking. I didn't want to think about what that look could mean, what that pain was for.

This could not be allowed to happen. It was not the end. I had seen my path, and my path was her. I had seen the end, seen my love for her and hers for me. I had seen everything. It was her. She was my everything. I would wait a thousand more years to experience those sights, but they would come to pass. They could not just be another of the zlomený. I wouldn't allow it.

"But, she is still sleeping... She's been sleeping for two weeks..." My eyes looked away from Dramin; I couldn't stand to try to explain something that I didn't understand. "How can she be..."

Dramin came to stand next to me, his hand moving to lay against Joclyn's face. His touch was soft against her cheek as he filled her with his magic. My eyes moved to glare into him as I felt his magic surge, the power of it right up against mine. I had never felt Dramin's magic so strongly. It wasn't the same deep magic of the Drak I was used to feeling; this was bright and strong. It almost felt powerful.

Dramin looked at me in wonder, the gleam in his eyes making it clear that he had found my new connection to Joclyn. He had known what the Black Water would do inside my veins after all.

I turned my hand toward him, showing him the angry welt that covered my palm. My face cringed as I let the pain show through my eyes, my chest still locking the rest of my pain inside.

Dramin's eyes went wide as they stared at my hand in silence. With one nod, he pushed more of his magic into her, the flow wide and strong. The burn on my hand had obviously opened up something inside me. It was more than the connection with Joclyn; I could feel the hidden strength of a Drak now. Our magic was able to work together for one minute before the connection changed.

Suddenly, I felt it inside of me, even though I knew it was inside of her. The repressive force of the heavy black mark that had hidden the thin strand of fine gold ribbon that her mind had followed to enter the Tòuha.

I found it.

I found *her*.

"It's a Vymàzat."

"What?" Dramin's hand pulled away from Joclyn's face, the mug in his other hand dropping to the floor in surprise. "How did you miss that? You tried everything—"

"I didn't miss it. It was hidden," I said as I pushed my magic into her, feeling it move through her as it would in me. My awareness of her body swelled within me. I felt everything. I felt the thick ridge of the curse inside the hollow cavity of her mind. The curse had spread like spider webs over her skull, so thin and fine, it was no wonder I had missed it. Whatever Edmund had done to her, he had hidden it well. Just not well enough.

I kept pushing my magic into her, my body beginning to feel weak and heavy as my power smothered her. I pushed as I worked to reverse the Vymàzat, to remove it from inside her.

"Ilyan, you can't possibly be saying what I think you are saying..." Dramin's voice just washed over me, my mind focused on the mountain of work before me.

I pushed into her, laying my magic over the curse repressively as I attacked it. I surged my magic violently through it until the thick strands of my father's curse began to break loose, the bands loosening away from her spinal column. It was there, with the sensation of her within me, that I felt her mind coming back.

Joclyn's mind, her soul, was clicking back into place as the Vymàzat loosened its grip on her. Her mind moved back into her, like a child playing with dominos—one piece falling after another as they moved into place. I could feel the heavy threads of her thoughts, the increased panic of her breathing, the elevated rate of her heart, and her hand against my shoulder.

24

ILYAN

I COULD FEEL her hand on my shoulder.

I almost lost contact with her at the touch. It felt so real and yet, she still lay unmoving below me. I could feel the touch of her skin against mine, the energy of her magic surging at the contact. It was her. My head spun toward the soft touch, my eyes widening at the broken, disheveled girl who stood beside me.

It was Joclyn, I could see it in the silver of her eyes and the angles of her face, but everything else was foreign. Her hair, once long and straight, was matted in long, tangled masses. Bloodied bits of scalp peeked through the large bald patches where the hair had been pulled out.

I scanned her body as my brain slowly began to register what I was seeing, as I began to understand the things that had happened to her. Her clothes were ripped and torn, the tattered fragments covered with dirt and blood as they hung from her emaciated body. Her skin was covered with bruises, cuts and burns.

I looked away from the horrific sight only to come back to the same beautiful face on the couch below me.

I looked back to the battered girl. My soul felt like it was being ripped in two by seeing her there; the giant rent began in my toes and moved through me in an earthquake of regret and fear, ripping my heart into pieces.

She looked at me with her silver eyes, the confidence I had watched her develop over the last few months so weak I could barely see it. Her power had been beaten out of her. As I watched her, I could see a shadow of that power return, the strength of her gaze growing as I stared into her, as I felt her memory click fully back into place.

My eyes darted back and forth from the girl I sat over to the ghostly apparition in front of me, my heart unwilling to accept the horrors I was seeing. My eyes had only returned to hers for a moment before I felt the shadow girl's hands hard against my chest, pushing me off the living girl's body. I fell to the floor, just as the hands of both girls rose in preparation to attack.

I yelled at the same time as Joclyn's broken body, her mouth moving as she spoke to someone that my vision would not allow me to see. No sound escaped her lips, even though I knew she was speaking. Her strength seeped back into her eyes as she screamed at whoever had been attacking her, as once again, she prepared to fight back.

There was barely a warning before Joclyn's hands exploded with energy, the magic soaring into the physical realm from the hands of the girl who lay sleeping on the faded upholstery.

My magic wrapped her in a heavy shield, her attack impacting with it, my soul acting on its own in response to her need. The attack disappeared as quickly as it had come, leaving us in silence once again. I watched for only a minute, waiting to see if more was to come, watching as both girls dropped their hands.

I was up in an instant, my heart fighting over which Joclyn to run to, yelling at me to find a way to bring the battered Joclyn home.

I had only made it a few steps before her weak voice met my ears, the sweet sound sending my heart into a frantic strum.

"Goodbye."

"No!" It was then I knew who I was running to, who needed me more. I ran to Joclyn's ghostly body, wrapping my arms around her as I surged my magic into both of them through the Štít. The shadow of her body was so cold, so small, compared to what she really was. I could feel her, the same way I had when the sight was first given to me. I could feel her gritty skin, the grease on her hair. Somehow, she was right there in my arms.

The Black Water had bridged the gap between us again, but this time I knew how to use that magic to bring her back. I could still feel the water burning through my veins, and hers, and even though I didn't want to, I forced its movement through me, through the Štít, and right to my heart. I felt the water burn alongside my magic, Joclyn's magic coming to the edge of the Štít as my power called to her. It was there that our magic mingled for the second time. The deep strength of it rocked through me with such an impact I was sure I would never be able to let her go again.

Her strong magic raged through me, my muscles tensed at the tingling ecstasy that washed over my nerve endings. The water continued its blissful movement until it began to pull away. Her magic seeped back into her, bringing her with it.

Without even knowing how, I felt her arms around me, warm and whole. I felt her presence leave mine, her mind whole again.

I pulled away from the warmth of her arms, scared about what I would see, my heart swelling at the unscathed, healthy face looking back at me.

"Ilyan." Her voice moved through me with the strength of a tidal wave. It crashed into my soul and took the breath out of my chest.

I looked into the silver sheen of her eyes, my soul undeniably lost to her, my heart belonging to her more than it ever had. Just as her sight had said.

She wrapped her hands around my neck and brought my forehead down onto hers, the contact of her skin igniting my blood. I could feel the fire of the Black Water speed up in my veins, its burn deep and yet so pleasant.

I would have gladly stayed there for hours, staring into her eyes, her skin against mine, but I could feel them coming. My magic had been so focused on Joclyn that I didn't feel their pulses until they were right on top of us.

I turned toward them as the door opened, stepping away from her in a panic, unsure as to how Joclyn would react at seeing Ryland.

He was the first one in the door, his blue eyes blazing as he searched for her. I looked toward Joclyn, expecting to see the heart-stopping joy I had seen light up her face before, but it was not there. The look of pain and fear that I had seen on the haggard girl's face had taken over Joclyn's beautiful features. Panic and fear ravaged her before her hands raised toward him, a pulse shooting through the air with more power than even I could conjure.

The glowing mass exploded from her hands with enough energy that the air rippled behind it, the deep earth magic reacting to Joclyn and strengthening the attack.

Time slowed as I watched the flame burn through the air, everyone slowly registering what was happening.

Joclyn's response to seeing Ryland was the exact opposite of what I had been expecting to happen.

Ryland pulled up his shield as a reflex reaction, although his confused face opened in a plea I barely heard above the panicked noise that had filled my suite.

I shielded Ryland quickly, knowing that even with both of our barriers her energy pulse would burn right through. The mass barreled toward Ryland's chest faster than a bullet. I could tell by the look on Joclyn's face that this wouldn't be the last attack. She was angry and terrified. Her eyes held more hatred than I had ever seen.

I surged my magic through the Štít and into her tense and frantic body, my magic soothing her mind to sleep as quickly as I could, just as Joclyn's attack made contact.

I expected the impact. I had yelled out against it, but it never hit Ryland. It hit Dramin.

I watched him as he moved in front of Ryland, his eyes hooded and sad. He was not panicked at what was about to collide with him, he was accepting. Dramin looked at Joclyn as her magic hit him, his face full of pity before he collapsed to the ground.

Everything froze in place as I felt Joclyn fall into sleep beside me, my magic removing her alert state and plunging her into a deep, dreamless sleep.

Joclyn's body sagged as Dramin's did, but it was Dramin's body that held my attention this time. The dull clunk of his head against the wood echoed through the quiet room, and through my heart. I could feel the surprise at what had just happened pulse through each of us for one breath before Thom's yell broke the stunned reverence we had been trapped in.

Thom yelled as he collapsed to the ground by his friend, his hands shaking as he reached for him, plunging his magic into him. His voice was the deep lolling of a keel, the sound of one lost to the deep pieties of the world. The sound of heartbreak.

All other thoughts left me as I dropped to Thom's side as he howled, my own yells joining his as he held onto his friend. My friend. All the times I had hidden him, protected him, and now he was just another one to fall.

"Dramin," I gasped, my voice inaudible above Thom's moans. "No... No... Dramin!"

I placed my shaking hands against Dramin's face, my magic moving into him in an attempt to find some evidence of life inside him, to find anything that would give me some hope.

I let my magic flow, my panic making it hard for me to regulate the amount that I plunged into him. I explored every inch of his body, my power covering him in my desperation to find something.

If it wasn't for the deep tick of the Black Water that would forever flow through me, I might not have felt the small spark that was hidden in his heart.

"He's not dead," I said firmly, the regality coming back into my voice as I fought the hopelessness that Dramin's injury had filled me with.

"What?" Ovailia's surprise mirrored my own, but the bitter sound within her voice was stronger than usual.

I grabbed Thom's magic that now snaked through Dramin's body to direct him to the spark of energy that I had found.

"Focus on that," I instructed him before pulling away.

My magic left him as I brought it back inside of myself, my heart thumping against my chest at what I was about to do.

"Please don't let me kill him," I spoke more to myself

than anyone else, but I knew that everyone had heard me, that everyone knew what I was going to do. It was what I had tried to do to my friend, Sarin, before I killed him a thousand years before. It was what I needed to do now in order to save Dramin's life.

My hands rested against Dramin's face, the skin contact warm and threatening. I breathed in, bringing my magic right to the surface, before breathing out and surging it into him. I let in just enough to jumpstart his entire body and hopefully, ignite his magic, but not enough to kill him—or so I hoped.

I looked up at Thom expectantly, hoping to see him looking at me, but his focus stayed on Dramin. The spark had obviously not ignited; his magic was still not strong enough to sustain his life.

I needed to perform the ozdobit třásněmi one more time.

I repeated the process, careful to keep my magic at just the right caliber inside of his body. This time, a small groan escaped Dramin's lips, his hand twitching in response to my jolt. My heart froze for one terrible moment before I gently pushed my magic back into his body, stretching it right to the small spark I had found, pleased to now find a fire.

I exhaled once I had felt the life inside of him, the knot in my back loosening. I looked up to Thom, his eyes meeting mine.

"He's alive?" he asked in awe, his voice a heavy rumble over Ryland's constantly mumbling voice behind us.

"Stěží." I answered Thom, careful to keep my voice low. Even though Ovailia was now standing next to Ryland and Joclyn, I knew she was listening.

"I've never seen anything like it," I gasped through the tense feeling in my shoulders.

"Me either," Thom said, his voice awed. "Even when we sparred back in the cave, after she gained full use of her power, she was never able to produce something that strong."

I sighed and ran my hand through my hair, forgetting that I had already cut off the long strands.

"Try to keep him alive, Thom," I pleaded, trying to make it plain that I needed his help.

"I will, but there is only so much I can do. With his magic so weak..." Thom's voice drifted off as he placed his hands against the skin of Dramin's face, his head shaking in worry. "Why did she attack Ryland like that in the first place? I thought she loved him."

"She did. She does," I corrected myself, ignoring the heavy thumping in my chest. I looked toward Ryland quickly, thankful to see both him and Ovailia absorbed in the sleeping girl before them. I needed to get over there. "Something must have happened in the Tŏuha," I continued, bringing my focus back to Thom. "He must have been attacking her somehow."

"Ryland was attacking her?" Thom asked, the alarm in his voice mirroring the anxiety that already burned through me, igniting the heavy Black Water inside of me again. I cringed against the burn, trying not to show the exhaustion the pain was cursing me with.

"I believe so."

"Is Ryland even safe to have here?" Thom's eyes darted over to where Ovailia hovered beside Ryland.

"Safer than Ovailia is at this point."

Thom's gaze darted away from our siblings, his eyes narrowing at my words, almost daring me to say what he wanted to hear.

"I need you to watch her."

"You need me to watch Ovailia *and* heal Dramin..."

I sighed and straightened my back. Thom had put into words exactly how terrible our situation was. I had foolishly thought that Joclyn's awakening would solve all of our problems, but now, somehow, she had only increased them.

"Ano," I said simply, knowing I was already asking too much of him. He only looked at me, nodding once in understanding, his own stress staring right back at me.

"Take him to his room, Thom. I'll be there shortly."

I stood as Thom carried Dramin's body out the door, the knot in my heart relaxing. Dramin would be okay if the spark of his magic stayed strong. I wasn't sure what Joclyn had hit him with, so I wasn't sure if what I had done was enough.

I turned to the others, unsurprised to see Ryland hovering over Joclyn. I could feel Ryland's magic inside of her, I could feel the foreign power infusing her through the edge of the Štít.

Ryland's voice filled the air around us, the English words sounding out of place as he whispered to her. I could still feel Ryland's magic right around the edges of my own, making it clear he was still there. I dutifully kept mine on the other side of the Štít, even though keeping it there was a physical pain to me now.

"He will live." I spoke more to myself than to the room, needing to hear the words for my own benefit.

"Honestly, I was surprised to see him remotely alive in the first place." Ovailia's voice was high and filled with fury.

I had known I couldn't avoid this confrontation for long. Instead of walking into the ruins of Rioseco to find just Joclyn and I, Ovailia had found two others—both of which she had thought to be dead. Thom and Dramin, one her brother and the other the son of her former mate.

Our eyes met and I refused to pull away, the intensity of our stares grew as each second passed. Given where she had just come from, this conversation could easily be used to my advantage, something I definitely needed in this game of cat and mouse that my father had set up.

I carefully fisted the burn on my hand, keeping it out of sight. Ovailia had laid her cards in front of me. I needed to play mine right. If I was going to get us out of this, then everything to do with the Black Water needed to stay hidden for my round to play out properly. Joclyn being a Drak was our greatest asset at this point, it was not information I would ever willingly hand over to Ovailia. Each of us continued to weigh our options as we danced around each other in a silent tango.

"Is she alive?" Ryland's accusatory voice was barely louder than a whisper, but it broke the tension between Ovailia and me.

"Yes, I just put her to sleep," I answered quickly, not able to focus on Ryland's misplaced worry.

"Why isn't she waking up, Ilyan?" Ryland's panicked voice cut through the silence as he shook her shoulders.

I turned toward him, my frustration flaring at his questions. Had he not noticed what had just happened? Did he not care that the man who had saved him was fighting for his life?

I brushed my irritation at his selfishness away. His hands were wrapped around hers as he whispered to her. I thought I had been prepared for this sight, but I was surprised by the uncomfortable thunk that sounded deep within my ironclad heart. I dutifully ignored it, instead moving toward them with my back straight and stoic in my usual way.

"I am keeping her asleep, Ryland."

"Wake her up!" he demanded, his desperation making him edgy. "I need to see her."

Ryland ran his hand over her hair, his fingers touching the skin of her face as he looked at me, waiting for me to act.

"I am not sure that is wise." Ryland's eyes widened at my response, my curiosity at his odd behavior peaking. "She just tried to kill you, Ryland."

He looked at me for only a minute before looking away, moving down to place his forehead against hers. I felt the pressure against my own head, and shook it off, surprised the bridge was still there even though I no longer had contact with her.

"She didn't mean it." Ryland's voice was heavy and low, his words spoken more to Joclyn than to me.

I looked toward Ovailia, expecting to receive some support, but she only looked back with a wicked gleam in her eye that I had only seen once before. The shine in her eyes prickled at my better judgment in warning.

"She woke up only a moment before you came in—"

"I know," Ryland interrupted me. "Thom told us she was sleeping before. She was just confused. She didn't know she had woken up. I need to tell her she is all right, Ilyan. Please. Let me do that."

I felt my protective instinct flare at his words, the desire to push him away from her strong and growing. "Why would she have need to attack you in a Tŏuha, Ryland?"

His eyes widened, they drifted from Ovailia to me uncomfortably, as if he was unsure what to say or how much he was allowed to reveal. The gesture made me wary, my fear rising quickly within me.

I had always counted on Ryland standing with me. He had gone out of his way multiple times to save me, to save Joclyn. He knew what her purpose was in this life, and yet, I could see the doubt in his eyes when he looked at me. He doubted that he could trust me, that I was telling the truth. The look triggered my own doubts about the situation, and I looked toward Ovailia, my eyes hardening.

Ryland's body stiffened, the large muscles in his shoulders bulging beneath his blue polo shirt. My body prickled as my magic flared in expectation of an outburst.

"She wouldn't... I mean..." Ryland's fingers began to dig into Joclyn's skin, his grip tightening with every word. "If you saw what he made us do... I mean... YOU CAN'T HAVE HER!" his voice roared, making the glass in the window rattle, his magic erupting out of him. The whirlwind of power circled through the room, ripping blankets, pictures and ornaments out of their places.

"SHE'S MINE!" Ryland yelled only a second later as the torrent continued, his hands digging into her, little drops of her blood trailing at his fingertips.

That was enough. Seeing her blood was all it took for my instincts to kick in, for my heart to thump for her safety. My magic surged as I threw him away from her, his body slamming into the stone wall of my suite where I restrained him.

The second he had left her side, I had gone to her, my arms resting over her in a physical shield.

Ryland looked at me in a panic, his eyes wild as he fought against me.

"Don't ever touch her like that," I snarled, aware that my composure had left.

"My, my, Ilyan," Ovailia soothed as she came up beside me. "Having trouble letting him near Joclyn, are we?"

"He was hurting her."

"That doesn't matter. He's her mate."

"That bond was broken. Or have you forgotten what it

takes to break a bond, Ovailia." I let my hard voice plague my words as I turned to face Ovailia, allowing my height to tower over her dauntingly. She met my hard gaze with a glare of her own, her lips turned up in that wicked, little half smile.

"Oh, now, how could I forget? No matter how much you wanted me to." She smiled wider, and I froze, my face in its hard mask.

I wanted her out of here, out of this room and out of the abbey. If I forced her out now, she would only instruct the Trpaslíks to attack. My father's plan was clicking into place now, his carefully woven web settling in around us. Like all webs, there was always a hole.

"I'll just take him to my suite for now, shall I?" Ovailia asked, the gleam in her eyes making it obvious she knew she had me. "He can come check on Joclyn in a few hours."

Ovailia moved toward Ryland as my magic released him, letting him slide to the floor.

"I can't leave her. I don't care what you say, Ilyan. I need her. I can't..." Ryland's voice was so weak, so pained, and I couldn't ignore the desperation that lined it.

"I know, Ryland. I will let you see her again soon. I promise."

Ryland opened his mouth to say something, but Ovailia stopped him. With one whispered word from her, his face hardened, his eyes dark as he followed Ovailia out without a word, his eyes never leaving Joclyn's sleeping body.

I had no choice, but to let them go, to leave Ryland in Ovailia's hands and let her manipulate him right in front of me. I could already feel the pieces of a larger game fall into place. Joclyn's sight from only a few weeks before rang in my ears, the words strong beside the vision that she had shared with me. The vision of Ovailia carrying Ryland down the hall.

'A tryst has been set in motion, one you cannot ignore. The father of the four is using his seed one against another, and in the end, none will fall until two lives are lost. It cannot be stopped. Beware where your trust lays.'

For once I needed time on my side, but in only a matter of minutes, time had already effectively ruined our chances.

25

ILYAN

I HADN'T SLEPT since yesterday morning. I hadn't dared. I couldn't relax after Joclyn had woken up, my name soft on her lips before she attempted to murder her mate. Former mate. I had to keep reminding myself that the bond was broken, broken by my father without their permission, their love tarnished for his wicked agenda. It made me sick to think about. Even though part of me pained at the thought, I just knew I had to find a way to get Joclyn past her fear of him.

My experiences over the last two weeks had been only a small touch of what Ryland must have felt while separated from Joclyn for so long, constantly praying for her health and safety. Then to see her again and have her attack you...

I shook my head. Part of me wanted to bring Ryland to her now, to let him be there to comfort her and protect her, while another part of me wanted him to stay far away.

No matter what I wanted, he couldn't come back. It wasn't safe for him here. Joclyn had proven that as she huddled against the toilet yesterday, her panic seeping into my soul. I had felt guilty leaving her alone since then, so I kept my visits with Thom and Dramin short, the ones with Ryland and Ovailia even shorter.

I had kept her asleep since her panicked outburst yesterday afternoon in an attempt to keep her mind clear of the nightmares that I knew would haunt her if I left her to sleep naturally. Instead, I chose to constantly replay my song within her mind in an effort to soothe her. It had seemed to work before. I hoped it would help to keep her calm and realize that she was safe.

While her sleep was kept dreamless, my waking hours were a nightmare. Joclyn had shown me the memories of the months she was trapped inside Cail's mind when she had been awake the day before. I had felt every bone break, every impact of her body against stone, walls and cement. I had watched in terror as she ran through bloodstained hallways, only to come face to face with Ryland who never ceased to find new ways to hurt her.

It wasn't really Ryland. It was a close enough likeness that even Joclyn had been fooled, but it was just a projection. A projection of Ryland that Cail had placed inside her mind to hurt her, to torture her, so that in the event she did escape, she would only be a weapon against him.

To be killed by your own mate; it was my father's sickest form of torture.

I replayed the memories as I dissected the words that were spoken, the way Cail yelled for Wynifred with his dying breath. Guilt filled me that I had not been able to keep my side of his bargain. A secret for a life, and he had lost his life anyway. I hoped Wyn was all right.

I replayed the way Cail led Joclyn through the maze of

his mind. Looking at it like this, I was able to relate every injury to an action, the connections only fueling my anger.

Anger bubbled up inside me like oil left too long in a pan, slow and smothering. I wasn't mad at Cail for what he had done. I wasn't even mad at Ryland for not getting her out in time. I was mad at myself for not protecting her, not demanding that the bond be broken before this could have happened.

I should have kept her safe, broken the bond when I had the chance, and protected her mind from the terrors that had changed her. I hadn't, though.

How could I have known what would happen? I could only assume what I felt ring true in Joclyn's heart: that Ryland was alive and soon they would be back together.

I wanted that for her.

My choice to give her the joy of her first love had only led to a terror I could never fathom.

I shook my head and continued down the halls, back toward my suite, back to where Joclyn still lay. My magic surged through her, keeping her asleep until I could return.

With no one extra on hand to watch her, I had left her alone with the door sealed, while I checked on Dramin. His room was bare except for mug after mug of Black Water. His body was still and cold as if death was unwilling to let him go. That was what I had thought when I first walked in—that he was dead. His magic was still strong inside of him after the restart, but everything else had seemed to shut down.

"Ilyan?"

I jumped at Ryland's voice, my body swinging around to face him. No one had snuck up on me in centuries. I could always feel everyone's magical impulses as they moved toward me, I could hear their breathing in my ears, and yet,

Ryland stood in front of me, nothing flowing off him, not a wave or a whisper. I had felt the deep green waves of Ryland's energy before, when he had released me from our father's torture chamber as a child and when I had seen him with Joclyn. Now, nothing was there.

"Yes?" My eyes narrowed in confusion, my magic surging toward him as I tried to figure out how he was restraining his magic to the point that I could not sense him.

"I... I thought you would come get me by now." I arched an eyebrow at him, not following. "To see Joclyn."

Ah yes, I should have known. It was wrong of me to keep him from her, but I worried. Worried what he would do to her and worried what she would do to him.

"It's not safe, Ryland, not yet." I kept my voice soft, hoping to speak with him like a brother, not a ruler.

"I can decide what is safe," Ryland snarled as he squared his strong shoulders. So much for a calm talk between brothers.

I kept my posture straight, while still trying to maintain my calm façade. I couldn't be the only levelheaded one around here, could I? "She tried to kill you, Ryland. That has not changed. When Cail trapped her in his mind, he used a projection of you to torture her. Right now, she doesn't see the difference."

Ryland's eyes widened as I spoke, the distrust showing in the furrowed lines of his forehead. I couldn't help the deep sigh that escaped me. Ovailia had already set her framework; getting him to see things differently was going to be difficult.

"She doesn't see the difference because you won't let her." Ryland's voice was deep and angry.

"That's not true, Ryland." I planted my feet as he began

to pace, his agitated movements alerting me to the fact that something much darker was dwelling within him.

"Ry?" He spun at my voice, as if he had forgotten I was there. His eyes widened in anger, and his hands began to shake, even though he had stopped pacing.

"Don't call me that." I stepped back on instinct, the snarl in his voice and the absence of his energy keeping me on high alert.

"Only Jos can call me that. She's the only one..." His fingers continued to flex as he spoke, his hands lifting to circle his head in agitation, his fingers glowing with power as his eyes darkened—and still I couldn't read him.

"All right," I said slowly, hoping to alleviate the pressure that was obviously building inside of him. "I didn't know that, Ryland. I won't do it again."

"She's all I have. I... She's mine." He snarled the last statement again, his hands continuing to open and close as his anger fueled his power.

I watched him for a moment, trying to get any kind of a read off him. Nothing triggered, nothing changed. He was obviously completely infused with his magic, but still I felt nothing.

"I know that, Ryland. She knows that. She risked everything to see you. Even when the dreams hurt, when the Tȯuha—"

"Then don't keep her from me!" I flinched at his words as his pacing returned, the agitated movements increasing in his arms.

I had to remind myself that he had only been released from his Vymȧzat a week ago. If his horrors were anything like what Joclyn had been forced to endure, then he had made amazing progress.

"I'm not keeping her from you, Ryland. She is afraid of

you. She wants to kill you. I am protecting you from her, as well as protecting her." I watched him as he moved, keeping my body still and my voice level in an effort to keep him calm.

"I don't believe you." He didn't even look at me as he paced, his eyes darting anywhere but at me.

"I would never lie to you, Ryland. You are my brother. You released me from our father's imprisonment. You saved my life. Now it is just my turn to return the favor."

"You don't know what he did to us!" he yelled, the palm of his hand moving to smack against his head in frustration.

I could already tell there would be no controlling Ryland's anger. It was too new. He reminded me of Thom when I had first met him, how the anger had been all that he had, what he held onto. It took Thom time, and Sain's guidance, to see how wrong that anger could be. I needed to get Ryland past it faster than Thom though. I needed him to see what he still had before it was all taken away by our father's games.

Ovailia had obviously led him to believe that I was keeping Joclyn from him. He needed to see that I hadn't taken her away from him, that I had no intention of holding them apart.

"I may not know what he did to you, but I know what he did to Joclyn," I whispered, my voice just loud enough to freeze him in place.

"He hurt her."

"Yes. In every nightmare. You were there, weren't you?" He only nodded; I tried to ignore the surge of pride at my lucky guess. "He hurt you, too."

It was a statement. Ryland looked up at me, his eyes calming as his breathing regulated. The moment his eyes met mine, I felt it. It was weak and only there for a moment, but his magic surged through the air before retreating again. I couldn't help but smile; I was calming him. I smiled and wondered at the fact that he could control himself so much that he could hide all of his power from my detection.

"They used me to hurt her." I visibly flinched at Ryland's words, at the way he clenched his chest as if the pain of the blood magic was still fresh on his mind. "I didn't want to, but when I fought them, when I warned her... Hurt Me!" His last words flew out in an angry rush, the disjointed nature of them alarming.

"I know."

"Hurt... hurt... hurt..." he repeated before hitting himself hard against the head with his palm again. As quick as it started, the deranged anger on his face left as he looked at me.

"I don't want to hurt her," he whispered. I nodded to him once, afraid of what speaking might bring out next. Ryland's hand moved to clench over his chest again, his eyes drifting back to me.

I didn't know how much Ryland remembered of the Vymäzat, or how much of what had been done was his own choice, but one thing was clear. He had suffered as much, if not more, than the rest of Edmund's children. If only for that, he deserved my patience.

"It wasn't your fault, Ryland. He has done it to all of us." I moved toward him slowly, keeping my voice level.

I needed Ryland on my side, I needed to regain the trust he had lost in me. Ovailia had moved him into position as a pawn, but he wasn't a pawn; he was a person. My brother. He was someone I cared for. If I could save him, I would.

"Everyone?" Ryland looked up at me from beneath his long bangs, the wicked gleam back in his eyes. I didn't know what was said to trigger his anger, but with one statement, we were right back where we began.

Fine. If he wanted to be angry, I would let him. I would not, however, let his foolish emotion affect me or my choices. If it were to be anything, it would be the other way around.

My skin prickled the way it always did in anticipation of battle, my magic surging as I smiled. I knew the wicked gleam was back in my eyes. I didn't try to hide it; I let it shine. I let the power behind my eyes move into my brother. He stepped back. Not a lot, but just enough to convey that the look in my eyes had done its job.

"Yes, Ryland, everyone. Most everyone has died at his hands. Zetta was killed at birth because of her brown eyes. Sylas was forcibly mated only to be killed when he never produced an heir. Mym tortured all her young life, turned into a five-year-old weapon. She never knew love until I rescued her, but even then, she struggled. How can you learn to recognize love if you've never felt it? Thom watched as his daughter was tortured and murdered at the hands of our father. He used to smear her blood on his face."

"Thom?" Ryland asked, the timber of his voice changing to one of sickened pity. Had no one told him yet? Had he not placed it together?

"Yes, Thom. He is your brother, too. Only the four of us remain. Some have escaped the horrors, others let them engulf them, and they are turned into heartless monsters. Joclyn fights her horrors every day; what will you do?"

"Joclyn..." His voice revered her, as if she was his deity. The anger was gone from his eyes now, his head hanging between his sagging shoulders. Right then, I could see the child who had saved me. He was scared, but so brave. In that moment, I knew that his strength was still there; it was the line between right and wrong that had been blurred.

We just needed to draw it again.

"I have kept her safe for you, Ryland. Just as I promised you I would. But I need to continue keeping her safe until she realizes that she doesn't need to be afraid of you."

Ryland's eyes looked up to me, and I felt my heart beat uncomfortably as it tried to escape the prison that I had trapped it in, as it tried to stop me from enacting on my heritage.

"She still loves you, Ryland. I can see it in her eyes. I saw it every day that she would talk about you, in the way she held out hope. She told me every day, Ryland. Her heart belongs to you."

Ryland listened through it all, his body relaxing and his eyes softening as he listened. He walked toward me slowly, his magical impulses finally released from wherever he had held them prisoner, the waves calm in the air.

"I will make this right and return her to you whole." I smiled, my face pulling up uncomfortably as my heart protested against my words.

"Thank you, Ilyan." Ryland's voice was soft in my ear as he embraced me, his body appearing only slightly younger than mine. I reluctantly returned the hug, my arms unsure how to respond to such a gesture.

"Samozřejmě, bratr. I will let you see her as soon as she is ready," I said, his slight smile appearing at my words.

Thom had been right from the very beginning. Handing her over was going to be harder than I had ever imagined.

It was duty, my role, to do what was right. There was no question that this was the right thing to do. I could not lead the few of us that remained if I was not honest and right.

And doing this, this was right.

The choices we make are not always easy, but it is the ones that are hard that matter. I could tell, looking into his eyes, that this was the one that mattered. This was the one that would make a difference.

This was the one that needed to be done; no matter how much it hurt.

26

ILYAN

I woke up with Joclyn in my arms, her body pressed against mine as I sang to her, my words flitting between Czech and English. I had finally fallen asleep at some point last night after making one last check on Dramin.

I had slept dreamlessly, but at some point, the restraint I had against her waking had slipped off and she had woke. She was scared. I could tell by the unsteady beat of her heart and the way her hand pressed roughly against me, as if she was trying to move into me. I tightened my arms against her, hoping the pressure would help to relax her.

I had seen her need for the security and the way she had come to get that from pressure as she wedged herself in between the toilet and vanity the other day. I had felt her need for the strength of something else when she could not find her own in the memories she had lent me.

Joclyn's body stiffened at my touch, a small flinch that shivered over her shoulder blades. Her breathing picked up and her heart rate increased, but I kept my arms tight around her, not willing to let her move into herself, not wanting her fears to take over. I pushed my magic into her, calming her, settling her frayed nerves.

I stayed silent as I held her, and she calmed. I wanted her to decide when she felt safe enough to speak. I wanted her to feel security come from me and then be able to find it in herself.

"Joclyn?" I kept my voice soft, my lips speaking gently against her dark hair.

She pressed against me at the noise, my arms helping her in her search for comfort as I tightened them around her.

"Are you okay?" I ran my hand over her hair, feeling the soft strands between my fingers, the act helping to slowly calm her heart.

Her head moved against me, the subtle nod of agreement one I hadn't expected. She was okay. Even though I could feel her fear, feel her panic, she still felt okay.

My heart beat in one wild thump before settling again, my hold on her lessening.

I kept her against me as I ran my hand over her hair, my other coming to press her back into me. I surrounded her in security, keeping her broken mind safe for just a moment.

She sighed, and I felt her body relax just enough to mold against me. I wished I could give her serenity in her waking moments, but it was not in my power to do so. There was one thing only I had power to give her right now.

I sang.

I hummed the melody of her song, our song, into her hair. Her body relaxed at the sound, her breath escaping in a warm rush against the skin of my chest. I smiled as I sang, and she calmed and breathed against me. I could still feel the stutter in her breath, the small half beat of her heart; but for one small moment, I didn't hear that, nor could I feel the tightness on her back, the tension in her joints. She was just Joclyn, in my arms once again.

She didn't know it now, but she was stronger than the demons that had filled her soul. I could feel it in the way she relaxed, in the steady strum of her heart. She could overcome this. She could become bigger than it. I just needed to help her find that path. To help her figure out how to put it behind her, to prove her own strength to her. I would help her find herself again.

I sang as I watched the sky lighten through the large arches of my room, the stars fading as the light of dawn took them. Minutes turned into hours, but still we lay, her body against mine, my song providing the calming security she so desperately needed.

I moved away from her slowly, surprised when she jerked as if the movement had been a lightning strike. I didn't dare go too far, only far enough to be able to look at her, to see her beautiful eyes stare into me. I had missed them, and in the morning light, they seemed to shine, the light of her soul sparkling through them and into me.

My hold on Joclyn loosened as I lifted my hand, the sun catching on the angry red burn that covered my palm and the inside of my fingers. The skin was red and raw, the moist flesh raised as if it had been partially eaten and cast aside.

It had taken centuries for the burns on my chest to heal, and the burn on my arm was still angry and red. This burn seemed much deeper than the others. The pain was definitely stronger and uncontrollable. I could already tell it would take much longer for this burn to heal, if it healed at all.

The connection that had been triggered by the touch of

the Black Water had left me, leaving me feeling strangely empty. Even with the magic of a bonding, such intimate connections weren't possible. To feel her heart, her body, within me, that wasn't something that had ever happened.

I just wished I knew what that connection meant. With all my training, with all the knowledge that had been demanded of me, the Drak's choice to keep this information hidden was one that would affect us in ways I didn't think I could ever understand.

Without analyzing the thought, I pressed my scarred hand against her cheek, a gasp escaping my lips as the connection restored itself. With one touch, my awareness of her increased. Her heartbeat was strong within me, and I could feel the steady thrum of her soul moving through me.

I couldn't help it. Even though I knew I shouldn't and my brain begged me not to, I let my finger trail down her neck and onto the raised skin of her mark. As my finger connected, the jolt that I had always felt shot through me, supercharging my magic in a surge of energy. It buzzed through me like the most addictive medicine.

I was surprised when I felt her heart seize as her own jolt shot through her, the shock of our joining magic strong in her body as well as my own. Before she could panic, before her heart rate could increase much further, she controlled it. She forced the fear down, forced the beat of her heart to keep a steady beat, even without my help.

She was amazing.

I couldn't keep the look of pure joy out of my eyes as I looked at her. She would never cease to amaze me. Everything that would be thrown at her she would overcome. I could tell that now. I was beyond honored to be the one to keep her safe, to be allowed to love her.

Her eyes looked into mine. Confusion and happiness

intermingled with each other before she gasped and moved into me; her hot breath against my chest sent waves of energy shooting over my skin.

I pulled her into me, my hold tight against her. I wanted so much to stay like this, our arms locked in each other's embrace, but it could not be. It was not right to dwell in a joy that was not yours, and sadly, that was just what I was doing.

"I'm going to go get you some Black Water. I'll be right back," I whispered in her ear before I pulled away, my muscles aching at the loss of her warmth.

Joclyn curled herself into a ball as I left, the loss of contact already affecting her. I needed to hurry, clear my head and come right back.

I moved swiftly out the door, careful to close it silently so as not to trigger any more of her panic attacks. The last thing I wanted was for her to panic without anyone there to calm her.

My magic surged through her as I raced to Dramin's room, grateful for his foresight in placing his chambers so close to my own.

Thom stood over Dramin, his hands on his head as he worked over him, healing his body and removing the burns that plagued his organs.

"Any change since last night?" I asked through the silence, but Thom only shook his head, a small sag in his shoulders telling me all I needed to know.

"Nothing."

"Keep trying, Thom. We can't lose him." I grabbed one of the full mugs before turning back to the pair, Thom's head hanging over his friend, his dreads making him look like he had been trapped in a cage.

"We can try to give him some Black Water later, perhaps

it will help." I raised the glass toward Thom, causing him to look toward me, his eyes shielded by his usual mask.

"At least that poison is good for something." He forced a laugh, the sound causing the lingering tension in the room to grow.

I opened my mouth to reply when a flare of my magic moved away from me and into Joclyn. Her panic had pulled it to her and I could feel her clinging to it like a lifeline. As it filled her, I felt the erratic beat of her heart and the pressure in her joints. The fear I had worked so carefully to remove from her had come back tenfold. Someone was there in the room with her. Something was wrong.

I said nothing to Thom as I placed the mug back on the table, my feet carrying me out of the room before I could even place the thought in my mind. I ran toward her as the fear grew within her, the panic turning into a yell on her lips, a yell that echoed through the walls of my ancient home.

The sound vibrated around me as I turned the last corner to find Ovailia leaning against the large, wooden door to my suite. She looked at me with her usual smug smile, her eyes flashing with a sheen of red I hadn't seen for hundreds of years.

"So, brother. Are you going to tell me what happened to your hand?" It was such a normal question, I couldn't believe that she would ask it here, in the hall, while she guarded the door to my own rooms, which she had obviously let Ryland through.

"I cut it," I lied, letting my feet take me closer to her, toward the door she leaned against and the girl I had to save.

Ovailia, however, didn't move. She stayed where she was

with her long frame leaning elegantly across the door. She looked at me with that wicked gleam she had perfected long ago, and I could tell at once that this would not go as planned.

"Get out of my way," I commanded, careful to keep my magic out of my voice.

"No. He deserves to see his mate. Unless you have taken her for yourself. Did you ruin his mate, brother? Tsk. Tsk. I knew you couldn't keep your hands off her." She spoke as if she was relating facts, not the disgusting lies that had just spewed from her lips. I could never do something so vulgar. By the look on her face, I could tell that she had already spread the seed of doubt in Ryland's mind.

"Don't say such vulgar things about me!" I yelled, fully aware that the power in my voice was shaking the door she still leaned against.

"Then why can't he see her?" She raised her voice to match mine, the increase in volume obviously only meant to fuel whatever was happening inside the room.

"Because she will kill him!"

"Oh, I doubt that, but if she does, it doesn't matter. It's what Father would want. They are both weapons, created only to kill each other," she sneered, the little twist of her lips identical to our father's, the action fueling my rage.

"Out of my way!" I roared, placing the magical strain in my voice this time. She started to move, her feet acting as if of their own accord as my magic forced her movements.

I had made it to the door when a yell of pain shot through the heavy wooden door to my suite. I surged my magic into Joclyn, my energy finding the bruised cells in her cheek automatically.

Ryland had punched her.

With one burst of energy, my magic sent Ovailia flying away from the door, her body hitting the wall opposite as it flew from its hinges. In two steps, I was inside. I only needed a glimpse of Ryland's arm pulling back in preparation for another punch before he, too, was forced away from her. His body hit stone with such force that a crack fanned away from him, breaking the ancient mortar that kept the wall steady.

I just caught a glimpse of Joclyn rolling off the bed, her small, scared body wedging itself into the small space underneath it, before Ryland recovered himself and Ovailia had moved to his side the moment she entered the room.

"Look what you have done, Ovailia!" I yelled at her in Czech, the look on Ryland's face making it clear he understood every word. "I won't play your games anymore."

"This wouldn't have happened if you had just let him see his mate. Why couldn't you do that, Ilyan? I don't understand. Why can't he see his mate?" Ovailia had placed just enough desperation in her voice to be able to claim sincerity. Her game was not very well covered, something I was positive she did on purpose.

"I'm trying to keep him safe."

"Are you sure? It looks like you are just trying to keep her for yourself."

I felt my muscles tense, the anger within me strong enough to overcome my breeding and rip out of me in a yell over her foolish lie.

"I'm not keeping her! I'm protecting her!" The royal façade had slipped, just as Ovailia wanted. My outcry only caused the ugly sneer on her lips to increase.

"But he didn't hurt her, did he?" Ovailia yelled as she transitioned smoothly to English.

"Ovailia, he punched her when I came into the room!" I eyed them as I moved to the side of the bed, my position and posture making it very clear I wasn't going to give her to them.

"I didn't see that," Ovailia lied smoothly, the laugh that escaped Ryland's mouth making it clear he believed her, that, like a child, he thought he had gotten away with something.

"He's going to lie anyway, Ovailia," Ryland said. "He's been feeding her lies. Just as you said." Both my, and Joclyn's, heart rate increased, but for entirely different reasons. Hers had accelerated in fear at the sound of Ryland's voice, mine in the realization of loss. My sister had played her game well. She had manipulated what was left of Ryland's mind just enough to turn him against me. I thought I had recovered enough of him when we had talked yesterday, but now I was not so sure.

"What lies have you been telling *him*, Ovailia?" I said.

"Nothing much. Two can play at this game, Ilyan." The wicked, honey texture of her voice flared as she smiled at me in exhilaration.

Before anyone could say anything else, Joclyn's heart rate increased. Her breathing picked up and her voice opened up into a howl so traumatized it wrenched through each of us. Even Ovailia looked surprised and somewhat pained. Ryland took a step forward, the desperation to comfort her evident, but I couldn't let him. I couldn't risk his life or put Joclyn through the pain.

He would have to be patient.

I looked at him, my eyes pleading for him to understand, begging him to give her space. He looked between Ovailia, whose wide eyes dug into him in warning, myself, and the bed, where Joclyn's cries continued to wail before moving back against the wall. His choice was obvious.

Even though Ovailia had taken away his trust in me, his longing for Joclyn was still stronger than the weak allegiance he had for Ovailia.

Ovailia saw his choice, and I saw her pride stutter for just a moment, her head spinning toward me, her eyes flashing as her long hair swirled around her.

"You'll regret this, Ilyan." I barely heard her voice above Joclyn's yells.

"I want you out, Ovailia! Leave the abbey, and take your pathetic game with you." I couldn't control the level of my voice. The anger I felt at the loss of my sister hit me far deeper than I would have expected.

Ovailia left quickly, the power in my voice not giving her a chance to question. Before the door had closed, I looked to Ryland, the pain was still evident in his face at not being able to help Joclyn, and his distrust of me rang strongly in his eyes. I couldn't trust him either, but right now, I needed to focus on Joclyn.

"Wait right outside the room, and keep the door open," I instructed him in Czech. "I will let you see her in a few minutes."

I did not intend to let him in to see her, not after what he had done to her face, but I needed his trust, and I needed him close. I would have to settle for some middle ground until I figured out what to do with the two damaged weapons that fate had placed in my care.

I dropped to the floor the second Ryland had left, pressing myself against it to look at Joclyn between the gap of the floor and the bed. With my full focus on her, I let my magic surge. It filled her completely as I calmed her, steadied her heart, and soothed her joints. She just looked at me with her beautiful eyes as her fear slowly dissipated.

When her heart rate was almost level, level enough not to trigger an attack, or so I hoped, I reached toward her, my hand extended in help, in safety. Even though I longed for it, she did not reach for me; her eyes only looked at the gesture for a moment before returning to my face, making it clear she had no interest in going anywhere yet.

I flattened myself against the floor, keeping my eyes on hers as I pressed myself against the bedframe, not able to make my body fit underneath the tiny gap.

"I'm sorry, Jos. I will make you safe. I will make you whole again," I whispered to her, not willing to take my eyes off her, letting the safety I wanted her to feel radiate off my skin.

She just stared at me, her bright eyes shining. I could see the hope in them, the small spark as her mind worked through what I had said.

Believe it. I said the words to myself, wishing there was a way to say them aloud, to make her feel them and know it was true.

It was the only promise I could give her, but one I would work until my dying day to make happen. I wanted her to be whole, to be happy. I wanted to see that smile on her face again.

Her eyes were welcoming and so I took a chance and moved myself under the frame, lifting the heavy wood just enough to make room. She didn't shy away from me; she kept still, so I continued to move until I was right up against her, our bodies wedged in the tiny space under the bed, a place that offered Joclyn security.

I lay near her, and we looked into each other's eyes, hers panicked, mine soft. Before I was even aware she had moved, her fingers reached up to run through the short hair that now lined the top of my head. My heart jolted at the contact, a smile coming to my lips as I moved a bit closer. I wanted her touch to continue, but her hand left, my movement obviously too much too fast.

"I cut it for you, after what you said in Italy. When you couldn't wake up... I was..." I had to stop. I didn't know what to say, how to explain what had happened. How do you tell the woman you love about the fear and pain you felt when you thought you had lost her? Even thinking about it brought the anxiety I had felt back into my gut.

Her fingers brushed my arm in apology before she moved into me, her body melding against mine. My arms moved around her as if they belonged there, even though they didn't. For this moment though, because she needed them, they did—they needed to. She could have whatever she needed from me until I could make her whole.

Our song filled our cramped space as I sang and held her against me. My lips brushed against the skin of her temple as I sang, the raw skin of my palm rubbing up and down her arm, opening the connection between us again.

I felt her heart as it beat alongside mine. I felt her breathing as it calmed and settled into a rate that was almost near my own. I let my magic surge into her, let it swirl through her as it calmed her and she became the strong girl she had been only a few weeks ago.

I could give her that back, and I would.

I would stand by her, love her and protect her until the day I died.

We stayed like that, pressed against each other for a few precious minutes. Minutes that would forever be marked in my mind as the last before everything fell apart.

The last moment until I heard a yell I thought I would

never hear. The sound of death and love and heartbreak all melded into a scream that I knew would signal the start of a war.

Ovailia's voice rang through the Abby, the sound of Sain's name on her lips.

27

ILYAN

JOCLYN JUMPED in my arms at the name, her heart beating rapidly in recognition. Her silver eyes looked into mine in longing and fear, the pupils growing as Ovailia's shout rang out again.

"Stay here," I instructed quietly, the words causing her heart to thump wildly. "Stay under the bed. I will shield you here and keep you safe."

She said nothing, and for once, I wished she would. I wished she would snap back at me about how I couldn't tell her what to do or make a joke about the ridiculous situation, but nothing came except a slow nod of understanding.

I looked into her eyes for one more second as another scream tore through the air.

"I love you, and I will always protect you." It was foolish of me to say, and I shouldn't have done it, but I couldn't stop myself. Hearing Sain's name echo through the abbey only triggered a million warnings of what was coming, and I wanted her to hear it. I wanted to leave her with one beautiful thing.

I was gone before she could respond. I left the shield

over her body as I took off through the door, only to signal for Ryland to follow me. We flew out through the window, my body speeding through the air to land in the large courtyard, the camps of the Trpaslíks glittering in the forest behind us.

Dirt and rocks exploded into the air on my landing, the ground rocking with my anger at what was unfolding before me.

Ovailia stood in the center of the garden ruins, her feet having taken her out of the abbey and directly into the path of an escaped pair seeking shelter.

I almost couldn't believe my eyes when I saw them.

Sain and Wynifred.

Sain was on the ground between Ovailia and me, his hair long and shaggy, a long beard plastered on his face. He looked even more haggard than when he had sought me out to tell me of Joclyn's existence. He cried toward Ovailia, pleading with her in Czech, French and Mandarin only for Ovailia to counter each plea angrily, her arms moving around and tossing a small, weak-looking figure through the air with each gesture.

Wynifred screamed as Ovailia flung her around, her body writhing in pain as she flopped through the air. Wynifred was weak, her clothes dirty and bloodstained, but it was the marks on her skin that yelled danger to me. They were what was causing her pain, not Ovailia.

The jagged spirals and flares had begun to move and shift, the dark black shifting over her skin like a living infection. I knew at once what had happened. When Cail had died his lock on the zánik curse had been removed. The marks were releasing their poison into her body, and after a hundred years, the curse was going to complete itself and end in Wynifred's death.

Once again, I was going to fail in my task to save someone. After hundreds of years working for me, Wynifred's sacrifice was going to be for nothing.

"Ovi! Let her go!" Sain's voice broke through the night air, his back to me as he yelled, his body doubled over as if he had just been attacked, which, judging by the look on Ovailia's face, I wouldn't doubt.

"Wyn! You're hurting her, Ovi!" Sain pleaded as I walked passed him, Ryland's steps stopping as he lowered himself to help the old man.

"Oh, hello, Ilyan." Ovailia spoke as if she was simply weeding a garden, not holding Wyn's body limply by her side. "Look what I found. She looks like she's hurt, and strangely, I think she remembers everything."

She held up Wynifred's small frame just as the girl yelled again. I moved toward her slowly, careful to keep my steps even, my face strong. I could tell by the look in her eyes that Ovailia had snapped. I needed to get Wynifred away from her before she did something stupid.

"It looks like someone hurt Cail. After all his hard work, too... poor Cail. Daddy won't like that." She smiled at me, her hold keeping Wyn's body dangling as she yelled.

"Daddy doesn't like it when you keep things from him. I don't like it either." She smiled, her eyes darting between Sain and myself.

I knew what was coming. She had no need for a cover; I had thrown her out of the abbey. Now she could say what was on her mind. I waited for the onslaught, waited for her to retreat so I could move closer and help Wynifred.

"Don't you?" I couldn't keep from answering. I didn't even try to keep the cutting edge out of my voice. At any other time, I would have at least tried, but Ovailia was staking her side. She was preparing herself for battle, so I let my maniacal power overtake me for a minute, making Ovailia flinch when she saw the look in my eyes.

"I thought you didn't like to wake the dead?"

"Maybe you should have let me die," she yelled, her face coming within an inch of my own.

"I didn't make that decision for you, Ovailia." My voice was hard and distant as I took two more steps nearer her.

"Well, you will," she smiled, her face glowing with the expectation of victory, "because I am coming right for you, with your worst enemy on my heels."

I just stared at her as she smiled, her warning mixed with Wyn's yells, ringing in my ears. I couldn't wait any longer.

With one blink of my eyes, I sent her flying, Wyn's body falling briefly before I caught her and brought her into my arms. Ovailia's yell rang in my ears as she righted herself, her posture strong as she defiantly faced me.

"Goodbye, Ovailia." It was all she needed to hear, her smile increasing before she stormed off to disappear into the forest.

I never saw her go. I never took another look at my sister; I just turned toward the abbey, Wynifred cradled in my arms. Her yells broke through the night as she writhed, the marks continuing their decent into her soul.

I seeped my magic into her, only to be burned by the powerful magic. The slow death her father had cast against her all those years ago had only become stronger. I withdrew my magic, not even able to numb her pain.

"Ian." I looked down at her, surprised to hear my code name from the centuries she had spied for me. "Tell Thom I'm sorry." She barely got the words out before she cried out incoherently again.

"He's here, Wynifred." I was not even sure she could

hear me, but I needed her to know that her last moments would not be alone.

I looked back at Ryland and Sain, Sain rushing forward, intent to help her in any way he could evident on his face. However, I knew it was no use. The curse was too strong. It had only grown stronger with time, and after a hundred years, there was no hope.

I moved into the abbey as quickly as I dared. I hoped my quick glance had conveyed the danger she was in and the need for them to follow me. Sain's pulse joined in my wake, Ryland's falling right into step beside him as I began to run, Wyn's body hanging in my arms.

I could feel the pulse of Thom's magic in his room and I knew at once that that was where we needed to go.

My magic pushed open the door to Thom's room before we had even arrived. I could see him turn, his hair whipping around at the unexpected movement. The movement alerted him, not the yells. He pulled the tiny ear buds of his iPod from his ears as we entered, the heartbreaking fear slamming into him as he registered who I was carrying.

"Wynifred!" His yell broke through the air like a knife. The sound of her name was loud and frightened.

I ignored him and the panic in his voice as I laid her down on the bed, her eyes closed as she writhed and yelled. The marks continued to snake across her skin, their number decreasing as they finished the work they had been sent out to do so long ago.

Thom was at her side in an instant, Ryland and Sain taking a place on either side of him as they entered the room. All three of them placed their hands on her, all three withdrawing as the supercharged curse stung their magic.

"That is dark magic," Sain noted, his voice shaking in

fear as he cradled his hand against his chest as if he had been burned.

Thom moved to try again when her body calmed momentarily, his hand moving to rest flat against her arm, right against the wiggling marks. I stopped him with one movement, my hand wrapping around his wrist. He pushed against me before looking up, a question in his eyes. Neither of us said anything, my face telling the whole story—there was nothing to be done.

Thom dropped his hand dejectedly, his shoulders sagging as he looked at her. Wynifred still yelled and writhed on the small bed I had laid her on.

"Her memories have returned," I whispered to Thom as he clung to her hand.

"Cail?" he asked, his voice panicked.

"Joclyn must have killed him when she escaped the Tȯuha. I didn't think so at first, but only Cail's death could release Wynifred's curse. It was either Joclyn or Edmund who killed him."

"It barely matters now. Can you bind it again?" I only shook my head.

"Talon?" Thom's voice was a whisper.

I could only shake my head; I didn't know.

"He's gone." My head snapped over to Sain, his voice scratchy, like sandpaper, against the loud chaos of the room. "He passed five days ago."

I was sure that my heart had stopped beating. Talon had been my best friend for as long as I could remember. We had been raised together, and he had been my guard until the day I dismissed him, on the day of his bonding with Wyn.

I wanted to destroy something. The pain that my loss was creating inside of me consumed me, made me want to turn the abbey to ash, run rampant and rain death through the Trpaslíks' camps.

I sucked in a breath, willing my soul to move past the pain, to hold the loss deep inside with all the others. I commanded it away from me and forced my upbringing forward, my back straightening as my veins ran icy for a moment.

"Wynifred." Thom's voice was calm as he spoke to her, her eyes growing wide with recognition.

"Thom?"

"I'm here," he whispered as she shifted her weight, her jaw clenching as she tried not to yell, but failed.

"Am I dead?" Wynifred's voice was deep and strong again, the way I had known it for centuries. She spoke the words through clenched teeth as she cringed against the pain.

"Not yet, sweetie, but I'll stay here until the end."

I could feel the sting in my eyes as Thom spoke to her, as he prepared her for what was coming. He clung to her, his hands wrapped around hers as he soothed her the only way he could. His focus was only on her, as was everyone else's. Ryland and Sain could only stare with tear-stained cheeks.

It was with a strained heart I realized what I was witnessing. Sain, Ryland and Wyn had been imprisoned together. They had suffered together. Ryland and Sain's tears suddenly made sense; they, too, were watching their friend die.

"Talon?" Wyn asked, her voice getting weaker.

"He will be there waiting for you. He's going to be right there... and... and you know who is going to be with him?"

"Rosaline?"

"Yeah, sweetie, she is going to be right there. Right there with Talon. She's been waiting for you, waiting... for her mommy." Thom's voice caught, and I had to look away. I couldn't think about what he was saying to her, what he was promising.

Instinctively, I pushed my magic toward Joclyn, needing to feel her, to feel her magic, to know that she was still okay. My eyes opened wider as I felt her presence right outside the door.

I looked back at Thom's goodbye to his best friend for only a minute before I moved out the door, finding Joclyn curled up in a ball against the floor, her hands wrapped around her knees and pulling herself into a tight fetal position. I dropped to the floor as my hands moved to touch the skin on her shoulders.

Joclyn's head snapped up at me, her wide, silver eyes blazing into me.

"Wyn." Her voice didn't shake as she said her friend's name, the intensity of the word making it clear what she wanted.

"She's dying, Joclyn." I ran my finger over her cheek, not knowing how to comfort her or even if she needed it.

I can save her.

I heard her voice in my head. My eyes widened in surprise, but her eyes continued to stare into mine, as if what she had just done was the simplest thing in the world.

"Ryland is in there." I tried to keep my voice level, not wanting to send her into a panic with the shock I was feeling at just having heard her voice in my head.

Don't let me see him. I will kill him if I see him.

I balked at her words, my jaw loosening in shock. I could hear the truth behind them, the conviction in her tones. She truly believed what she was saying. It couldn't be. I wished I could blame her misplaced intentions on what the imitation of Ryland had done to her in the Tōuha, but I had heard

Ovailia's words. Edmund had intentionally marred them both, making them weapons against each other. Joclyn's words only confirmed it.

I struggled to keep my anger restrained before it threatened to explode. The pain of hearing Wynifred's screams and of losing Talon mixed with the anger I felt at what Edmund had done to Joclyn and Ryland. He had manipulated them for his own use.

"Joclyn..." I began, unsure of what to say.

I can do it. Take me to her.

I said nothing. I didn't know what else could be said.

Joclyn only looked at me for a second before closing her eyes, her hand wrapping firmly around mine as she stood, her body bent and crippled from the torture her mind had gone through.

Wyn yelled again, and I knew I couldn't wait. I wrapped my arm around Joclyn, bringing her close against me as I led her through the door.

Sain and Ryland stiffened when I brought her in, both men taking a step toward her in longing. Both men drawn to her for different reasons. I shook my head at them frantically, hoping they would understand. Ryland still attempted to move toward us, but Sain wrapped his hand around Ryland's strong bicep, bringing him back against him.

"Do you remember when we took her to the beach?" Thom's voice was soft as he tried to keep Wynifred calm with memories of her long forgotten past. He didn't notice us until we were right in front of him, Joclyn's body moving toward Wynifred as if she sensed exactly where she was.

Thom sat back as Joclyn fell on top of her friend, her torso draping over Wynifred's, her hands extending to cover the moving marks on her arm. I could feel Joclyn's magic surge at the touch, the air around her sending a powerful aura right into me. I felt the surge a moment before everyone else could see it.

The air around Joclyn rippled as her magic continued to swell. She pulled the magic out of the air, the stone and the earth. She brought it into her, using the power as she would her own. Her control was above any I had ever seen.

The air continued to ripple visibly, the breaths of everyone held in place as they watched. Silence filled the room as Joclyn's body and magic smothered Wynifred's pain. Even with the energy Joclyn was channeling, the marks still moved on Wyn's arms, the curse still seeping into her heart in an effort to kill her.

"N-n-need m-more." Joclyn's voice was quiet, her magic straining as she began to sweat.

I moved closer to her, my body hovering over hers as I leaned down to whisper in her ear. I could see Ryland shift uncomfortably at my close proximity, his intent to injure me obvious. Without Sain and Thom there to restrain him, he probably would have.

"Use me; take it through the Štít," I whispered softly, not wanting Ryland or Sain to hear.

I began to push my magic into her, the full strength of it filling her for one moment before she grabbed it and pushed it into Wynifred. As soon as she did, I could feel Wynifred, feel the curse, but I could also feel that my magic was not fully mine. I could feel it. I could recognize what it was doing, but it was Joclyn who controlled it.

"M... more... Il... Ilyan..." Her voice dropped as she began to pant, the work involved in healing Wyn becoming too much for her.

I looked away from her to the three men at the other side of the room. They watched our actions with fear, amazement and anger spread across each of their faces. I knew what my next action would mean to Ryland, to Sain, but it had to be done.

I moved Joclyn's hair out of the way, shifting it around her neck to reveal the raised dragon-shaped brand on her neck. The kiss stared at me from her smooth skin as I unwrapped my bandaged hand, letting the smooth covering fall to the floor and revealing the angry, red scar of the burn.

I didn't hesitate. I didn't look to the gasps that sounded as they each recognized the angry red marks that covered the palm of my hand. I lowered my body to press against Joclyn's back, my hand hovering over the mark for just a moment before I lowered it onto her skin.

The razor sharp jolt sprung through our bodies simultaneously, the connection the Black Water had forged between us coming to life and combining with the jolt from the kiss. Our voices called out in harmony as the shock the connection forged between us rippled through our bodies. I could feel Joclyn's exertion, her weakness, and her mad need to heal her friend. More than that, I could feel our mingled magic surging strong through Wynifred. The amount of power rushing into her should have been enough to kill her instantly, but somehow Joclyn controlled it. Joclyn maintained the magical pulse and Wynifred's life in perfect harmony.

The black marks on Wynifred's arm that had been moving into her heart were fast, but strangely, Joclyn was faster. She moved seamlessly in a way that even I would not have been able to. Her power was obviously beyond even that which I had been born with.

I opened my eyes; the three men staring in amazement as Wyn's marks not only stopped moving, but also began to fade from her skin.

Hold me.

I didn't need to be told twice. I looked away from the three pairs of eyes that stared at us and wrapped my free hand around Joclyn's waist, keeping my scarred hand against her mark as I brought her body against me.

No sooner had I pressed myself against her back than both girls began to scream, their voices matched in pitch, the sound ringing out like a song rather than the agonizing pain I could feel mirrored in my own body.

The scream ended only moments after it had come. Joclyn gasped for breath before she rocked away from Wynifred's body and threw both of us away from the bed.

Wynifred's yell lasted for a moment longer before her mouth opened wider, her jaw extended like a cat on the hunt. She writhed on the bed, her back arching eerily before her body released a plume of black smoke. It spewed from her gaping mouth like the steam from an engine, the blackness rising and curling dangerously into the air before disappearing.

I held Joclyn's body against mine, my eyes darting down to Wyn, whose body was now relaxed and her marks all but gone.

No one dared to move, least of all me. We all knew just by looking that Joclyn had done something even I couldn't.

Cover my eyes.

I did as she asked, recognizing the change that was coming over her. Her body stiffened and her head spun within me. Her breathing picked up as her mind was filled with a sight, her spine tensing for only a moment before she spoke.

"T-take th...the l-left." Her deep voice filled the room. Thom barely looked at her before rushing back to Wyn's side.

Sain's eyes widened as he pieced together what had just had happened, but Ryland hadn't seemed to notice, he just looked at her with that desperate longing in his eyes again. I did not even think he realized that there was something different in her voice.

I looked at Sain, pleading with him not to say anything, to keep this secret. I still wasn't sure I could trust Ryland. I needed to keep Joclyn safe, and letting this get out would not help her.

Sain nodded once in understanding, the action letting my muscles relax.

"She's fine," Thom's voice cut through my silent exchange, bringing us all back to what had just happened. "Joclyn healed her."

I couldn't help but smile as I brought her body into mine, keeping her close to me.

I told you I could.

I jerked my eyes back down to her. Her eyes were still closed, and her face was pressed against my chest. She could have been sleeping.

I slowly removed my finger from the mark, allowing the connection to begin to fade from my mind. I wished I knew how she was doing that, how she was filling my mind with her voice. No one had ever managed anything past crude pictures—not since the first were born from the mud. To hear her voice, without the stutter, inside my mind... it was as beautiful as she was.

She was amazing.

Thank you.

28

JOCLYN

Fireflies.

When I was growing up, I thought fireflies were magic. I thought they were like fairies. I would try to catch them in jars and take them home to convince them to grant my wish.

I was four when I caught my first one. I had put him in a glass jar and watched him glow as he fluttered and banged against the glass. He was going to grant my wish. My father had sat with me and ran his finger over the glass, the firefly drawn to him. When my father's finger was there, the firefly didn't bang his head against the glass anymore; he just followed my father's finger.

Dad asked me what my wish was, but at four all I could think of was a pony, a pony and the ability to fly. My father smiled and told me that magic was inside of you, not in bugs. I asked him if I had magic then, and he got that face that parents get when they are caught in a lie. I knew it then, that magic wasn't real, but I didn't care.

I had laughed as we set my little firefly free, sad for the loss of a wish, but happy that the bug was free.

It was one of my only memories of my father.

Then, many years later, I found out what magic really was. And just like the firefly, I wished I could just open the jar and let it go free.

I still wanted to think of fireflies as magic. I watched them as they danced outside the window of Ilyan's room, and I wanted to dance with them, but I couldn't. I couldn't move my body out of the heavy blanket I had found on the couch. I was too scared to move from the small alcove of stone that looked out onto the balcony. So I watched the fireflies, and felt my magic surge and flow through the air, the power wild and unrestrained within me.

My magic flew away from me as I watched, desperate to be out of the small container my body provided it. It flowed through the air and over the yards of the abbey like water. It fanned away from me and brought back signs and signals from everyone around me.

I could feel the armies that surrounded us and their eagerness for a battle that they knew was coming. I could feel Thom's joy as he sat next to Wyn, closeted up in his room where I had left them only a few minutes before. I could feel Wyn's sadness at losing her mate. I wished I could tell her that I could still feel Talon inside of her, but I didn't dare speak. Not yet.

I had sat with them as Wyn woke up, my eyes closed as I hid myself in Ilyan's chest. I could feel them all around me. I could feel my father's magic. I could feel everything. In that tiny room, I was trapped.

As soon as Wyn woke, the questions came, the voices all sounding at once. They asked questions and demanded answers, their voices growing louder and panicking me. The touching followed, my father's hands on my skin in excitement, Thom reaching out to me in thanks, and though I understood their desires, my body curled into itself. I couldn't stop the howling that escaped from my chest.

I pushed myself into Ilyan, the only security I knew, and let his comfort take the fear away. I wasn't ready to talk to any of them. I wasn't ready to look into my father's eyes and relive all that had happened since he had left. So instead, my father had hugged me as I sat on Ilyan's lap and whispered in my ear how much he loved me. Ilyan had passed on my words to him before taking me from the room.

I had crawled to the balcony after he left me, my movements slow as the twitches kept coming, my heart thumping as it continued to struggle with reality.

I kept my magic trained on Ilyan as I watched the fireflies. I pulled his magic through the Štít in desperation, trying to feel his comfort, to feel safe. His magic was the reminder that I was okay.

Everything was getting clearer, but I still hadn't broken free. I didn't think I ever would.

I could feel the pulse of Ilyan's magic from where he stood with Sain as they healed his son, my brother. I could feel Ilyan's emotions, the heightened connection giving me access to loose pieces of his thoughts. Ilyan was nervous about me; he wanted to leave, but he was fighting it, knowing he needed to stay there, too, that he had responsibilities that he could not ignore.

I felt Ilyan's anxiety as Sain began to tell him all that had happened. His anxiety triggered my own; my magic surging through him as my own peaked, confusing me as to whether I should calm him or myself.

If I focused, I could hear their conversation. I could pretend to be well enough to be around them, but they weren't alone. There was someone else with them. I knew that if I heard his voice, I couldn't be sure what I would do.

Ilyan.

I let my magic grow and sent my voice into his head, the word traveling through the Štít and into him. I wasn't sure how I had done it the first time. I had sat huddled on the floor as Wyn screamed, and I could feel my magic grow into something that it hadn't been before. I looked into Ilyan's eyes and my soul had told me what to do. It didn't take more of a thought than that.

I felt Ilyan's excitement increase at my message, his thoughts changing from stress over what he was being told toward me, his thoughts heavy with worry.

I'm fine, Ilyan.

A moment passed as he talked, but soon his thoughts were torn between wondering what I needed and trying to focus on what Sain was telling him.

I stayed still as I felt the ebb and flow of Ilyan's emotions, small words of his thoughts filtering through. I didn't know what had caused me to call to him; I knew he would come when he was done. I could feel that conviction inside of him already. Besides, I had my fireflies to keep me company.

My body shook the longer I sat, my hands twitching underneath the blanket. I could feel the anxiety rise, the uncertainty taking over. I focused on the panic, trying to calm it, but knowing it would come no matter what I did.

My tension grew, but Ilyan's song filled my mind, the thought flowing from Ilyan into me, my own lips following suit as I whispered the words to myself. The anxiety I had felt lessened as Ilyan's magic filled me from a distance.

The song ended just as the door creaked open and he entered a few minutes later. I knew it was Ilyan, but I couldn't stop the tension from filling my joints or the way my head moved toward my chest. I kept my body still against the stone of the wall as I felt Ilyan's magic move closer to me, the ebbs growing as he calmed me.

I turned my eyes enough to watch as he sat next to me, his legs crossed beneath him, just far enough away that I couldn't touch him easily. I curled into myself instinctively, part of me wishing I wouldn't. I could hear that part of me scream for his contact, but the jitters begged otherwise.

Even through the fear, I still wanted to touch him. I pushed the thought away, choosing instead to focus on his blue eyes and how they dug into me, the way his fingers twitched in desperation to touch me, and the way his lips turned up in a calm joy when I looked at him.

I watched him, and I felt the tension leave, my heart rate slowing. Not for the first time, just the sight of him calmed me.

"Ilyan," I breathed, my voice calm. I wasn't sure I could manage more than that one word though.

He smiled at the sound of his name on my tongue, his magic surging in response.

"Are you talking now?" he asked, his voice a cross between amusement and worry.

No. I sent the one word into his mind, but instead of sadness, he only smiled. I didn't see what was so funny, but he obviously did. I wrapped my hands around myself, my body tensing at what that smile could mean. It was nothing. It had to be nothing but happiness. *I will only talk to you.*

Ilyan smiled again, his gaze darting away from mine to his hands before coming back to rest on me, the soft blue light of his eyes glossed over.

"And I will cherish every second of your voice that you

give me." He smiled again, the warmth of his face seeping into me, soothing my nerves.

My body loosened a bit, and I couldn't help but let my own small smile filter onto my face. A smile. It felt weird and foreign on my face. I had forgotten what it felt like. I had forgotten what happiness felt like.

"Y... you w-w-will?" My smile left as the stutter took over, the shake of my voice taking my newfound happiness away.

"I will," he sighed, his body shifting to move closer to me. His knees pressed against the heavy blanket I had covered myself with. I focused on the pressure, leaning into it. I leaned into the warmth I felt from his touch and the ripples of heat coming off his body, my body hovering precariously away from the pressure the alcove provided me.

"How are you feeling?"

My eyes widened at his question, at the barely concealed worry behind it. I didn't know why, but his worry seemed to calm me. Just knowing how much he cared seemed to steady my frayed nerves.

I'm not sure if I am fine or if I am broken.

"It's okay to be both, Joclyn." He sighed again, his hand moving to rest against my cheek, but it wasn't skin I felt.

I turned my head toward him in confusion, my eyes narrowing at the heavy bandage he had covered his hand with. My heart beat quickly at seeing it there. Ilyan had hurt himself. For the first time, I worried about what had happened while I had been trapped in hell, while I had been tortured. Ilyan had been injured. Heavy emotions swirled through me, once forgotten and now foreign, as I began to remove the heavy bandage.

Ilyan's heart quickened as I removed the covering, my breathing shaking as the angry red marks came into view.

The red welts stood up from his hand like a burn, but the skin was still wet in places.

What happened? I asked, my fear for him overriding my personal demons for the moment. He didn't need to tell me. I could see the moment replayed in his head, the horrors of those last moments in my hell a swirl of color and fear in his eyes.

This is how you brought me back? The Black Water?

He nodded once, and I pulled the hand toward me, my back arching as I brought the scars against my face, another mark that Ilyan would bear forever, another scar he had taken for me.

Thank you.

"Haven't I told you enough? I would do anything for you." His voice was so soft I barely heard him.

I leaned toward him as I pressed his hand against me, his magic pulsing through me. It was so warm and delicate within me. I could feel it reach into every part of me, cradling me as if I was something precious, which is how I knew he looked at me.

I could feel his emotions whisper it to me now. I could feel his heart ache; his love for me that was always held behind the strict barriers of what he felt was right broke through and was bared between us. I stared at him as his thoughts and emotions swirled toward me.

Then, they changed. He second-guessed himself somewhere along the way, his emotions withdrawing and his insecurities taking their place.

As his doubts and fears took hold of him, they also seeped into me. I moved away from him. I wanted that feeling back, that love that I had felt emanating from him only a moment ago. I felt my heart hunger for it, need it.

What's wrong? I asked, unable to keep my worry inside of

me, not wanting to let it change into something else if I held it back.

I should have tried harder to keep my thoughts at bay. Ilyan looked at me with pain in his eyes, his mind pouring out his sadness before his mouth even opened. His first word brought the panic I had kept at bay until this point.

"Ryland has asked me—"

"No!" My voice caught him off guard, his eyes widening at the power behind my one word.

I couldn't stop the panic that flowed through my body. I moaned as I curled into the blanket, every nerve ending tensing in agony, in fear of what was to come. I felt Ilyan's magic surge into me and my own magic joining his as I attempted to calm myself, to take the fear away.

I could see Ilyan's thoughts in front of me, his worry for his brother and his friend and his desperate need for me, and I could hear Ryland's words in his head. I tensed as they hit my mind, my body tightly wound before Ilyan's magic was able to calm me again.

I will not see him, I answered the unasked question inside his head. *I will kill him if I see him. I* want *to kill him.* I narrowed my eyes at him, my jaw tensing at the calm agony his eyes showed me.

I curled into the wall, my mind fighting against my better judgment as it begged me to run away.

"You won't kill him," Ilyan said as calmly as he could, and I felt my anger rise and my magic pulse. For one fleeting second it was stronger than the crazed anxiety that still overtook me.

I will.

"No, Jos," he whispered, and I couldn't help the thunk of my heart at my nickname on his lips. "You don't want that, not really."

I do, Ilyan, I begged him. I begged through the panic, the fear. I needed him to understand this. To understand my need. The anger was a fire inside of me, the need for revenge fanning it ever higher. *He hurt me... he...*

My thoughts stopped as Ilyan's hand moved against my neck, the sharp jolt as his skin made contact with my mark stopping my words. I sighed at the sensation, at the pleasurable heat it gave me, before staring into Ilyan, knowing it had been his intention to stop me.

"You don't want to hurt him. You don't want to kill him. It's not really *you* that feels that way. You think it is because you are still so scared and confused at what has happened. You were hurt, Joclyn, but not by him."

His eyes dug into me as he spoke, his words pleading with me to believe him, but I couldn't. I couldn't see beyond the panic and pain. It consumed me. A part of me wanted it to. In some ways, the pain and the anxiety made me remember that I was alive.

It was him, I spat as I pushed Ilyan away, as I let the anxiety mix with the hate. I could feel my magic surge and pulse, but it wasn't like when I had healed Wyn; this was uncontrollable, like I myself was the danger, as if I would explode.

"No, my love," Ilyan said calmly, his eyes scanning me as I continued to try to move into myself and my breathing picked up. "It was a farce, a projection in Cail's mind meant to confuse you so that you would kill him if you ever got the chance."

I could feel Ilyan's magic move into me and take away the frayed edges of my panic. I wanted to hold it to me and relax in the pain, but I couldn't. I couldn't tear my mind away from what Ilyan was saying, what he was trying so foolishly to get me to believe.

I couldn't ignore the pulse of anger that moved through me. I couldn't ignore the way that just talking about him was awakening my panic, causing my body to shake and curl into itself. Ryland needed to pay for what he had done to me.

It was him, Ilyan. I know—

"How do you know it was?" The desperation in his words stopped me, my eyes widening. Why did he doubt me? Why was he pushing me? What had Ryland told him? What had my father said?

I had shown Ilyan everything; I had filled his mind with those memories. Why couldn't he see that I knew? I knew by the way that he had walked, the way that his hair curled. I could have admitted that there had been something different about him, but I couldn't tell what it was. I didn't want to.

I twitched as I focused on the memories, the images letting that strong fear back into my heart. My body moved even further into the wall as I tried to keep the fear at bay, as I tried to hold onto reality.

How do you know that it wasn't? I countered, my voice snide in his head.

Ilyan closed his eyes for a moment, and I could hear the replay of the last hour in his mind, the conversation he had had with Sain. I didn't want to hear it. Even though I could tell he was trying to give me the thoughts, I wouldn't let them in. I wasn't interested.

"They did the same to him, Jos." He sighed, his breath exhaling as he lifted his eyes to look at me again. "They turned him into a weapon to hurt you. It's why he punched you. He still sees you as the enemy they haunted him with. He is trying to fight it, but I am not sure he can."

I just stared at him, the words sinking into a place deep

inside of me that I wanted so desperately to ignore. Ilyan's eyes were soft, the truth behind them penetrating. I sighed as I leaned my head against the wall, not willing to except it, more willing to let my panic take over.

How do you know that I am meant to be a weapon now?

Ilyan stared and moved closer, his body folding as he leaned toward me.

"It's what my father does, Joclyn." His fingers twitched in desperation to hold me again. "It is what he has always done. You know this."

I did. I had seen it even before he had done it to me. I had seen it in Thom, and I had heard the stories of my father. I had no reason to doubt any of them.

"You need to let go of that anger, Joclyn," Ilyan continued when I said nothing, his hand finally moving to rest against the blanket that covered me. "You can't let the pain control you."

I can't, Ilyan. If I let go of it, then there is nothing left. I have nothing behind that. It's all I am anymore.

"That's not true," Ilyan said, his hand moving to rub my body in comfort through the blanket.

It's all I feel. I sighed, pulling the blanket around me tighter. I felt the jagged edge within me as it threatened to turn into panic. I pushed it away as I buried my face into the wall, refusing to look at him. I knew the look he would have if I did.

"You have to look beyond it, my love," he whispered, his voice soft as his hand moved from the blanket to the skin of my face. I fought the temptation to lean into the touch, to bask in it.

There is nothing behind it, I said, the voice in my head breaking in my sadness.

Ilyan sighed, and his hand moved over my skin before

343

he dropped it, before he leaned away from me. The movement scared me, and I looked toward him. His eyes were looking right at me, the bright blue shocking as they raged with a heady emotion that took my breath away.

"My father hung me from a tree shortly after it became obvious that I was the one challenging him. He caught me, whipped me and burned my skin with irons. I thought I would go mad, but I didn't."

He didn't move as he spoke, his eyes never leaving mine. I had always excluded Ilyan from the pain Edmund had caused his children. I didn't know why, but Ilyan seemed untouchable. Now he was telling me that he had been hurt. He had thought he would go crazy, but he didn't.

How?

He smiled at my question, and for the first time since I met him, I could tell he was nervous. I could feel the anxiety in his mind; hear the thump of his heart.

His heart called to me, and I leaned toward him, the heavy blanket moving away as I reached for his hands and wrapped my own around his.

"Ilyan?" I asked aloud, loving the way his name felt on my tongue.

"I thought of you, of the vision. I basked in the way you felt in my arms, the smell of your hair. I thought of every vision I had seen in the sight and I knew I was bigger than the pain. I looked beyond it, and I found love."

Love.

The look in his eyes, the way his magic felt within me, none of it was wild, none of it was scary. Everything about Ilyan was calm. He was love.

He was light.

I had felt it before, before Wyn's screams had broken open the façade I had plastered together. Ilyan was love.

He wasn't love simply because I knew he loved me. Because I did know that. Without question, he had proved that to me again and again. No, he was love because I loved him.

I loved him.

"What is beyond your anger, Joclyn? What is your pain hiding?"

I didn't look away from him as he asked his questions. I didn't dare take my eyes off him. I stared at Ilyan as my body leaned toward him, as my hands moved from his. My fingers moved on their own, trailing up his shirt and over the skin of his neck.

I held my breath as I touched his face, the soft skin I had never touched before. I ran the pads of my fingers over his eyebrows, his defined cheek bones, and through the hairline of his short cut.

My heart pulsed wildly inside of me as I let my fingers trail over the scruff from a beard I had never seen, prickly and sharp, before dragging to his lips. I froze.

I froze at the sound of my pulse in my ears. I froze at the calm that had overtaken me. I froze at the desire that circled through Ilyan's mind and the willpower he was exerting to keep it there.

I watched his breathing. I felt the heat of his breath against my fingers, the pulse of his magic hot under his skin.

What was behind the anger?

"Ilyan," I said again, his eyes opening slowly to stare at me, "you are behind my anger."

I smiled at my words, my heart thumping even more at the clarity they brought, at the way each word formed perfectly.

Ilyan's lips upturned underneath my touch, the skin

parting as he kissed the pads of my fingers, the wetness of his lips soft against my skin.

"I always will be," he whispered as my fingers fell from his lips and I moved closer.

As I kissed him.

ALSO BY REBECCA ETHINGTON

THE WORLD OF IMDALIND

THE IMDALIND SERIES

KISS OF FIRE, IMDALIND #1

EYES OF EMBER, IMDALIND #2

SCORCHED TREACHERY, IMDALIND #3

SOUL OF FLAME, IMDALIND #4

BURNT DEVOTION, IMDALIND #5

BRAND OF BETRAYAL, IMDALIND #6

DAWN OF ASH, IMDALIND #7

CROWN OF CINDERS, IMDALIND #8

ILYAN, IMDALIND #9

THE KING OF IMDALIND SERIES

SPARK OF VENGEANCE, BOOK 1

FLARE OF VILLAINY, BOOK 2 (COMING 2019)

BOOKS 3-6 TBA

THE CIRCUS OF SHIFTERS

THE PHOENIX'S ASHES SERIES

RISE OF THE WITCH, BOOK ONE

FALL OF THE DRAGON, BOOK TWO

FLIGHT OF THE KING, BOOK THREE

FLAME OF THE PHOENIX, BOOK FOUR

THE DRAGON QUEEN SERIES
RISING FLAME (COMING MARCH 2019)
BOOKS 2-4 TBA

THE OTHER WORLDS

THE THROUGH GLASS SERIES
BOOK ONE: THE DARK
BOOK TWO: THE BLUE
BOOK THREE: THE ROSE
BOOK FOUR: THE CUT
BOOK FIVE: THE LIGHT (COMING 2019)
BOOK SIX: THE ASCENDED (COMING 2019)

OF RIVER AND RAYNN, THE SERIES
THE CATALYST: ACT ONE (RERELEASES 2019)
THE REQUISITE: ACT TWO (COMING 2019)

ABOUT THE AUTHOR

Rebecca Ethington is an internationally bestselling author with almost 700,000 books sold. Her breakout debut, The Imdalind Series, has been featured on bestseller lists since its debut in 2012, reaching thousands of adoring fans worldwide and cited as "Interesting and Intense" by *USA Today's Happily Ever After Blog*.

From writing horror to romance and creating every sort of magical creature in between, Rebecca's imagination weaves vibrant worlds that transport readers into the pages of her books. Her writing has been described as fresh, original, and groundbreaking, with stories that bend genres and create fantastical worlds.

Born and raised under the lights of a stage, Rebecca has written stories by the ghost light, told them in whispers in dark corridors, and never stopped creating within the pages of a notebook.

Find me online
www.rebeccaethington.com
contact@rebeccaethington.com

IMDALIND CONTINUES IN BOOK FOUR

The Full Series is Available Now